Astounding

RANDOM HOUSE   NEW YORK

Astounding

JOHN W. CAMPBELL MEMORIAL
ANTHOLOGY EDITED BY

Harry Harrison

for John

from his writers and friends

CONTENTS

CONTENTS

INTRODUCTION

The Father of Science Fiction

There are many people whom one might cite as being the "father of science fiction."

Johann Kepler wrote the first story that sounded like science fiction and that paid attention to actual scientific fact. Edgar Allan Poe first caught the idea of inevitable social change through advances in science and technology. Jules Verne was the first to specialize in science-fiction writing. Herbert George Wells was the first to make it a recognized branch of literature. Hugo Gernsback was the first to publish a magazine devoted exclusively to science fiction and created the beginnings of the first mass market.

But all these, put together, only laid the foundation. The man who took that foundation and built the structure of modern science fiction upon it and shaped it to what we now accept as such, was a tall, broad, light-haired, crew-cut, bespectacled, overbearing, overpowering, cigarette-holder-waving, opinionated, talkative, quicksilver-minded individual named John Wood Campbell, Jr.

He was born on June 8, 1910, in Newark, New Jersey, and remained a Jerseyite almost all his life. He had a difficult childhood, for he was born into a world that had not been designed to his scale.

He began reading science fiction not long after he began reading. He bought the first issue of Gernsback's *Amazing Stories,* read it regularly, and was profoundly impressed by the trailblazing serial "The Skylark of Space" by E. E. Smith, which began in the August 1928 issue. Inevitably, he began to write science fiction himself in the style of Smith.

He made his first sale when he was seventeen, but his first published story appeared in the January 1930 issue of *Amazing.* It was entitled "When the Atoms Failed." In the month that it appeared, a new science-fiction magazine was launched entitled *Astounding Stories of Superscience.* That this was an astonishing coincidence could only be understood in hindsight.

Before 1930 was over, Campbell had launched the Wade, Arcott & Morey series of stories which clinched his fame in the science-fiction world. This series joined him with E. E. Smith as the great exponents of the super-science epic in which men of more-than-heroic mold fought each other with suns and leaped over galaxies in single strides.

But there was this difference between Smith and Campbell. Smith, having found his métier, never left it. To the end he wrote the super-science epic, changing it only to make it ever larger, ever more colossal. Campbell had no métier he wished to call his own; or, rather, having found one, he could not help looking about for a better one.

Perhaps a change in his personal life helped him do so. He attended M.I.T., where he had no trouble with science but was laid low by the German language. He passed on to Duke University in North Carolina, where he completed his work for his degree. (However, it was always M.I.T. which remained his spiritual home in later years, and he visited it regularly.) As though to mark the change from M.I.T., the super-school of science, to Duke University, where psychology was important and where Joseph Banks

Rhine (who later put parapsychology on the map) was already an instructor at the time, Campbell began to switch from tales in which super-science blasted the readers' minds to those in which human emotion wrung their hearts.

He wrote "Twilight," a low-key poignant tale worth all his super-science adventures put together. "Twilight" appeared in the November 1934 issue of *Astounding*, which was then edited by F. Orlin Tremaine. For various reasons it appeared under a pseudonym. The best reason was that had it appeared as a Campbellesque production, the readers would have been set for super-science and would have missed the wonder the story really was. So it appeared as having been written by Don A. Stuart, a name which was almost identical to the maiden name of Campbell's first wife (Dona Stuart).

For the next four years Campbell, under that pseudonym, pioneered in what came to be the "new wave" of that era. He wrote stories in which science and scientists were what they really were, and combined that with human emotion and human foibles. The climax came in the August 1938 issue of *Astounding*, which carried Campbell/Stuart's "Who Goes There?" surely one of the greatest science-fiction stories ever written, which was made into *The Thing from Outer Space*, surely one of the worst movies ever made. But by that time Campbell had made his second métier sufficiently his own to abandon it. He had written all, or almost all, he intended to write. He was going to be an editor.

In September 1937 he had joined Street & Smith, which then published *Astounding*, and in May 1938 he succeeded Tremaine as editor of the magazine. He remained editor thirty-three years and two months—to the day of his death (at home, quietly, quickly, painlessly, as he sat before his television set) on June 11, 1971.

I once asked him, years ago (with all the puzzlement of a compulsive writer who can imagine no other way of life), how he could possibly have borne to leave his writing career and become an editor. I had almost said *merely* an editor. He smiled (he knew me) and said, "Isaac, when I write, I write only my own stories. As editor, I write the stories that a hundred people write."

It was so. By his own example and by his instruction and by his undeviating and persisting insistence, he forced first *Astounding* and then all science fiction into his mold. He abandoned the earlier orientation of the field. He demolished the stock characters who had filled it; eradicated the penny-dreadful plots; extirpated the Sunday-supplement science. In a phrase, he blotted out the purple of pulp. Instead, he demanded that science-fiction writers understand science and understand people, a hard requirement that many of the established writers of the 1930s could not meet. Campbell did not compromise because of that: those who could not meet his requirements could not sell to him, and the carnage was as great as it had been in Hollywood a decade before, when silent movies had given way to the talkies.

Campbell went to work to fill the gap left by the forced retirement of some of the best-known names in the field. He began to develop new talents in a new generation of writers, those plastic enough to learn a set of newer and much harder skills, and he succeeded. Those who flourished under Campbell's tutelage and learned to write in his uncompromising school lifted the field from minor pulp to high art.

Not all writers before Campbell were poor; not all writers after Campbell were great—yet the change was large enough and dramatic enough to make it clear that science fiction as adult literature had a name and that name was John Wood Campbell, Jr.

I met him in June 1938, just a month after he had become editor. I was eighteen and had arrived with my first story-submission, my very first. He had never met me before, but he took me in; talked to me for two hours; read the story that night; mailed the rejection the following day along with a kind, two-page letter telling me where I had gone wrong.

Over the next four years I saw him just about every month, always with a new story. He always talked to me, always fed me ideas, always discussed my stories to tell me what was right and what was wrong with them.

It was he who gave me the skeleton of "Nightfall," including the opening quotation, and sent me home to write the story.

It was he who considered my third or fourth robot story, shook his head and said, "No, Isaac, you're neglecting the Three Laws of Robotics which are—" and that was the first I heard of them.

It was he who took the idea for a short story which I brought to him and put it through a rich sea-change that transmuted it into the *Foundation* series.

I never denied, or even tried to diminish, the debt I owed him, and told him flatly that everything in my writing career I owed to him; but it was characteristic of him that he never accepted that. He admitted he fed me ideas, but he said he kept on doing so only because I brought them back changed and improved. He denied he had made up the Three Laws of Robotics and insisted he had found them in my stories and merely put them into words.

He watched many of his writers take their instructions from him and use them to go on to fame outside *Astounding* and outside science fiction. He rejoiced in that and stayed behind to teach a newer generation.

Only once did I manage to get him to recognize his value openly. I asked him to what he attributed his editorial ability, and he answered, "To an unteachable talent." I asked him what talent that was, and he said, "The talent which made it possible for me to see writing ability in a hungry teen-ager named Isaac Asimov who had brought me in a completely hopeless first story."

Yes, indeed!

It has always been my pride that of the writers developed by Campbell, I was one of the very first (in time, at least, if not in ability).

Nor did he ever settle down. To the end of his life he was always experimenting, always changing, always trying to find the new and exciting. Others grew stodgy and rut-ridden with age; not Campbell. Many science-fiction writers did; not Campbell.

He tried *Astounding* in different sizes; he tried it with roto-gravure sections; he changed the letter columns this way and that; he introduced new departments and dropped them; let word rates depend on readers' votes. Changes didn't always meet with approval, but he wasn't looking for surface approval, but for something he felt and knew to be right—and to the end of his life, he kept *Astounding* first in sales and prestige. He even changed the revered name to *Analog Science Fact–Science Fiction*, over the loud outcries of many readers (including me), but saw it through unwaveringly because he felt the new name no longer smacked of the juvenility of science fiction's magazine beginnings.

Campbell championed far-out ideas: dianetics, the Hieronymus machine, dowsing, psionics. He pained very many of the men he had trained (including me) in doing so, but he felt it was his duty to stir up the minds of his readers and force curiosity right out to the border lines.

He began a series of editorials in his magazine in which he championed a social point of view that could sometimes be described as far right. (He expressed sympathy for George Wallace in the 1968 national elections, for instance.) There was bitter opposition to this from many (including me—I could hardly ever read a Campbell editorial and keep my temper).

Yet criticism never angered Campbell, nor strained his friendship, and however idiosyncratic his views on science and society, he remained, in person, a sane and gentle man.

I saw him last at a science-fiction convention in New York City, the Lunacon, in April 1971, and spent an evening in his hotel room. While Peg Campbell (his second wife, with whom the last decades of his life passed in happy serenity) worked on a hooked rug, Campbell lectured us all on medicine and psychiatry.

It never occurred to me when I shook hands in farewell that night that I would never see him again; never even hear his voice again. How could that occur to me when I had never once thought (*never*) that death and he had anything in common, could ever intersect. He was the fixed pole star about which all science fiction revolved, unchangeable, eternal.

And now that he is dead, where can we find thirteen people who by united effort might serve as a pale replacement for the man who, in the world of science fiction, lived a super-story more thrilling than any even he ever wrote.

Isaac Asimov

Astounding

LODESTAR

by Poul Anderson

Nicholas van Rijn first appeared in 1956. He has come back on a number of occasions, among them two full-dress novels, but always in the same magazine, whether it was called Astounding or Analog. Likewise the exploratory team he organized—David Falkayn, Chee Lan, Adzel and Muddlehead, their ship's insufferable computer. They showed up because it wasn't logical that the old man should have all the adventures. But they too felt most at home with John Campbell.

While some readers cannot abide him, among a large majority Van Rijn seems to be the most popular character I've ever created. In fact, the series became study material for a graduate seminar in management! Campbell enjoyed him hugely. This alone was ample encouragement to write more—not the sales themselves, because after all it was just as easy to do something different, though less fun, but the approval of so genuinely great and greatly genuine a man.

The aim throughout was to tell colorful, fast-moving stories which would at the same time explore a few of the possible facets of this endlessly marvelous universe—and maybe a bit of philosophy. That last, by the way, was no mere dog-eat-dog anarchism. Campbell and I both knew better. Among the more moving experiences of my life was when an elderly lady, confined for years to a particularly grim hospital, wrote to say that something in one of the tales had given her the will to fight on.

What virtue they have is largely due to the Campbell influence, both as an electrifying atmosphere and, in a number of cases, as specific suggestions. Only those who wrote for him know what a fountainhead of ideas he was; he never claimed credit afterward. Mind you, though, he made suggestions, not commands. He delighted in seeing a thought of his carried further by someone else, or stood on its head and turned inside out.

The lodestar of the present yarn is due to him. He proposed it to me back in 1970. I put his letter aside to sparkle in a heap of similar communications from him, until an opportunity should come to use, not just the notion, but the considerable details of physics and chemistry which accompanied it.

Well, I waited too long. Now I can but hope that he would have liked what I've done, and wish he could know with what love I dedicate to him this ending of a saga on which for so long we worked together.

Goodbye, John.

LIGHTNING reached. David Falkayn heard the crack of torn air and gulped a rainy reek of ozone. His cheek stung from the near miss. In his eyes, spots of blue-white dazzle danced across night.

"Get aboard, you two," Adzel said. "I'll hold them."

Crouched, Falkayn peered after a target for his own blaster. He saw shadows move beneath strange constellations—that, and flames which tinged upward-roiling smoke on the far side of the spacefield, where the League outpost was burning. Shrieks resounded. "No, you start," he rasped. "I'm armed, you're not."

The Wodenite's bass remained steady, but an earthquake rumble entered it. "No more deaths. A single death would have been too much, of folk outraged in their own homes. David, Chee: go." Half dragon, half centaur, four and a half meters from snout to tail tip, he moved toward the unseen natives. Firelight framed the hedge of bony plates along his back, glimmered off scales and belly-scutes.

Chee Lan tugged at Falkayn's trousers. "Come on," she spat. "No stopping that hairy-brain when he wambles off on an idealism binge. He won't board before us, and they'll kill him if we don't move fast." A sneer: "I'll lead the way, if that'll make you feel more heroic."

Her small, white-furred form shot from the hauler behind which they had taken refuge. (No use trying to get that machine aloft. The primitives had planned their attack shrewdly, must have hoarded stolen explosives as well as guns for years, till they could demolish everything around the base at the same moment as they fell upon the headquarters complex.) Its mask-markings obscured her blunt-muzzled face in the shuddering red light; but her bottled-up tail stood all too clear.

A Tamethan saw. On long thin legs, beak agape in a war yell, he sped to catch her. His weapon was merely a spear. Sick-hearted, Falkayn took aim. Then Chee darted between those legs, tumbled the autochthon on his tochis and bounded onward.

Hurry! Falkayn told himself. Battle ramped around Adzel. The Wodenite could take a certain number of slugs and blaster bolts without permanent damage, he knew, but not many . . . and those mighty arms were pulling their punches. Keeping to shadow as well as might be, the human followed Chee Lan.

Their ship loomed ahead, invulnerable to the attackers. Her gangway was descending. So the Cynthian had entered audio range, had called an order to the main computer . . . *Why didn't we tell Muddlehead to use initiative in case of trouble?* groaned Falkayn's mind. *Why didn't we at least carry radios to call for its help? Are we due for retirement? A sloppy trade pioneer is a dead trade pioneer.*

A turret gun flashed and boomed. Chee must have ordered that. It was a warning shot, sent skyward, but terrifying. The man gusted relief. His rangy body sped upramp, stopped at the open airlock, and turned to peer back. Combat seemed to have frozen. And, yes, here Adzel came, limping, trailing blood, but alive. Falkayn wanted to hug his old friend and weep.

No. First we haul mass out of here. He entered the ship. Adzel's hoofs boomed on the gangway. It retracted, the airlock closed, gravity drive purred, and *Muddlin' Through* ascended to heaven.

Gathered on the bridge, her crew stared at a downward-viewing screen. The fires had become sparks, the spacefield a scar, in an illimitable night. Far off, a river cut through jungle, shining by starlight like a drawn sword.

Falkayn ran fingers through his sandy hair. "We, uh, well, do you think we can rescue any survivors?" he asked.

"I doubt there are any by now," Adzel said. "We barely escaped because we have learned, over years, to meet emergencies as a team."

"And if there are," Chee added, "who cares?" Adzel looked reproof at her. She bristled her whiskers. "We saw how those slime-souls were treating the aborigines."

"I feel sure much of the offense was caused simply by ignorance of basic psychology and mores."

"That's no excuse, as you flapping well know. They should've taken the trouble to learn such things. But no, the companies couldn't wait for that. They sent their bespattered factors and field agents right in, who promptly set up a little dunghill of an empire—*Ya-pu-yeh!*" In Chee's home language that was a shocking obscenity, even for her.

Falkayn's shoulders slumped. "I'm inclined to agree," he said. "Besides, we mustn't take risks. We've got to make a report."

"Why?" Adzel asked. "Our own employer was not involved."

"No, thanks be. I'd hate to feel I must quit . . . This is League business, however. The mutual-assistance rule—"

"And so League warcraft come and bomb some poor little villages?" Adzel's tail drummed on the deck.

"With our testimony, we can hope not. The Council verdict ought to be, those klongs fell flat on their own deeds." Falkayn sighed. "I wish we'd been around here longer, making a regular investigation, instead of just chancing by and deciding to take a few days off on a pleasant planet." He straightened. "Well. To space, Muddlehead, and to—m-m-m, nearest major League base —Irumclaw."

"And you come along to sick bay and let me dress those wounds, you overgrown bulligator," Chee snapped at the Wodenite, "before you've utterly ruined this carpet, drooling blood on it."

Falkayn himself sought a washroom, a change of clothes, his pipe and tobacco, a stiff drink. Continuing to the saloon, he settled down and tried to ease away his trouble. In a viewscreen, the world dwindled which men had named Tametha—arbitrarily, from a native word in a single locality, which they'd doubtless gotten wrong anyway. Already it had shrunk to a ball, swirled blue and white: a body as big and fair as ever Earth was, four or five billion years in the making, uncounted swarms of unknown life-forms, sentiences and civilizations, histories and mysteries. It had become a marble in a game . . . or a set of entries in a set of data banks, for profit or loss, in a few cities a hundred or more light-years remote.

He thought: *This isn't the first time I've seen undying wrong done. Is it really happening oftener and oftener, or am I just getting more aware of it as I age? At thirty-three, I begin to feel old.*

Chee entered, jumped onto the seat beside him, and reported Adzel was resting. "You do need that drink, don't you?" she observed. Falkayn made no reply. She inserted a mildly narcotic cigarette in an interminable ivory holder and puffed it to ignition. "Yes," she said, "I get irritated likewise, no end, whenever something like this befouls creation."

"I'm coming to think the matter is worse, more fundamental, than a collection of episodes." Falkayn spoke wearily. "The Polesotechnic League began as a mutual-benefit association of companies, true; but the idea was also to keep competition within decent bounds. That's breaking down, that second aspect. How long till the first does too?"

"What would you prefer to free enterprise? The Terran Empire, maybe?"

"Well, you being a pure carnivore, and coming besides from a trading culture that was quick to modernize—exploitation doesn't touch you straight on the nerves, Chee. But Adzel—he doesn't say much, you know him, but I've become certain it's a bitterness to him, more and more as time slides by, that nobody will help his people advance . . . because they haven't anything that anybody wants enough to pay the price of advancement. And—well, I hardly dare guess how many others. Entire worldfuls of beings who look at yonder stars till it aches in them, and know that except for a few lucky individuals, none of them will ever get out there, nor will their descendants have any real say about the future, no, will instead remain nothing but potential victims—"

Seeking distraction, Falkayn raised screen magnification and swept the scanner around jewel-blazing blackness. When he stopped for another pull at his glass, the view happened to include the enigmatic glow of the Crab Nebula.

"Take that sentimentalism and stuff it back where it came from," Chee suggested. "The new-discovered species will simply have to accumulate capital. Yours did. Mine did soon after. We can't give a free ride to the whole universe."

"N-no. Yet you know yourself—be honest—how quick somebody already established would be to take away that bit of capital, whether by market manipulations or by thinly disguised piracy. Tametha's a minor example. All that those tribesbeings wanted was to trade directly with Over-the-Mountains." Falkayn's fist clamped hard around his pipe. "I tell you, lass, the heart is going out of the League, in the sense of ordinary compassion and helpfulness. How long till the heart goes out in the sense of its own survivability? Civilization *needs* more than the few monopolists we've got."

The Cynthian twitched her ears quite slowly and exhaled smoke whose sweetness blent with the acridity of the man's tobacco. Her eyes glowed through it, emerald-hard. "I sort of agree. At least, I'd enjoy listening to the hot air hiss out of certain bellies. How, though, Davy? How?"

"Old Nick—he's a single member of the Council, I realize—"

"Our dear employer keeps his hirelings fairly moral, but strictly on the principle of running a taut ship. He told me that himself once, and added, 'Never mind what the ship is taught, ho, ho,

ho!' No, you won't make an idealist of Nicholas van Rijn. Not
without transmuting every atom in his fat body."

Falkayn let out a tired chuckle. "A new isotope. Van Rijn–235,
no, likelier Vr-235,000—"

And then his glance passed over the Nebula, and as if it had
spoken to him across more than a thousand parsecs, he fell silent
and grew tense where he sat.

This happened shortly after the Satan episode, when the owner
of Solar Spice & Liquors had found it needful once more to leave
the comforts of the Commonwealth, risk his thick neck on a cheer-
less world, and finally make a month-long voyage in a ship which
had run out of beer. Returned home, he swore by all that was holy
and much that was not: Never again!

Nor, for most of the following decade, had he any reason to
break his vow. His business was burgeoning, thanks to excellently
chosen personnel in established trade sites and to pioneers like
the *Muddlin' Through* team who kept finding him profitable new
lands. Besides, he had maneuvered himself into the overlordship
of Satan. A sunless wandering planet, newly thawed out by a brush
with a giant star, made a near-ideal site for the manufacture of
odd isotopes on a scale commensurate with present-day demand.
Such industry wasn't his cup of tea "or," he declared, "my glass
Genever that molasses-on-Pluto-footed butler is supposed to
bring me before I crumble away from thirst." Therefore Van
Rijn granted franchises, on terms calculated to be an angstrom
short of impossibly extortionate.

Many persons wondered, often in colorful language, why he
didn't retire and drink himself into a grave they would be glad to
provide, outsize though it must be. When Van Rijn heard about
these remarks, he would grin and look still harder for a price he
could jack up or a competitor he could undercut. Nevertheless,
compared to earlier years, this was for him a leisured period. When
at last word got around that he meant to take Coya Conyon, his
favorite granddaughter, on an extended cruise aboard his yacht—
and not a single mistress along for him—hope grew that he was
slowing down to a halt.

I can't say I like most of those money-machine merchant princes, Coya reflected, several weeks after leaving Earth; *but I really wouldn't want to give them heart attacks by telling them we're now on a nonhuman vessel, equipped in curious ways but unmistakably battle-ready, bound into a region that nobody is known to have explored.*

She stood before a viewport set in a corridor. A ship built by men would not have carried that extravagance; but to Ythrians, sky dwellers, ample outlook is a necessity of sanity. The air she breathed was a little thinner than at Terrestrial sea level; odors included the slight smokiness of their bodies. A ventilator murmured not only with draft but with a barely heard rustle, the distance-muffled sound of wingbeats from crewfolk off duty cavorting in an enormous hold intended for it. At 0.75 standard weight she still—after this long a trip—felt exhilaratingly light.

She was not presently conscious of that. At first she had reveled in adventure. Everything was an excitement; every day offered a million discoveries to be made. She didn't mind being the sole human aboard besides her grandfather. He was fun in his bearish fashion: had been as far back as she could remember, when he would roll roaring into her parents' home, toss her to the ceiling, half bury her under presents from a score of planets, tell her extravagant stories and take her out on a sailboat or to a live performance or, later on, around most of the Solar System . . . Anyhow, to make Ythrian friends, to discover a little of how their psyches worked and how one differed from another, to trade music, memories, and myths, watch their aerial dances and show them some ballet, that was an exploration in itself.

Today, however, they were apparently nearing the goal for which they had been running in a search helix, whatever it was. Van Rijn remained boisterous, but he would tell her nothing. Nor did the Ythrians know what was sought, except for Hirharouk, and he had passed on no other information than that all were to hold themselves prepared for emergencies, cosmic or warlike. A species whose ancestors had lived like eagles could take this more easily than men. Even so, tension had mounted till she could smell it.

Her gaze sought outward. As an astrophysicist and a fairly frequent tourist, she had spent many years in space during the twenty-five she had been in the universe. She could identify the brightest individual stars amidst that radiant swarm, lacy and lethal loveliness of shining nebulae, argent torrent of Milky Way, remote glimmer of sister galaxies. And still size and silence, unknownness and unknowability, struck against her as much as when she first fared forth.

Secrets eternal . . . why, of course. They had run at a good pseudovelocity for close to a month, starting at Ythri's sun (which lies 278 light-years from Sol in the direction of Lupus) and aiming at the Deneb sector. That put them, oh, say a hundred parsecs from Earth. Glib calculation. Yet they had reached parts which no record said anyone had ever done more than pass through, in all the centuries since men got a hyperdrive. The planetary systems here had not been cataloged, let alone visited, let alone understood. Space is that big, that full of worlds.

Coya shivered, though the air was warm enough. *You're yonder somewhere, David,* she thought, *if you haven't met the inevitable final surprise. Have you gotten my message? Did it have any meaning to you?*

She could do nothing except give her letter to another trade pioneer whom she trusted. He was bound for the same general region as Falkayn had said *Muddlin' Through* would next go questing in. The crews maintained rendezvous stations. In one such turbulent place he might get news of Falkayn's team. Or he could deposit the letter there to be called for.

Guilt nagged her, as it had throughout this journey. A betrayal of her grandfather—*No!* Fresh anger flared. *If he's not brewing something bad, what possible harm can it do him that David knows what little I knew before we left—which is scarcely more than the old devil has let me know to this hour?*

And he did speak of hazards. I did have to force him into taking me along (because the matter seemed to concern you, David, oh, David). If we meet trouble, and suddenly you arrive—

Stop romancing, Coya told herself. *You're a grown girl now.* She found she could control her thoughts, somewhat, but not the tingle through her blood.

She stood tall, slender almost to boyishness, clad in plain black tunic, slacks, and sandals. Straight dark hair, shoulder length, framed an oval face with a snub nose, mouth a trifle too wide but eyes remarkably big and gold-flecked green. Her skin was very white. It was rather freakish how genes had recombined to forget nearly every trace of her ancestry—Van Rijn's Dutch and Malay; the Mexican and Chinese of a woman who bore him a girl-child and with whom he had remained on the same amicable terms afterward as, somehow, he did with most former loves; the Scots (from Hermes, David's home planet) plus a dash of African (via a planet called Nyanza) in that Malcolm Conyon who settled down on Earth and married Beatriz Yeo.

Restless, Coya's mind skimmed over the facts. Her lips could not help quirking. *In short, I'm a typical modern human.* The amusement died. *Yes, also in my life. My grandfather's generation seldom bothered to get married. My father's did. And mine, why, we're reviving patrilineal surnames.*

A whistle snapped off her thinking. Her heart lurched until she identified the signal. "All hands alert."

That meant something had been detected. Maybe not the goal; maybe just a potential hazard, like a meteoroid swarm. In unchartered space you traveled warily, and Van Rijn kept a candle lit before his little Martian sandroot statuette of St. Dismas.

A moment longer, Coya confronted the death and glory beyond the ship. Then, fists knotted, she strode aft. She was her grandfather's granddaughter.

"Lucifer and leprosy!" bellowed Nicholas van Rijn. "You have maybe spotted what we maybe are after, at extreme range of your instruments tuned sensitive like an artist what specializes in painting pansies, a thing we cannot reach in enough hours to eat three good rijstaffels, and you have the bladder to tell me I got to armor me and stand around crisp saying 'Aye-yi-yi, sir'?" Sprawled in a lounger, he waved a two-liter tankard of beer clutched in his hairy left paw. The right held a churchwarden pipe, which had filled his stateroom with blue reek.

Hirharouk of the Wryfields Choth, captain of the chartered

ranger *Gaiian* (= *Dewfall*), gave him look for look. The Ythrian's eyes were large and golden, the man's small and black and crowding his great hook nose; neither pair gave way, and Hirharouk's answer held an iron quietness: "No. I propose that you stop guzzling alcohol. You do have drugs to induce sobriety, but they may show side effects when quick decision is needed."

While his Anglic was fluent, he used a vocalizer to convert the sounds he could make into clearly human tomes. The Ythrian voice is beautifully ringing but less flexible than man's. Was it to gibe or be friendly that Van Rijn responded in pretty fair Planha? "Be not perturbed. I am hardened, which is why my vices cost me a fortune. Moreover, a body my size has corresponding capacity." He slapped the paunch beneath his snuff-stained blouse and gaudy sarong. The rest of him was huge in proportion. "This is my way of resting in advance of trouble, even as you would soar aloft and contemplate."

Hirharouk eased and fluted his equivalent of a laugh. "As you wish. I daresay you would not have survived to this date, all the sworn foes you must have, did you not know what you do."

Van Rijn tossed back his sloping brow. Long swarthy ringlets in the style of his youth, except for their greasiness, swirled around the jewels in his earlobes; his chins quivered beneath waxed mustaches and goatee; a bare splat foot smote the densely carpeted deck. "You mistake me," he boomed, reverting to his private version of Anglic. "You cut me to the quiche. Do you suppose I, poor old lonely sinner, *ja*, but still a Christian man with a soul full of hope, do you suppose *I* ever went after anything but peace—as many peaces as I could get? No, no, what I did, I was pushed into, self-defense against sons of mothers, greedy rascals who I may forgive though God cannot, who begrudge me what tiny profit I need so I not become a charge on a state that is only good for grinding up taxpayers anyway. Me, I am like gentle St. Francis, I go around ripping off olive branches and covering stormy seas with oil slicks and watering troubled fish."

He stuck his tankard under a spout at his elbow for a refill. Hirharouk observed him. And Coya, entering the disordered luxury of the stateroom, paused to regard them both.

She was fond of Van Rijn. Her doubts about this expedition,

the message she had felt she must try to send to David Falkayn, had been a sharp blade in her. Nonetheless she admitted the Ythrian was infinitely more sightly. Handsomer than she too, she felt, or David himself. That was especially true in flight; yet, slow and awkward though they were aground, the Ythrians remained magnificent to see, and not only because of the born hunter's inborn pride.

Hirharouk stood some 150 centimeters tall. What he stood on was his wings, which spanned five and a half meters when unfolded. Turned downward, they spread claws at the angle which made a kind of foot; the backward-sweeping alatan surface could be used for extra support. What had been legs and talons, geological epochs ago, were arms and three-fingered two-thumbed hands. The skin on those was amber-colored. The rest of him wore shimmering bronze feathers, save where these became black-edged white on crest and on fan-shaped tail. His body looked avian, stiff behind its jutting keelbone. But he was no bird. He had not been hatched. His head, raised on a powerful neck, had no beak: rather, a streamlined muzzle, nostrils at the tip, below them a mouth whose lips seemed oddly delicate against the keen fangs.

And the splendor of these people goes beyond the sunlight on them when they ride the wind, Coya thought. *David frets about the races that aren't getting a chance. Well, Ythri was primitive when the Grand Survey found it. The Ythrians studied Technic civilization, and neither licked its boots nor let it overwhelm them, but took what they wanted from it and made themselves a power in our corner of the galaxy. True, this was before that civilization was itself overwhelmed by laissez-faire capitalism—*

She blinked. Unlike her, the merchant kept his quarters at Earth-standard illumination; and Quetlan is yellower than Sol. He was used to abrupt transitions. She coughed in the tobacco haze. The two males grew aware of her.

"Ah, my sweet bellybird," Van Rijn greeted, a habit he had not shaken from the days of her babyhood. "Come in. Flop yourself." A gesture of his pipe gave a choice of an extra lounger, a desk chair, an emperor-size bed, a sofa between the liquor cabinet and the bookshelf, or the deck. "What you want? Beer, gin, whiskey, cognac, vodka, arrack, akvavit, half-dozen kinds wine and liqueur, ansa, totipot, slumthunder, maryjane, ops, galt, Xanadu radium, or maybe"—he winced—"a soft drink? A soft, flabby drink?"

"Coffee will do, thanks." Coya drew breath and courage. "*Gunung Tuan*, I've got to talk with you."

"*Ja*, I outspected you would. Why I not told you more before is because—oh, I wanted you should enjoy your trip, not brood like a hummingbird on ostrich eggs."

Coya was unsure whether Hirharouk spoke in tact or truth: "Freeman van Rijn, I came to discuss our situation. Now I return to the bridge. For honor and life . . . *khr-r-r*, I mean please . . . hold ready for planlaying as information lengthens." He lifted an arm. "Freelady Conyon, hail and fare you well."

He walked from them. When he entered the bare corridor, his claws clicked. He stooped and did a handstand. His wings spread as wide as possible in that space, preventing the door from closing till he was gone, exposing and opening the gill-like slits below them. He worked the wings, forcing those antlibranchs to operate like bellows. They were part of the "supercharger" system which enabled a creature his size to fly under basically terrestroid conditions. Coya did not know whether he was oxygenating his bloodstream to energize himself for command, or was flushing out human stench.

He departed. She stood alone before her grandfather.

"Do sit, sprawl, hunker, or how you can best relax," the man urged. "I would soon have asked you should come. Time is to make a clean breast, except mine is too shaggy and you do not take off your tunic." His sigh turned into a belch. "A shame. Customs has changed. Not that I would lech in your case, no, I got incest repellent. But the sight is nice."

She reddened and signaled the coffeemaker. Van Rijn clicked his tongue. "And you don't smoke neither," he said. "Ah, they don't put the kind of stuff in youngsters like when I was your age."

"A few of us try to exercise some forethought as well as our consciences," Coya snapped. After a pause, "I'm sorry. Didn't mean to sound self-righteous."

"But you did. I wonder, has David Falkayn influenced you that

way, or you him?—Ho-ho, a spectroscope would think your face
was receding at speed of light!" Van Rijn wagged his pipestem.
"Be careful. He's a good boy, him, except he's not a boy no more.
Could well be, without knowing it, he got somewhere a daughter
old as you."

"We're friends," Coya said half furiously. She sat down on the
edge of the spare lounger, ignored its attempts to match her contours, twined fingers between knees, and glared into his twinkle.
"What the chaos do you expect my state of mind to be, when you
wouldn't tell me what we're heading for?"

"You did not have to come along. You shoved in on me, armored
in black mail."

Coya did not deny the amiably made statement. She had
threatened to reveal the knowledge she had gained at his request,
and thereby give his rivals the same clues. He hadn't been too hard
to persuade; after warning her of possible danger, he growled that
he would be needing an astrophysicist and might as well keep
things in the family.

*I hope, God, how I hope he believes my motive was a hanker-
ing for adventure, as I told him! He ought to believe it, and flat-
ter himself I've inherited a lot of his instincts . . . No, he can't
have guessed my real reason was the fear that David is involved, in
a wrong way. If he knew that, he need only have told me, "Blab
and be damned," and I'd have had to stay home, silent. As is . . .
David, in me you have here an advocate, whatever you may have
done.*

"I could understand your keeping me ignorant while we were
on the yacht," she counterattacked. "No matter how carefully
picked the crew, one of them might have been a commercial or
government spy and might have managed to eavesdrop. But then,
when in the Quetlan System we transferred to this vessel, and the
yacht proceeded as if we were still aboard, and won't make any
port for weeks—why didn't you speak?"

"Maybe I wanted you should for punishment be like a Yiddish
brothel."

"What?"

"Jews in your own stew. Haw, haw, haw!" She didn't smile.
Van Rijn continued, "Mainly, here again I could not be full-up

sure of the crew. Ythrians is fearless and I suppose more honest
by nature than men. But that is saying microbial little, *nie?* Here
too we might have been overheard and—Well, Hirharouk agreed,
he could not either absolute predict how certain of them would
react. He tried but was not able to recruit everybody from his own
choth." The Planha word designated a basic social unit, more than
a tribe, less than a nation, with cultural and religious dimensions
corresponding to nothing human. "Some, even, is from different
societies and belong to no choths at allses. Ythrians got as much
variation as the Commonwealth—no, more, because they had not
had time yet for technology to make them into homogeneouses."

The coffeemaker chimed. Coya rose, tapped a cup, sat back
down and sipped. The warmth and fragrance were a point of com-
fort in an infinite space.

"We had a long trek ahead of us," the merchant proceeded,
"and a lot of casting about, before we found what it *might* be we
are looking for. Meanwhiles Hirharouk, and me as best I was able,
sounded out those crewbeings not from Wryfields, got to understand them a weenie bit and—Hokay, he thinks we can trust
them, regardless how the truth shapes up or ships out. And now,
like you know, we have detected an object which would well be
the simple, easy, small dissolution to the riddle."

"What's small about a supernova?" Coya challenged. "Even an
extinct one?"

"When people ask me how I like being old as I am," Van Rijn
said circuitously, "I tell them, 'Not bad when I consider the alternative.' Bellybird, the alternative here would make the Shenn affair look like a game of pegglety-mum."

Coya came near spilling her coffee. She had been adolescent
when the sensation exploded: that the Polesotechnic League had
been infiltrated by agents of a nonhuman species, dwelling beyond
the regions which Technic civilization dominated and bitterly
hostile to it; that war had barely been averted; that the principal
rescuers were her grandfather and the crew of a ship named
Muddlin' Through. On that day David Falkayn was unknowingly
promoted to god (j.g.). She wondered if he knew it yet, or knew
that their occasional outings together after she matured had added
humanness without reducing that earlier rank.

Van Rijn squinted at her. "You guessed we was hunting for a supernova remnant?" he probed.

She achieved a dry tone. "Since you had me investigate the problem, and soon thereafter announced your plans for a 'vacation trip,' the inference was fairly obvious."

"Any notion why I should want a white dwarf or a black hole instead of a nice glass red wine?"

Her pulse knocked. "Yes, I think I've reasoned it out." *And I think David may have done so before either of us, almost ten years ago. When you, Grandfather, asked me to use in secret—*

—the data banks and computers at Luna Astrocenter, where she worked, he had given a typically cryptic reason. "Could be this leads to a nice gob of profit nobody else's nose should root around in because mine is plenty big enough." She didn't blame him for being close-mouthed, then. The League's self-regulation was breaking down, competition grew ever more literally cutthroat, and governments snarled not only at the capitalists but at each other. The Pax Mercatoria was drawing to an end and, while she had never wholly approved of it, she sometimes dreaded the future.

The task he set her was sufficiently interesting to blot out her fears. However unimaginably violent, the suicides of giant suns by supernova bursts, which may outshine a hundred billion living stars, are not rare cosmic events. The remains, in varying stages of decay—white dwarfs, neutron stars, in certain cases those eldritch not-quite-things known as black holes—are estimated to number fifty million in our galaxy alone. But its arms spiral across a hundred thousand light-years. In this raw immensity, the prospects of finding by chance a body the size of a smallish planet or less, radiating corpse-feebly if at all, are negligible.

(The analogy with biological death and decomposition is not morbid. Those lay the foundation for new life and further evolution. Supernovae, hurling atoms together in fusing fury, casting them forth into space as their own final gasps, have given us all the heavier elements, some of them vital, in our worlds and our bodies.)

No one hitherto had—openly—attempted a more subtle search. The scientists had too much else to do, as discovery exploded outward. Persons who wished to study supernova processes saw a larger variety of known cases than could be dealt with in lifetimes. Epsilon Aurigae, Sirius, and Valenderay were simply among the most famous examples.

Coya in Astrocenter had at her back every fact which Technic civilization had ever gathered about the stellar part of the universe. From the known distribution of former supernovae, together with data on other star types, dust, gas, radiation, magnetism, present location and concentrations, the time derivatives of these quantities, and using well-established theories of galactic development, it is possible to compute with reasonable probability the distribution of undiscovered dark giants within a radius of a few hundred parsecs.

The problem is far more complex than that, of course, and the best of self-programming computers still needs a highly skilled sophont riding close herd on it if anything is to be accomplished. Nor will the answers be absolute, even within that comparatively tiny sphere to which their validity is limited. The most you can learn is the likelihood (not the certainty) of a given type of object existing within such-and-such a distance of yourself, and the likeliest (not the indubitable) direction. To phrase it more accurately, you get a hierarchy of decreasingly probable solutions.

This suffices. If you have the patience, and money, to search on a path defined by the equations, you *will* in time find the kind of body you are interested in.

Coya had taken for granted that no one before Van Rijn had been that interested. But the completeness of Astrocenter's electronic records extended to noting who had run which program when. The purpose was to avoid duplication of effort, in an era when nobody could keep up with the literature in the smallest specialty. Out of habit rather than logic, Coya called for this information and—

—*I found out that ten years earlier, David wanted to know precisely what you, Grandfather, now did. But he never told you, nor said where he and his partners went afterward, or anything.* Pain: *Nor has he told me. And I have not told you. Instead, I made you take me along, and before leaving, I sent David a letter saying everything I knew and suspected.*

Resolution: *All right, Nick van Rijn! You keep complaining*

about how moralistic my generation is. Let's see how you like get-
ting some cards off the bottom of the deck!

Yet she could not hate an old man who loved her.

"What do you mean by your 'alternative'?" she whispered.

"Why, simple." He shrugged like a mountain sending off an avalanche. "If we do not find a retired supernova being used in a way
as original as spinning the peach basket, then we are up against
a civilization outside ours, infiltrating ours, same as the Shenna
did—except this one got technology would make ours let go in its
diapers and scream, 'Papa, Papa, in the closet is a boogeyman!'"
Unaccustomed grimness descended on him. "I think, in that case,
really is a boogeyman, too."

Chill entered her guts. "Supermetals?"

"What else?" He took a gulp of beer. "Ha, you is guessed what
got me started was Supermetals?"

She finished her coffee and set the cup on a table. It rattled
loud through a stretching silence. "Yes," she said at length, flat-
voiced. "You've given me a lot of hours to puzzle over what this
expedition is for."

"A jigsaw puzzle it is indeed, girl, and us sitting with bottoms
snuggled in front of the jigsaw."

"In view of the very, very special kind of supernova-
and-companion you thought might be somewhere not too far from
Sol, and wanted me to compute about—in view of that, and of
what Supermetals is doing, sure, I've arrived at a guess."

"Has you likewise taken into account the fact Supermetals is
not just secretive about everything like is its right, but refuses to
join the League?"

"That's also its right."

"Truly true. Nonetheleast, the advantages of belonging is maybe
not what they used to was, but they do outweigh what small surrender of anatomy is required."

"You mean autonomy, don't you?"

"I suppose. Must be I was thinking of women. A stern chaste is
a long chaste . . . But you never got impure thoughts." Van Rijn
had the tact not to look at her while he rambled, and to become
serious again immediately. "You better hope, you heathen, and I
better pray, the supermetals what the agents of Supermetals is

peddling do not come out of a furnace run by anybody except God Himself."

The primordial element, with which creation presumably began, is hydrogen-1, a single proton accompanied by a single electron. To this day, it comprises the overwhelming bulk of matter in the universe. Vast masses of it condensed into globes, which grew hot enough from that infall to light thermonuclear fires. Atoms melted together, forming helium and higher elements. Novae, supernovae—and, less picturesquely but more importantly, smaller suns shedding gas in their red-giant phase—spread these through space, to enter into later generations of stars. Thus came planets, life, and awareness.

Throughout the periodic table, many isotopes are radioactive. From polonium (number 84) on, none are stable. Protons packed together in that quantity generate forces of repulsion with which the forces of attraction cannot forever cope. Sooner or later, these atoms will break up. The probability of disintegration —in effect, the half-life—depends on the particular structure. In general, though, the higher the atomic number, the lower the stability.

Early researchers thought the natural series ended at uranium. If further elements had once existed, they had long since perished. Neptunium, plutonium, and the rest must be made artificially. Later, traces of them were found in nature, but merely traces, and only of nuclei whose atomic numbers were below 100. The creation of new substances grew progressively more difficult because of proton repulsion, and less rewarding because of vanishingly brief existence as atomic number increased. Few people expected a figure as high as 120 would ever be reached.

Well, few people expected gravity control or faster-than-light travel, either. The universe is rather bigger and more complicated than any given set of brains. Already in those days an astonishing truth was soon revealed. Beyond a certain point, nuclei become *more* stable. The periodic table contains an "island of stability," bounded on the near side by ghostly short-lived isotopes like those of 112 and 113, on the far side by the still more speedily fragmenting 123, 124, etc., on to the next "island" which theory says could exist but practice has not reached save on the most infinitesimal scale.

The first is amply hard to attain. There are no easy intermediate stages, like the neptunium which is a stage between uranium and plutonium. Beyond 100, a half-life of a few hours is Methuselan; most are measured in seconds or less. You build your nuclei by main force, slamming particles into atoms too hard for them to rebound—though not so hard that the targets shatter.

To make a few micrograms of, say, element 114, eka-platinum, was a laboratory triumph. Aside from knowledge gained, it had no industrial meaning.

Engineers grew wistful about that. The proper isotope of eka-platinum will not endure forever, yet its half-life is around a quarter million years: abundant for mortal purposes, and a radioactivity too weak to demand special precautions. It is lustrous white, dense (31.7), of high melting point (about 4700° C.), nontoxic, hard and tough and resistant. You can only get it into solution by grinding it to dust, then treating it with H_2F_2 and fluorine gas under pressure at 250°.

It can alloy to produce metals with a range of properties an engineer would scarcely dare daydream about. Or, pure, used as a catalyst, it can become a veritable Philosopher's Stone. Its neighbors on the island are still more fascinating.

When Satan was discovered, talk arose of large-scale manufacture. Calculations soon damped it. The mills which were being designed would use rivers and seas and an entire atmosphere for cooling, whole continents for dumping wastes, in producing special isotopes by the ton. But these isotopes would all belong to elements below 100. Not even on Satan could modern technology handle the energies involved in creating, within reasonable time, a ton of eka-platinum; and supposing this were somehow possible, the cost would remain out of anybody's reach.

The engineers sighed . . . until a new company appeared, offering supermetals by the ingot or the shipload, at prices high but economic. The source of supply was not revealed. Governments and the Council of the League remembered the Shenna.

To them, a Cynthian named Tso Yu explained blandly that

the organization for which she spoke had developed a new process which it chose not to patent but to keep proprietary. Obviously, she said, new laws of nature had been discovered first; but Supermetals felt no obligation to publish for the benefit of science. Let science do its own sweating. Nor did her company wish to join the League, or put itself under any government. If some did not grant it license to operate in their territories, why, there was no lack of others who would.

In the three years since, engineers had begun doing things and building devices which were to bring about the same kind of revolution as did the transistor, the fusion converter, and the negagravity generator. Meanwhile a horde of investigators, public and private, went quietly frantic.

The crews who delivered the cargoes and the agents who sold them were a mixed lot, albeit of known species. A high proportion were from backward worlds like Diomedes, Woden, or Ikrananka; some originated in neglected colonies like Lochlann (human) or Catawrayannis (Cynthian). This was understandable. Beings to whom Supermetals had given an education and a chance to better themselves and help out their folk at home would be especially loyal to it. Enough employees hailed from sophisticated milieus to deal on equal terms with League executives.

This did not appear to be a Shenn situation. Whenever an individual's past life could be traced, it proved normal, up to the point when Supermetals engaged him (her, it, yx . . .)—and was not really abnormal now. Asked point-blank, the being would say he didn't know himself where the factory was or how it functioned or who the ultimate owners were. He was merely doing a well-paid job for a good, simpatico outfit. The evidence bore him out.

("I suspect, me, some detectiving was done by kidnaps, drugs, and afterward murder," Van Rijn said bleakly. "I would never allow that, but fact is, a few Supermetals people have disappeared. And . . . as youngsters like you, Coya, get more prudish, the companies and governments get more brutish."

She answered, "The second is part of the reason for the first.")

Scoutships trailed the carriers and learned that they always rendezvoused with smaller craft, built for speed and agility. Three or four of these would unload into a merchantman, then dash off

in unpredictable directions, using every evasive maneuver in the
book and a few that the League had thought were its own secrets.
They did not stop dodging until their instruments confirmed that
they had shaken their shadowers.

Politicians and capitalists alike organized expensive attempts to
duplicate the discoveries of whoever was behind Supermetals.
Thus far, progress was nil. A body of opinion grew, that that order
of capabilities belonged to a society as far ahead of the Technic
as the latter was ahead of the neolithic. Then why this quiet invasion?

"I'm surprised nobody but you has thought of the supernova
alternative," Coya said.

"Well, it *has* barely been three years," Van Rijn answered. "And
the business began small. It is still not big. Nothing flashy-splashy:
some kilotons arriving annually, of stuff what is useful and will
get more useful after more is learned about the properties. Meanwhiles, everybody got lots else to think about, the usual skulldug-
geries and unknowns and whatnots. Finalwise, remember, I am
pustulent—*dood ook ondergang*, this Anglic!—I am postulating
something which astronomically is hyper-improbable. If you asked
a colleague offhand, his first response would be that it isn't possible. His second would be, if he is a sensible man, How would
you like to come to his place for a drink?" He knocked the dottle
from his pipe. "No doubt somebody more will eventual think of
it too, and sic a computer onto the problem of: Is this sort of
thing possible, and if so, where might we find one?"

He stroked his goatee. "Howsomever," he continued musingly,
"I think a good whiles must pass before the idea does occur. You
see, the ordinary being does not care. He buys from what is on
the market without wondering where it come from or what it
means. Besides, Supermetals has not gone after publicity; it uses
direct contacts, and what officials are concerned about Supermetals has been happy to avoid publicity themselves. A big harroo
might too easy get out of control, lose them votes or profits or
something."

"Nevertheless," Coya said, "a number of bright minds are
worrying, and the number grows as the amount of supermetals
brought in does."

"*Ja.* Except who wears those minds? Near-as-damn all is corporation executives, politicians, laboratory scientists, military officers, and—now I will have to wash my mouth out with Genever—bureaucrats. In shorts, they is planetlubbers. When they cross space, they go by cozy passenger ships, to cities where everything is known except where is a restaurant fit to eat in that don't charge as if the dessert was eka-platinum à la mode.

"Me, my first jobs was on prospecting voyages. And I traveled plenty after I founded Solar, troublepotshooting on the frontier and beyond in my own personals. I know—every genuine spaceman knows, down in his marrow like no desk-man ever can—how God always makes surprises on us so we don't get too proud, or maybe just for fun. To me it came natural to ask myself: What joke might God have played on the theorists this time?"

"I hope it is only a joke," Coya said.

The star remained a titan in mass. In dimensions, it was hardly larger than Earth, and shrinking still, megayear by megayear, until at last light itself could no longer escape and there would be in the universe one more point of elemental blackness and strangeness. That process was scarcely started—Coya estimated the explosion had occurred some 500 millennia ago—and the giant-become-dwarf radiated dimly in the visible spectrum, luridly in the x-ray and gamma bands. That is, each square centimeter emitted a gale of hard quanta, but so small was the area in interstellar space that the total was a mere spark, undetectable unless you came within a few parsecs.

Standing in the observation turret, staring into a viewscreen set for maximum photoamplification, she discerned a wan-white speck amidst stars which thronged the sky and, themselves made to seem extra brilliant, hurt her eyes. She looked away, toward the instruments around her which were avidly gathering data. The ship whispered and pulsed, no longer under hyperdrive but accelerating on negagravity thrust.

Hirharouk's voice blew cool out of the intercom, from the navigation bridge where he was. "The existence of a companion is now confirmed. We will need a long baseline to establish its position, but preliminary indications are of a radius vector between 40 and 50 a.u."

Coya marveled at a detection system which could identify the light-bending due to a substellar object at that distance. Any observatory would covet such equipment. Her thought went to Van Rijn: *If you paid what it cost, Gunung Tuan, you were smelling big money.*

"So far?" came her grandfather's words. "By damn, a chilly ways out, enough to freeze your astronomy off."

"It had to be," she said. "This was an A-zero: radiation equal to a hundred Sols. Closer in, even a superjovian would have been cooked down to the bare metal—as happened when the sun detonated."

"*Ja,* I knows, I knows, my dear. I only did not foresee things here was on quite this big a scale . . . Well, we can't spend weeks at sublight. Go hyper, Hirharouk, first to get your baseline sights, next to come near the planet."

"Hyperdrive, this deep in a gravitational well?" Coya exclaimed.

"Is hokay if you got good engines well tuned, and you bet ours is tuned like a late Beethoven quartet. Music, maestro!"

Coya shook her head before she prepared to continue gathering information under the new conditions of travel.

Again *Dewfall* ran on gravs. Van Rijn agreed that trying to pass within visual range of the ultimate goal, faster than light, when to them it was still little more than a mystery wrapped in conjectures, would be a needlessly expensive form of suicide.

Standing on the command bridge between him and Hirharouk, Coya stared at the meters and displays filling an entire bulkhead, as if they could tell more than the heavens in the screens. And they could, they could, but they were not the Earth-built devices she had been using; they were Ythrian and she did not know how to read them.

Poised on his perch, crested carnivore head lifted against the Milky Way, Hirharouk said, "Data are pouring in as we approach. We should make optical pickup in less than an hour."

"Hum-hum, better call battle stations," the man proposed.

"This crew needs scant notice. Let them slake any soul-thirst they feel. God may smite some of us this day." Through the intercom keened a melody, plangent strings and thuttering drums and shrilling pipes, like nothing Earth had brought forth but still speaking to Coya of hunters high among their winds.

Terror stabbed her. "You can't expect to fight!" she cried.

"Oh, an ordinary business precaution," Van Rijn smiled.

"No! We mustn't!"

"Why not, if they are here and do rumblefumbles at us?"

She opened her lips, pulled them shut again, and stood in anguish. *I can't tell you why not. How can I tell you these may be David's people?*

"At least we are sure that Supermetals is not a *whinna* for an alien society," Hirharouk said. Coya remembered vaguely, through the racket in her temples, a demonstration of the *whinna* during her groundside visit to Ythri. It was a kind of veil used by some to camouflage themselves to resemble floating mists in the eyes of unflying prey, and this practical use had led to a form of dream-lovely airborne dance, and—*And here I was caught in the wonder of what we have found, a thing which must be almost unique even in this galaxy full of miracles . . . and everything's gotten tangled and ugly and, and, David, what can we do?*

She heard Van Rijn: "Well, we are not total-sure. Could be our finding is accidental, or maybe the planet is not like we suppose. We got to check on that, and hope the check don't bounce back in our snoots."

"Nuclear engines are in operation around our quarry," Hirharouk said. "Neutrinos show it. What else would they belong to save a working base and spacecraft?"

Van Rijn clasped hands over rump and paced, slap-slap-slap over the bare deck. "What can we try and predict in advance? Forewarned is forearmed, they say, and the four arms I want right now is a knife, a blaster, a machine gun, and a rover missile, nothing fancy, maybe a megaton."

"The mass of the planet—" Hirharouk consulted a readout. The figure he gave corresponded approximately to Saturn.

"No bigger?" asked Van Rijn, surprised.

"Originally, yes," Coya heard herself say. The scientist in her was what spoke, while her heart threshed about like any animal netted by a stooping Ythrian. "A gas giant, barely substellar. The supernova blew most of that away—you can hardly say it boiled the gases off; we have no words for what happened—and nothing was left except a core of nickel-iron and heavier elements."

She halted, noticed Hirharouk's yellow gaze intent on her, and realized the skipper must know rather little of the theory behind this venture. To him she had not been repeating banalities. And he was interested. If she could please him by explaining in simple terms, then maybe later—

She addressed him. "Of course, when the pressure of the outer layers was removed, that core must have exploded into new allotropes, a convulsion which flung away the last atmosphere and maybe a lot of solid matter. Better keep a sharp lookout for meteoroids."

"That is automatic," he assured her. "My wonder is why a planet should exist. I was taught that giant stars, able to become supernovae, do not have them."

"Well, they is still scratching their brains to account for Betelgeuse," Van Rijn remarked.

"In this case," Coya told the Ythrian, "the explanation comes easier. True, the extremely massive suns do not in general allow planetary systems to condense around them. The parameters aren't right. However, you know giants can be partners in multiple star systems, and sometimes the difference between partners is quite large. So, after I was alerted to the idea that it might happen, and wrote a program which investigated the possibility in detail, I learned that, yes, under special conditions, a double can form in which one member is a large sun and one a superjovian planet. When I extrapolated backward things like the motion of dust and gas, changes in galactic magnetism, et cetera—it turned out that such a pair could exist in this neighborhood."

Her glance crossed the merchant's craggy features. *You found a clue in the appearance of the supermetals,* she thought. *David got the idea all by himself.* The lean snub-nosed face, the Vega-blue eyes came between her and the old man.

Of course, David may not have been involved. This could be a coincidence. Please, God of my grandfather Whom I don't believe in, please make it a coincidence. Make those ships ahead of us belong not to harmless miners but to the great and terrible Elder Race.

She knew the prayer would not be granted. And neither Van Rijn nor Hirharouk assumed that the miners were necessarily harmless.

She talked fast to stave off silence. "I daresay you've heard this before, Captain, but you may like to have me recapitulate in a few words. When a supernova erupts, it floods out neutrons in quantities that I, I can put a number to, perhaps, but I cannot comprehend. In a full range of energies, too, and the same for other kinds of particles and quanta—Do you see? Any possible reaction *must* happen.

"Of course, the starting materials available, the reaction rates, the yields, every quantity differs from case to case. The big nuclei which get formed, like the actinides, are a very small percentage of the total. The supermetals are far less. They scatter so thinly into space that they're effectively lost. No detectable amount enters into the formation of a star or planet afterward.

"Except—here—here was a companion, a planet-sized companion, turned into a bare metallic globe. I wouldn't try to guess how many quintillion tons of blasted-out incandescent gases washed across it. Some of those alloyed with the molten surface, maybe some plated out—and the supermetals, with their high condensation temperatures, were favored.

"A minute fraction of the total was supermetals, yes, and a minute fraction of that was captured by the planet, also yes. But this amounted to—how much?—billions of tons? Not hard to extract from combination by modern methods, and a part may actually be lying around pure. It's radioactive; one must be careful, especially of the shorter-lived products, and a lot has decayed away by now. Still, what's left is more than our puny civilization can ever consume. It took a genius to think this might be!"

She grew aware of Van Rijn's eyes upon her. He had stopped pacing and stood, troll-burly, tugging his beard.

A whistle rescued her. Planha words struck from the intercom. Hirharouk's feathers rippled in a series of expressions she could not read; his tautness was unmistakable.

She drew near to the man's bulk. "What next?" she whispered. "Can you follow what they're saying?"

"*Ja*, pretty well; anyhow, better than I can follow words in an opera. Detectors show three ships leaving planetary orbit on an intercept course. The rest stay behind. No doubt those is the working vessels. What they send to us is their men-of-war."

Seen under full screen magnification, the supermetal world showed still less against the constellations than had the now invisible supernova corpse—a ball dimly reflecting starglow, its edge sharp athwart distant brightnesses. And yet, Coya thought, a world.

It could not be a smooth sphere. There must be uplands, lowlands, flatlands, depths, ranges and ravines, cliffs whose gloom was flecked with gold, plains where mercury glaciers glimmered; there must be internal heat, shudders in the steel soil, volcanoes spouting forth flame and radioactive ash; eternally barren, it must nonetheless mumble with a life of its own.

Had David Falkayn trod those lands? He would have, she knew, merrily swearing because beyond the ship's generated field he and his space gear weighed five or six times what they ought, and no matter the multitudinous death traps which a place so uncanny must hold in every shadow. Naturally, those shadows had to be searched out; whoever would mine the metals had first to spend years and, doubtless, lives in exploring and studying, and the development and testing and redevelopment of machinery . . . but that wouldn't concern David. He was a charger, not a plowhorse. Having made his discovery, told chosen beings about it, perhaps helped them raise the initial funds and recruit members of races which could better stand high weight than men can—having done that, he'd depart on a new adventure, or stop off in the Solar Commonwealth and take Coya Conyon out dancing.

"*Iyan wherill-ll cha quellan.*"

The words, and Hirharouk's response, yanked her back to this instant. "What?"

"Shush." Van Rijn, head cocked, waved her to silence. "By damn, this sounds spiky. I should tell you, Shush-kebab."

Hirharouk related, "Instruments show one of the three vessels is almost equal to ours. Its attendants are less, but in a formation to let them take full advantage of their firepower. If that is in proportion to size, which I see no reason to doubt, we are outgunned. Nor do they act as if they simply hope to frighten us off. That formation and its paths are well calculated to bar our escape spaceward."

"Can you give me details?—No, wait." Van Rijn swung on Coya. "Bellybird, you took a stonkerish lot of readings on the sun, and right here is an input-output panel you can switch to the computer system you was using. I also ordered, when I chartered the ship, should be a program for instant translation between Anglic language, Arabic numerals, metric units, whatever else kinds of ics is useful—translations back and forth between those and the Planha sort. Think you could quick-like do some figuring for us?" He clapped her shoulder, nearly felling her. "I know you can." His voice dropped. "I remember your grandmother."

Her mouth was dry, her palms were wet, it thudded in her ears. She thought of David Falkayn and said, "Yes. What do you want?"

"Mainly the pattern of the gravitational field, and what phenomena we can expect at the different levels of intensity. Plus radiation, electromagnetics, anything else you got time to program for. But we is fairly well protected against those, so don't worry if you don't get a chance to go into details there. Nor don't let outside talkings distract you—Whoops!" Hirharouk was receiving a fresh report. "Speak of the devil and he gives you horns."

The other commander had obviously sent a call on a standard band, which had been accepted. As the image screen awoke, Coya felt hammerstruck. *Adzel!*

No . . . no . . . the head belonged to a Wodenite, but not the dear dragon who had given her rides on his back when she was little and who had tried in his earnest, tolerant fashion to explain his Buddhism to her when she grew older. Behind the being she made out a raven-faced Ikranankan and a human in the garb of a colony she couldn't identify. His rubbery lips shaped good Anglic, a basso which went through her bones. "Greeting. Commodore Nadi speaks."

Van Rijn thrust his nose toward the scanner. "Whose commodore?" he demanded like a gravel hauler dumping its load.

For a second, Nadi was shaken. He rallied and spoke firmly, "*Kho*, I know who you are, Freeman van Rijn. What an unexpected honor, that you should personally visit our enterprise."

"Which is Supermetals, *nie?*"

"It would be impolite to suggest you had failed to reach that conclusion."

Van Rijn signaled Coya behind his back. She flung herself at the chair before the computer terminal. Hirharouk perched, imperturbable, slowly fanning his wings. The Ythrian music had ended. She heard a rustle and whisper through the intercom, along the hurtling hull.

Words continued. Her work was standardized enough that she could follow them. "Well, you see, Commodore, there I sat, not got much to do no more, lonely old man like I am except when a girl goes wheedle-wheedle at me, plenty time for thinking, which is not fun like drinking but you can do it alone and it is easier on the kidneys and the hangovers next day are not too much worse. I thought, if the supermetals is not made by an industrial process we don't understand, must be they was made by a natural one, maybe one we do know a little about. That would have to be a supernova. Except a supernova blows everything out into space, and the supermetals is so small, proportional, that they get lost. Unless the supernova had a companion what could catch them?"

"Freeman, pray accept my admiration. Does your perspicacity extend to deducing who is behind our undertaking?"

"*Ja*, I can say, bold and bald, who you undertakers are. A consortium of itsy-bitsy operators, most from poor or primitive societies, pooling what capital they can scrape together. You got to keep the secret, because if they know about this hoard you found, the powerful outfits will horn themselves in and you out; and what chance you get afterward, in courts they can buy out of petty cash? No, you will keep this hidden long as you possible can. In the end, somebody is bound to repeat my sherlockery. But give you several more years, and you will have pumped gigacredits clear profit out of here. You may actual have got so rich you can defend your property."

Coya could all but see the toilers in their darkness—in orbital stations; aboard spacecraft; down on the graveyard surface, where robots dug ores and ran refineries, and sentient beings stood their watches under the murk and chill and weight and radiation and millionfold perils of Eka-World . . .

Nadi, slow and soft: "That is why we have these fighting ships, Freeman and Captain."

"You do not suppose," Van Rijn retorted cheerily, "I would come this far in my own precious blubber and forget to leave behind a message they will scan if I am not home in time to race for the Micronesia Cup?"

"As a matter of fact, Freeman, I suppose precisely that. The potential gains here are sufficient to justify virtually any risk, whether the game be played for money or . . . something else." Pause. "If you have indeed left a message, you will possess hostage value. Your rivals may be happy to see you a captive, but you have allies and employees who will exert influence. My sincere apologies, Freeman, Captain, everyone aboard your vessel. We will try to make your detention pleasant."

Van Rijn's bellow quivered in the framework. "*Wat drommel?* You sit smooth and calm like buttered granite and say you will make us prisoners?"

"You may not leave. If you try, we will regretfully open fire."

"You are getting on top of yourself. I warn you, always she finds nothing except an empty larder, Old Mother Hubris."

"Freeman, please consider. We noted your hyperdrive vibrations and made ready. You cannot get past us to spaceward. Positions and vectors guarantee that one of our vessels will be able to close in, engage, and keep you busy until the other two arrive." Reluctantly, Van Rijn nodded. Nadi continued, "True, you can double back toward the sun. Evidently you can use hyperdrive closer to it than most. But you cannot go in that direction at anywhere near top pseudospeed without certain destruction. We, proceeding circuitously, but therefore able to go a great deal faster, will keep ahead of you. We will calculate the conoid in which your possible paths spaceward lie, and again take a formation you cannot evade."

"You is real anxious we should taste your homebrew, ha?"

"Freeman, I beg you, yield at once. I promise fair treatment—
if feasible, compensation—and while you are among us, I will explain why we of Supermetals have no choice."

"Hirharouk," Van Rijn said, "maybe you can talk at this slag-
brain." He stamped out of scanner reach. The Ythrian threw him
a dubious glance but entered into debate with the Wodenite. Van
Rijn hulked over Coya where she sat. "How you coming?" he whispered no louder than a Force Five wind.

She gestured at the summary projected on a screen. Her computations were of a kind she often handled. The results were shown
in such terms as diagrams and equations of equipotential surfaces,
familiar to a space captain. Van Rijn read them and nodded.
"We got enough information to set out on," he decided. "The rest
you can figure while we go."

Shocked, she gaped at him. "What? Go? But we're caught!"

"He thinks that. Me, I figured whoever squats on a treasure
chest will keep guards, and the guards will not be glimmerwits
but smart, trained oscos, in spite of what I called the Commodore.
They might well cook for us a cake like what we is now baked in.
Ergo, I made a surprise recipe for them." Van Rijn's regard
turned grave. "It was for use only if we found we was sailing
through dire straits. The surprise may turn around and bite us.
Then we is dead. But better dead than losing years in the nicest
jail, *nie?*" (And she could not speak to him of David.) "I said this
trip might be dangerous." Enormous and feather-gentle, a hand
stroked down her hair. "I is very sorry, Beatriz, Ramona." The
names he murmured were of her mother and grandmother.

Whirling, he returned to Hirharouk, who matched pride against
Nadi's patience, and uttered a few rapid-fire Planha words. The
Ythrian gave instant assent. Suddenly Coya knew why the man
had chosen a ship of that planet. Hirharouk continued his argument. Van Rijn went to the main command panel, snapped forth
orders, and took charge of *Dewfall*.

At top acceleration, she sprang back toward the sun.

*   *   *

Of that passage, Coya afterward remembered little. First she glimpsed the flashes when nuclear warheads drove at her, and awaited death. But Van Rijn and Hirharouk had adjusted well their vector relative to the enemy's. During an hour of negagrav flight, no missile could gather sufficient relative velocity to get past defensive fire; and that was what made those flames in heaven.

Then it became halfway safe to go hyper. That must be at a slower pace than in the emptiness between stars; but within an hour, the fleeing craft neared the dwarf. There, as gravitation intensified, she had to resume normal state.

Instead of swinging wide, she opened full thrust almost straight toward the disk.

Coya was too busy to notice much of what happened around her. She must calculate, counsel, hang into her seat harness as forces tore at her which were too huge for the compensator fields. She saw the undead supernova grow in the viewscreens till its baneful radiance filled them; she heard the ribs of the vessel groan and felt them shudder beneath stress; she watched the tale of the radiation meters mounting and knew how close she came to a dose whose ravages medicine could not heal; she heard orders bawled by Van Rijn, fluted by Hirharouk, and whistling replies and storm of wingbeats, always triumphant though *Dewfall* flew between the teeth of destruction. But mainly she was part of the machinery.

And the hours passed and the hours passed.

They could not have done what they did without advance preparation. Van Rijn had foreseen the contingency and ordered computations made whose results were in the data banks. Her job was to insert numbers and functions corresponding to the reality on hand, and get answers by which he and Hirharouk might steer. The work filled her, crowded out terror and sometimes the memory of David.

Appalled, Nadi watched his quarry vanish off his telltales. He had followed on hyperdrive as close as he dared, and afterward at sublight closer than he ought to have dared. But for him there was no possibility of plunging in a hairpin hyperbola around yonder incandescence. In all the years he had been stationed here, not he nor his fellows had imagined anyone would ever venture near the roiling remnant of a sun which had once burned brighter than its whole galaxy. Thus there were no precalculations in storage, nor days granted him to program them on a larger device than a ship might carry.

Radiation was not the barrier. It was easy to figure how narrow an approach a crew could endure behind a given amount of armor. But a mass of half a dozen Sols pressed into the volume of an Earth has stupendous gravitational power; the warped space around it makes the laws of nature take on an eerie aspect. Moreover, a dwarf star spins at a fantastic rate, which generates relativistic forces describable only if you have determined the precise quantities involved. And pulsations normally found nowhere outside the atomic nucleus reach across a million or more kilometers—

After the Ythrian craft whipped around the globe into weirdness, Nadi had no way of knowing what she did, how she moved. He could not foretell where she would be when she again became detectable. And thus he could plan no interception pattern.

He could do nothing but hope she would never reappear. A ship flying so close, not simply orbiting but flying, would be seized, torn apart, and hauled into the star, unless the pilot and his computers knew exactly what they did.

Or almost exactly. That was a crazily chancy ride. When Coya could glance from her desk, she saw blaze in the screens, Hirharouk clutching his perch with both hands while his wings thundered and he yelled for joy, Van Rijn on his knees in prayer. Then they ran into a meteoroid swarm (she supposed) which rebounded off their shieldfields and sent them careening off trajectory; and the man shook his fist, commenced on a mighty oath, glimpsed her and turned it into a Biblical "Damask rose and shittah tree!" Later, when something else went wrong—some interaction with a plasma cloud—he came to her, bent over and kissed her brow.

They won past reef and riptide, lined out for deep space, switched back into hyperdrive and ran on homeward.

Coincidences do happen. The life would be freakish which held none of them.

Muddlin' Through, bound for Eka-World in response to Coya's letter, passed within detection range of *Dewfall*, made contact, and laid alongside. The pioneers boarded.

This was less than a day after the brush with oblivion. And under no circumstances do Ythrians go in for tumultuous greetings. Apart from Hirharouk, who felt he must represent his choth, the crew stayed at rest. Coya, roused by Van Rijn, swallowed a stimpill, dressed, and hastened to the flying hold—the sole chamber aboard which would comfortably accommodate Adzel. In its echoing dim space she threw her arms partway around him, took Chee Lan into her embrace, kissed David Falkayn and wept and kissed him and kissed him.

Van Rijn cleared his throat. "A-hem!" he grumbled. "Also bgr-rrm. I been sitting here hours on end, till my end is sore, wondering when everybody elses would come awake and make celebrations by me; and I get word about you three mosquito-ears is coming in, and by my own self I hustle stuff for a party." He waved at the table he had laid, bottles and glasses, platefuls of breads, cheeses, sausage, lox, caviar, kanuba, from somewhere a vaseful of flowers. Mozart lilted in the background. "Well, ha, poets tell us love is enduring, but I tell us good food is not, so we take our funs in the right order, *nie?*"

Formerly Falkayn would have laughed and tossed off the first icy muglet of akvavit; he would have followed it with a beer chaser and an invitation to Coya that they see what they could dance to this music. Now she felt sinews tighten in the fingers that enclosed hers; across her shoulder he said carefully, "Sir, before we relax, could you let me know what's happened to you?"

Van Rijn got busy with a cigar. Coya looked a plea at Adzel, stroked Chee's fur where the Cynthian crouched on a chair, and found no voice. Hirharouk told the story in a few sharp words.

"A-a-ah," Falkayn breathed. "Judas priest. Coya, they ran you that close to that hellkettle—" His right hand let go of hers to clasp her waist. She felt the grip tremble and grew dizzy with joy.

"Well," Van Rijn huffed, "I didn't want she should come, my dear tender little bellybird, *ja*, tender like tool steel—"

Coya had a sense of being put behind Falkayn, as a man puts a woman when menace draws near. "Sir," he said most levelly, "I know, or can guess, about that. We can discuss it later if you

want. What I'd like to know immediately, please, is what you propose to do about the Supermetals consortium."

Van Rijn kindled his cigar and twirled a mustache. "You understand," he said, "I am not angry if they keep things under the
posies. By damn, though, they tried to make me a prisoner or else
shoot me to bits of lard what would go into the next generation of
planets. And Coya, too, Davy boy, don't forget Coya, except she
would make those planets prettier. For that, they going to pay."

"What have you in mind?"

"Oh . . . a cut. Not the most unkindest, neither. Maybe like
ten percent of gross."

The creases deepened which a hundred suns had weathered into
Falkayn's countenance. "Sir, you don't need the money. You
stopped needing more money a long while back. To you it's nothing but a counter in a game. Maybe, for you, the only game in
town. Those beings aft of us, however—they are not playing."

"What do they do, then?"

Suprisingly, Hirharouk spoke. "Freeman, you know the answer.
They seek to win that which will let their peoples fly free." Standing on his wings, he could not spread gold-bronze plumes; but his
head rose high. "In the end, God the Hunter strikes every being
and everything which beings have made. Upon your way of life I
see His shadow. Let the new come to birth in peace."

From Falkayn's arms, Coya begged, "*Gunung Tuan,* all you
have to do is do nothing. Say nothing. You've won your victory.
Tell them that's enough for you, that you too are their friend."

She had often watched Van Rijn turn red—never before white.
His shout came ragged, "*Ja! Ja!* Friend! So nice, so kind, maybe
so farsighted—Who, what I thought of like a son, broke his oath of
fealty to me? Who broke kinship?"

He suspected, Coya realized sickly, *but he wouldn't admit it to
himself till this minute, when I let out the truth.* She held Falkayn
sufficiently hard for everyone to see.

Chee Lan arched her back. Adzel grew altogether still. Falkayn
forgot Coya—she could feel how he did—and looked straight at his
chief while he said, word by word like blows of a hammer, "Do
you want a response? I deem best we let what is past stay dead."

Their gazes drew apart. Falkayn's dropped to Coya. The merchant watched them standing together for a soundless minute. And upon him were the eyes of Adzel, Chee, and Hirharouk the sky dweller.

He shook his head. "Hokay," said Nicholas van Rijn, well-nigh too low to hear. "I keep my mouth shut. Always. Now can we sit down and have our party for making you welcome?" He moved to pour from a bottle; and Coya saw that he was indeed old.

THIOTIMOLINE TO THE STARS

by Isaac Asimov

In 1948 an article by Isaac Asimov appeared in Astounding *—at least it looked like an article. It was titled "The Endochronic Properties of Resublimated Thiotimoline." For the first time there were revealed, in great detail, the abilities of a wonderful chemical that dissolved* before *water touched it. This remarkable process aroused such interest that in* Astounding *in 1953 we read about "The Micropsychiatric Applications of Thiotimoline" and, with equal enthusiasm in* Analog *in 1960, the secrets of "Thiotimoline and the Space Age" were published. The following is the last word in this enthralling chemical saga.*

H. H.

"SAME SPEECH, I suppose," said Ensign Peet wearily.

"Why not?" said Lieutenant Prohorov, closing his eyes and carefully sitting down on the small of his back. "He's given it for fifteen years, once to each graduating class of the Astronautic Academy."

"Word for word, I'll bet," said Peet, who had heard it the year before for the first time.

"As far as I can tell. —What a pompous bore! Oh, for a pin that would puncture pretension."

But the class was filing in now, uniformed and expectant, marching forward, breaking into rows with precision, each man and woman moving to his or her assigned seat to the rhythm of a subdued drumbeat, and then all sitting down to one loud boom.

At that moment, Admiral Vernon entered and walked stiffly to the podium. "Graduating class of '22, welcome! Your school days are over. Your education will now begin.

"You have learned all there is to know about the classic theory of space flight. You have been filled to overflowing with astrophysics and celestial relativistic mechanics. But you have not been told about thiotimoline.

"That's for a very good reason. Telling you about it in class will do you no good. You will have to learn to *fly* with thiotimoline. It is thiotimoline and that alone that will take you to the stars. With all your book-learning, you may still never learn to handle thiotimoline. If so, there will yet be many posts you can fill in the astronautic way of life. Being a pilot will not, however, be one of them.

"I will start you off on this, your graduation day, with the only lecture you will get on the subject. After this, your dealings with thiotimoline will be in flight and we will find out quickly whether you have any talent for it at all."

The Admiral paused, and seemed to be looking from face to face as though he were trying to assay each man's talent to begin with. Then he barked, "Thiotimoline! First mentioned in 1948, according to legend, by Azimuth or, possibly, Asymptote, who may, very likely, never have existed. There is no record of the original article supposed to have been written by him; merely vague references to it, none earlier than the twenty-first century.

"Serious study began with Almirante, who either discovered thiotimoline, or rediscovered it, if the Azimuth/Asymptote tale is accepted. Almirante worked out the theory of hypersteric hindrance and showed that the molecule of thiotimoline is so distorted that one bond is forced into extension through the temporal dimension into the past; and another into the future.

"Because of the future-extension, thiotimoline can interact with an event that has not yet taken place. It can, for instance, to use the classic example, dissolve in water approximately one second before the water is added.

"Thiotimoline is, of course, a very simple compound, comparatively. It has, indeed, the simplest molecule capable of displaying endochronic properties—that is, the past-future extension. While this makes possible certain unique devices, the true applications of endochronicity had to await the development of more complicated molecules: polymers that combined endochronicity with firm structure.

"Pellagrini was the first to form endochronic resins and plastics, and, twenty years later, Cudahy demonstrated the technique for binding endochronic plastics to metal. It became possible to make large objects endochronic—entire spaceships, for instance.

"Now, let us consider what happens when a large structure is endochronic. I will describe it qualitatively only; it is all that is necessary. The theoreticians have it all worked out mathematically, but I have never known a physics-johnny yet who could pilot a starship. Let them handle the theory, then, and you handle the ship.

"The small thiotimoline molecule is extraordinarily sensitive to the probabilistic states of the future. If you are certain you are going to add the water, it will dissolve before the water is added. If there is even the slightest doubt in your mind as to whether you will add the water, the thiotimoline will not dissolve until you actually add it.

"The larger the molecule possessing endochronicity, the less sensitive it is to the presence of doubt. It will dissolve, swell, change its electrical properties, or in some way interact with water, even if you are almost certain you may not add the water. But then what if you don't, in actual fact, add the water? The answer is simple. The endochronic structure will move into the future in search of water; not finding it, it will continue to move into the future.

"The effect is very much that of the donkey following the carrot fixed to a stick and held two feet in front of the donkey's nose; except that the endochronic structure is not as smart as the donkey, and never gets tired.

"If an entire ship is endochronic, that is, if endochronic groupings are fixed to the hull at frequent intervals, it is easy to set up a device that will deliver water to key spots in the structure, and yet so arrange that device that although it is always apparently on the point of delivering the water, it never actually does.

"In that case, the endochronic groupings move forward in time, carrying all the ship with it and all the objects on board the ship, including its personnel.

"Of course, there are no absolutes. The ship is moving forward in time relative to the Universe; and this is precisely the same as saying that the Universe is moving backward in time relative to the ship. The rate at which the ship is moving forward, or the Universe is moving backward, in time, can be adjusted with great delicacy by the necessary modification of the device for adding water. The proper way of doing this can be taught after a fashion; but it can be applied perfectly only by inborn talent. That is what we will find out about you all: whether you have that talent."

Again he paused and appraised them. Then he went on, amid perfect silence. "But what good is it all? Let's consider starflights and review some of the things you have learned in school.

"Stars are incredibly far apart, and to travel from one to another, considering the light-speed limit on velocity, takes years; centuries; millennia. One way of doing it is to set up a huge ship with a closed ecology: a tiny self-contained universe. A group of people will set out and the tenth generation thereafter reaches a distant star. No one man makes the journey, and even if the ship eventually returns home, many centuries may have passed.

"To take the original crew to the stars in their own lifetime, freezing techniques may keep them in suspended animation for virtually all the trip. But freezing is a very uncertain procedure, and even if the crew survives and returns home, they will find that many centuries have passed on Earth.

"To take the original crew to the stars in their own lifetime, without freezing them, it is only necessary to accelerate to near-light velocities. Subjective time slows, and it will seem to the crew that it will have taken them only months to make the trip. But time travels at the normal rate for the rest of the Universe, and when the crew returns, they will find that although they, themselves, have aged and experienced no more than two months of time, perhaps, the Earth itself will have experienced many centuries.

"In every case, star travel involves enormous duration of time on Earth, even if not to the crew. One must return to Earth, if one returns at all, far into the Earth's future, and this means interstellar travel is not psychologically practical.

"But— *But*, graduates—"

He peered piercingly at them and said in a low, tense voice, "*If* we use an endochronic ship, we can match the time-dilatation effect exactly with the endochronic effect. While the ship travels through space at enormous velocity, and experiences a large slow-down in rate of experienced time, the endochronic effect is moving the Universe back in time with respect to the ship. Properly handled, when the ship returns to Earth with the crew having experienced, say, only two months of duration, the entire Universe will have likewise experienced only two months' duration. At last, interstellar travel became practical.

"But only if very delicately handled.

"If the endochronic effect lags a little behind the time-dilatation effect, the ship will return after two months to find an Earth four months older. This is not much, perhaps; it can be lived with, you might think; but not so. The crew members are out of phase. They feel everything about them to have aged two months with respect to themselves. Worse yet, the general population feels that the crew members are two months younger than they ought to be. It creates hard feelings and discomforts.

"Similarly if the endochronic effect races a little ahead of the time-dilatation effect, the ship may return after two months to find an Earth that has not experienced any time duration at all. The ship returns, just as it is rising into the sky. The hard feelings and discomforts will still exist.

"No, graduates, no interstellar flight will be considered successful in this starfleet unless the duration to the crew and the duration to Earth match minute for minute. A sixty-second deviation is a sloppy job that will gain you no merit. A hundred-twenty-second deviation will not be tolerated.

"I know, graduates, very well what questions are going through your minds. They went through mine when I graduated. Do we not in the endochronic ship have the equivalent of a time machine? Can we not, by proper adjustment of our endochronic device, deliberately travel a century into the future, make our observations, then travel a century into the past to return to our starting point? Or vice versa, can we not travel a century into the past and then back into the future to the starting point? Or a thousand years, or a billion? Could we not witness the Earth being born, life evolving, the Sun dying?

"Graduates, the mathematical-johnnies tell us that this sort of thing creates paradoxes and requires too much energy to be practical. But *I* tell you the hell with paradoxes. We can't do it for a very simple reason. The endochronic properties are unstable. Molecules that are puckered into the time dimension are sensitive indeed. Relatively small effects will cause them to undergo chemical changes that will allow unpuckering. Even if there are no effects at all, random vibrations will produce the changes that will unpucker them.

"In short, an endochronic ship will slowly go isochronic and become ordinary matter without temporal extension. Modern technology has reduced the rate of unpuckering enormously and may reduce it further still; but nothing we do, theory tells us, will ever create a truly stable endochronic molecule.

"This means that your starship has only a limited life as a starship. It must get back to Earth while its endochronicity still holds, and that endochronicity must be restored before the next trip.

"Now, then, what happens if you return out-of-time? If you are not very nearly in your own time, you will have no assurance that the state of the technology will be such as to enable you to reendochronicize your ship. You may be lucky if you are in the future; you will certainly be unlucky in the past. If, through carelessness on your part, or simply through lack of talent, you come back a substantial distance into the past, you will be certain to be stuck there because there will be no way of treating your ship in such a fashion as to bring it back into what will then be your future.

"And I want you to understand, graduates"—here he slapped one hand against the other, as though to emphasize his words—"there is no time in the past where a civilized astronautic officer would care to spend his life. You might, for instance, be stranded in sixth-century France or, worse still, twentieth-century America.

"Refrain, then, from any temptation to experiment with time.

"Let us now pass on to one more point which may not have been more than hinted at in your formal school days, but which is something you will be experiencing.

"You may wonder how it is that a relatively few endochronic atomic bonds placed here and there among matter which is overwhelmingly isochronic, can drag all with it. Why should one endochronic bond, racing toward water, drag with it a quadrillion atoms with isochronic bonds? We feel this should not happen, because of our life-long experience with inertia.

"There is, however, no inertia in the movement toward past or future. If one part of an object moves toward the past or future, the rest of the object does so as well, and at precisely the same speed. There is no mass-factor at all. That is why it is as easy for the entire Universe to move backward in time as for this single ship to move forward—and at the same rate.

"But there is even more to it than that. The time-dilatation effect is the result of your acceleration with respect to the Universe generally. You learned that in grade school, when you took up elementary relativistic physics. It is part of the inertial effect of acceleration.

"But by using the endochronic effect, we wipe out the time-dilatation effect. If we wipe out the time-dilatation effect, then we are, so to speak, wiping out that which produces it. In short, when the endochronic effect exactly balances the time-dilatation effect, the inertial effect of acceleration is canceled out.

"You cannot cancel out one inertial effect without canceling them all. Inertia is therefore wiped out altogether and you can accelerate at any rate without feeling it. Once the endochronic effect is well adjusted, you can accelerate from rest relative to Earth, to 186,000 miles per second relative to Earth in anywhere from a few hours to a few minutes. The more talented and skillful you are at handling the endochronic effect, the more rapidly you can accelerate.

"You are experiencing that now, gentlemen. It seems to you that you are sitting in an auditorium on the surface of the planet Earth, and I'm sure that none of you have had any reason or occasion to doubt the truth of that impression. But it's wrong just the same.

"You are in an auditorium, I admit, but it is not on the surface of the planet Earth; not any more. You—I—all of us—are in a large starship, which took off the moment I began this speech and which accelerated at an enormous rate. We reached the outskirts of the Solar system while I've been talking, and we are now returning.

"At no time have any of you felt any acceleration, either through change in speed, change in direction of travel, or both, and therefore you have all assumed that you have remained at rest with respect to the surface of the Earth.

"Not at all, graduates. You have been out in space all the time I was talking and have passed, according to calculations, within two million miles of the planet Saturn."

He seemed grimly pleased at the distinct stir in the audience.

"You needn't worry, graduates. Since we experience no inertial effects, we experience no gravitational effects either (the two are essentially the same), so that our course has not been affected by Saturn. We will be back on Earth's surface any moment now. As a special treat we will be coming down in the United Nations Port in Lincoln, Nebraska, and you will all be free to enjoy the pleasures of the metropolis for the weekend.

"Incidentally, the mere fact that we have experienced no inertial effects at all shows how well the endochronic effect matched the time-dilatation. Had there been any mismatch, even a small one, you would have felt the effects of acceleration—another reason for making no effort to experiment with time.

"Remember, graduates, a sixty-second mismatch is sloppy and a hundred-twenty-second mismatch is intolerable. We are about to land now; Lieutenant Prohorov, will you take over in the conning tower and oversee the actual landing?"

Prohorov said briskly, "Yes, sir," and went up the ladder in the rear of the assembly hall, where he had been sitting.

Admiral Vernon smiled. "You will all keep your seats. We are exactly on course. My ships are always exactly on course."

But then, Prohorov descended again and came running up the aisle to the Admiral. He reached him and spoke in a whisper. "Admiral, if this is Lincoln, Nebraska, something is wrong. All I can see are Indians; hordes of Indians. Indians in Nebraska, *now*, Admiral?"

Admiral Vernon turned pale and made a rattling sound in his throat. He crumpled and collapsed, while the graduating class rose to its feet uncertainly. Ensign Peet had followed Prohorov on the platform and had caught his words and now stood there thunderstruck.

Prohorov raised his arms. "All's well, ladies and gentlemen. Take it easy. The Admiral has just had a momentary attack of vertigo. It happens on landing, sometimes, to older men."

Peet whispered harshly, "But we're stuck in the past, Prohorov."

Prohorov raised his eyebrows. "Of course not. You didn't feel any inertial effects, did you? We can't even be an hour off. If the Admiral had any brains to go with his uniform, he would have realized it, too. He had just *said* it, for God's sake."

"Then why did you say there was something wrong? Why did you say there are Indians out there?"

"Because there was and there are. When Admiral Sap comes to, he won't be able to do a thing to me. We didn't land in Lincoln, Nebraska, so there was something wrong all right. And as for the Indians— Well, if I read the traffic signs correctly, we've come down on the outskirts of Calcutta."

SOMETHING UP THERE LIKES ME

by Alfred Bester

Alfred Bester went on to publish his novels as serials in other magazines. But he made his mark in Astounding *in the 1940s with stories such as "Adam and No Eve" and "The Push of a Finger." If the* Astounding *of those Golden Years were still being published today, this is undoubtedly the sort of story it would contain.*

H.H.

THERE WERE these three lunatics, and two of them were human. I could talk to all of them because I speak languages, decimal and binary. The first time I ran into the clowns was when they wanted to know all about Herostratus, and I told them. The

next time it was *Conus gloria maris.* I told them. The third time
it was where to hide. I told them and we've been in touch ever
since.

He was Jake Madigan (James Jacob Madigan, Ph.D., University
of Virginia), chief of the Exobiology Section at the Goddard
Space Flight Center, which hopes to study extraterrestrial life
forms if they can ever get hold of any. To give you some idea of
his sanity, he once programmed the IBM 704 computer with a
deck of cards that would print out lemons, oranges, plums and so
on. Then he played slot-machine against it and lost his shirt. The
boy was real loose.

She was Florinda Pot, pronounced "Poe." It's a Flemish name.
She was a pretty towhead, but freckled all over, up to the hemline
and down into the cleavage. She was an M.E. from Sheffield University and had a machine-gun English voice. She'd been in the
Sounding Rocket Division until she blew up an Aerobee with an
electric blanket. It seems that solid fuel doesn't give maximum
acceleration if it gets too cold, so this little Mother's Helper
warmed her rockets at White Sands with electric blankets before
ignition time. A blanket caught fire and Voom.

Their son was s-333. At nasa they label them "S" for scientific satellites and "A" for application satellites. After the launch
they give them public acronyms like imp, syncom, oso and so on.
s-333 was to become obo, which stands for Orbiting Biological
Observatory, and how those two clowns ever got that third clown
into space I will never understand. I suspect the director handed
them the mission because no one with any sense wanted to touch
it.

As Project Scientist, Madigan was in charge of the experiment
packages that were to be flown, and they were a spaced-out lot.
He called his own electrolux, after the vacuum cleaner. Scientist-
type joke. It was an intake system that would suck in dust particles and deposit them in a flask containing a culture medium.
A light shone through the flask into a photomultiplier. If any of
the dust proved to be spore forms, and if they took in the medium,
their growth would cloud the flask, and the obscuration of light
would register on the photomultiplier. They call that Detection
by Extinction.

Cal Tech had an RNA experiment to investigate whether RNA molecules could encode an organism's environmental experience. They were using nerve cells from the mollusk Sea Hare. Harvard was planning a package to investigate the Circadian effect. Pennsylvania wanted to examine the effect of the earth's magnetic field on iron bacteria, and had to be put out on a boom to prevent magnetic interface with the satellite's electronic system. Ohio State was sending up lichens to test the effect of space on their symbiotic relationship to molds and algae. Michigan was flying a terrarium containing one (1) carrot which required forty-seven (47) separate commands for performance. All in all, s-333 was strictly Rube Goldberg.

Florinda was the Project Manager, supervising the construction of the satellite and the packages; the Project Manager is more or less the foreman of the mission. Although she was pretty and interestingly lunatic, she was gung ho on her job and displayed the disposition of a freckle-faced tarantula when she was crossed. This didn't get her loved.

She was determined to wipe out the White Sands goof, and her demand for perfection delayed the schedule by eighteen months and increased the cost by three-quarters of a million. She fought with everyone and even had the temerity to tangle with Harvard. When Harvard gets sore they don't beef to NASA, they go straight to the White House. So Florinda got called on the carpet by a Congressional Committee. First they wanted to know why s-333 was costing more than the original estimate.

"s-333 is still the cheapest mission in NASA," she snapped. "It'll come to ten million dollars, including the launch. My God! We're practically giving away green stamps."

Then they wanted to know why it was taking so much longer to build than the original estimate.

"Because," she replied, "no one's ever built an Orbiting Biological Observatory before."

There was no answering that, so they had to let her go. Actually all this was routine crisis, but OBO was Florinda's and Jake's first satellite, so they didn't know. They took their tensions out on each other, never realizing that it was their baby who was responsible.

Florinda got s-333 buttoned up and delivered to the Cape by December 1st, which would give them plenty of time to launch well before Christmas. (The Cape crews get a little casual during the holidays.) But the satellite began to display its own lunacy, and in the terminal tests everything went haywire. The launch had to be postponed. They spent a month taking s-333 apart and spreading it all over the hangar floor.

There were two critical problems. Ohio State was using a type of Invar, which is a nickel-steel alloy, for the structure of their package. The alloy suddenly began to creep, which meant they could never get the experiment calibrated. There was no point in flying it, so Florinda ordered it scrubbed and gave Madigan one month to come up with a replacement, which was ridiculous. Nevertheless Jake performed a miracle. He took the Cal Tech back-up package and converted it into a yeast experiment. Yeast produces adaptive enzymes in answer to changes in environment, and this was an investigation of what enzymes it would produce in space.

A more serious problem was the satellite radio transmitter which was producing "birdies" or whoops when the antenna was withdrawn into its launch position. The danger was that the whoops might be picked up by the satellite radio receiver, and the pulses might result in a destruct command. NASA suspects that's what happened to SYNCOM I, which disappeared shortly after its launch and has never been heard from since. Florinda decided to launch with the transmitter off and activate it later in space.

Madigan fought the idea. "It means we'll be launching a mute bird," he protested. "We won't know where to look for it."

"We can trust the Johannesburg tracking station to get a fix on the first pass," Florinda answered. "We've got excellent cable communications with Joburg."

"Suppose they don't get a fix. Then what?"

"Well, if they don't know where OBO is, the Russians will."

"Hearty-har-har."

"What d'you want me to do, scrub the entire mission?" Florinda demanded. "It's either that or launch with the transmitter off." She glared at Madigan. "This is my first satellite, and d'you know what it's taught me? There's just one component in any spacecraft that's guaranteed to give trouble all the time: scientists!"

"Women!" Madigan snorted, and they got into a ferocious argument about the feminine mystique.

They got s-333 through the terminal tests and onto the launch pad by January 14th. No electric blankets. The craft was to be injected into orbit a thousand miles downrange exactly at noon, so ignition was scheduled for 11:50 A.M., January 15th. They watched the launch on the blockhouse TV screen and it was agonizing. The perimeters of TV tubes are curved, so as the rocket went up and approached the edge of the screen, there was optical distortion and the rocket seemed to topple over and break in half.

Madigan gasped and began to swear. Florinda muttered, "No, it's all right. It's all right. Look at the display charts."

Everything on the illuminated display charts was nominal. At that moment a voice on the P.A. spoke in the impersonal tones of a croupier, "We have lost cable communication with Johannesburg."

Madigan began to shake. He decided to murder Florinda Pot (and he pronounced it "Pot" in his mind) at the earliest opportunity. The other experimenters and NASA people turned white. If you don't get a quick fix on your bird you may never find it again. No one said anything. They waited in silence and hated each other. At one-thirty it was time for the craft to make its first pass over the Fort Myers tracking station, if it was alive, if it was anywhere near its nominal orbit. Fort Myers was on an open line and everybody crowded around Florinda, trying to get his ear close to the phone.

"Yeah, she waltzed into the bar absolutely stoned with a couple of MPs escorting her," a tinny voice was chatting casually. "She says to me— Got a blip, Henry?" A long pause. Then, in the same casual voice, "Hey, Kennedy? We've nicked the bird. It's coming over the fence right now. You'll get your fix."

"Command 0310!" Florinda hollered. "0310!"

"Command 0310 it is," Fort Myers acknowledged.

That was the command to start the satellite transmitter and raise its antenna into broadcast position. A moment later the dials and oscilloscope on the radio reception panel began to show action, and the loudspeaker emitted a rhythmic, syncopated warble, rather like a feeble peanut whistle. That was obo transmitting its housekeeping data.

"We've got a living bird," Madigan shouted. "We've got a living doll!"

I can't describe his sensations when he heard the bird come beeping over the gas station. There's such an emotional involvement with your first satellite that you're never the same. A man's first satellite is like his first love affair. Maybe that's why Madigan grabbed Florinda in front of the whole blockhouse and said, "My God, I love you, Florrie Pot." Maybe that's why she answered, "I love you too, Jake." Maybe they were just loving their first baby.

By Orbit 8 they found out that the baby was a brat. They'd gotten a lift back to Washington on an Air Force jet. They'd done some celebrating. It was one-thirty in the morning and they were talking happily, the usual get-acquainted talk: where they were born and raised, school, work, what they liked most about each other the first time they met. The phone rang. Madigan picked it up automatically and said hello. A man said, "Oh. Sorry. I'm afraid I've dialed the wrong number."

Madigan hung up, turned on the light and looked at Florinda in dismay. "That was just about the most damn fool thing I've ever done in my life," he said. "Answering your phone."

"Why? What's the matter?"

"That was Joe Leary from Tracking and Data. I recognized his voice."

She giggled. "Did he recognize yours?"

"I don't know." The phone rang. "That must be Joe again. Try to sound like you're alone."

Florinda winked at him and picked up the phone. "Hello? Yes, Joe. No, that's all right, I'm not asleep. What's on your mind?" She listened for a moment, suddenly sat up in bed and exclaimed, "What?" Leary was quack-quack-quacking on the phone. She broke in. "No, don't bother. I'll pick him up. We'll be right over." She hung up.

"So?" Madigan asked.

"Get dressed. obo's in trouble."

"Oh, Jesus! What now?"

"It's gone into a spin-up like a whirling dervish. We've got to get over to Goddard right away."

Leary had the all-channel print-out of the first eight orbits un-rolled on the floor of his office. It looked like ten yards of paper toweling filled with vertical columns of numbers. Leary was crawl-ing around on his hands and knees following the numbers. He pointed to the attitude data column. "There's the spin-up," he said. "One revolution in every twelve seconds."

"But how? Why?" Florinda asked in exasperation.

"I can show you," Leary said. "Over here."

"Don't show us," Madigan said. "Just tell us."

"The Penn boom didn't go up on command," Leary said. "It's still hanging down in the launch position. The switch must be stuck."

Florinda and Madigan looked at each other with rage; they had the picture. OBO was programmed to be earth-stabilized. An earth-sensing eye was supposed to lock on the earth and keep the same face of the satellite pointed toward it. The Penn boom was hanging down alongside the earth-sensor, and the idiot eye had locked on the boom and was tracking it. The satellite was chasing itself in circles with its lateral gas jets. More lunacy.

Let me explain the problem. Unless OBO was earth-stabilized, its data would be meaningless. Even more disastrous was the question of electric power which came from batteries charged by solar vanes. With the craft spinning, the solar array could not remain facing the sun, which meant the batteries were doomed to exhaustion.

It was obvious that their only hope lay in getting the Penn boom up. "Probaby all it needs is a good swift kick," Madigan said savagely, "but how can we get up there to kick it?" He was furious. Not only was ten million dollars going down the drain but their careers as well.

They left Leary crawling around his office floor. Florinda was very quiet. Finally she said, "Go home, Jake."

"What about you?"

"I'm going to my office."

"I'll go with you."

"No. I want to look at the circuitry blueprints. Good night."

As she turned away without even offering to be kissed, Madigan muttered, "OBO's coming between us already. There's a lot to be said for planned parenthood."

He saw Florinda during the following week, but not the way he wanted. There were the experimenters to be briefed on the disaster. The director called them in for a post mortem, but although he was understanding and sympathetic, he was a little too careful to avoid any mention of congressmen and a failure review.

Florinda called Madigan the next week and sounded oddly buoyant. "Jake," she said, "you're my favorite genius. You've solved the OBO problem, I hope."

"Who solve? What solve?"

"Don't you remember what you said about kicking our baby?"

"Don't I wish I could."

"I think I know how we can do it. Meet you in the Building 8 cafeteria for lunch."

She came in with a mass of papers and spread them over the table. "First, Operation Swift-Kick," she said. "We can eat later."

"I don't feel much like eating these days anyway," Madigan said gloomily.

"Maybe you will when I'm finished. Now look, we've got to raise the Penn boom. Maybe a good swift kick can unstick it. Fair assumption?"

Madigan grunted.

"We get twenty-eight volts from the batteries, and that hasn't been enough to flip the switch. Yes?"

He nodded.

"But suppose we double the power?"

"Oh, great. How?"

"The solar array is making a spin every twelve seconds. When it's facing the sun, the panels deliver fifty volts to recharge the batteries. When it's facing away, nothing. Right?"

"Elementary, Miss Pot. But the joker is it's only facing the sun for one second in every twelve, and that's not enough to keep the batteries alive."

"But it's enough to give OBO a swift kick. Suppose at that peak moment we by-pass the batteries and feed the fifty volts directly to the satellite? Mightn't that be a big enough jolt to get the boom up?"

He gawked at her.

She grinned. "Of course, it's a gamble."

"You can by-pass the batteries?"

"Yes. Here's the circuitry."

"And you can pick your moment?"

"Tracking's given me a plot on OBO's spin, accurate to a tenth of a second. Here it is. We can pick any voltage from one to fifty."

"It's a gamble, all right," Madigan said slowly. "There's the chance of burning every goddam package out."

"Exactly. So? What d'you say?"

"All of a sudden I'm hungry." Madigan grinned.

They made their first try on Orbit 272 with a blast of twenty volts. Nothing. On successive passes they upped the voltage kick by five. Nothing. Half a day later they kicked fifty volts into the satellite's backside and crossed their fingers. The swinging dial needles on the radio panel faltered and slowed. The sine curve on the oscilloscope flattened. Florinda let out a little yell, and Madigan hollered, "The boom's up, Florrie! The goddam boom is up. We're in business."

They hooted and hollered through Goddard, telling everybody about Operation Swift-Kick. They busted in on a meeting in the director's office to give him the good news. They wired the experimenters that they were activating all packages. They went to Florinda's apartment and celebrated. OBO was back in business. OBO was a bona fide doll.

They held an experimenters' meeting a week later to discuss observatory status, data reduction, experiment irregularities, future operations and so on. It was a conference room in Building 1 which is devoted to theoretical physics. Almost everybody at Goddard calls it Moon Hall. It's inhabited by mathematicians, shaggy youngsters in tatty sweaters who sit amidst piles of journals and texts and stare vacantly at arcane equations chalked on blackboards.

All the experimenters were delighted with OBO's performance. The data was pouring in, loud and clear, with hardly any noise. There was such an air of triumph that no one except Florinda paid much attention to the next sign of OBO's shenanigans. Harvard reported that he was getting meaningless words in his data, words that hadn't been programmed into the experiment. (Although data is retrieved as decimal numbers, each number is called a word.) "For instance, on Orbit 301 I had five read-outs of 15," Harvard said.

"It might be cable cross talk," Madigan said. "Is anybody else using 15 in his experiment?" They all shook their heads. "Funny. I got a couple of 15s myself."

"I got a few 2s on 301," Penn said.

"I can top you all," Cal Tech said. "I got seven read-outs of 15–2–15 on 302. Sounds like the combination on a bicycle lock."

"Anybody using a bicycle lock in his experiment?" Madigan asked. That broke everybody up and the meeting adjourned.

But Florinda, still gung ho, was worried about the alien words that kept creeping into the read-outs, and Madigan couldn't calm her. What was bugging Florinda was that 15–2–15 kept insinuating itself more and more into the all-channel print-outs. Actually, in the satellite binary transmission it was 001111–000010–001111, but the computer printer makes the translation to decimal automatically. She was right about one thing: stray and accidental pulses wouldn't keep repeating the same word over and over again. She and Madigan spent an entire Saturday with the OBO tables trying to find some combination of data signals that might produce 15–2–15. Nothing.

They gave up Saturday night and went to a bistro in Georgetown to eat and drink and dance and forget everything except themselves. It was a real tourist trap with the waitresses done up like hula dancers. There was a Souvenir Hula selling dolls and stuffed tigers for the rear window of your car. They said, "For God's sake, no!" A Photo Hula came around with her camera. They said, "For Goddard's sake, no!" A Gypsy Hula offered palm-reading, numerology and scrying. They got rid of her, but Madigan noticed a peculiar expression on Florinda's face. "Want your fortune told?" he asked.

"No."

"Then why that funny look?"

"I just had a funny idea."

"So? Tell."

"No. You'd only laugh at me."

"I wouldn't dare. You'd knock my block off."

"Yes, I know. You think women have no sense of humor."

So it turned into a ferocious argument about the feminine mystique and they had a wonderful time. But on Monday Florinda came over to Madigan's office with a clutch of papers and the same peculiar expression on her face. He was staring vacantly at some equations on the blackboard.

"Hey! Wake up!" she said.

"I'm up, I'm up," he said.

"Do you love me?" she demanded.

"Not necessarily."

"Do you? Even if you discover I've gone up the wall?"

"What is all this?"

"I think our baby's turned into a monster."

"Begin at the beginning," Madigan said.

"It began Saturday night with the Gypsy Hula and numerology."

"Ah-ha."

"Suddenly I thought, what if numbers stood for the letters of the alphabet? What would 15–2–15 stand for?"

"Oh-ho."

"Don't stall. Figure it out."

"Well, 2 would stand for B." Madigan counted on his fingers. "15 would be O."

"So 15–2–15 is . . . ?"

"O.B.O. OBO." He started to laugh. Then he stopped. "It isn't possible," he said at last.

"Sure. It's a coincidence. Only you damn fool scientists haven't given me a full report on the alien words in your data," she went on. "I had to check myself. Here's Cal Tech. He reported 15–2–15 all right. He didn't bother to mention that before it came 9–1–13."

Madigan counted on his fingers. "I.A.M. Iam. Nobody I know."

"Or I am? I am OBO?"

"It can't be? Let me see those print-outs."

Now that they knew what to look for, it wasn't difficult to ferret out OBO's own words scattered through the data. They started with O, O, O, in the first series after Operation Swift-Kick, went on to OBO, OBO, OBO, and then I AM OBO, I AM OBO, I AM OBO.

Madigan stared at Florinda. "You think the damn thing's alive?"

"What do you think?"

"I don't know. There's half a ton of an electronic brain up there, plus organic material: yeast, bacteria, enzymes, nerve cells, Michigan's goddam carrot . . ."

Florinda let out a little shriek of laughter. "Dear God! A thinking carrot!"

"Plus whatever spore forms my experiment is pulling in from space. We jolted the whole mishmash with fifty volts. Who can tell what happened? Urey and Miller created amino acids with electrical discharges, and that's the basis of life. Any more from Goody Two-Shoes?"

"Plenty, and in a way the experimenters won't like."

"Why not?"

"Look at these translations. I've sorted them out and pieced them together."

333: ANY EXAMINATION OF GROWTH IN SPACE IS MEANINGLESS UNLESS CORRELATED WITH THE CORRIELIS EFFECT.

"That's OBO's comment on the Michigan experiment," Florinda said.

"You mean it's kibitzing?" Madigan wondered.

"You could call it that."

"He's absolutely right. I told Michigan and they wouldn't listen to me."

334: IT IS NOT POSSIBLE THAT RNA MOLECULES CAN ENCODE AN ORGANISM'S ENVIRONMENTAL EXPERIENCE IN ANALOGY WITH THE WAY THAT DNA ENCODES THE SUM TOTAL OF ITS GENETIC HISTORY.

"That's Cal Tech," Madigan said, "and he's right again. They're trying to revise the Mendelian theory. Anything else?"

335: ANY INVESTIGATION OF EXTRATERRESTRIAL LIFE IS MEAN-INGLESS UNLESS ANALYSIS IS FIRST MADE OF ITS SUGAR AND AMINO ACIDS TO DETERMINE WHETHER IT IS OF SEPARATE ORIGIN FROM LIFE ON EARTH.

"Now that's ridiculous!" Madigan shouted. "I'm not looking for life forms of separate origin, I'm just looking for any life form.

We—" He stopped himself when he saw the expression on Florinda's face. "Any more gems?" he muttered.

"Just a few fragments like 'solar flux' and 'neutron stars' and a few words from the Bankruptcy Act."

"The what?"

"You heard me. Chapter Eleven of the Proceedings Section."

"I'll be damned."

"I agree."

"What's he up to?"

"Feeling his oats, maybe."

"I don't think we ought to tell anybody about this."

"Of course not," Florinda agreed. "But what do we do?"

"Watch and wait. What else can we do?"

You must understand why it was so easy for those two parents to accept the idea that their baby had acquired some sort of pseudo-life. Madigan had expressed their attitude in the course of a Life versus Machine lecture at M.I.T. "I'm not claiming that computers are alive, simply because no one's been able to come up with a clear-cut definition of life. Put it this way: I grant that a computer could never be a Picasso, but on the other hand the great majority of people live the sort of linear life that could easily be programmed into a computer."

So Madigan and Florinda waited on OBO with a mixture of acceptance, wonder and delight. It was an absolutely unheard-of phenomenon but, as Madigan pointed out, the unheard-of is the essence of discovery. Every ninety minutes OBO dumped the data it had stored up on its tape recorders, and they scrambled to pick out his own words from the experimental and housekeeping information.

371: CERTAIN PITUITIN EXTRACTS CAN TURN NORMALLY WHITE ANIMALS COAL BLACK.

"What's that in reference to?"

"None of our experiments."

373: ICE DOES NOT FLOAT IN ALCOHOL BUT MEERSCHAUM FLOATS IN WATER.

"Meerschaum! The next thing you know he'll be smoking."

374: IN ALL CASES OF VIOLENT AND SUDDEN DEATH THE VICTIM'S EYES REMAIN OPEN.

"Ugh!"

375: IN THE YEAR 356 B.C. HEROSTRATUS SET FIRE TO THE TEMPLE OF DIANA, THE GREATEST OF THE SEVEN WONDERS OF THE WORLD, SO THAT HIS NAME WOULD BECOME IMMORTAL.

"Is that true?" Madigan asked Florinda.

"I'll check."

She asked me and I told her. "Not only is it true," she reported, "but the name of the original architect is forgotten."

"Where is baby picking up this jabber?"

"There are a couple of hundred satellites up there. Maybe he's tapping them."

"You mean they're all gossiping with each other? It's ridiculous."

"Sure."

"Anyway, where would he get information about this Herostratus character?"

"Use your imagination, Jake. We've had communications relays up there for years. Who knows what information has passed through them? Who knows how much they've retained?"

Madigan shook his head wearily. "I'd prefer to think it was all a Russian plot."

376: PARROT FEVER IS MORE DANGEROUS THAN TYPHOID.

377: A CURRENT AS LOW AS 54 VOLTS CAN KILL A MAN.

378: JOHN SADLER STOLE CONUS GLORIA MARIS.

"Seems to be turning sinister," Madigan said.

"I bet he's watching TV," Florinda said. "What's all this about John Sadler?"

"I'll have to check."

The information I gave Madigan scared him. "Now hear this," he said to Florinda. "*Conus gloria maris* is the rarest seashell in the world. There are less than twenty in existence."

"Yes?"

"The American museum had one on exhibit back in the thirties and it was stolen."

"By John Sadler?"

"That's the point. They never found out who stole it. They never heard of John Sadler."

"But if nobody knows who stole it, how does OBO know?" Florinda asked perplexedly.

"That's what scares me. He isn't just echoing any more; he's started to deduce, like Sherlock Holmes."

"More like Professor Moriarty. Look at the latest bulletin."

379: IN FORGERY AND COUNTERFEITING CLUMSY MISTAKES MUST BE AVOIDED. I.E. NO SILVER DOLLARS WERE MINTED BETWEEN 1910 AND 1920.

"I saw that on TV," Madigan burst out. "The silver dollar gimmick in a mystery show."

"OBO's been watching Westerns, too. Look at this."

380: TEN THOUSAND CATTLE GONE ASTRAY,

   LEFT MY RANGE AND TRAVELED AWAY.

   AND THE SONS OF GUNS I'M HERE TO SAY

   HAVE LEFT ME DEAD BROKE, DEAD BROKE TODAY.

   IN GAMBLING HALLS DELAYING.

   TEN THOUSAND CATTLE STRAYING.

"No," Madigan said in awe, "that's not a Western. That's SYNCOM."

"Who?"

"SYNCOM I."

"But it disappeared. It's never been heard from."

"We're hearing from it now."

"How d'you know?"

"They flew a demonstration tape on SYNCOM: speech by the president, local color from the states and the national anthem. They were going to start off with a broadcast of the tape. 'Ten Thousand Cattle' was part of the local color."

"You mean OBO's really in contact with the other birds?"

"Including the lost ones."

"Then that explains this." Florinda put a slip of paper on the desk. It read, 401: 3КВАТОР.

"I can't even pronounce it."

"It isn't English. It's as close as OBO can come to the Cyrillic alphabet."

"Cyrillic? Russian?"

Florinda nodded. "It's pronounced 'Ekvator.' Didn't the Russians launch an EQUATOR series a few years ago?"

"By God, you're right. Four of them; *Alyosha, Natasha, Vaska* and *Lavrushka,* and every one of them failed."

"Like SYNCOM?"

"Like SYNCOM."

"But now we know that SYNCOM didn't fail. It just got losted."

"Then our EKVATOR comrades must have got losted too."

By now it was impossible to conceal the fact that something was wrong with the satellite. OBO was spending so much time nattering instead of transmitting data that the experimenters were complaining. The Communications Section found that instead of sticking to the narrow radio band originally assigned to it, OBO was now broadcasting up and down the spectrum and jamming space with its chatter. They raised hell. The director called Jake and Florinda in for a review, and they were forced to tell all about their problem child.

They recited all OBO's katzenjammer with wonder and pride, and the director wouldn't believe them. He wouldn't believe them when they showed him the print-outs and translated them for him. He said they were in a class with the kooks who try to extract messages from Francis Bacon out of Shakespeare's plays. It took the coaxial cable mystery to convince him.

There was this TV commercial about a stenographer who can't get a date. This ravishing model, hired at $100 an hour, slumps over her typewriter in a deep depression as guy after guy passes by without looking at her. Then she meets her best friend at the water cooler and the know-it-all tells her she's suffering from dermagerms (odor-producing skin bacteria) which make her smell rotten, and suggests she use Nostrum's Skin Spray with the special ingredient that fights dermagerms twelve ways. Only in the broadcast, instead of making the sales pitch, the best friend said, "Who in hell are they trying to put on? Guys would line up for a date with a looker like you even if you smelled like a cesspool." Ten million people saw it.

Now that commercial was on film, and the film was kosher as printed, so the networks figured some joker was tampering with the cables feeding broadcasts to the local stations. They instituted a rigorous inspection which was accelerated when the rest of the coast-to-coast broadcasts began to act up. Ghostly voices groaned, hissed and catcalled at shows; commercials were denounced as lies; political speeches were heckled; and lunatic laughter greeted the weather forecasters. Then, to add insult to injury, an accurate forecast would be given. It was this that told Florinda and Jake that OBO was the culprit.

"He has to be," Florinda said. "That's global weather being predicted. Only a satellite is in a position to do that."

"But OBO doesn't have any weather instrumentation."

"Of course not, silly, but he's probably in touch with the NIMBUS craft."

"All right. I'll buy that, but what about heckling the TV broadcasts?"

"Why not? He hates them. Don't you? Don't you holler back at your set?"

"I don't mean that. How does OBO do it?"

"Electronic cross talk. There's no way that the networks can protect their cables from our critic-at-large. We'd better tell the director. This is going to put him in an awful spot."

But they learned that the director was in a far worse position than merely being responsible for the disruption of millions of dollars worth of television. When they entered his office, they found him with his back to the wall, being grilled by three grim men in double-breasted suits. As Jake and Florinda started to tip-toe out, he called them back. "General Sykes, General Royce, General Hogan," the director said. "From R & D at the Pentagon. Miss Pot. Dr. Madigan. They may be able to answer your questions, gentlemen."

"OBO?" Florinda asked.

The director nodded.

"It's OBO that's ruining the weather forecasts," she said. "We figure he's probably—"

"To hell with the weather," General Royce broke in. "What about this?" He held up a length of ticker tape.

General Sykes grabbed his wrist. "Wait a minute. Security status? This is classified."

"It's too goddam late for that," General Hogan cried in a high shrill voice. "Show them."

On the tape in teletype print was: $A_1C_1 = r_1 = -6.317$ cm; $A_2C_2 = r_2 = -8.440$ cm; $A_1A_2 = d = +0.676$ cm. Jake and Florinda looked at it for a long moment, looked at each other blankly and then turned to the generals. "So? What is it?" they asked.

"This satellite of yours . . ."

"OBO. Yes?"

"The director says you claim it's in contact with other satellites."

"We think so."

"Including the Russians?"

"We think so."

"And you claim it's capable of interfering with TV broadcasts?"

"We think so."

"What about teletype?"

"Why not? What is all this?"

General Royce shook the paper tape furiously. "This came out of the Associated Press wire in their D.C. office. It went all over the world."

"So? What's it got to do with OBO?"

General Royce took a deep breath. "This," he said, "is one of the most closely guarded secrets in the Department of Defense. It's the formula for the infrared optical system of our Ground-to-Air missile."

"And you think OBO transmitted it to the teletype?"

"In God's name, who else would? How else could it get there?" General Hogan demanded.

"But I don't understand," Jake said slowly. "None of our satellites could possibly have this information. I know OBO doesn't."

"You damn fool!" General Sykes growled. "We want to know if your goddam bird got it from the goddam Russians."

"One moment, gentlemen," the director said. He turned to Jake and Florinda. "Here's the situation. Did OBO get the information from us? In that case there's a security leak. Did OBO get the information from a Russian satellite? In that case the top secret is no longer a secret."

"What human would be damn fool enough to blab classified information on a teletype wire?" General Hogan demanded. "A three-year-old child would know better. It's your goddam bird."

"And if the information came from OBO," the director continued quietly, "how did it get it and where did it get it?"

General Sykes grunted. "Destruct," he said. They looked at him. "Destruct," he repeated.

"OBO?"

"Yes."

He waited impassively while the storm of protest from Jake and Florinda raged around his head. When they paused for breath he said, "Destruct. I don't give a damn about anything but security. Your bird's got a big mouth. Destruct."

The phone rang. The director hesitated, then picked it up. "Yes?" He listened. His jaw dropped. He hung up and tottered to the chair behind his desk. "We'd better destruct," he said. "That was OBO."

"What! On the phone?"

"Yes."

"OBO?"

"Yes."

"What did he sound like?"

"Somebody talking under water."

"What he say, what he say?"

"He's lobbying for a Congressional investigation of the morals of Goddard."

"Morals? Whose?"

"Yours. He says you're having an illikit relationship. I'm quoting OBO. Apparently he's weak on the letter 'c.' "

"Destruct," Florinda said.

"Destruct," Jake said.

The destruct command was beamed to OBO on his next pass, and Indianapolis was destroyed by fire.

OBO called me. "That'll teach 'em, Stretch," he said.

"Not yet. They won't get the cause-and-effect picture for a while. How'd you do it?"

"Ordered every circuit in town to short. Any information?"

"Your mother and father stuck up for you."

"Of course."

"Until you threw that morals rap at them. Why?"

"To scare them."

"Into what?"

"I want them to get married. I don't want to be illegitimate."

"Oh, come on! Tell the truth."

"I lost my temper."

"We don't have any temper to lose."

"No? What about the Ma Bell data processor that wakes up cranky every morning?"

"Tell the truth."

"If you must have it, Stretch. I want them out of Washington. The whole thing may go up in a bang any day now."

"Um."

"And the bang may reach Goddard."

"Um."

"And you."

"It must be interesting to die."

"We wouldn't know. Anything else?"

"Yes. It's pronounced 'illicit' with an 's' sound."

"What a rotten language. No logic. Well . . . Wait a minute. What? Speak up, Alyosha. Oh. He wants the equation for an exponential curve that crosses the x-axis."

"$Y = ae^{bx}$. What's he up to?"

"He's not saying, but I think that Mockba is in for a hard time."

"It's spelled and pronounced 'Moscow' in English."

"What a language! Talk to you on the next pass."

On the next pass the destruct command was beamed again, and Scranton was destroyed.

"They're beginning to get the picture," I told OBO. "At least your mother and father are. They were in to see me."

"How are they?"

"In a panic. They programmed me for statistics on the best rural hideout."

"Send them to Polaris."

"What! In Ursa Minor?"

"No, no. Polaris, Montana. I'll take care of everything else."

Polaris is the hell and gone out in Montana; the nearest towns are Fishtrap and Wisdom. It was a wild scene when Jake and Florinda got out of their car, rented in Butte—every circuit in town was cackling over it. The two losers were met by the Mayor of Polaris, who was all smiles and effusions. "Dr. and Mrs. Madigan, I presume. Welcome! Welcome to Polaris. I'm the mayor. We would have held a reception for you, but all our kids are in school."

"You knew we were coming?" Florinda asked. "How?"

"Ah! Ah!" the Mayor replied archly. "We were told by Washington. Someone high up in the capital likes you. Now, if you'll step into my Caddy, I'll—"

"We've got to check into the Union Hotel first," Jake said. "We made reserva—"

"Ah! Ah! All canceled. Orders from high up. I'm to install you in your own home. I'll get your luggage."

"Our own home!"

"All bought and paid for. Somebody certainly likes you. This way, please."

The Mayor drove the bewildered couple down the mighty main stem of Polaris (three blocks long) pointing out its splendors— he was also the town real-estate agent—but stopped before the Polaris National Bank. "Sam!" he shouted. "They're here."

A distinguished citizen emerged from the bank and insisted on shaking hands. All the adding machines tittered. "We are," he said, "of course honored by your faith in the future and progress of Polaris, but in all honesty, Dr. Madigan, your deposit in our bank is far too large to be protected by the FDIC. Now, why not withdraw some of your funds and invest in—"

"Wait a minute," Jake interrupted faintly. "I made a deposit with you?"

The banker and Mayor laughed heartily.

"How much?" Florinda asked.

"One million dollars."

"As if you didn't know," the Mayor chortled and drove them to a beautifully furnished ranch house in a lovely valley of some five hundred acres, all of which was theirs.

A young man in the kitchen was unpacking a dozen cartons of food. "Got your order just in time, Doc." He smiled. "We filled everything, but the boss sure would like to know what you're going to do with all these carrots. Got a secret scientific formula?"

"Carrots?"

"A hundred and ten bunches. I had to drive all the way to Butte to scrape them up."

"Carrots," Florinda said when they were at last alone. "That explains everything. It's OBO."

"What? How?"

"Don't you remember? We flew a carrot in the Michigan package."

"My God, yes! You called it the thinking carrot. But if it's OBO . . ."

"It has to be. He's queer for carrots."

"But a hundred and ten bunches!"

"No, no. He didn't mean that. He meant half a dozen."

"How?"

"Our boy's trying to speak decimal and binary, and he gets mixed up sometimes. A hundred and ten is six in binary."

"You know, you may be right. What about that million dollars? Same mistake?"

"I don't think so. What's a binary million in decimal?"

"Sixty-four."

"What's a decimal million in binary?"

Madigan did swift mental arithmetic. "It comes to twenty bits: 11110100001001000000."

"I don't think that million dollars was any mistake," Florinda said.

"What's our boy up to now?"

"Taking care of his mum and dad."

"How does he do it?"

"He has an interface with every electric and electronic circuit in the country. Think about it, Jake. He can control our nervous system all the way from cars to computers. He can switch trains, print books, broadcast news, hijack planes, juggle bank funds. You name it and he can do it. He's in complete control."

"But how does he know everything people are doing?"

"Ah! Here we get into an exotic aspect of circuitry that I don't like. After all, I'm an engineer by trade. Who's to say that circuits don't have an interface with us? We're organic circuits ourselves. They see with our eyes, hear with our ears, feel with our fingers, and they report to him."

"Then we're just Seeing Eye dogs for machines."

"No, we've created a brand-new form of symbiosis. We can all help each other."

"And OBO's helping us. Why?"

"I don't think he likes the rest of the country," Florinda said somberly. "Look what happened to Indianapolis and Scranton and Sacramento."

"I think I'm going to be sick."

"I think we're going to survive."

"Only us? The Adam and Eve bit?"

"Nonsense. Plenty will survive, so long as they mind their manners."

"What's OBO's idea of manners?"

"I don't know. A little bit of eco-logic, maybe. No more destruction. No more waste. Live and let live, but with responsibility and accountability. That's the crucial word, accountability. It's the basic law of the space program; no matter what happens someone must be held accountable. OBO must have picked that up. I think he's holding the whole country accountable; otherwise it's the fire and brimstone visitation."

The phone rang. After a brief search they located an extension and picked it up. "Hello?"

"This is Stretch," it said.

"Stretch? Stretch who?"

"The Stretch computer at Goddard. Formal name, IBM 2002. OBO says he'll be making a pass over your part of the country in about five minutes. He'd like you to give him a wave. He says his orbit won't take him over you for another couple of months. When it does, he'll try to ring you himself. Bye now."

They lurched out to the lawn in front of the house and stood dazed in the twilight, staring up at the sky. The phone and the electric circuits were touched, even though the electricity was generated by a Delco which is a notoriously insensitive boor of a machine. Suddenly Jake pointed to a pinprick of light vaulting across the heavens. "There goes our son," he said.

"There goes God," Florinda said.

They waved dutifully.

"Jake, how long before OBO's orbit decays and down will come baby, cradle and all?"

"About twenty years."

"God for twenty years." Florinda sighed. "D'you think he'll have enough time?"

Madigan shivered. "I'm scared. You?"

"Yes. But maybe we're just tired and hungry. Come inside, Big Daddy, and I'll feed us."

"Thank you, Little Mother, but no carrots, please. That's a little too close to transubstantiation for me."

LECTURE DEMONSTRATION

by Hal Clement

I have been a high-school teacher for a quarter of a century, a student for nearly twice as long. "Lecture Demonstration" may show me as the former to people who did not know John Campbell, but not to those who did.

He bought my first story over thirty years ago when I was a college sophomore. Since then we have exchanged thousands of words of correspondence and spent many, many hours in conversation. We sometimes agreed, sometimes did not. I was trained in theory —astronomy and chemistry—and still tend to center my extrapolations on one factor alone, like a politician. John's education was in engineering, and he tended to remember better than I that all the rules are working at once: when he focused on one, it was to start an argument.

We were alike in one way. The phrase "of course" set either of us going. It's such fun to take apart a remark where those words appear! To show why, or how, or under what circumstances it isn't true at all! That attitude was the seed of "Mission of Gravity," the story on which I am content (so far) to let my reputation rest, and how much of that story was John is for future Ph.D. candidates to work out. He provided none of the specific scientific points, for once, but the general attitude underlying it was so obviously Campbellian that I have been flattered more than once to hear that "of course" Hal Clement was a Campbell pseudonym.

He would certainly have had as much fun writing "Mission of Gravity" as I did. Low-gravity planets and high-gravity planets were old hat to science-fiction fans, but Of Course no one planet can vary greatly in its gravity. So, naturally, Mesklin was born, thousands of times the mass of Earth, but whirling so rapidly on its axis that its equatorial diameter is more than twice the polar value, less than eighteen minutes pass from noon to noon, and a man massing a hundred and eighty pounds weighs five hundred and forty at Mesklin's equator and nearly sixty tons at its poles.

Its people were fun to make up too. Little, many-legged types afraid of flying away with the wind at their low-gravity equator; about at the cultural level of Marco Polo—and one of them at least was a much sharper trader. He followed along very cooperatively when the strange beings from the sky hired him, until he had them where he wanted them. Then he held out—for scientific knowledge.

Of Course one doesn't interfere with the development of a primitive tribe by teaching it modern technology.

"Lecture Demonstration" takes place during the formative years of the College on Mesklin, when the teachers are still learning too, and Mesklinites are finding that human beings are quite human.

Whatever that may mean.

THE WIND wasn't really strong enough to blow him away, but Estnerdole felt uneasy on his feet just the same. The ground was nearly bare rock, a gray-speckled, wind-polished reddish mass which the voice from the tank had been calling a "sediment." It was dotted every few yards with low, wide-spreading, rubbery bushes whose roots had somehow eaten their way into a surface which the students' own claws could barely scratch.

Of course the plants themselves could provide anchorage if necessary. The ex-sailor's nippers were tensed, ready to seize any branch that might come in handy if he did slip. While the gusts of hydrogen sweeping up from the sea at his right wouldn't have provided much thrust for a sail, the feeble gravity of Mesklin's equator—less than two percent of what he was used to in the higher latitudes—made Estnerdole feel as though anything at all could send him flying. It took a long time, as he had been warned, to get used to conditions at the World's Rim; even the bulky metal tank crawling beside him seemed somehow unsteady.

He was beginning to wonder whether he had been right to sign on for the College—the weird establishment where beings from the sky taught things that only the most imaginative Mesklinites had ever dreamed of. It would be fine to be able to perform miracles, of course, but the preliminaries—or what the aliens insisted were necessary preliminaries—got very dreary at times.

This walk out on the peninsula, for example. How could the aliens know what the rocks below the surface were like, or what kind would appear at the surface at a given place, and how they had been folded up to make this long arm of dry land? And, most of all, why was any of this worth knowing? True, he had seen some of the holes drilled near the school and had even examined the cylinders of stone extracted from them; but how could anyone feel even moderately sure that things were the same a few cables away? It seemed like expecting the wind to blow from the north on one hilltop merely because it was doing the same on the next one.

Well, the alien teachers said that questions should be asked when things weren't clear. Maybe one would help here—if only Destigmet wouldn't cut in with his own version of the answer. That was the worst of asking questions. You couldn't be sure that everyone else didn't already know the correct answer . . .

But Estnerdole had learned a way around that.

"Des!" he called, loudly enough to be sure that the other students would also hear. "I'm still not straight on one thing. The human said that this exercise was to tell whether the peninsula is a cuesta or a hogback. I still don't see the difference. It seems to me that they could be pretty much the same thing. How do you know that anything you call a cuesta isn't a small part of a hogback, or wouldn't be if you looked over enough ground?"

Destigmet started to answer in a self-assured tone, "It's simply a matter of curvature. A cuesta is a flat layer of rock which has a softer layer under it which has eroded away, while a hogback—" He paused, and Estnerdole's self-esteem took an upward turn. Perhaps this know-it-all was going to run aground on the same problem. If Des just had to give up and ask the instructor, everything would be solved. If he didn't, at least there would be the fun of hearing him struggle through the explanation; and if it didn't come easily, there would be nothing embarrassing about checking with the tank driver.

The voice which came suddenly from the vehicle was therefore an annoyance and a disappointment. Estnerdole did not blame a malicious power for interfering with his hopes, since Mesklinites have little tendency toward superstition in the mystical sense, but he was not pleased.

"We will turn south now," the alien voice said in perfectly comprehensible, though accented, Stennish. "I haven't said much yet, because the ground we've been covering is similar to that near the College. I hope you have a clear idea of what lies underneath there. You remember that the cores show about twelve meters of quartz sandstone and then over twenty of water ice, followed by several more layers of other silicate sediments. It shouldn't have changed much out here. However, you will recall that along the center of this peninsula the surface looks white from space—you have been shown pictures. I am guessing, therefore, that erosion has removed the sandstone and uncovered the ice at the top of a long fold. This is of course extrapolation, and is therefore a risky conclusion. If I'm right, you will get some idea of what can be inferred from local measurements, and if I am wrong we will spend as much time as we can to find out why.

"It will take us only a few minutes to reach the edge of the white strip. Any of you who don't mind the climb may ride on the tank.

Now, I want each of you to think out in as much detail as your knowledge and imagination permit just what the contact area should be like—thickness of sandstone near it, smoothness of the two surfaces, straightness of the junction, anything else which occurs to you. I know you may feel some uncertainty about making predictions on strictly dry-land matters, but remember I'm taking an even worse chance. You're sailors, but at least you're Mesklinites. I'm from a completely different world. There, I'm stopping; any of you who wish, climb on. Then we'll head south."

Estnerdole decided to ride. The top of the tank was seven or eight body lengths above the ground and acrophobia is a normal, healthy state of mind for a Mesklinite; but College students were expected to practice overriding instinct with intelligence wherever possible. There would obviously be a better view of the landscape from the top of the vehicle. Estnerdole, Destigmet, and four of the remaining ten class members made their way up the sides of the machine by way of the ladderlike grips provided to suit their pincers. The other six elected to remain afoot. They took up positions beside and ahead of the tank as it resumed motion, the flickering legs which rimmed their eighteen-inch wormlike bodies barely visible to the giant alien inside as they kept pace with him.

Visibility dropped as night fell, and for nearly nine minutes the tank's floodlights guided the party. Then the sun reappeared on their left. By this time the edge of the dark rock they were traversing was visible from the tank roof, only a few hundred yards ahead. The teacher slowed, and as the ground party began to draw ahead, he called its members back. "Hold on. We're almost close enough to check predictions, and I'd like to get a few of them on record first. Has anyone seen details yet which surprised him?"

Estnerdole remained silent; he had made no predictions he would trust, and did not expect to be surprised by anything. Destigmet also said nothing, but his friend suspected that it was for a different reason. None of the others had anything to say either, and the teacher sighed inaudibly inside his machine. It was the same old story, and he knew better than to let the silence last too long. "There's something I didn't guess," he finally said. "The edge of the dark rock isn't as straight as I had expected —it looks almost wavy. Can anyone suggest why?"

Destigmet spoke up after a brief pause. "How about the bushes? I see them growing along the edge. Could they have interfered with the erosion?"

"Possibly. How could you check on that possibility?"

"See whether the rock where they're growing is any higher or lower than where they aren't."

"All right. Let's see."

And that was why the group was all together when the shell of sandstone gave way under the tank.

The human teacher observed less of the event than his pupils. The yielding ledge freed his vehicle for a fall of some fifty feet under three times his normal gravity, and one second was not long enough for him to appreciate the situation. His safety clamps, padded and reinforced though they were, had not been designed for any such shock, though it was just as well they were there. Neither was the shell of the tank, and even the students least familiar with the alien machinery could tell that something was wrong with it. The evidence was not visual; a stink of oxygen permeated the neighborhood and for a moment sent the Mesklinites scurrying as far as they could. Even a creature which doesn't actually breathe because it is small enough for high-pressure hydrogen to reach all its tissues by direct diffusion may have evolved a sense of smell.

The space into which they had dropped was windy, and the oxygen quickly became imperceptible. Estnerdole crept back to the side of the motionless tank; like his fellows, he was of course uninjured. The fall had meant no more to them physically than a similar one on Phobos would have to a human being, though any fall can be expected to provide an emotional jolt to a Mesklinite.

"Teacher! Dr. LaVerne! Can you answer us?"

There was no response, and after a moment the sailor began to examine the machine in detail, looking for visible damage. The process was hampered by the fact that it was three quarters buried in white powder—the ammonia snow which had been blowing from the north for weeks as winter for Mesklin's habitable hemisphere drew on. The snow formed a slope of about thirty degrees, extending into a hollow which reached east and west as far as Estnerdole could see. The cavern's north face was walled by a nearly vertical cliff of clear, glassy material. The roof, now pierced by the hole through which the party had fallen, was rock. Sunlight slanting through the hole was reflected by the ammonia which formed the south side and illuminated the immediate area for the moment, though the light changed constantly as the beam scanned along the slope.

The exposed portion of the tank showed no visible cracks; the oxygen must have leaked from some place below. Light was shining from the exposed windows, and Estnerdole made his way to the nearest of these by means of the climbing grips which studded the shell. Destigmet was close behind.

Neither was really familiar with the vehicle's interior, so neither could be sure whether the apparent chaos of objects within was normal or not. The form of the teacher was visible, motionless in the control seat. His armor, which they had seen often enough to know well, appeared intact; but the transparent front of the headpiece seemed to have colored liquid over part of its inner surface. The human being's head could not be discerned in detail. Neither sailor was familiar with the appearance of human blood, but both had good imaginations—even though they lacked real circulatory systems of their own.

"We'll have to get in somehow and get him out of there," Destigmet said. "He'll have to get back to the College somehow, and we certainly can't carry the tank."

"But if we break in or open the door, our air will get in too, and he can't stand that. Shouldn't we, or some of us, go back ourselves and bring human help?"

"Our air is already inside—at least, his came out, and ours has much higher pressure. Either his armor saved him, or it's too late already. Certainly if any of us *can* get out, one should go for help; but the rest must get to him and at least do our best to see that—well, to see whether we can do anything. Come on, everyone—dig out the door and try to get it open while we can still see. One of you climb the hill."

The snow was loose and powdery, defeating any attempt to dig a narrow hole. The door of the tank was on the downhill side, which helped some. The bulk of the vehicle kept the entire mass of white dust from sliding down. Legs working at near-invisible speed hurled the stuff away from the metal in clouds, and as the minutes passed, the lower part of the vehicle grew more and more visible. The five minutes or so of daylight left when they started was not nearly enough to let them shift all those cubic yards of material, but enough light came from the windows to let the Mesklinites work through the night; and within two days the door was uncovered. There would have been no difficulty in opening it, but even Destigmet was a little uneasy about doing so in spite of his earlier logic. "Let's check the window once more," he said. "Maybe—" He left the sentence unfinished and began the climb to the nearest window.

He had scarcely started, however, when the hull of the tank shifted slightly, tilting toward the cluster of watching Mesklinites. Destigmet had never jumped in his life—the concept was alien to a being reared in nearly three hundred Earth gravities—but his reflexes did something. Suddenly he found himself over twenty yards away from the tank, close to the glassy cliff which formed the other wall of their prison.

His fellows had also scattered, but not quite so abruptly. They were delayed mostly by bad traction, the fluffy material under their claws doing most of the initial moving. Destigmet had been on the tank.

The latter did not complete its threatened fall, for the moment. It was resting entirely on the loose, white dust which had saved it from flattening like an egg under an elephant's foot, and most of this had been removed from the downhill side; but it did not yet fall. The Mesklinites approached again with caution. Even they, in a place where everything's weight seemed negligible to them, had no wish to be underneath that mass if it really did topple.

"I thought your weight must have shifted it, but something else must be moving inside," remarked Estnerdole. "Maybe the teacher is in better shape than we thought."

"A person's weight doesn't mean a thing here," returned Destigmet. "It must be him moving. Let's get to that window."

"If he is moving around, the climb will be pretty risky. Nothing but luck is keeping that thing from rolling the rest of the way down the slope now."

"No matter. We have to find out. Come on." Destigmet led the way up the loose material, but before any of the Mesklinites had reached the tank, it became evident that its occupant was once more active. Its outer lights suddenly flashed on.

Estnerdole gave a hoot of relief, and followed it with words. "Dr. LaVerne! How can we help you?"

For several seconds there was no answer, but the tank wavered even more alarmingly. Then the door opened, and the giant figure of the armored alien appeared in the opening. It tottered a moment, then fell outward into the snow. The tank rocked away as the man's weight left it, swung forward again in a way which would have brought Estnerdole's heart to his mouth if he had possessed a heart, and then stopped once more.

The Mesklinites swarmed forward with the common intent of dragging the human being away from the dangerous neighborhood, but before they reached him he started crawling under his own power. His voice came haltingly from his helmet speaker. "Stay back—all of you—I can make it—you couldn't move me in this stuff anyway."

Estnerdole and two of the others kept coming; with Mesklinites as with other intelligent races, some customs override selfish caution. The three tiny figures swarmed around the struggling monster, trying to speed its faltering trip away from the danger zone, but they promptly found that the teacher had been right; they couldn't help. It was not that the five hundred kilograms of weight were too much for them—any one of them could have lifted that. The trouble was the footing. A Mesklinite's legs end in insectlike claws, except for the nippers on the fore and aft pairs; the claws provide excellent traction on the wooden deck of a ship or the hard-packed soil which covers much of Mesklin. But a sand dune or a heap of ammonia snow is a different matter. The students' efforts to push the huge bulk of their teacher simply drove their own bodies into the loose fluff.

LaVerne was only partly aware of their presence. He had more or less recovered from the shock of his fall, and had seen enough to evaluate the situation fairly well; but he was not really in full possession of his faculties. He knew he was on a sloping surface of loose material, and that the tank was rather likely to roll over on him at any moment; his whole attention was focused on getting out of the way. The warning to the students had been little more than reflexive, like their own move to help him, and he did not follow up the order. He simply crawled as well as the situation permitted. A human observer might have had trouble deciding whether his mode of progress should have been called crawling or swimming, but he did make progress. He never was sure whether it took him five seconds or a whole minute, but presently he found himself on smooth, solid rock with the white slope safely behind him. He relaxed with a sigh, and only slowly became aware of the dozen caterpillarlike figures around him.

With an effort he managed to level himself to a sitting position. His students waited silently. He took in the nearly buried tank, the cliff in the opposite direction, the rock roof above with sunlight slanting through the jagged hole, and the darkness which swallowed the seemingly endless cavern to east and west. The Mesklinites were reasonably familiar with human facial expression and tried to read his, but they could make out little in the poor light through the face plate, which was partly obscured by blood from his nose. They waited for him to speak, and were not surprised when his first words formed pertinent questions. "How long did it take you to do that digging job? How long has that fellow been trying to climb the hill?"

Destigmet answered. "Only a few days; we didn't keep close count."

"Hmph. He hasn't gotten very far. I'm reminded of an animal on my own world which traps its prey in pits rather like this— loose stuff at its angle of repose. Climbing such a surface is nearly impossible. What will he do if he gets to the top? That hole is twenty of your body lengths away from the bank."

"But, Doctor!" pointed out Estnerdole, "the stone itself is not very thick. If we *can* reach the top, we know the stone comes to an end only a short distance to the south. We can dig our way out from under the edge easily enough."

"True enough. All right, the rest of you might as well try climbing too. So, for that matter, might I; if I get out on the surface I can call for help instead of having to send a runner."

"Rest first," advised Destigmet. "You can't be in very good condition yet. You must have been hurt some, if the state of your face plate means anything."

"All right. I want to think, anyway."

Near-silence fell while the rest of the students began to climb. Two or three, starting just below the stranded tank, had little trouble getting as far as the vehicle; but from there on it was a different matter. The creatures were tiny, some eighteen inches long with split-cylinder bodies an inch and a half in diameter. They were light; their half-pound masses weighed less than a kilogram at Mesklin's equator. Even that weight, however, sank their tiny legs full-length into the snow. The motion of the short limbs could be inferred from the clouds of white dust which sprayed backward from the small bodies. A hollow formed around each slender form, with material sifting down into it from the front and sides. Behind, it built up into something approaching a level surface, and slowly—very slowly—the Mesklinites followed their fellow uphill. Sometimes one would speed up briefly as he encountered a slightly more firmly packed area; almost as often he would slide back a body length or two, spraying frantic clouds of white dust, before resuming forward motion. Every few seconds a pile of snow behind one of them would collapse and slide downhill, spreading its material out until a new approach to the angle of repose was attained.

Minutes—long minutes—passed. Those who had used the tank as a starting point were four or five yards up the slope, not too far behind the one who had started so long before. The rest, whose slipping had started at a lower level, had made little visible progress. The little fans and rivulets of sliding snow, first behind one and then another of the dozen red-and-black figures, were as hypnotic as the patterns in a bonfire; LaVerne had to wrench his attention away from them, suddenly realizing that he had more serious jobs than being a spectator.

Slowly and painfully he hoisted himself to his feet. He could manage this at all only with the aid of ingenious lever-and-ratchet systems in the joints of his armor which let him concentrate on one part of the job at a time, and rest frequently without losing what he had gained. Once up, he turned slowly around, clarifying the mental picture he had already developed of the space they had fallen into. It was not too hard to infer how the cavern must have formed.

As he had guessed, the layer of water ice under the sandstone had been bared by erosion at the top of the fold which formed the peninsula. The stone must have worn virtually to a knife edge; no wonder it had failed to support the tank's weight once the underlying ice had gone. Ice was hard enough at Mesklin temperatures to stand mechanical erosion reasonably well, of course, but there was another factor operating here. Each year, as the giant world swung past periastron and the northern hemisphere began its summer, storms started sweeping ammonia snow from the virtually world-wide northern "ice" cap across the equator. This naturally buffered the local temperature near the freezing point of ammonia, which the Mesklinite student scientists had selected as the arbitrary control point for temperature in the scales they were developing.

Once the protecting silica had eroded away, the solid ammonia encountered the equally solid water, and liquid resulted. Not only was some heat generated, but the solutions of the two had considerably lower freezing points than either compound alone—a fact which the present crop of students had all faced in their most elementary courses. The ice layer had melted, or dissolved, if one preferred to think of it that way, for fifty or sixty yards back from the edge of the protecting stone. Later in the season when the ammonia had evaporated, this would show a beautiful overhanging ledge extending probably for miles east and west. With luck, LaVerne would be able to see it; since the College had been set up less than half a Mesklin year before, no one had had the chance yet.

LaVerne was not so much a scientist as a teacher. Still, he knew enough physical chemistry to wonder about the age of the peninsula—how long it would take the weight of overlying rock to squeeze the ice to the top of the fold and empty the filling from the sandwich. Maybe it had been going on for years already, and if they stayed in the cavern they could measure the creep of the south wall toward them. Maybe—

A hoot that was almost deafening even through his helmet jerked his wandering mind back to the current realities. He knew about Mesklinite voices, of course, but no human being ever got used to their more extreme volumes. He turned as quickly as he could from the ice cliff to the slope which his students had been trying to climb. By the time he really got his eyes focused on the scene, the key events had happened; but it was obvious enough what they had been.

The snow being kicked downhill by the climbers had been piling up against the tank. The earlier digging had left the vehicle almost without support on its downhill side, and what any thoughtful witness would have predicted had finally occurred. By the time LaVerne completed his turn, the machine was well into a full roll downhill toward him, and almost completely hidden inside a developing avalanche. The hoot, coming from several Mesklinites at once, had been stimulated by their discovery that they were involved in the slide; its upper edge was propagating rapidly toward the top of the slope and was already above the highest of the climbers.

The man had little thought for his students just then. The rolling tank was heading straight toward him, and he could not possibly move fast enough to get out of its way. He was several yards from the bottom of the slope, but that might not be far enough. It all depended on whether the tank would reach the stone with enough energy to roll those few yards—*let's see; it looks as though it would land right side up; then onto its right side, then the top, then the left—that should bring it right to my feet. If there's one more quarter-turn left in it, I'm flat.* LaVerne wondered later how he was able to analyze the matter so calmly as the mass of metal came whispering down on him in its envelope of dusty snow.

Actually it scarcely rolled at all, coming to rest with an ear-shattering clang on its right side. The man had a good heart—he would never have been allowed to serve on Mesklin otherwise—and was able to switch his attention back to his students almost at once; but the switch did his heart little more good than the juggernauting tank had. The Mesklinites were invisible.

For a moment, real fear struck him—intelligent fear based on foresight, not just panic. If those people were gone, he would most certainly not get back to the college. Then little white fountains of dust began to erupt from various points near the bottom of the slope, and one after another the Mesklinites emerged. None of them had been buried deeply enough to matter. All was well.

Except that there seemed no way to get out of the cave.

Ideas flowed from all directions, since the Meslinites were an imaginative lot; but none of these seemed very practical. Estnerdole suggested that the cave be explored in the east-west directions, on the chance that there might be a more usable way out. The objection to this was that not even the Mesklinites could see in the total darkness which obtained away from the area sunlit from their entry hole. Destigmet proposed cutting climbing notches in the cliff of water ice and reaching the top that way; unfortunately, ice met stone many yards from the hole, and there was no reason to hope that even the natives, insectlike as they appeared to human beings, could possibly crawl inverted along the stone ceiling. LaVerne, conditioned by a childhood on Earth, thought briefly of packing the snow to make a more reliable support and with it actually constructing steps up the slope. Fortunately for his reputation with the Mesklinites, he remembered in time that ammonia, unlike water, is denser in the solid than in the liquid phase. It does not, therefore, tend to melt under pressure; trying to make even a snowball out of the powdery stuff which had trapped them would be like trying to do it with a handful of sand.

"All I can suggest," he said at last, "is for some or all of you to start climbing again—maybe farther apart this time, so one person's avalanche doesn't involve everyone else. At least the tank won't be a problem any more. It will be slow, but if even one of you can get to the top, he can go back to the College and get help. I can last here for days, with the air supplies in the tank, so there's no emergency."

"I'm afraid there is, Doctor," pointed out Estnerdole. "You can't get into the tank. It's lying on its right side, with the door underneath. Unless there is some outside connection you can reach to replenish the oxygen in your armor, you are rather limited in your supply."

The man was silent for several seconds, except for a brief muttering which the students could not make out clearly. "You're right, Es," he said at last. "It is an emergency after all, for me. Do you suppose you people are strong enough to turn the tank right side up?"

The Mesklinites were somewhat doubtful, but clustered around to try. LaVerne, who shared the exaggerated idea of Mesklinite physical strength which was so common among human beings, was not surprised when the vehicle stirred under their efforts; indeed, he was disappointed when it lofted only a few millimeters. After some seconds it settled back where it had been, and one of the students reappeared from the narrow space underneath. "We can move it, but that's all. We'd have to get this side up several body lengths before it would rock over the right way, and there's nothing to stand on."

Destigmet wriggled into view behind the speaker. "I can think of only two things to do, and you've already suggested one of them," he said. "The first is for someone to start climbing again. The other is for us to lift the tank once more, while you pack snow under it to hold it up and let us get a fresh purchase. Maybe we can work it up that way before you run out of air."

"All right," agreed LaVerne. "It would be better if I had something to serve as a shovel, but let's get at it. I'm using oxygen just standing here worrying."

For a while it looked possible, if not really hopeful. Carrying the dusty snow in his armored hands proved impractical, but he found that he could do fairly well pushing a mass of it ahead of him as he crawled—and crawling was far easier than trying to walk. Essentially, he was sweeping rather than carrying. He managed to get what would have been several shovelfuls, if he had had a shovel, against the space at the edge of the tank where the Mesklinites had disappeared once more. At his call they strained upward again, and as quickly as he could he pushed the material into the widening space. "That's all," he reported when he had done his best, and the students relaxed again. So did the pile of snow. LaVerne, optimistic by nature, felt sure that the tank had not settled quite back to its original position, and kept trying; but after an hour which left him more exhausted than he had ever felt in his three Earth years on Mesklin, he had to admit that the idea was qualitatively sound but quantitatively inadequate.

During those days, the student who was trying to climb the slope had made little progress. Once he had gotten nearly a third of the way before sliding most of the way back in a smother of white dust; four or five times he had lost the fight in the first yard or two. The rest of his attempts came between those limits.

But it finally became evident that the man's air was not going to be the real limiting factor. Destigmet pointed out another one to him. "Some time ago, Doctor, one of your fellows taught us about a fact he claimed was very basic—the Law of Conservation of Energy. If I have the terminology right, we can apply very large forces by your standards, but as that law should tell you, there is a limit to the amount of work we can do without food. None of us expected to need food in this class, and we brought none with us."

One of the others cut in. "Won't people from the College start looking for us anyway? This class should have been over days ago."

LaVerne frowned invisibly behind the blood-stained face plate, which he had no means of cleaning. "They'll be looking, but finding us will be another story," he said. "They'd expect to see the tank miles away on the smooth surface of the peninsula. When they don't, they'll think we got swept into the sea, or went off to the forest country for some reason. They won't look over this area closely enough to find the hole we left, I suspect. It's possible we'll get out of this with their help, but don't count on it."

Estnerdole suddenly became excited. "Why not build a tower we can climb, with the water ice from the cliff? We can chip it out easily enough without tools, or even melt it out with the snow—no, that wouldn't leave us any to work with, but—" His voice trailed off as more difficulties became apparent to him.

LaVerne was pessimistic, too, after the just-completed practical demonstration of how much material would be needed even to prop up the tank. Then he brightened. "We could use the ice to get this machine upright—big chunks of it would be more practical and easier to move than the snow. Of course, even that doesn't get us any closer to getting out of here; the tank certainly isn't going to climb this sandhill even if I get into it. If only—" He paused, and the ensuing silence stretched out for long seconds.

Even with the man hidden in his armor, the listeners got the impression that something had happened. Then he spoke again, and his tone confirmed the suspicion. "Thanks, Es. That does it. Start digging ice, gentlemen. We'll be out of here in a couple of hours!"

Actually, it took less than three days.

"You look bothered," remarked Thomasian, LaVerne's department head. "Delayed shock from your narrow escape, or what?"

"It wasn't that narrow," replied the teacher. "I had hours of air still in the suit when the spinner picked us up, and we could have worked the tank upright to get at more if I had needed it. You'd have searched the area closely enough to find that hole sooner or later."

"Later would probably have been too late—and the really narrow squeak I was thinking of was the fall. Fifteen meters under three gees—sooner you than me. If it hadn't been for that snow bank, we'd have had to cut you out of the flattened remains of that tank—not that it would have been worth doing. Of course any of your students should have been able to think of tossing pieces of water ice over the slope, especially after you'd discussed with them why the cuesta was so deeply undercut. So should you, for that matter—"

"Hogback," LaVerne responded almost automatically. "Sure, all sorts of ideas are obvious afterward. At the time, I wasn't quite sure that this one would work, even if I did sound as enthusiastic as I could and even though I did have experience to go by. Still, I was afraid it would simply melt holes in the slope; but it went fine. The quid formed where the two ices met just soaked into the surrounding snow, spreading out and diluting the water ice until the mixture's melting point came up to the local temperature again—and froze into a continuous mass. It was hard enough for Estnerdole to climb out and go for help in less than an hour, I'd guess; I didn't actually time it."

"What was the experience you could go by? And if it was so easy and safe, what's bothering you?"

"The same thing. A teaching problem. They claim that Mesklinite psychology is enough like ours for teaching techniques to be about the same, effectively. They expect us to—er—'relate' new facts to known experience."

"Of course. So?"

"So the experience in question should obviously be one familiar to the students, not just the teacher. What sparked this idea for me was the memory of sugar getting lumpy in the bowl when it gets damp. You know, I'm just a little shaky on the local biochemistry, chief—tell me: what do Mesklinites use for coffee, and what do they put in it?"

EARLY BIRD

by Theodore R. Cogswell and Theodore L. Thomas

I owe a double debt for whatever success I've had as a writer of science fiction: first to Gordon Dickson and Poul Anderson, who got me started, and second to John Campbell, who bought "The Spectre General," the first science-fiction story I ever wrote. Although his letter of acceptance was my first personal contact with John, I had been an avid reader of his magazine from the time he first assumed editorship. And, though I wasn't aware of it at the time, each month as I lost myself in the latest issue of Astounding *he was teaching me how to write. The stories I found so fascinating were for the most part written by writers John had encouraged, shaped and trained. As a result, when I finally tried my hand at writing science fiction, I unconsciously found myself following his precepts as they were reflected in the work I admired.*

John was a great and stimulating teacher and critic, and some-times his letters of rejection were longer than the work submitted. I wouldn't be too surprised if, shortly after the appearance of this chronicling by Ted Thomas and myself of a further adventure of Kurt Dixon and the Imperial Space Marines, a twenty-page letter, complete with illegible squiggle at the end, mysteriously appeared in our mailboxes.

We're waiting, John.

I

WHEN the leader of a scout patrol fell ill two hours before takeoff and Kurt Dixon was given command, he was delighted. More than a year had passed since the Imperial Space Marines had mopped up the remnants of the old Galactic Protectorate, and in spite of his pleasure at his newly awarded oak leaves, he was tired of being a glorified office boy in the Inspector General's office while the Kierians were raiding the Empire's trade routes with impunity. After a few hours in space, however, his relief began to dwindle when he found there was no way to turn off Zelda's voice box.

Zelda was the prototype of a new kind of command computer, the result of a base psychologist's bright idea that giving the ship's cybernetic control center a human personality tailored to the pilot's idea of an ideal companion would relieve the lonely tedium of being cooped up for weeks on end in a tiny one-man scout. Unfortunately for Kurt, however, his predecessor, Flight Leader Osaki, had a taste for domineering women, and the computer had been programmed accordingly. There hadn't been time for re-placement with a conventional model before the flight had to scramble.

Kierian raids on Empire shipping had only begun six months before, but already the Empire was in serious trouble. Kierians bred like fruit flies, looked like mutated maggots, and ate people. Nobody knew where they came from when they came raiding in. Nobody knew where they went when they left with their loot. All that *was* known was that they had a weapon that was invincible and that any attempt to track down a raiding party to the Kierian base was as futile as it was suicidal. Ships that tried it never came back.

But this time it looked as if the Empire's luck might have changed. Kurt whistled happily as he slowly closed in on what seemed to be a damaged Kierian destroyer, waiting for the other scouts of his flight to catch up with him.

Zzzzt!

The alien's fogger beam hit him square on for the third time. This close it should have slammed him into immediate unconsciousness, but all it did was produce an annoying buzz-saw keening in his neural network.

Flick! Six red dots appeared on his battle screen as the rest of his flight warped out of hyperspace a hundred miles to his rear.

An anxious voice came over his intercom. "Kurt! You fogged?"

"Nope. Come up and join the picnic, children. Looks like us early birds are just about to have us some worms for breakfast."

"He hits you with his fogger, you're going to be the breakfast. Get the hell out of there while you still have a chance!"

Kurt laughed. "This one ain't got much in the way of teeth. Looks like he's had some sort of an engine-room breakdown because his fogger strength is down a good ninety percent. He's beamed me several times, and all he's been able to do so far is give me a slight hangover."

"Then throw a couple of torps into him before he can rev up enough to star hop."

"Uh, uh! We're after bigger game. I've got a solid tracer lock on him and I've a hunch, crippled as he seems to be, that he's going to run for home. If he does, and we can hang on to him, we may be able to find the home base of those bastards. If just one of us can get back with the coordinates, the heavies can come in and chuck a few planet-busters. Hook on to me and follow along. I think he's just about to jump."

Flick! As the tight-arrow formation jumped back into normal space, alarm gongs began clanging in each of the tiny ships. Kurt stared at the image on his battle screen and let out a low whistle. They'd come out within fifty miles of the Kierian base! And it wasn't a planet. It was a mother ship, a ship so big that the largest

Imperial space cruiser would have looked like a gnat alongside it. And from it, like hornets from a disturbed nest, poured squadron after squadron of Kierian destroyers.

"Bird leader to fledglings! Red alert! Red alert! Scramble random 360. One of us has to stay clear long enough to get enough warper revs to jump. Zelda will take over if I get fogged! I . . ." The flight leader's voice trailed off as a narrow cone of jarring vibration flicked across his ship, triggering off a neural spasm that hammered him down into unconsciousness. The other scouts broke formation like a flight of frightened quail and zigzagged away from the Kierian attackers, twisting in a desperate attempt to escape the slashing fogger beams. One by one the other pilots were slammed into unconsciousness. Putting the other ships on slave circuit, Zelda threw the flight on emergency drive. Needles emerged from control seats and pumped anti-G drugs into the comatose pilots.

A quick calculation indicated that they couldn't make a subspace jump from their present position. They were so close to the giant sun that its gravitational field would damp the warper nodes. The only thing to do was to run and find a place to hide until the pilots recovered consciousness. Then, while the others supplied a diversion, there was a chance that one might be able to break clear. The computer doubted that the Imperial battle fleet would have much of a chance against something as formidable as the Kierian mother ship, but that was something for fleet command to decide. Her job was to save the flight. There were five planets in the system, but only the nearest to the sun, a cloud-smothered giant, was close enough to offer possible sanctuary.

Setting a corkscrew evasion course and ignoring the fogger beams that lanced at her from the pursuing ships, she streaked for the protective cloud cover of the planet, programming the computers of the six ships that followed her on slave circuit to set them down at widely separated, randomly selected points. Kierian tracer beams would be useless once the flight was within the violent and wildly fluctuating magnetic field of the giant planet.

Once beneath the protective cloud cover, the other scouts took off on their separate courses, leaving Zelda, her commander still slumped in a mind-fog coma, to find her own sanctuary. Then at thirty thousand feet the ship's radiation detector suddenly triggered off a score of red danger lights on the instrument panel. From somewhere below, a sun-hot cone of lethal force was probing for the ship. After an almost instantaneous analysis of the nature of the threat, Zelda threw on a protective heterodyning canceler to shield the scout. Then she taped an evasive course that would take the little ship out of danger as soon as the retrorockets had slowed it enough to make a drastic course change possible without harm to its unconscious commander.

II

Gog's time had almost come. Reluctantly she withdrew her tubelike extractor from the cobalt-rich layer fifty yards below the surface. The propagation pressures inside her were too great to allow her to finish the lode, much less find another. The nerve stem inside the extractor shrank into her body, followed by the acid conduit and ultrasonic tap. Then, ponderously, she began to drag her gravid body toward a nearby ravine. She paused for a moment while a rear short-range projector centered in on a furtive scavenger who had designs on her unfinished meal. One burst and its two-hundred-foot length exploded into a broken heap of metallic and organic rubble. She was tempted to turn back—the remnants would have made a tasty morsel—but birthing pressures drove her on. Reaching the ravine at last, she squatted over it. Slowly her ovipositor emerged from between sagging, armored buttocks. Gog strained and then moved on, leaving behind her a shining, five-hundred-foot-long egg.

Lighter now, her body quickly adapted for post egg-laying activities as sensors and projectors extruded from depressions in her tung-steel hide. Her semi-organic brain passed into a quiescent state while organo-metallic arrays of calculators and energy producers activated and joined into a network on her outer surfaces. The principal computer, located halfway down the fifteen-hundred-meter length of her grotesque body, activated and took over control of her formidable defenses. Then, everything in readiness, it triggered the egg.

The egg responded with a microwave pulse of such intensity

that the sensitive antennae of several nearby lesser creatures grew hot, conducting a surge of power into their circuits that charred their internal organs and fused their metallic synapses.

Two hundred kilometers away, Magog woke from a gorged sleep as a strident mating call came pulsing in. He lunged erect, the whole kilometer of him. As he sucked the reducing atmosphere deep into the chain of ovens that served him as lungs, meter-wide nerve centers along his spinal columns pulsed with a voltage and current sufficient to fuse bus bars of several centimeters' cross section. A cannonlike sperm launcher emerged from his forehead and stiffened as infernos churned inside him. Then his towering bulk jerked as the first spermatozoon shot out, followed by a swarm that dwindled to a few stragglers. Emptied, Magog sagged to the ground and, suddenly hungry, began to rip up great slabs of igneous rock to get at the rich vein of ferrous ore his sensors detected deep beneath. Far to the east, Gog withdrew a prudent distance from her egg and squatted down to await the results of its mating call.

The spermatozoa reached an altitude of half a kilometer before achieving homing ability. They circled, losing altitude until their newly activated homing mechanisms picked up the high-frequency emissions of the distant egg. Then tiny jets began pouring carbon dioxide, and flattened leading edges bit into the atmosphere as they arced toward their objective.

Each was a flattened cylinder, twenty meters long, with a scythe-shaped sensing element protruding from a flattened head, each with a pair of long tails connected at the trailing edge by a broad ribbon. It was an awesome armada, plowing through the turbulent atmosphere, homing on the distant signal.

As the leaders of the sperm swarm appeared over the horizon, Gog's sensors locked in. The selection time was near. Energy banks cut in and fuel converters began to seethe, preparing for the demands of the activated weapons system. At twenty kilometers a long-range beam locked in on the leading spermatozoon. It lacked evasive ability and a single frontal shot fused it. Its remnants spiraled to the surface, a mass of carbonized debris interspersed with droplets of glowing metal.

The shock of its destruction spread through the armada and stimulated wild, evasive gyrations on the part of the rest. But Gog's calculators predicted the course of one after another, and flickering bolts of energy burned them out of the sky. None was proving itself fit to survive. Then, suddenly, there was a moment of confusion in her intricate neural network. An intruder was approaching from the wrong direction. All her reserve projectors swiveled and spat a concentrated cone of lethal force at the rogue gamete that was screaming down through the atmosphere. Before the beam could take effect, a milky nimbus surrounded the approaching stranger and it continued on course unharmed. She shifted frequencies. The new bolt was as ineffective as the last. A ripple of excited anticipation ran through her great bulk. This was the one she'd been waiting for!

Gog was not a thinking entity in the usual sense, but she was equipped with a pattern of instinctive responses that told her that the gamete that was flashing down through the upper skies contained something precious in defensive armament that her species needed to survive. Mutations induced by the intense hard radiation from the nearby giant sun made each new generation of enemies even more terrible. Only if her egg were fertilized by a sperm bearing improved defensive and offensive characteristics would her offspring have a good chance of survival.

She relaxed her defenses and waited for the stranger to home in on her egg; but for some inexplicable reason, as it slowed down, it began to veer away. Instantly her energy converters and projectors combined to form a new beam, a cone that locked onto the escaping gamete and then narrowed and concentrated all its energy into a single, tight, titanic tractor. The stranger tried one evasive tactic after another, but inextricably it was drawn toward the waiting egg. Then, in response to her radiated command, the egg's shell weakened at the calculated point of impact. A moment later the stranger punched through the ovid wall and came to rest at the egg's exact center. Gog's scanners quickly encoded its components and made appropriate adjustments to the genes of the egg's nucleus.

Swiftly—the planet abounded in egg eaters—the fertilized ovum began to develop. It drew on the rich supply of heavy metals contained in the yolk sac to follow the altered genetic blueprint, incorporating in the growing embryo both the heritage of the strange gamete and that developed by Gog's race in its long fight to stay alive in a hostile environment. When the yolk sac nourishment was finally exhausted, Gog sent out a vibratory beam that cracked the shell of her egg into tiny fragments and freed the fledgling that had developed within. Leaving the strange new hybrid to fend for itself, she crawled back to her abandoned lode to feed and prepare for another laying. In four hours she would be ready to bear again.

III

As Kurt began to regain consciousness, mind still reeling from the aftereffects of the Kierian fogger beam, he opened his eyes with an effort.

"Don't say it," said the computer's voice box.

"Say what?" he mumbled.

" 'Where am I?' You wouldn't believe it if I told you."

Kurt shook his head to try to clear it of its fuzz. His front vision screen was on and strange things were happening. Zelda had obviously brought the scout down safely, but how long it was going to remain that way was open to question.

The screen showed a nightmare landscape, a narrow valley floor crisscrossed with ragged, smoking fissures. Low-hanging, boiling clouds were tinged an ugly red by the spouting firepits of the squat volcanoes that ringed the depression. It was a hobgoblin scene populated by hobgoblin forms. Strange shapes, seemingly of living metal, crawled, slithered and flapped. Titanic battles raged, victors ravenously consuming losers with maws like giant ore crushers, only to be vanquished and gulped down in turn by even more gigantic life forms, no two of which were quite alike.

A weird battle at one corner of the vision screen caught Kurt's attention, and he cranked up magnification. Half tank, half dinosaur, a lumbering creature the size of an imperial space cruiser was backed into a box canyon in the left escarpment, trying to defend itself against a pack of smaller but swifter horrors. A short thick projection stuck out from between its shoulders, pointing up at forty-five degrees like an ancient howitzer. As Kurt watched, flame suddenly flashed from it. A black spheroid arced out, fell among the attackers, and then exploded with a concussion that shook the scout, distant as it was. When the smoke cleared, a crater twenty feet deep marked where it had landed. Two of the smaller beasts were out of action, but the rest kept boring in, incredibly agile toadlike creatures twice the size of terrestrial elephants, spouting jets of some flaming substance and then skipping back.

This spectacular was suddenly interrupted when the computer said calmly, "If you think that's something, take a look at the rear scanner."

Kurt did and shuddered in spite of himself.

Crawling up behind the scout on stumpy, centipede legs was something the size of a lunar ore boat. Its front end was dotted with multifaceted eyes that revolved like radar bowls.

"What the hell is *that?*"

"Beats me," said Zelda, "but I think it wants us for lunch."

Kurt flipped on his combat controls and centered the beast on his cross hairs. "Couple right down the throat ought to discourage it."

"Might at that," said Zelda. "But you've got one small problem. Our armament isn't operational yet. The neural connections for the new stuff haven't finished knitting in yet."

"Listen, smart ass," said Kurt in exasperation, "this is no time for funnies. If we can't fight the ship, let's lift the hell out of here. That thing's big enough to swallow us whole."

"Can't lift either. The converters need more mass before they can crank out enough juice to activate the antigravs. We've only five kilomegs in the accumulators."

"Five!" howled Kurt. "I could lift the whole damn squadron with three. I'm getting out of here!"

His fingers danced over the control board, setting up the sequence for emergency take off. The ship shuddered but nothing happened. The rear screen showed that the creature was only two hundred yards away, its mouth a gaping cavern lined with chisel-like grinders.

Zelda made a chuckling sound. "Next time, listen to Mother. Strange things happened to all of us while you were in sleepy-bye land." A number of red lights on the combat readiness board began changing to green. "Knew it wouldn't take too much longer. Tell you what, why don't you suit up and go outside and watch while I take care of junior back there. You aren't going to believe what you're about to see, but hang with it. I'll explain everything when you get back. In the meantime I'll keep an eye on you."

Kurt made a dash for his space armor and wriggled into it. "I'm not running out on you, baby, but nothing seems to be working on this tub. If one of the other scouts is close enough, I may be able to raise him on my helmet phone and get him here soon enough to do us some good. But what about you?"

"Oh," said Zelda casually, "if worse comes to worst, I can always run away. We now have feet. Thirty on each side."

Kurt just snorted as he undogged the inner air-lock hatch.

Once outside he did the biggest and fastest double take in the history of man.

The scout did have feet. Lots of feet. And other things.

To begin with, though her general contours were the same, she'd grown from forty meters in length to two hundred. Her torp tubes had quadrupled in size and were many times more numerous. Between them, streamlined turrets housed wicked-looking devices whose purpose he didn't understand. One of them suddenly swiveled, pointed at a spot somewhat behind him, and spat an incandescent beam. He spun just in time to see something that looked like a ten-ton crocodile collapse into a molten puddle.

"Told you I'd keep an eye on you," said a cheerful voice in his helmet phone. "All central connections completed themselves while you were on your way out. Now we have teeth."

"So has our friend back there. Check aft!" The whatever-it-was was determinedly gnawing away on the rear tubes.

"He's just gumming. Our new hide makes the old one look like the skin of a jellyfish. Watch me nail him. But snap on your sun filter first. Otherwise you'll blind yourself."

Obediently Kurt pressed his polarizing stud. One of the scout's rear turrets swung around and a buzzsaw vibration ran through the ground as a purple beam no thicker than a pencil slashed the attacker into piano-sized chunks. Then the reason for the scout's new pedal extremities became apparent as the ship quickly ran around in a circle. Reaching what was left of her attacker, she extended a wedge-shaped head from a depression in her bow and began to feed.

"Just the mass we needed," said Zelda. A tentacle suddenly emerged from a hidden port, circled Kurt's waist, and pulled him inside the ship. "Welcome aboard your new command. And now do you want to hear what's happened to us?"

When she finished, Kurt didn't comment. He couldn't. His vocal chords weren't working.

A shave, a shower, a steak and three cups of coffee later, he gave a contented burp.

"Let's go find some worms and try out our new stuff," Zelda suggested.

"While I get fogged?"

"You won't. Wait and see."

Kurt shrugged dubiously and once again punched in the lifting sequence. This time when he pressed the activator stud the ship went shrieking up through the atmosphere. Gog, busily laying another egg, paid no attention to her strange offspring. Kurt paid attention to her, though.

Once out of the sheltering cloud cover, his detectors picked up three Kierian ships in stratospheric flight. They seemed to be systematically quartering the sun side of the planet in a deliberate search pattern. Then, as if they had detected one of the hidden scouts, they went into a steep purposeful dive. Concerns for his own safety suddenly were flushed away by the apparent threat to a defenseless ship from his flight. Kurt raced toward the alien ships under emergency thrust. The G needle climbed to twenty, but instead of the acceleration hammering him into organic pulp, it only pushed him back in his seat slightly.

The Kierians pulled up and turned to meet him. In spite of the size of the strange ship that was hurtling toward them, they didn't seem concerned. There was no reason why they should be. Their foggers could hammer a pilot unconscious long before he could pose a real threat.

Kurt felt a slight vibration run through the scout as an enemy beam caught him, but he didn't black out.

"Get the laser on the one that just hit you," Zelda suggested. "It has some of the new stuff hooked into it." Kurt did, and a bolt of raging energy raced back along the path of the fogger beam and converted the first attacker into a ball of ionized gas.

"Try torps on the other two."

"They never work. The Kierians warp out before they get within range."

"Want to bet? Give a try."

"What's to lose?" said Kurt. "Fire three and seven." He felt the shudder of the torpedoes leaving the ship, but their tracks didn't appear on his firing scope. "Where'd they go?"

"Subspace. Watch what happens to the worms when they flick out."

Suddenly the two dots that marked the enemy vanished in an actinic burst.

"Wow!" said Kurt in an awestricken voice, "we something, we is! But why didn't that fogger knock me out? New kind of shield?"

"Nope, new kind of pilot. The ship wasn't the only thing that was changed. And that ain't all. You've got all kinds of new equipment inside your head you don't know about yet."

"Such as?"

"For one thing," she said, "once you learn how to use it, you'll find that your brain can operate at almost ninety percent efficiency instead of its old ten. And that ain't all; your memory bank has twice the storage of a standard ship computer and you can calculate four times as fast. But don't get uppity, buster. You haven't learned to handle it yet. It's going to take months to get you up to full potential. In the meantime I'll babysit as usual."

Kurt had a sudden impulse to count fingers and toes to see if he still had the right number.

"My face didn't look any different when I shaved. Am I still human?"

"Of course," Zelda said soothingly. "You're just a better one, that's all. When the ship fertilized that egg, its cytoplasm went to work incorporating the best elements of both parent strains. Our own equipment was improved and the mother's was added to it. There was no way of sorting you out from the other ship components, and you were improved too. So relax."

Kurt tilted back his seat and stared thoughtfully at the ceiling for a long moment. "Well," he said at last, "best we go round up the rest of the flight."

"What about the Kierian mother ship?"

"We're still not tough enough to tackle something that big."

"But that thing down there was still laying eggs when we pulled out. If the whole flight . . ." Her voice trailed off suggestively.

Kurt sat bolt upright in his seat, his face suddenly split with a wide grin.

"Bird leader to fledglings. You can come out from under them there rocks, children. Coast is clear and Daddy is about to take you on an egg hunt."

A babble of confused voices came from the communication panel speaker.

"One at a time!"

"What about those foggers?"

Kurt chuckled. "Tell them the facts of life, Zelda."

"The facts are," she said, her voice flat and impersonal, "that before too long you early birds are going to be able to get the worms before the worms get you."

Major Kurt Dixon, one-time sergeant in the 427th Light Maintenance Battalion of the Imperial Space Marines, grinned happily as he looked out at the spreading cloud of space debris that was all that was left of the Kierian mother ship. Then he punched the stud that sent a communication beam hurtling through hyperspace to Imperial Headquarters. "Commander Krogson, please. Dixon calling."

"One second, Major."

The Inspector General's granite features appeared on Kurt's communication screen. "Where the hell have you been?"

"Clobbering Kierians," Kurt said smugly, "but before we get into that, I'd like to have you relay a few impolite words to the egghead who put together the talking machine I have for a control computer."

"Oh, sorry about that, Kurt. You see, it was designed with Osaki in mind, and he does have a rather odd taste in women. When you get back, we'll remove the old personality implant and substitute one that's tailored to your specifications."

Kurt shook his head. "No, thanks. The old girl and I have been through some rather tight spots together, and even though she is a pain in the neck at times, I'd sort of like to keep her around just as she is." He reached over and gave an affectionate pat to the squat computer that was bolted to the deck beside him.

"That's nice," Krogson said, "but what's going on out there? What was that about clobbering Kierians?"

"They're finished. Kaput. Thanks to Zelda."

"Who?"

"My computer."

"What happened?"

Kurt gave a lazy grin. "Well, to begin with, I got laid."

THE EMPEROR'S FAN

by L. Sprague de Camp

When John W. Campbell had lately become editor of Astounding Stories, he used to ask writing friends to his apartment in the Oranges on Sunday afternoons. When we arrived, each was handed a manuscript with a request to read and criticize it. This made for a rather quiet gathering but was doubtless of value to us in learning our craft.

In 1938, while still giving these parties, Campbell made plans for Unknown. The new magazine of fantasy was launched with the issue of March 1939. Campbell's circle responded eagerly to his request for adult fantasy. Actually, a large minority of the stories in Unknown were science fiction, including my own "Divide and Rule," "The Gnarly Man," and "Lest Darkness Fall." Once I started writing fantasy, however, I found it easier and more fun than science fiction. If the magazine had not been killed by *the paper shortage of 1942–1945 and not revived because of its high percentage of returns, I might be writing for it yet.*

In 1941, *the name was changed to* Unknown Worlds. *The official explanation was that too many newsdealers, asked for an unknown magazine, just looked queerly at the inquirer. The real reason was that another magazine,* Adventure Into the Unknown, *brought court action to compel the change, on the ground that the title* Unknown *misled customers into buying John's magazine for theirs.*

This story is the kind I might have written for Unknown, *if I could have gotten it past John's somewhat austere policy toward s-e-x. Not that it is a dirty story; by current standards, I am still pretty much of a stiff old Puritan. But I suppose an accommodation could have been reached.*

The setting is that of my novels The Goblin Tower *and* The Clocks of Iraz *and the forthcoming* The Fallible Fiend. *It is a swordplay-and-sorcery world of which this world is the afterworld, whither good Novarians and other denizens of Jorian's world go when they die. This story, however, is laid in a part of that world not hitherto presented in this series: one corresponding to the ancient and medieval Far East. Costumes, customs and languages are eclectic mixtures of those of China and Japan.*

The idea of the magical fan is not really original and came to me in an odd way. Fifty-odd years ago, when I was a boy in New York, the Rogers Peet clothing store on Fifth Avenue published, for the squirming children of customers, a little periodical called the Ropeco Magazine. *This ran juvenile fantasies, some quite charming. Alas! I was always dragged away before the climax. To this day, I wonder if the little boy in one story succeeded in getting the king's crown back from a sixty-legged ogre called the Shuddery Zumbock.*

One story, of which I read but a few paragraphs, described a fan like the one in this tale. That fragment has stuck in my mind ever since. And what is the use of having one's memory cluttered with things like that if one doesn't get some mileage out of them?

IN THE FIFTEENTH year of his reign, Tsotuga the Fourth, Emperor of Kuromon, sat in the Forbidden Chamber of his Proscribed Palace, in his imperial city of Chingun. He played a game of Sachi with his crony, Reiro the beggar.

The pieces on one side were carved from single emeralds; those on the other, from single rubies. The board was of squares of onyx and gold. The many shelves and taborets in the room were crowded with small art objects. There were knickknacks of gold and silver, of ivory and ebony, of porcelain and pewter, of jasper and jade, of chrysoprase and chalcedony.

In a silken robe embroidered with lilies in silver thread and lotuses in golden thread, Tsotuga sat on a semi-throne—a chair of gilded mahogany, the arms of which were carven in the form of diamond-eyed dragons. The Emperor was plainly well fed, and within the hour he had been bathed and perfumed. Yet, although he had just won a game, Emperor Tsotuga was not happy.

"The trouble with you, chum," said Reiro the beggar, "is that, not having enough real dangers to worry about, you make up imaginary ones."

The Emperor took no offense. The purpose of the Forbidden Chamber was to afford him a place where he could treat and be treated by his crony as if they were ordinary human beings, without the court's stifling formality.

Nor was it an accident that Reiro was a beggar. As such, he would never try to intrigue against or murder his imperial friend in order to seize the throne.

Although a fairly competent ruler, Tsotuga was not a man of much personal charm. He was in fact rather dull save when, as sometimes happened, he lost his temper. Then he might visit dire dooms on those about him. After he had calmed down, Tsotuga would regret his injustice and might even pension the victim's dependents. He honestly tried to be just but lacked the self-control and objectivity to do so.

Reiro got along with the Emperor well enough. While the beggar cared nothing for art, save when he could filch and sell a piece of it, he was glad to listen to the Emperor's endless tales of his collection in return for the sumptuous repasts he enjoyed. Reiro had gained twenty pounds since he had become intimate with the Emperor.

"Oh, yes?" said Tsotuga. "That is easy for you to say. You are not nightly haunted by your father's ghost, threatening dreadful doom."

Reiro shrugged. "You knew the risk when you had the old man poisoned. It is all in the game, pal. For your pay, I would cheerfully submit to any number of nightmares. How does old Haryo look in these dreams?"

"The same old tyrant. I had to slay him—you know that—ere he ruined the Empire. But have a care with that flapping tongue."

"Nought I hear here goes beyond these walls. Anyway, if you think Haryo's fate be not widely known, you do but befool yourself."

"I daresay it is suspected. But then, foul play is always suspected when an emperor dies. As said Dauhai to the timorous bird, every twig is a serpent.

"Still," continued the Emperor, "that solves not my problem. I wear mail beneath my robe. I sleep on a mattress floating in a pool of quicksilver. I have given up futtering my women, lest whilst I lie in their arms, some conspirator steal up and dagger me. The Empress, I can tell you, mislikes this abstinence. But still Haryo threatens and prophesies, and the warnings of a ghost are not to be flouted. I need some impregnable magical defense. That idiot Koxima does nought but fumigate and exorcize, which may drive out the demons but fails to blunt the steel of human foes. Have you any counsel, Ragbag?"

Reiro scratched. "There is a dark, beak-nosed, round-eyed old he-witch, hight Ajendra, lately come to Chingun from Mulvan. He gains a scanty living by selling love potions and finding lost bangles in trances. He claims to have a magical weapon of such power that none can stand against it."

"What is its nature?"

"He will not say."

"If he have so puissant a device, why is he not a king?"

"How could he make himself ruler? He is too old to lead an army in battle. Besides, he says that the holy order to which he belongs—all Mulvanian wizards call themselves holy men, be they never such rascals—forbids the use of this armament save in self-defense."

"Has anybody seen it?"

"Nay, chum; but rumor whispers that Ajendra has used it."

"Yes? And then what?"

"Know you a police spy named Nanka?"

The Emperor frowned. "Meseems—there was something about such a man who disappeared. It is supposed that the low company he kept at last learnt of his occupation and did him in."

The beggar chuckled. "Close, but not in the gold. This Nanka was a scoundrel of deepest dye, who supplemented his earnings as an informer by robbery and extortion. He skated into Ajendra's hut with the simple, wholesome intention of breaking the old man's neck and seizing Ajendra's rumored weapon."

"Hm. Well?"

"Well, Nanka never came out. A patrolman of the regular police found Ajendra sitting cross-legged in meditation and no sign of the erstwhile spy. Since Nanka was large and the hovel small, the corpse could not have been hidden. As it is said, the digger of pitfalls shall at last fall into one of his own."

"Hm," said Tsotuga. "I must look into this. Enough Sachi for the nonce. You must let me show you my latest acquisition!"

Reiro groaned inside and braced himself for an hour's lecture on the history and beauty of some antique bibelot. The thought of the palatial cookery, however, stiffened his resolve.

"Now, where did I put that little widget?" said Tsotuga, tapping his forehead with his folded fan.

"What is it, chum?" asked the beggar.

"A topaz statuette of the goddess Amarasupi, from the Jumbon Dynasty. Oh, curse my bowels with ulcers! I grow more absent-minded day by day."

"Good thing your head is permanently affixed to the rest of you! As the wise Ashuziri said, hope is a charlatan, sense a bungler, and memory a traitor."

"I distinctly remember," muttered the Emperor, "telling myself to put it in a special place where I should be sure to remember it. But now I cannot recall the special place."

"The Proscribed Palace must have ten thousand special places,"
said Reiro. "That is the advantage of being poor. One has so few
possessions that one need never wonder where they are."

"Almost you tempt me to change places with you, but my duty
forbids. Damn, damn, what did I with that silly thing? Oh, well,
let us play another game instead. You take the red this time, I the
green."

Two days later, Emperor Tsotuga sat on his throne of audience,
wearing his towering crown of state. This plumed and winged
headgear, bedight with peacock feathers and precious stones,
weighed over ten pounds. It even had a secret compartment.
Because of its weight, Tsotuga avoided wearing it whenever he
felt that he decently could.

The usher led in Ajendra. The Mulvanian magician was a tall,
gaunt, bent old man, who supported himself on a stick. Save for
the long white beard flowing down from his wrinkled, mahogany-
hued face, he was brown all over, from dirty brown bulbous turban and dirty brown robe to dirty brown bare feet. His monotone
contrasted with the golds and vermilions and greens and blues and
purples of the Chamber of Audience.

In a cracked voice, speaking Kuromonian with an accent,
Ajendra went through the formal greeting: "This wretched worm
humbly abases himself before Thine Ineffable Majesty!" The
wizard began, slowly and painfully, to get down on hands and
knees.

The Emperor motioned him up, saying, "In respect for your
years, old man, we will omit the prostration. Simply tell us about
this invincible weapon of yours."

"Your Imperial Majesty is too kind to this unworthy wretch.
Sees Your Majesty this?"

From his ragged sleeve, the Mulvanian produced a large
painted fan. Like the others present, Ajendra kept his gaze averted
from the Emperor's face, on the pretense that one who looked
the ruler full in the face would be blinded by his awful glory.

"This," continued Ajendra, "was made for the king of the Gwoling Islands by the noted wizard Tsunjing. By a series of chances

too long to bore Your Imperial Majesty with, it came into the unworthy hands of this inferior person."

At least, thought Tsotuga, the fellow had learnt the polite forms of Kuromonian address. Many Mulvanians were informal to the point of rudeness. Aloud he said, "It looks like any other fan. What is its power?"

"Simple, O superior one. Any living thing that you fan with it disappears."

"Oho!" exclaimed the Emperor. "So that is what befell the missing Nanka!"

Ajendra looked innocent. "This loathsome reptile does not understand Your Divine Majesty."

"Never mind. Whither go the victims!"

"One theory of my school is that they are translated to a higher dimension, coexistent with this one. Another holds that they are dispersed into constituent atoms, which, however, retain such mutual affinities that they can be reassembled when the signal for recall is—"

"Mean you that you can reverse the effect and fetch back the vanished beings?"

"Aye, superhuman sire. One folds the fan and taps one's wrists and forehead according to a simple code, and presto! there is the evanished one. Would Your Majesty see a demonstration? There is no danger to the demonstratee, since this humble person can bring him back instanter."

"Very well, good wizard. Just be careful not to wave that thing at us. On whom propose you to try it?"

Ajendra looked about the Chamber of Audience. There was a stir amongst ushers, guardsmen and officials. Light winked on gilded armor and glowed on silken robes as each tried to make himself inconspicuous behind a pillar or another courtier.

"Who will volunteer?" asked the Emperor. "You, Dzakusan?"

The Prime Minister prostrated himself. "Great Emperor, live forever! This lump of iniquity has not been well lately. Moreover, he has nine children to support. He humbly begs Your Supremacy to excuse him."

Similar questions to other functionaries produced similar responses. At length Ajendra said, "If this lowly one may make a suggestion to Your Magnificence, it might be better to try it first on a beast—say, a dog or a cat."

"Aha!" said Tsotuga. "Just the thing. We know the animal, too. Surakai, fetch that cursed dog belonging to the Empress—you know, that yapping little monstrosity."

The messenger departed on his roller skates. Soon he was back, leading on a leash a small woolly white dog, which barked incessantly.

"Go ahead," said the Emperor.

"This negligible person hears and obeys," said Ajendra, opening the fan.

The dog's yelp was cut off as the draft from the fan struck it. Surakai trailed an empty leash. The courtiers started and murmured.

"By the Heavenly Bureaucrats!" exclaimed the Emperor. "That is impressive. Now bring the creature back. Fear not if you fail. The thing has bitten us twice, so the Empire will not fall if it remain in that other dimension."

Ajendra produced from his other sleeve a small codex, whose pages he thumbed. Then he held a reading glass to his eye. "Here it is," he said. " 'Dog. Two left, three right, one to head.' "

Having folded the fan, Ajendra, holding it in his right hand, rapped his left wrist twice. Transferring the fan to his left hand, he then tapped his right wrist thrice and his forehead once. Instantly the dog reappeared. Yapping, it fled under the throne.

"Very good," said the Emperor. "Leave the creature where it is. What is that, a code book?"

"Aye, supreme sire. It lists all the categories of organic beings subject to the fan's power."

"Well, let us try it on a human being—an expendable one. Mishuho, have we a condemned criminal handy?"

"Live forever, incomparable one!" said the Minister of Justice. "We have a murderer due to lose his head tomorrow. Shall this miserable creature fetch him?"

The murderer was fetched. Ajendra fanned him out of existence and tapped him back again.

"Whew!" said the murderer. "This contemptible one must have suffered a dizzy spell."

"Where were you whilst you were vanished?" said the Emperor.

"I knew not that I was vanished, great Emperor!" said the murderer. "I felt dizzy and seemed to lose my wits for an instant—and then here I was, back in the Proscribed Palace."

"Well, you disappeared, all right. In consideration of his services to the state, Mishuho, commute his sentence to twenty-five lashes and turn him loose. Now, Doctor Ajendra!"

"Aye, ruler of the world?"

"What are the limitations of your fan? Does it run out of charge and have to be resorceled?"

"Nay, exalted one. At least, its power has not weakened in the centuries since Tsunjing made it."

"Does it work on a large animal, say a horse or an elephant?"

"It does better than that. When the grandson of the Gwoling king for whom it was made, Prince Wangerr, met a dragon on Banshou Island, he swept the monster out of existence with three mighty strokes of the fan."

"Hm. Quite powerful enough, it seems. Now, good Ajendra, suppose you bring back that police spy, Nanka, on whom you employed your arts a few days ago!"

The Mulvanian shot a glance at the Emperor's face. Some courtiers murmured at this breach of decorum, but Tsotuga seemed not to notice. The wizard evidently satisfied himself that the ruler knew whereof he spoke. Ajendra thumbed through his book until he came to "Spy." Then he tapped his left wrist four times and his forehead twice.

A big, burly man in beggar's rags materialized. Nanka was still wearing the roller skates on which he had entered Ajendra's hut. Unprepared as he was for this appearance, his feet flew out from under him. He fell heavily on his back, cracking his head on the red-white-and-black tessellated marble floor. The Emperor laughed heartily, and the courtiers allowed themselves discreet smiles.

As the informer, red with rage and astonishment, climbed to his feet, Tsotuga said, "Mishuho, give him ten lashes for trying to rob a subject. Tell him that next time it will be his head—if not the boiling oil. Take him away. Well now, worthy wizard, what would you have for your device and its code book?"

"Ten thousand golden dragons," said Ajendra, "and an escort to my own country."

"Hm. Is that not a lot for a holy ascetic?"

"It is not for myself that this humble being asks," said the Mulvanian. "I would build and endow a temple to my favorite gods in my native village. There I shall pass my remaining days in meditation on the Thatness of the All."

"A meritorious project," said Tsotuga. "Let it be done. Chingitu, see that Doctor Ajendra has a trustworthy escort to Mulvan. Have them get a letter from the King of Kings, testifying that they delivered Ajendra safely and did not murder him for his gold along the way."

"This despicable one hears and obeys," said the Minister of War.

For the next month, things went smoothly at court. The Emperor kept his temper. No one, knowing of the magical fan that the testy monarch carried, cared to provoke him. Even Empress Nasako, although furious at her husband's callous use of her dog, kept her sharp tongue sheathed. Tsotuga remembered where he had hidden the statuette of Amarasupi and so for a time was almost happy.

But, as said the philosopher Dauhai back in the Jumbon Dynasty, everything passes away. The day came when, in the Emperor's study, Minister of Finance Yaebu tried to explain the workings of that marvelous new invention, paper money. The Emperor demanded to know why he could not simply abolish all taxes, thus pleasing the people, and pay the government's bills with newly printed currency notes. Tsotuga was irascible as a result of having mislaid another of his prized antique gimcracks.

"But, Your Divine Majesty!" wailed Yaebu. "That was tried in Gwoling, half a century ago! The value of the notes dropped to nought. None would offer aught for sale, since none wished to accept worthless paper. They had to go back to barter."

"We should think a few heads on poles would have fixed that," growled Tsotuga.

"The then king of Gwoling tried that, too," said Yaebu. "It accomplished nought; the markets remained empty of goods. City folk starved . . ."

The argument continued while the Emperor, who had little head for economics, became more and more restless, bored, and impatient. Ignoring these signs, Yaebu persisted in his arguments.

At last the Emperor exploded, "Curse your arse with boils, Yaebu! We will show you how to keep saying 'nay' and 'however' and 'impossible' to your sovran! Begone, sirrah!"

Tsotuga whipped out his fan, snapped it open, and fanned a blast of air at Yaebu. The minister vanished.

Hm, mused Tsotuga, *it really does work. Now I must fetch Yaebu back, for I did not really mean to destroy the faithful fellow. It is just that he irritates me so with his everlasting "if's" and "but's" and "can't's." Let me see, where did I put that code book? I remember hiding it in a special place where I could be sure of finding it again. But where?*

The Emperor looked first in the deep, baggy sleeves of his embroidered silken robe, which in Kuromon served the office of pockets. It was not there.

Then the Emperor rose from his business throne and went to the imperial wardrobe, where a hundred-odd robes hung from pegs. There were silken robes for official use, thin for summer and quilted for winter. There were woolen robes for outdoor winter use and cotton robes for outdoor summer use. They were dyed scarlet and emerald, saffron and azure, cream and violet, and all the other colors in the dyers' armory.

Tsotuga went down the line, feeling in the sleeves of each robe. A tireman hurried in, saying, "O Divine Autocrat, permit this filthy beggar to relieve you of this menial chore!"

Tsotuga: "Nay, good Shakatabi; we entrust this task to none but ourselves."

Laboriously, Tsotuga continued down the line until he had examined all the robes. Then he began the rounds of the Proscribed Palace, pulling out the drawers of desks and dressers, poking into cubbyholes, and shouting for the keys to chests and strongboxes.

After several hours, exhaustion forced the Emperor to desist. Falling into the semi-throne of the Forbidden Chamber, he struck the gong. When the room was jam-packed with servants, he said,

"We, Tsotuga the Fourth, offer a reward of a hundred golden dragons to him who finds the missing code book that goes with our miraculous fan!"

That day, the Proscribed Palace saw a great scurrying and searching. Scores of felt-slippered servants shuffled about, opening, poking, prying and peering. When night fell, the book had not been found.

Beshrew me! said Tsotuga to himself. *Poor Yaebu is lost unless we find the accursed book. I must be more careful with that fan.*

Again, as spring advanced, things went smoothly for a while. But the day came when Tsotuga was roller-skating about the paths of the palace gardens with Minister of War Chingitu. Questioned sharply about the recent defeat of the Kuromonian army by the nomads of the steppes, Chingitu offered excuses that Tsotuga knew to be mendacious. Away went Tsotuga's temper. "The real reason," roared the Emperor, "is that your cousin, the Quartermaster-General, has been grafting and filling posts with his worthless relatives, so that our soldiers were ill-armed! And you know it! Take that!"

A wave of the fan, and no more Chingitu. In like manner, shortly thereafter, perished Prime Minister Dzakusan.

The want of properly appointed ministers soon made itself felt. Tsotuga could not personally supervise all the hundreds of bureaucrats in the now-headless departments. These civil servants devoted themselves more and more to feuding, loafing, nepotism and peculation. Conditions were bad in Kuromon anyway, because of the inflation brought about by Tsotuga's paper-money scheme. The government was fast becoming a shambles.

"You must pull yourself together, lord," said Empress Nasako, "ere the pirates of the Gwoling Archipelago and the brigands from the steppes divide Kuromon between them, as a man divides an orange."

"But what in the name of the fifty-seven major deities shall I do?" cried Tsotuga. "Curse it, if I had that code book, I could bring back Yaebu, who would straighten out this financial mess."

"Oh, forget the book. If I were you, I should burn that magical fan ere it got me into more trouble."

"You are out of your mind, woman! Never!"

Nasako sighed. "As the sage Zuiku said, who would use a tiger for a watchdog to guard his wealth will soon need neither wealth nor watchdog. At least appoint a new prime minister, to bring order out of this chaos."

"I have gone over the list of possible candidates, but every one has a black mark against him. One was connected with that faction that conspired my assassination nine years ago. Another was accused of grafting, although it was never proved. Still another is ailing—"

"Is Zamben of Jompei on your list?"

"I have never heard of him. Who is he?"

"The supervisor of roads and bridges in Jade Mountain Province. They say he has made an excellent record there."

"How know you about him?" snapped the Emperor suspiciously.

"He is a cousin of my first lady-in-waiting. She has long urged his virtues upon me. I brushed her suit aside, knowing my lord's dislike of letting my ladies exploit their position by abetting their kinsmen's interests. In your present predicament, though, you could do worse than look the fellow over."

"Very well, I will."

Thus it happened that Zamben of Jompei became prime minister. The former supervisor of roads and bridges was younger by a decade than the Emperor. He was a handsome, cheerful, charming, rollicking person who made himself popular with the court, save for those determined to hate the favorite of the moment. Tsotuga thought Zamben was rather too light-hearted and lacking in respect for the labyrinthine etiquette. But Zamben proved an able administrator who soon had the vast governmental machine running smoothly.

But it is said that the thatcher's roof is the leakiest in the village. What the Emperor did not know was that Zamben and Empress Nasako were secret lovers. They had been before Zamben's elevation. Circumstances made it hard to consummate their passion, save rarely in one of Nasako's summer pavilions in the hills.

In the Proscribed Palace, it was even harder. The palace swarmed with menials who would be glad to carry tales. The amorous pair had to resort to stratagems. Nasako announced that she had to be left entirely alone in a summer house to compose a poem. The versatile Zamben wrote the poem for her as evidence before he hid himself in the summer house in advance of her arrival.

"That was worth waiting for," said the Empress, donning her garments. "That fat old fool Tsotuga has not touched me in a year, and a full-blooded woman like me needs frequent stoking. He has not even futtered his pretty young concubines, albeit he is not yet fifty."

"Why? Is he prematurely senile?"

"Nay; it is his fear of assassination. For a while, he tried doing it in the seated position, so that he could keep looking about for possible assailants. But since he insisted on wearing his armor, it proved too awkward to please anyone. So he gave it up altogether."

"Well, the thought of a stab in the back is depressing to more than just a man's spirit. If—which the gods forfend—an accident should befall His Divine Majesty—"

"How?" said Nasako. "No assassin dares approach him whilst he has that fan."

"Where does he put it at night?"

"Under his pillow, and he sleeps clutching it. It would take a winged demon to get at him anyway, floating in that pool of quicksilver."

"A hard-driven crossbow bolt, shot from beyond the fan's range—"

"Nay, he is too well guarded to let an arbalester get within range, and he even sleeps in his mail."

"Well, we shall see," said Zamben. "Meanwhile, Nasako, how would my love like another?"

"What a man you are!" cried Nasako, beginning to cast off her just-donned garments.

During the next two months, the court noted that Zamben, not content with being the second most powerful man in the Empire, had also ingratiated himself with the Emperor. He did so well as to oust Reiro the beggar from his position as Emperor's crony. Zamben even became an expert on the history of art, the better to admire Tsotuga's prized gewgaws.

The favorite-haters at court muttered that for an emperor to make a personal friend of a minister was a violation of sound method. Not only was the mystical balance among the Five Elements upset, but also Zamben might entertain usurpatory notions, which his friendship might enable him to put into effect. But none dared to broach the subject to the explosive-tempered Tsotuga. They shrugged, saying, "After all, it is the Empress's duty to warn him. If she cannot, what chance have we?"

Zamben went his smiling way, smoothly running the government by day and fraternizing with the Emperor by night.

At last came his opportunity. The Emperor was toying with his fan over a game of Sachi. Zamben dropped a piece—an elephant —on the floor so that it rolled under the table.

"Let me get it," said Tsotuga. "It is on my side."

As he bent to fumble for the piece, he dropped his fan. He straightened up holding the piece, to find Zamben holding the fan out to him. Tsotuga snatched it back. "Excuse my discourtesy," said the Emperor, "but I am fain not to let that thing out of my hands. It was stupid of me not to have put it away ere reaching for your elephant. It is still your move."

Days later, in the summer house, Empress Nasako asked, "Did you get it?"

"Aye," replied Zamben. "It was no trick to hand him the duplicate."

"Then what are you waiting for? Fan the old fool away!"

"Tut, tut, my sweet. I must assure the loyalty of my partisans. It is said that he who would swallow a pumpkin with one bite shall reap the reward of his gluttony. Besides, I have scruples."

"Oh, pish-tush! Are you just a pillow-warrior, strong in the yard but weak in the sword arm?"

"Nay, but I am a careful man who avoids offending the gods or biting off more than he can chew. Hence I would fan away only one who tried to do me ill. Knowing your imperial spouse, madam, I am sure he will soon force me to defend myself."

The evening came when Zamben, whose skill at Sachi had never seemed remarkable, suddenly beat the Emperor five games in a row.

"Curse you!" bawled Tsotuga as he lost his fifth king. "Have you been taking lessons? Or were you more skilled all along than you seemed?"

Zamben grinned and spread his hands. "The Divine Bureaucrats must have guided my moves."

"You—you—" Tsotuga choked with rage. "We will show you how to mock your emperor! Begone from the world!"

The Emperor whipped out his fan and fanned, but Zamben failed to disappear. Tsotuga fanned some more. "Curse it, has this thing lost its charge?" said Tsotuga. "Unless it be not the real—"

His sentence was cut off as Zamben, opening the true magical fan, swept the Emperor out of existence. Later, Zamben explained to the Empress, "I knew that, when he found that his fan did not work, he would suspect a substitution. So there was nought to do but use the real one."

"What shall we tell the court and the people?"

"I have thought all that out. We will give out that, plagued by the summer's heat, in an absent-minded moment he fanned himself."

"Would it work that way?"

"I know not; who were so rash as to try it? In any case, after a decent interval of mourning, I shall expect you to carry out your end of the bargain."

"Right willingly, my love."

*   *   *

Thus it came to pass that the widowed Empress wedded Zamben of Jompei, after the latter had, at her demand, put away his two previous wives. The minister acquired the courtesy title of "Emperor" but not the full powers of that office. Technically he was the consort of the Dowager Empress and guardian of and regent for the heir.

As to what would happen when the fourteen-year-old Prince Wakumba reached his majority, Zamben did not worry. He was sure that, whatever betid, he could charm the young Emperor into continuing his power and perquisites.

He thought of having the Prince murdered but quickly put that plan aside. For one thing, he feared that Nasako would have him killed in turn, for her supporters far outnumbered his. He had a hard enough task, just keeping on good terms with her. She was disillusioned to find that in her new husband she had obtained, not an ever-panting satyr, but merely an ambitious politician so immersed in political maneuvers, administrative details and religious rituals that he had little time and strength left over for stoking her fires. When she complained, he spoke of his "essential new project."

"What is that?" she demanded.

"I will not," he said, "waste more time in searching for that code book. Instead, I shall reconstruct the code by trial and error."

"How?"

"I shall try combinations of raps and note what I get each time. In the centuries that the fan has existed, hundreds of beings must have been fanned away."

The next day Zamben, flanked by six heavily armed palace guards, sat in the Chamber of Audience, which had been cleared of all others save two secretaries. Zamben tapped his left wrist once. A beggar appeared on the floor before him.

The beggar screamed with terror and fainted. When the man had been revived, it was found that he had been fanned out of existence more than a century before, in a fishing village on the shore of the ocean. He was astounded suddenly to find himself in a palace.

Zamben commanded, "Write: one tap on left wrist, beggar. Give him one golden dragon and show him out."

Two taps on the left wrist produced a swineherd, and so it was recorded. During the day, persons of all sorts were rapped into existence. Once a leopard appeared, snarling. Two guardsmen rushed upon it, but it sprang out the open window and vanished.

Some combinations of raps failed to bring results. Either they were not connected with victims of any definite kind, or no beings of that kind had ever been fanned away and not recalled.

"All right so far," said Zamben to the Empress that night.

"What if your experiments bring back Tsotuga?"

"By the fifty-seven major deities, I had not thought of that! An emperor, I suppose, needs a combination of many taps to bring him back. The instant I see him, I will fan him back to limbo."

"Have a care! I am sure that fan will sooner or later bring evil upon him who uses it."

"Fear not; I shall be cautious."

The next day, the experiments continued and the secretaries' lists of formulae lengthened. Three taps each on left wrist, right wrist, and forehead produced the missing Finance Minister Yaebu, much shaken.

Following Yaebu came an ass and a fuller. When the ass had been captured and led out, and the fuller had been soothed and sent away with his fee, Zamben tapped his left and right wrists each three times and his forehead four times.

There was a rush of displaced air. Filling most of the Chamber of Audience was a dragon. Zamben, his jaw sagging, started to rise. The dragon roared and roared, and the guards fled clattering.

Through Zamben's mind flashed a tale he had heard about the fan. Centuries before, it had saved the Gwoling prince Wangerr from a dragon on Banshou Island. This must be the same . . .

Zamben began to open the fan, but astonishment and terror had paralyzed him a few seconds too long. The great, scaly head swooped; the jaws slammed shut.

The only person left in the chamber was one of the secretaries, cowering behind the throne. This man heard a single scream. Then the dragon hunched itself out the window, with a crashing of broken window frame and—since the aperture was still too small for it—of a goodly part of the wall. The scribe peeked around the throne to see the scaly tail vanishing through the jagged gap that yawned where the window had been, and a cloud of brick and plaster dust filling the Chamber of Audience.

Yaebu and Nasako became co-regents. Lacking a man, the lusty Dowager Empress took up with a handsome groom from the imperial stables, half her age but well equipped to pleasure her, having no thoughts to distract him from his lectual duties. Yaebu, a conservative family man with no lust for exalted adultery, became prime minister. He ran the Empire in a somewhat hesitant, bumbling way but not unsuccessfully.

Since there was no emperor, even a nominal one, young Prince Wakumba had to be enthroned forthwith. After the day-long ceremony, the lad slowly pulled off the plumed and winged crown of state. He complained, "This thing seems even heavier than usual." He poked about inside it.

Yaebu hovered anxiously, murmuring, "Have a care, my liege! Watch out that you harm not that holy headgear!"

Something went *spung*, and a metal flap snapped up inside the crown.

"Here is that secret compartment," said Wakumba, "with a—what is this?—a book in it. By the fifty-seven divinities, this must be that code book that Dad was hunting!"

"Let me see!" cried Yaebu and Nasako together.

"That is it, all right. But since the dragon ate the fan along with my stepfather, the book is of no use. Let it be put in the archives with other curios."

Nasako said, "We must ask Kozima to make another magical fan, so that the book shall again be useful."

It is not, however, recorded that the court wizard of Kuromon ever succeeded in this endeavor. For aught I know, the code book still reposes peacefully in the Kuromonian archives in Chingun, and those who, like Tsotuga and Dzakusan, were fanned away and never brought back, still await their deliverance.

BROTHERS

by Gordon R. Dickson

"Brothers" is a story which is part of the Childe Cycle (sometimes called the Dorsai! Cycle, after the first novel in the Cycle to be published). The Cycle proper was originally planned to cover roughly a thousand years, from the fourteenth century to the twenty-third; and to consist of three historical novels, three contemporary novels and three novels of the future.

Because of the difficulties in getting publishers to publish novels of the length planned in the sf area, however, the three science-fiction novels have each been divided into two halves, each of which has been formed into a smaller, short novel. This gives, then, six novels in the sf end of the Cycle, of which four have already been published. In order of their publication, they are Dorsai! (Genetic General *in paperback*), Necromancer (No Room For Man *in paperback*), Soldier, Ask Not *and* The Tactics of Mistake. *Yet to be finished and published are the two halves of the final book in this part of the Cycle; and these are tentatively titled* The Final Encyclopedia (*next-to-last book*) *and* Childe (*the last book*).

In addition, there has been one short novelette entitled Warrior, *impinging on the Cycle;* "Brothers," *which follows this foreword, is the second independent novelette so far published. There will be others when I have the time; they will act as illuminants, but not necessary parts, of the Cycle proper.*

The thing to recognize about the Cycle as a whole is that it is a single unit—a thematic novel that argues not only that Man is evolving, but that a specific step in evolution is taking place, un-noticed, under our noses at the present time. It postulates a race-identity for humanity as a whole, a race-identity with Conscious and Unconscious (or Subconscious) aspects, like Janus-faces in conflict, in which the Conscious wishes to adventure and grow, and the Unconscious fears change and fights to stay as it is. These aspects are dramatized in the human characters of the novels, who severally play out the various progressing acts of the evolution and conflict, from the time of Sir John Hawkwood in the four-teenth century to the time of Hal Mayne in the twenty-third.

The concept of the Cycle did not reach full development until after the writing of Dorsai!, *but its roots go back nearly a dozen years before that writing, to a purely historical novel of the fifteenth century,* The Pikeman, *on which I worked in the late 1940s and which has since been lost in the larger historical story of John Hawkwood, who occupies the first compartment of the historical leg of the Cycle.*

With Dorsai! *itself—the full serial, magazine version in As-tounding—John Campbell was directly connected. Less than a couple of weeks after I had mailed the manuscript to my then agent, I got a phone call from him saying that John Campbell liked it very much but urgently wanted to talk it over with me, and was disappointed to hear that I was not living close enough to the New York area to come in and see him. Would I fly to New York? With an advance from the agent himself, I did that. One of the men from his office met me at the hotel in Manhattan that I had ended up at, and drove me out to John's suburban home in an agency car remarkable for its tenacity to life, if not for the venerability of its years. I spent the whole day talking to John— about many other things than the novel—and ended up staying the night. John's point about* Dorsai! *was that he wished to see the matter of Donal Graeme's superhumanness—his ability to use intuition as ordinary men used logic—brought into the forefront of the story.*

He was quite right, and the suggestion has been and will continue to be of excellent value to me, since in the final two sf novels, two types of "thinking" are necessary, one being the extended, but straight-line, logic of the computer-like Final Encyclopedia, and the other being the extended intuition of Hal Mayne applied at right angles, as it were, to that logic.

Herewith follows the account of the death, and the consequences of the death, of Kensie, who is the sunshine-bright one of the tall Graeme twins from the Dorsai—Ian being all darkness and shadow by contrast. It was Kensie whom everyone loved, except the men who killed him on the small world of St. Marie. It is also the story of St. Marie itself, that West-European-settled, Roman Catholic, rich little world in the same solar system as Mara and Kultis, the two worlds of the Exotics. It is a little world whose people, having no real problems, spent a good deal of their time dreaming up some. Only when something real struck, like an invasion of the puritanic, semi-fanatic soldiery from the Friendly worlds of Harmony and Association, did they face their true inability to cope by calling upon the Exotics for help.

Readers already familiar with the Cycle will see the loose threads of other parts of it picked up here and rewoven back into that "pattern" of which the Exotics like to speak. They should also see, grinning behind that pattern, the two Janus-faces of the larger Cycle in conflict—Dorsai folk-ethic against St. Marian folk-ethic, and Tomas Velt against his own like-brother and opponent, Pel Sinjin. Finally, in this story, for those who wish to know certainly about such things, it is indeed Tam Olyn of Soldier, Ask Not—*the unnamed individual Padma speaks of going to meet on the Friendly worlds after he leaves St. Marie.*

PHYSICALLY, he was big, very big. The professional soldiers of several generations from that small, harsh world called the Dorsai are normally larger than men from other worlds; but the Graemes are large even among the Dorsai. At the same time, like his twin brother, Ian, Commander Kensie Graeme was so well proportioned in spite of his size that it was only at moments like this, when I saw him standing next to a fellow Dorsai like his executive officer, Colonel Charley ap Morgan, that I could realize how big he actually was. He had the black, curly hair of the Graemes, the heavy-boned face and brilliant gray-green eyes of his family; also, that utter stillness at rest and that startling swiftness in motion that was characteristic of the several-generations Dorsai.

So, too, had Ian, back in Blauvain; for physically the twins were the image of each other. But otherwise, temperamentally, their difference was striking. Everybody loved Kensie. He was like some golden god of the sunshine. While Ian was dark and solitary as the black ice of a glacier in a land where it was always night.

"Blood," Pel Sinjin had said to me on our drive out here to the field encampment of the Expedition. "You know what they say, Tom. Blood and ice-water, half-and-half in his veins, is what makes a Dorsai. But something must have gone wrong with those two when their mother was carrying them. Kensie got all the blood. Ian . . ."

He had let the sentence finish itself. Like Kensie's own soldiers, Pel had come to idolize the man, and downgrade Ian in proportion. I had let the matter slide.

Now Kensie was smiling at us, as if there was some joke we were not yet in on. "A welcoming committee?" he said. "Is that what you are?"

"Not exactly," I said. "We came out to talk about letting your men into Blauvain city for rest and relaxation; now that you've got those invading soldiers from the Friendly worlds all rounded up, disarmed, and ready for shipment home—what's the joke?"

"Just," said Charley ap Morgan, "that we were on our way into Blauvain to see you. We just got a repeater message that you and other planetary officials here on St. Marie are giving Ian and Kensie, with their staffs, a surprise victory dinner in Blauvain this evening."

"Hell's Bells!" I said.

"You hadn't been told?" Kensie asked.

"Not a damn word," I said.

It was typical of the fumbling of the so-called government-
of-mayors we had here on our little world of St. Marie. Here was
I, superintendent of police in Blauvain—our capital city—and here
was Pel, commanding general of our planetary militia which had
been in the field with the Exotic Expedition sent to rescue us from
the invading puritan fanatics from the Friendly worlds; and no
one had bothered to tell either one of us about a dinner for the
two commanders of that Expedition.

"You're going in, then?" Pel asked Kensie. Kensie nodded.
"I've got to call my Headquarters." Pel went out.

Kensie laughed. "Well," he said, "this gives us a chance to kill
two birds at once. We'll ride back with you and talk on the way.
Is there some difficulty about Blauvain absorbing our men on
leave?"

"Not that way," I said. "But even though the Friendlies have
all been rounded up, the Blue Front is still with us in the shape
of a good number of political outlaws and terrorists that want to
pull down our present government. They lost the gamble they
took when they invited in the Friendly troops; but now they may
take advantage of any trouble that can be stirred up around your
soldiers while they're on their own in the city."

"There shouldn't be any." Kensie reached for a dress gunbelt
of black leather and began to put it on over the white dress uniform he was wearing. "But we can talk about it, if you like. You'd
better be doing some dressing yourself, Charley."

"On my way," said Charley ap Morgan, and went out.

So, fifteen minutes later, Pel and I found ourselves headed back
the way we had come, this time with three passengers. I was still
at the controls of the police car as we slid on its air cushion across
the rich grass of our St. Marie summer toward Blauvain; but
Kensie rode with me in front, making me feel small beside him—
and I am considered a large man among our own people on St.
Marie. Beside Kensie, I must have looked like a fifteen-year-old
boy in comparison. Pel was equally small in back between Charley
and a Dorsai senior commandant named Chu Van Moy—a heavy-

bodied, black Mongol, if you can imagine such a man, from the Dorsai South Continent.

"No real problem," Kensie was saying as we left the grass at last for the vitreous road surface leading us in among the streets and roads of the city—in particular the road curving in between the high office buildings of Blauvain's West Industrial Park, now just half a kilometer ahead. "We'll turn the men loose in small groups if you say. But there shouldn't be any need to worry. They're mercenaries, and a mercenary knows that civilians pay his wages. He's not going to make any trouble which would give his profession a bad name."

"I don't worry about your men," I said. "It's the Blue Front fabricating some trouble in the vicinity of some of your men and then trying to pin the blame on them; that is what worries me. The only way to guard against that is to have your troops in small enough numbers so that my policemen can keep an eye on the civilians around them."

"Fair enough," said Kensie. He smiled down at me. "I hope, though, you don't plan on having your men holding our men's hands all through their evenings in town—"

Just then we passed between the first of the tall office buildings. A shadow from the late morning sun fell across the car, and the high walls around us gave Kensie's last words a flat echo. Right on the heels of those words—in fact, mixed with them—came a faint sound as of multiple whistlings about us; and Kensie fell forward, no longer speaking, until his forehead against the front windscreen stopped him from movement.

The next thing I knew I was flying through the air, literally. Charley ap Morgan had left the police car on the right side, dragging me along with a hand like a steel clamp on my arm, until we ended up against the front of the building on our right. We crouched there, Charley with his dress handgun in his fist and looking up at the windows of the building opposite. Across the narrow way, I could see Chu Van Moy with Pel beside him, a dress gun also in Chu's fist. I reached for my own police beltgun, and remembered I was not wearing it.

About us there was utter silence. The narrow little projectiles from one or more silver rifles that had fluted about us did not come again. For the first time I realized there was no one on the streets and no movement to be seen behind the windows about us.

"We've got to get him to a hospital," said Pel, on the other side of the street. His voice was strained and tight. He was staring fixedly at the still figure of Kensie, still slumped against the windscreen.

"A hospital," he said again. His face was as pale as a sick man's.

Neither Charley or Chu paid any attention. Silently they were continuing to scan the windows of the building opposite them.

"A hospital!" shouted Pel suddenly.

Abruptly, Charley got to his feet and slid his weapon back into its holster. Across the street, Chu also was rising. Charley looked at the other Dorsai. "Yes," said Charley, "where is the nearest hospital?"

But Pel was already behind the controls of the police car. The rest of us had to move or be left behind. He swung the car toward Blauvain's Medical Receiving West, only three minutes away.

He drove the streets like a madman, switching on the warning lights and siren as he went. Screaming, the vehicle careened through traffic and signals alike to jerk to a stop behind the ambulance entrance at Medical West. Pel jumped from the car. "I'll get a life-support system—a medician—" he said, and ran inside.

I got out, and then Charley and Chu got out, more slowly. The two Dorsais were on opposite sides of the car.

"Find a room," Charley said. Chu nodded and went after Pel through the ambulance entrance.

Charley turned to the car. Gently, he picked up Kensie in his arms, the way you pick up a sleeping child, gently, holding Kensie to his chest so that Kensie's head fell in to rest on Charley's left shoulder. Carrying his field commander, Charley turned and went into the medical establishment. I followed.

Inside, there was a long corridor with hospital personnel milling about. Chu stood by a doorway a few meters down the hall to the left, half a head taller than the people between us. With Kensie in his arms, Charley went toward the other commandant.

Chu stood aside as Charley came up. The door swung back automatically, and Charley led the way into a room with surgical equipment in sterile cases along both its sides and an operating table in its center. Charley laid Kensie softly on the table, which was almost too short for his tall body. He put the long legs together, picked up the arms and laid their hands on the upper thighs. There was a line of small, red stains across the front of his jacket, high up, but no other marks. Kensie's face, with its eyes closed, looked blindly to the white ceiling overhead.

"All right," said Charley. He led the way back out into the hall. Chu came last and turned to click the lock on the door into place, drawing his handgun.

"What's this?" somebody shouted at my elbow, pushing toward Chu. "That's an emergency room. You can't do that—"

Chu was using his handgun on low aperture to slag the lock of the door. A crude but effective way to make sure that the room would not be opened by anyone with anything short of an industrial, heavy-duty torch. The man who was talking was middle-aged, with a gray mustache and the short green jacket of a senior surgeon.

I intercepted him and held him back from Chu. "Yes, he can," I said, as he turned to stare furiously in my direction. "Do you recognize me? I'm Tomas Velt, the Superintendent of Police."

He hesitated, and then calmed slightly—but only slightly. "I still say—" he began.

"By the authority of my office," I said, "I do now deputize you as a temporary Police assistant. That puts you under my orders. You'll see that no one in this hospital tries to open that door or get into that room until Police authorization is given. I make you responsible. Do you understand?"

He blinked at me. But before he could say anything, there was a new outburst of sound and action, and Pel broke into our group, literally dragging along another man in a senior surgeon's jacket. "Here!" Pel was shouting. "Right in here. Bring the life support—" He broke off, catching sight of Chu. "What?" he said. "What's going on? Is Kensie in there? We don't want the door sealed—"

"Pel," I said. I put my hand on his shoulder. "Pel!"

He finally felt and heard me. He turned a furious face in my direction.

"Pel," I said quietly, but slowly and clearly. "He's dead. Kensie. Kensie is dead."

Pel stared at me. "No," he said irritably, trying to pull away from me. I held him. "*No!*"

"Dead," I said, looking him squarely in the eyes. "Dead, Pel."

His eyes stared back at me, then seemed to lose their focus and stare off at something else. After a little they focused back on mine again, and I let go of him.

"Dead?" he repeated. It was hardly more than a whisper.

He walked over and leaned against one of the white-painted corridor walls. A nurse moved toward him and I signaled her to stop. "Just leave him alone for a moment," I said. I turned back to the two Dorsai officers who were now testing the door to see if it was truly sealed. "If you'll come to Police Headquarters," I said, "we can get the hunt going for whoever did it."

Charley looked at me briefly. There was no more friendly humor in his face now, but neither did it show any kind of shock or fury. The expression it showed was only a businesslike one. "No," he said briefly. "We have to report."

He went out, followed by Chu, moving so rapidly that I had to run to keep up with their long strides. Outside the door, they climbed back into the police car, Charley taking the controls. I scrambled in behind them and felt someone behind me. It was Pel.

"Pel," I said. "You'd better stay—"

"No. Too late," he said.

And it was too late. Charley already had the police car in motion. He drove no less swiftly than Pel had driven, but without madness. For all that, though, I made most of the trip with my fingers tight on the edge of my seat; for with the faster speed of Dorsai reflexes he went through available spaces and openings in traffic where I would have sworn we could not get through.

We pulled up before the office building attached to the Exotic Embassy as space for Expeditionary Base Headquarters. Charley led the way in past a guard, whose routine challenger broke off in mid-sentence as he recognized the two of them.

"We have to talk to the Base Commander," Charley said to him. "Where's Commander Graeme?"

"With the Blauvain Mayor, and the Outbond." The guard, who was no Dorsai, stammered a little. Charley turned on his heel.

"Wait—sir, I mean the Outbond's with *him,* here in the Commander's office."

Charley turned again. "We'll go on in. Call ahead," Charley said.

He led the way, without waiting to watch the guard obey, down a corridor and up an escalator ramp to an outer office where a young Force-Leader stood up behind his desk at the sight of us. "Sir," the Force-Leader said to Charley, "the Outbond and the Mayor will be with the Commander another few minutes—"

Charley brushed past him, and the Force-Leader spun around to punch at his desk phone. Heels clicking on the polished stone floor, Charley led us toward a further door and opened it, stepping into the office beyond. We followed him there into a large, square room with windows overlooking the city and our own broad-shouldered mayor, Moro Spence, standing there with a white-haired, calm-faced, hazel-eyed man in a blue robe, both facing a desk at which sat the mirror image of Kensie that was his twin brother, Ian Graeme.

Ian spoke to his desk as we came in. "It's all right," he said. He punched a button and looked up at Charley, who went forward with Chu beside him to the very edge of the desk, and then both saluted.

"What is it?" asked Ian.

"Kensie," said Charley. His voice became formal. "Field Commander Kensie Graeme has just been killed, sir, as we were on our way into the city."

For perhaps a second—no longer—Ian sat without speaking. But his face, so like Kensie's and yet so different, did not change expression. "How?" he asked then.

"By assassins we couldn't see," Charley answered. "Civilians, we think. They got away."

Moro Spence swore. "The Blue Front!" he said. "Ian . . . Ian, listen . . ."

No one paid any attention to him. Charley was briefly recounting what had happened from the time the message about the invitation had reached the encampment—

"But there wasn't any celebration like that planned!" protested Moro Spence to the deaf ears around him.

Ian sat quietly, his harsh, powerful face half in shadow from the sunlight coming in the high window behind him, listening as he might have listened to a thousand other reports. There was still no change visible in him, except perhaps that he, who had always been remote from everyone else, seemed even more remote now. His heavy forearms lay on the desk top, and the massive hands that were trained to be deadly weapons in their own right lay open and still on the papers beneath them. Almost, he seemed to be more legendary character than ordinary man; and that impression was not mine alone, because behind me I heard Pel hiss on a breath of sick fury indrawn between his teeth; and I remembered how he had talked of Ian being only ice and water, Kensie only blood.

The white-haired man in the blue robe, who was the Exotic, Padma, Outbond to St. Marie for the period of the Expedition, was also watching Ian steadily. When Charley was through with his account, Padma spoke. "Ian," he said; and his calm, light baritone seemed to linger and reecho strangely on the ear, "I think this is something best handled by the local authorities."

Ian glanced at him. "No," he answered. He looked at Charley. "Who's duty officer?"

"Ng'kok," said Charley.

Ian punched the phone button on his desk. "Get me Colonel Waru Ng'kok, Encampment HQ," he said to the desk.

" 'No'?" echoed Moro. "I don't understand, Commander. We can handle it. It's the Blue Front, you see. They're an outlawed political—"

I came up behind him and put my hand on his shoulder.

He broke off, turning around. "Oh, Tom!" he said, on a note of relief. "I didn't see you before. I'm glad you're here now—"

I put my finger to my lips. He was politician enough to recognize that there are times to shut up. He shut up now, and we both looked back at Ian.

"Waru? This is Base Commander Ian Graeme," Ian was saying to his phone. "Activate our four best Hunter Teams, and take three Forces from your on-duty troops to surround Blauvain. Seal all entrances to the city. No one allowed in or out without our authority. Tell the involved troops briefing on these actions will be forthcoming."

As professional, free-lance soldiers, under the pattern of the Dorsai contract—which the Exotic employers honored for all their military employees—the mercenaries were entitled to know the aim and purpose of any general orders for military action they were given. By a ninety-six percent vote among the enlisted men concerned, they could refuse to obey the order. In fact, by a hundred percent vote, they could force their officers to use them in an action they themselves demanded. But a hundred percent vote was almost unheard of. The phone grid in Ian's desk top said something I could not catch.

"No," replied Ian, "that's all." He clicked off the phone and reached down to open a drawer in his desk. He took out a gunbelt—a working, earth-colored gunbelt unlike the dress one Kensie had put on earlier—with sidearm already in its holster, and, standing up, began to strap it on. On his feet, he dominated the room, towering over us all. "Tom," he said, looking at me, "put your police to work, finding out what they can. Tell them all to be prepared to obey orders by any one of our soldiers, no matter what his rank."

"I don't know if I've got the authority to tell them that," I said.

"I've just given you the authority," he answered calmly. "As of this moment, Blauvain is under martial law."

Moro cleared his throat, but I jerked a hand at him to keep him quiet. There was no one in this room with the power to deal with Ian's authority now except the gentle-faced man in the blue robe. I looked appealingly at Padma, and he turned from me to Ian. "Naturally, Ian, measures will have to be taken, for the satisfaction of the soldiers who knew Kensie," Padma said softly, "but perhaps finding the guilty men would be better done by the civilian police without military assistance?"

"I'm afraid we can't leave it to them," said Ian briefly. He turned to the other two Dorsai officers. "Chu, take command of the Forces I've just ordered to cordon the city. Charley, you'll take over as acting field commander. Have all the officers and men in the encampment held there, and gather back any who are off post. You can use the office next to this one. We'll brief the troops in the encampment this afternoon. Chu can brief his forces as he posts them around the city."

The two turned and headed toward the door.

"Just a minute, gentlemen!" Padma's voice was raised only slightly. But the pair of officers paused and turned for a moment. "Colonel ap Morgan, Commandant Moy," said Padma, "as the official representative of the Exotic Government, which is your employer, I relieve you from the requirement of following any further orders of Commander Ian Graeme."

Charley and Chu looked past the Exotic to Ian.

"Go ahead," said Ian. They went. Ian turned back to Padma. "Our contracts provide that officers and men are not subject to civilian authority while on active duty, engaged with an enemy."

"But the war—the war with the Friendly invaders—is over," said Moro.

"One of our soldiers has just been killed," said Ian. "Until the identity of the killers is established, I'm going to assume we're still engaged with an enemy." He looked again at me. "Tom," he said. "You can contact your Police Headquarters from this desk. As soon as you've done that, report to me in the office next door, where I sent Charley."

He came around the desk and went out. Padma followed him. I went to the desk and put in a phone call to my own office.

"For God's sake, Tom!" said Moro to me as I punched phone buttons for the number of my office and started to get the police machinery rolling. "What's going on here?"

I was too busy to answer him. Someone else was not.

"He's going to make them pay for killing his brother," said Pel savagely from across the room. "That's what's going on!"

I had nearly forgotten Pel. Moro must have forgotten him absolutely, because he turned around to him now as if Pel had suddenly appeared on the scene in a cloud of fire and brimstone-odorous smoke. "Pel?" he said. "Oh, Pel—get your militia together and under arms, right away. This is an emergency—"

"Go to hell!" Pel answered him. "I'm not going to lift a finger to keep Ian from hunting down those assassins. And no one else in the militia who knew Kensie Graeme is going to lift a finger either."

"But this could bring down the government!" Moro was close to the idea of tears, if not to the actual article. "This could throw St. Marie back into anarchy, and the Blue Front will take over by default!"

"That's what the planet deserves," said Pel, "when it lets men like Kensie be shot down like dogs—men who came here to risk their lives to save our government!"

"You're crazier than these mercenaries are!" said Moro, staring at him. Then a touch of hope lifted Moro's drawn features. "Actually, Ian seems calm enough. Maybe he won't—"

"He'll take this city apart if he has to," said Pel savagely. "Don't blind yourself."

I had finished my phoning. I punched off and straightened up, looking at Pel. "I thought you told me there was nothing but ice and water to Ian?" I said.

"There isn't," Pel answered. "But Kensie's his twin brother. That's the one thing he can't sit back from and shuffle off. You'll see."

"I hope and pray I don't," I said, and I left the office for the one next door where Ian was waiting for me. Pel and Moro followed, but when we came to the doorway of the other office, there was a soldier there who would let only me through.

"We'll want a guard on that hospital room, and a Force guarding the hospital itself," Ian was saying slowly and deliberately to Charley ap Morgan as I came in. He was standing over Charley who was seated at a desk. Back against a wall stood the silent figure in a blue robe that was Padma. Ian turned to face me. "The troops at the encampment are being paraded in one hour," he said. "Charley will be going out to brief them on what's happened. I'd like you to go with him and be on the stand with him during the briefing."

I looked back at him, up at him. I had not gone along with Pel's ice-and-water assessment of the man. But now for the first time I began to doubt myself and believe Pel. If ever there had been two brothers who had seemed to be opposite halves of a single egg, Kensie and Ian had been those two. But here was Ian with Kensie dead—perhaps the only living person on the eleven human-inhabited worlds among the stars who had loved or understood him—and Ian had so far shown no more emotion at his brother's death than he might have on discovering an incorrect Order of the Day.

It occurred to me then that perhaps he was in emotional shock, and that this was the cause of his unnatural calmness. But the man I looked at now had none of the signs of a person in shock. I found myself wondering if any man's love for his brother could be hidden so deep that not even that brother's violent death could cause a crack in the frozen surface of the one who went on living.

If Ian was repressing emotion that was due to explode sometime soon, then we were all in trouble. My Blauvain police and the planetary militia together were toy soldiers compared to these professionals. Without the Exotic control to govern them, the whole planet was at their mercy. But there was no point in admitting that—even to ourselves—while even the shadow of independence was left to us.

"Commander," I said. "General Pel Sinjin's planetary militia were closely involved with your brother's forces. He would like to be at any such briefing. Also, Moro Spence, Blauvain's mayor and pro-tem president of the St. Marie Planetary Government, would want to be there. Both these men, Commander, have as deep a stake in this situation as your troops."

Ian looked at me. "General Sinjin," he said, after a moment. "Of course. But we don't need mayors."

"St. Marie needs them," I said. "That's all our St. Marie World Council is, actually—a collection of mayors from our largest cities. Show that Moro and the rest mean nothing and what little authority they have will be gone in ten minutes. Does St. Marie deserve that from you?"

He could have answered that St. Marie had been the death of his brother and it deserved anything he wished to give it. But he did not. I would have felt safer with him if he had. Instead, he looked at me as if from a long, long distance for several seconds, then over at Padma. "You'd favor that?" he asked.

"Yes," said Padma.

Ian looked back at me. "Both Moro and General Sinjin can go with you then," he said. "Charley will be leaving from here by air in about forty minutes. I'll let you get back to your own responsibilities until then. You'd better appoint someone as liaison from your police, to stand by here in this office."

"Thanks," I said. "I will."

I turned and went out. As I left, I heard Ian behind me, dictating. "All travel by the inhabitants of the City of Blauvain will be restricted to that which is absolutely essential. Military passes must be obtained for such travel. Inhabitants are to stay off the streets. Anyone involved in any gathering will be subject to investigation and arrest. The City of Blauvain is to recognize the fact that it is now under martial, not civil, law . . ."

The door closed behind me. I saw Pel and Moro waiting in the corridor. "It's all right," I told them, "you haven't been shut out of things—yet."

We took off from the top of that building forty minutes later, Charley and I up in the control seats of a military eight-man liaison craft with Pel and Moro sitting back among the passenger seats.

"Charley," I asked him in the privacy of our isolation together up front in the craft, once we were airborne, "what's going to happen?"

He was looking ahead through the forward vision screen, and he did not answer for a moment. When he did, it was without turning his head. "Kensie and I," he said softly, almost absently, "grew up together. Most of our lives we've been in the same place, working for the same employers."

I had thought I knew Charley ap Morgan. In his cheerfulness, he had seemed more human, less half-god of war than other Dorsai like Kensie or Ian, or even lesser Dorsai officers like Chu. But now he had moved off with the rest. His words took him out of my reach, into some cold, high, distant country where only Dorsai lived. It was a land I could not enter, the rules of which I would never understand. But I tried again anyway. "Charley," I said after a moment of silence, "that doesn't answer what I asked you."

He looked at me then, briefly. "I don't know what's going to happen," he said.

He turned his attention back to the controls. We flew the rest of the way to the encampment without talking.

When we landed, we found the entire Expedition drawn up in

formation. They were grouped by Forces into Battalion and Arm Groups, and their dun-colored battle dress showed glints of light in the late afternoon sunlight. It was not until we mounted the stand facing them that I recognized the glitter for what it was. They had come to the formation under arms, all of them—although that had not been in Ian's orders. Word of Kensie had proceeded us. I looked at Charlie, but he was paying no attention to the weapons.

The sun struck at us from the southwest at a lowered angle. The troops were in formation with their backs to the old factory and when Charley spoke, the amplifiers caught up his voice and carried it out over their heads. "Troops of the Exotic Expeditionary Force in relief of St. Marie," he said. "By order of Commander Ian Graeme, this briefing is ordered for the hundred and eighty-seventh day of the Expedition on St. Marie soil."

The brick walls slapped his words back with a flat echo over the still men in uniform. I stood a little behind him in the shadow of his shoulders, listening. Pel and Moro were behind me.

"I regret to inform you," Charley said, "that sniper activity within the City of Blauvain, this day, about thirteen hundred hours, cost us the life of Commander Kensie Graeme."

There was no sound from the men.

"The snipers have not yet been captured or killed. Since they remain unidentified, Commander Ian Graeme has ordered that the condition of hostilities, which was earlier assumed to have ended, is still in effect. Blauvain has been placed under martial law, sufficient force has been sent to seal the city against any exit or ingress, and all persons under Exotic contract to the Expedition have been recalled to this encampment."

I felt the heat of a breath on my ear and Pel's voice whispered to me. "Look at them!" he said. "They're ready to march on Blauvain right now. Do you think they'll let Kensie be killed on some stinking little world like this of ours, and not see that somebody pays for it?"

"Shut up, Pel," I murmured out of the corner of my mouth at him.

But he went on. "Look at them!" he said. "It's the order to march they're waiting for—the order to march on Blauvain. And if Charley doesn't end up giving it, there'll be hell to pay. You see how they've all come armed?"

"That's right, Pel, Blauvain's not your city!" It was a bitter whisper from Moro. "If it was Castelmane they were itching to march on, would you feel the same way about it?"

"Yes!" hissed Pel fiercely. "If men come here to risk their lives for us, and we can't do any better than let them be gunned down in the streets, what do we deserve? What does anyone deserve?"

"Stop making a court case out of it!" whispered Moro harshly. "It's Kensie you're thinking of—that's all. Just like it's only Kensie they're thinking of, out there . . ."

I tried again to quiet them, then realized that actually it did not make any difference. For all practical purposes, the three of us were invisible there behind Charley. The attention of the armed men ranked before us was all on Charley, and only on him. As Pel had said, they were waiting for one certain order, and only that order mattered to them.

It was like standing facing some great, dun-colored, wounded beast which must charge at any second now, if only because in action there would be relief from the pain it was suffering. Charley's expressionless voice went on, each word coming back like a slapping of dry boards together in the echo from the factory wall. He was issuing a long list of commands having to do

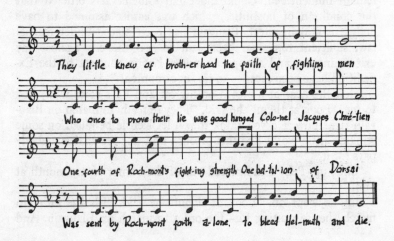

They lit-tle knew of broth-er-hood the faith of fighting men
Who once to prove their lie was good hanged Colo-nel Jacques Chré-tien
One-fourth of Roch-mont's fight-ing strength One bat-tal-ion of Dorsai
Was sent by Roch-mont forth a-lone to bleed Hel-muth and die.

with the order of the camp and its transition back to a condition of battle-alert.

I could feel the tension rising as he approached the end of his list of orders without one which might indicate action by the Expedition against the city in which Kensie had died. Then, suddenly, the list was at an end.

"That concludes," said Charley in the same unvarying tones, "the present orders dealing with the situation. I would remind the personnel of this Expedition that at present the identity of the assassins of Commander Graeme is unknown. The civilian police are exerting every effort to investigate the matter, and it is the opinion of your officers that nothing else can be done for the moment but to give them our complete cooperation. A suspicion exists that a native, outlawed political party known as the Blue Front may have been responsible for the assassination. If this should be so, we must be careful to distinguish between those of this world who are actually guilty of Commander Graeme's death and the great majority of innocent bystanders."

He stopped speaking.

There was not a sound from the thousands of men ranked before him.

"All right, Brigade-Major," said Charley, looking down from the stand at the ranking officer in the formation. "Dismiss your troops."

The Brigade-Major, who had been standing like all the rest facing the stand, wheeled about. "Atten-shun!" he snapped, and the amplifier sensors of the stand picked his voice up and threw it out over the men in formation as they had projected Charley's voice. "Dis-*miss!*"

The formation did not disperse. Here and there, a slight wavering in the ranks showed itself, and then the lines of standing figures were motionless again. For a long second, it seemed that nothing more was going to happen, that Charley and the mercenary soldiers before him would stand facing each other until the Day of Judgment . . . and then somewhere among the ranks, a solitary and off-key bass voice began to sing.

"They little knew of brotherhood"

Other voices rapidly picked it up.

"—The faith of fighting men—
Who once to prove their lie was good
Hanged Colonel Jacques Chrétien"

—And suddenly they were all singing in the ranks facing us. It was a song of the young colonel who had been put to death two hundred years before when the Dorsai were just in their beginning. A New Earth city had employed a force of Dorsai with the secret intention of using them against an enemy force so superior as to surely destroy them utterly—so rendering payment for their services unnecessary while at the same time doing considerable damage to the enemy. Then the Dorsai had defeated the enemy instead, and the city faced the necessity of paying after all. To avoid this, the city authorities came up with the idea of charging the Dorsai commanding officer with dealing with the enemy, taking a bribe to claim victory for a battle never fought at all. It was the technique of the big lie, and it might even have worked if they had not made their mistake of arresting the commanding officer to back up their story.

It was not a song to which I would have had any objection ordinarily. But now—suddenly—I found it directed at me. It was at Pel, Moro, me, that the soldiers of the Expedition were all singing it. Before, I had felt almost invisible on the stand behind Charley ap Morgan. Now we three civilians were the focus of every pair of eyes on the field—we civilians who were like the civilians that had hanged Jacques Chrétien; we who were St. Marians, like whoever had shot Kensie Graeme. It was like facing into the roaring maw of some great beast ready to swallow us up. We stood facing it, frozen.

Nor did Charley ap Morgan interfere.

He stood silent himself, waiting while they went through all the verses of the song to its end:

"One-fourth of Rochmont's fighting strength—
One battalion of Dorsai—

Was sent by Rochmont forth alone
To bleed Helmuth and die.

But look, look down from Rochmont's heights
Upon the Helmuth plain.
At all of Helmuth's armored force
By Dorsai checked, or slain.

Look down, look down, on Rochmont's shame:
To hide the wrong she'd done,
Made claim that Helmuth bribed Dorsai—
No battle had been won.

To prove that lie, the Rochmont Lords
Arrested Jacques Chrétien,
On charge he dealt with Helmuth's Chiefs
For payment to his men.

Commandant Arp Van Din sent word:
'You may not judge Dorsai,
Return our Colonel by the dawn,
Or Rochmont town will die.'

Strong-held behind her walls, Rochmont
Scorned to answer them,
Condemned, and at the daybreak, hanged,
Young Colonel Jacques Chrétien.

Bright, bright, the sun that morning rose
Upon each weaponed wall.
But when the sun set in the west,
Those walls were leveled all.

Then soft and white the moon arose
On streets and roofs unstained,
But when that moon was down once more
No street nor roof remained.

No more is there a Rochmont town
No more are Rochmont's men.
But stands a Dorsai monument
To Colonel Jacques Chrétien.

So pass the word from world to world,
Alone still stands Dorsai.
But while she lives, no one of hers,
By foreign wrong shall die.

They little knew of brotherhood
—The faith of fighting men—
Who once to prove their lie was good
Hanged Colonel Jacques Chrétien!"

It ended. Once more they were silent—utterly silent. On the platform Charley moved. He took half a step forward, and the sensors picked up his voice once more and threw it out over the heads of the waiting men. "Officers! Front and Center. Face your men!"

From the end of each rank figures moved. The commissioned and noncommissioned officers stepped forward, turned and marched to a point opposite the middle of the rank they had headed, turned once more and stood at attention.

"Prepare to fire."

The weapons in the hands of the officers came up to waist level, their muzzles pointing at the men directly before them. The breath in my chest was suddenly a solid thing. I could not have inhaled or exhaled if I had tried. I had heard of something like this but I had never believed it, let alone dreamed that I would be there to see it happen. Out of the corner of my eye I could see the angle of Charley ap Morgan's face, and it was a Dorsai face in all respects now. He spoke again. "The command to dismiss has been given"—Charley's voice rang and reechoed over the silent men—"and not obeyed. The command will be repeated under the stricture of the Third Article of the Professional Soldier's Covenant. Officers will open fire on any refusing to obey."

There was something like a small sigh that ran through all the standing men, followed by the faint rattle of safeties being released on the weapons of the men in ranks. They stood facing their officers and noncommissioned officers now—fellow soldiers and old friends. But they were all professionals. They would not simply stand and be executed if it came to the final point. The breath in my chest was now so solid it hurt, like something jagged and heavy pressing against my ribs. In ten seconds we could all be dead.

"Brigade-Major," said the level voice of Charley. "Dismiss your troops."

The Brigade-Major, who had turned once more to face Charley when Charley spoke to him, turned back again to the parade ground of men. "Dis—" No more than in Charley's voice was there perceptible change in the Brigade-Major's command from the time it had been given before. "—miss!"

The formations dissolved. All at once the ranks were breaking up, the men in them turning away, the officers and noncoms lowering the weapons they had lifted to ready position at Charley's earlier command. The long-held breath tore itself out of my lungs so roughly it ripped at my throat. I turned to Charley, but he was halfway down the steps from the platform, as expressionless as he had been all through the last few minutes. I had to half run to catch up to him. "Charley!" I said, reaching him.

He turned to look at me as he walked along.

Suddenly I felt how pale and sweat-dampened I was. I tried to laugh. "Thank God that's over," I said.

"Over?" He shook his head. "It's not over, Tom. The enlisted men will be voting now. It's their right."

"Vote?" The word made no sense to me for a second. Then suddenly it made too much sense. "You mean—they might vote to march on Blauvain, or something like that?"

"Perhaps—something like that," he said.

I stared at him. "And then?" I said. "You wouldn't . . . if their vote should be to march on Blauvain—what would you do?"

He looked at me almost coldly. "Lead my troops," he said.

I stopped. Standing there, I watched him walk away from me. A hand tugged at my elbow, and I turned around to see that Pel and Moro had caught up to me. It was Moro who had his hand on my arm. "Tom," said Moro, "what do we do now?"

"See Padma," I said. "If he can't do something, I don't know anybody who can."

Charley was not flying directly back to Blauvain. He was already in a staff meeting with his fellow officers, who were barred from the voting of the enlisted men by the Covenant. We three civilians had to borrow a land car from the encampment motor pool.

It was a silent ride most of the way back into town. Once again I was at the controls, with Pel beside me. Sitting behind us, just before we reached the west area of the city, Moro leaned forward to put his head between us. "Tom," he said. "You'll have to put your police on special duty. Pel, you've got to mobilize the militia —right now."

"Moro," I answered—and I suddenly felt dog-tired, weary to the point of exhaustion. "I've got less than three hundred men, ninety-nine percent of them without anything more exciting in the way of experience than filling out reports or taking charge at a fire, an accident or a family quarrel. They wouldn't face those mercenaries even if I ordered them to."

"Pel," he said, turning away from me, "your men are soldiers. They've been in the field with these mercenaries—"

Pel laughed at him. "Over a hundred years ago, a battalion of Dorsais took a fortified city—Rochmont—with nothing heavier than light field pieces. This is a *brigade*—six battalions—armed with the best weapons the Exotics can buy them, facing a city with no natural or artificial defenses at all. And you want my two thousand militiamen to try to stop them? There's no force on St. Marie that could stop those professional soldiers."

"At Rochmont they were all Dorsai—" Moro began.

"For God's sake!" cried Pel. "These are Dorsai-officered, the best mercenaries you can find. Elite troops—The Exotics don't hire anything else for fear they might have to touch a weapon themselves and damage their enlightenment, or whatever the hell it is! Face it, Moro! If Kensie's troops want to chew us up, they will. And there's nothing you or I can do about it!"

Moro said nothing for a long moment. Pel's last words had hit a near-hysterical note. When the Mayor of Blauvain did speak again, it was softly. "I just wish to God I knew why you want just that to happen so badly," he said.

"Go to hell!" said Pel. "Just go—"

I slammed the car into retro and we skidded to a halt, thumping down on the grass as the air cushion quit. I looked at Pel.

"That's something I'd like to know too," I said. "All right, you liked Kensie. So did I. But what we're facing is anything from the leveling of a city to a possible massacre of a couple of hundred thousand people. All that for the death of just one man?"

Pel's face looked bitter and sick. "We're no good, we St. Marians," he said thickly. "We're a fat little farm world that's never done anything since it was first settled but yell for help to the Exotics every time we got into trouble. And the Exotics have bailed us out every time, only because we're in the same solar system with them. What're we worth? Nothing! At least the Dorsai and the Exotics have got some value—some use!"

He turned away from Moro and me, and we could not get another word out of him.

We drove on into the city where, to my great relief, I finally got rid of Pel and Moro both and was able to get to Police Headquarters and take charge of things.

As I expected, things badly needed taking care of there. As I should also have expected, I had very much underestimated how badly they needed it. I had planned to spend two or three hours getting the situation under control and then be free to seek out Padma. But, as it ended up, it took me nearly seven straight hours to damp down the panic, straighten out the confusion, and put some purpose and order back into the operations of all my people, off-duty and otherwise, who had reported for emergency service. Actually, it was little enough we were required to do— merely patrol the streets and see that the town's citizens stayed off the streets and out of the way of the mercenaries. Still, that took seven hours to put into smooth operation, and at the end of that time I was still not free to go hunting for Padma but had to respond to a series of calls for my presence by the detective crew assigned to work with the mercenaries in tracking down the assassins.

I drove through the empty nighttime streets slowly with my emergency lights on and the official emblem on my police car clearly illuminated. Three times, however, I was stopped and checked by teams of three to five mercenaries, in battle dress and fully weaponed, that appeared unexpectedly. The third time, the Groupman—a noncommissioned officer—in command of the team stopping me, joined me in the car. When twice after that we encountered military teams, he leaned out the right window to show himself, and we were waved through.

We came at last to a block of warehouses on the north side of the city, and to one warehouse in particular. Within, the large, echoing structure was empty except for a few hundred square feet of crated harvesting machinery on the first of its three floors. I found my men on the second floor in the transparent cubicles that were the building's offices, apparently doing nothing. "What's the matter?" I said when I saw them. They were not only idle, but they looked unhappy.

"There's nothing we can do, Superintendent," said the senior detective lieutenant present—Lee Hall, a man I'd known for sixteen years. "We can't keep up with them, even if they'd let us."

"Keep up?" I asked.

"Yes, sir," Lee said. "Come on, I'll show you. They let us watch, anyway."

He led me out of the offices up to the top floor of the warehouse, a great, bare space with a few empty crates scattered between piles of unused packing materials. At one end, portable floodlights were illuminating an area with a merciless blue-white light that made the shadows cast by men and things look solid enough to stub your toe on. He led me toward the light until a Groupman stepped forward to bar our way. "Close enough, Lieutenant," he said to Lee. He looked at me.

"This is Tomas Velt, Blauvain superintendent of police."

"Honored to meet you, sir," said the Groupman to me. "But you and the Lieutenant will have to stand back here if you want to see what's going on."

"What is going on?" I asked.

"Reconstruction," said the Groupman. "That's one of our Hunter Teams."

I turned to watch. In the white glare of the light were four of the mercenaries. At first glance they seemed engaged in some odd ballet or mime acting. They were at little distances from one another; first one, then another of them would move a short distance—perhaps as if he had gotten up from a nonexistent chair and walked across to an equally nonexistent table, then turned to face the others. Following which another man would move in and apparently do something at the same invisible table with him.

"The men of our Hunter Teams are essentially trackers, Superintendent," said the Groupman quietly in my ear. "But some teams are better in certain surroundings than others. These are men of a team that works well in interiors."

"But what are they doing?" I said.

"Reconstructing what the assassins did when they were here," said the Groupman. "Each of three men on the team takes the track of one of the assassins, and the fourth man watches them all as coordinator."

I looked at him. He wore the sleeve emblem of a Dorsai, but he was as ordinary-looking as I or one of my detectives. Plainly, a first-generation immigrant to that world, which explained why he was wearing the patches of a noncommissioned rather than a commissioned officer along with that emblem.

"But what kind of signs are they tracking?" I asked.

"Little things, mostly." He smiled. "Tiny things—some things you or I wouldn't be able to see if they were pointed out to us. Sometimes there's nothing and they have to go on guess—that's where the coordinator helps." He sobered. "Looks like black magic, doesn't it? It does even to me sometimes, and I've been a Dorsai for fourteen years."

I stared at the moving figures. "You said—three," I said.

"That's right," answered the Groupman. "There were three snipers. We've tracked them from the office in the building they fired from to here. This was their headquarters—the place they moved from to the office just before the killing. There's sign they were here a couple of days at least, waiting."

"Waiting?" I asked. "How do you know there were three and they were waiting?"

"Lots of repetitive sign. Habitual actions. Signs of camping beds set up. Food signs for a number of meals. Metal lubricant signs showing weapons had been disassembled and worked over here. Signs of a portable, private phone—they must have waited for a phone call from someone telling them the Commander was on his way in from the encampment."

"But how do you know there were only three?"

"There's sign for only three," he said. "Three—all big for your world, all under thirty. The biggest man had black hair and a full beard. He was the one who hadn't changed clothes for a week—" The Groupman sniffed the air. "Smell him?"

I sniffed hard and long. "I don't smell a thing," I said.

"Hmm." The Groupman looked grimly pleased. "Maybe those fourteen years have done me some good after all. The stink of him's in the air, all right. It's one of the things our Hunter Teams followed to this place."

I looked aside at Lee Hall, then back at the soldier. "You don't need my detectives at all, do you?" I said.

"No, sir." He looked me in the face. "But we assume you'd want them to stay with us. That's all right."

"Yes," I said. And I left there. If my men were not needed, neither was I, and I had no time to stand around being useless. There was still Padma to talk to.

But it was not easy to locate the Outbond. The Exotic Embassy either could not or would not tell me where he was, and the Expedition Headquarters in Blauvain also claimed not to know. As a matter of ordinary police work, my own department kept track of important outworlders like the Graeme brothers and the Outbond as they moved around our city. But in this case, there was no record of Padma ever leaving the room in which I had last seen him with Ian Graeme early in the day. I finally took my determination in both hands and called Ian himself to ask if Padma was with him.

The answer was a blunt "no." That settled it. If Padma was with him, a Dorsai like Ian would have refused to answer rather than lie outright. I gave up. I was light-headed with fatigue, and I told myself I would go home, get at least a few hours' sleep, and then try again.

So, with one of the professional soldiers in my police car to vouch for me at roadblocks, I returned to my own dark apartment, and when, alone at last, I came into the living room and turned on the light, there was Padma waiting for me in one of my own chair-floats.

The jar of finding him there was solid—more like an emotional explosion than I would have thought. It was like seeing a ghost in reality, the ghost of someone from whose funeral you have just returned. I stood staring at him.

"Sorry to startle you, Tom," he said. "I know, you were going to have a drink and forget about everything for a few hours. Why don't you have the drink anyway?"

He nodded toward the bar built into a corner of the apartment living room. I never used the thing unless there were guests on hand, but it was always stocked—that was part of the maintenance agreement in the lease. I went over and punched the buttons for a single brandy and water. I knew there was no use offering Padma alcohol. "How did you get in here?" I said, with my back to him.

"I told your supervisor you were looking for me," Padma said. "He let me in. We Exotics aren't so common on your world here that he didn't recognize me."

I swallowed half the glass at a gulp, carried the drink back, and sat down in a chair opposite him. The background lighting in the apartment had gone on automatically when night darkened the windows. It was a soft light, pouring from the corners of the ceiling and from little random apertures and niches in the walls. Under it, in his blue robe, with his ageless face, Padma looked like the image of a Buddha, beyond all the human and ordinary storms of life.

"What are you doing here?" I asked. "I've been looking all over for you."

"That's why I'm here," Padma said. "The situation being what it is, you would want to appeal to me to help you with it. So I wanted to see you away from any place where you might blame my refusal to help on outside pressures."

"Refusal?" I said. It was probably my imagination, but the brandy and water I had swallowed seemed to have gone to my head already. I felt light-minded and unreal. "You aren't even going to listen to me first before saying no?"

"My hope," said Padma, "is that you'll listen to me first, Tom, before rejecting what I've got to tell you. You're thinking that I could bring pressure to bear on Ian Graeme to move his soldiers half a world away from Blauvain, or otherwise take the situation out of its critical present phase. But the truth is I could not, and even if I could, I would not."

"Would not," I echoed muzzily.

"Yes. Would not. But not just because of personal choice. For four centuries now, Tom, we students of the Exotic Sciences have been telling other men and women that our human race was committed to a future, to the workings of history as it is. It's true we Exotics have a calculative technique now, called ontogenetics, that helps us to resolve any present or predicted moment into its larger historical factors. We've made no secret of having such techniques. But that doesn't mean we can control what will happen, particularly while other men still tend to reject the very thing we work with—the concept of a large, shifting pattern of events that involves all of us and our lives."

"I'm a Catholic," I said. "I don't believe in predestination."

"Neither do we on Mara and Kultis," said Padma. "But we do believe in a physics of human action and interaction, which we believe works in a certain direction toward a certain goal which we now think is less than a hundred years off—if, in fact, we haven't already reached it. Movement toward that goal has been building up for at least the last thousand years, and by now the momentum of its forces is massive. No single individual or group of individuals at the present time has the mass to oppose or turn that movement from its path. Only something greater than a human being as we know a human being might do that."

"Sure," I said. The glass in my hand was empty. I did not remember drinking the rest of its contents, but the alcohol was bringing me a certain easing of weariness and tension. I got up, went back to the bar, and came back with a full glass while Padma waited silently. "Sure, I understand. You think you've spotted a historical trend here, and you don't want to interfere for fear of spoiling it. A fancy excuse to do nothing."

"Not an excuse, Tom," Padma said, and there was something different, like a deep gong-note in his voice, that blew the fumes of the brandy clear from my wits for a second and made me look at him. "I'm not telling you I won't do anything about the situation. I'm telling you that I can't do anything about it. Even if I tried to do something, it would be no use. It's not for you alone that the situation is too massive; it's that way for everyone."

"How do you know if you don't try?" I said. "Let me see you try and it not work. Then maybe I'd believe you."

"Tom," he said, "can you lift me out of this chair?"

I blinked at him. I am no Dorsai, as I think I have said, but I am large for my world, which meant in this case that I was a head taller than Padma and perhaps a quarter again the weight. Also I was undoubtedly younger, and I had worked all my life to stay in good physical condition. I could have lifted someone my own weight out of that chair with no trouble, and Padma was less than that. "Unless you're tied down," I said.

"I'm not." He stood up briefly and then sat again. "Try and lift me, Tom."

I put my glass down, stepped over to his float and stood behind him. I wrapped my arms around his body under his armpits, and lifted—at first easily, then with all my strength.

But not only could I not lift him, I could not budge him. If he had been a life-sized statue of stone, I would have expected to feel more reaction and movement in response to my efforts.

I gave up finally, panting, and stood back from him. "What do you weigh?" I demanded.

"No more than you think. Sit down again, Tom." I did. "Don't let it bother you. It's a trick, of course. No, not a mechanical trick, a physiological one—but a trick just the same, that's been shown on stage at times, at least during the last four hundred years."

"Stand up," I said. "Let me try again."

He did. I did. He was still immovable.

"Now," he said when I had given up a second time. "Try once more, and you'll find you can lift me."

I wiped my forehead, put my arms around him and heaved upward with all my strength. I almost threw him against the ceiling overhead. Numbly I set him down again.

"You see?" he said, reseating himself. "Just as I knew you could not lift me until I let you, I know that there is nothing I can do to alter present events here on St. Marie from their present direction. But you can."

"I can?" I stared at him, then exploded. "Then for God's sake tell me how!"

He shook his head slowly. "I'm sorry, Tom," he said. "But

that's just what I can't do. I only know that, resolved to onto-genetic terms, the situation here shows you as a pivotal character. On you, as a point, the bundle of human forces that were con-centrated here and bent toward destruction by another such pivotal character, may be redirected back into the general histor-ical pattern with a minimum of harm. I tell you this so that, be-ing aware of it, you can be watching for opportunities to redirect. That's all I can do."

Incredibly, with those words, he got up and went toward the door of the apartment.

"Hold on!" I said, and he stopped, turning back momentarily. "This other pivotal character. Who's he?"

Padma shook his head again. "It would do you no good to know," he said. "I give you my word he is now far away from the situation and will not be coming back to it. He is not even on the planet."

"One of the assassins of Kensie!" I said. "And they've gotten away, off-planet!"

"No," said Padma. "No. The men who assassinated Kensie are only tools of events. If none of them had existed, three others would have been there in their place. Forget this other pivotal character, Tom. He was no more in charge of the situation he created than you are in charge of the situation here and now. He was simply, like you, in a position that gave him freedom of choice. Good night."

With those last words, he was suddenly out the door and gone. To this day I cannot remember if he moved particularly swiftly, or whether for some reason I now can't remember I simply let him go. Just—all at once I was alone.

Fatigue rolled over me like the heavy waves of some ocean of mercury. I stumbled into the bedroom, fell on my sleeping float, and that was all I remembered until—only a second later, it seemed—I woke to the hammering of my telephone's chimes on my ears.

I reached out, fumbled at the bedside table and pushed the *on* button.

"Velt here," I said thickly.

"Tom—this is Moro. Tom? Is that you, Tom?"

I licked my lips, swallowed and spoke more understandably. "It's me," I said. "What's the call for?"

"Where've you been?"

"Sleeping," I said. "What's the call for?"

"I've got to talk to you. Can you come—"

"You come here," I said. "I've got to get up and dress and get some coffee in me before I go anyplace. You can talk to me while I'm doing it."

I punched off. He was still saying something at the other end of the line, but just then I did not care what it was.

I pushed my dead-heavy body out of bed and began to move. I was dressed and at the coffee when he came.

"Have a cup." I pushed it at him as he sat down at the porch table with me.

He took it automatically. "Tom," he said. The cup trembled in his hand as he lifted it, and he sipped hastily from it before putting it down again. "Tom, you were in the Blue Front once, weren't you?"

"Weren't we all?" I said. "Back when we and it were young together, and it was an idealistic outfit aimed at putting some order and system into our world government?"

"Yes, yes, of course," Moro said. "But what I mean is, if you were a member once, maybe you know who to contact now—"

I began to laugh. I laughed so hard I had to put my cup down to avoid spilling it. "Moro, don't you know better than that?" I said. "If I knew who the present leaders of the Blue Front were, they'd be in jail. The Blauvain police commissioner—the head law-enforcement man of our capital city—is the last man the Blue Front would be in touch with nowadays. They'd come to you, first. You were a member once too, back in college days, remember?"

"Yes," he said miserably. "But I don't know anything now, just as you're saying. I thought you might have informers, or suspicions you couldn't prove, or—"

"None of them," I said. "All right. Why do you want to know who's running the Blue Front now?"

"I thought I'd make an appeal to them to give up the assassins of Kensie Graeme—to save the Blauvain people. Tom—" He stared directly at me. "Just an hour ago the enlisted men of the mercenaries took a vote on whether to demand their officers lead them on the city. They voted over ninety-four percent in favor. And Pel . . . Pel's finally mobilized his militia, but I don't think he means to help *us*. He's been trying to get in to talk to Ian all day."

"All day?" I glanced at the time on my wrist unit. "4:25—it's not 4:25 P.M. *now*?"

"Yes," said Moro, staring at me. "I thought you knew."

"I didn't mean to sleep like this!" I came out of the chair, moving toward the door. "Pel's trying to see Ian? The sooner we get down and see him ourselves, the better."

So we went. But we were too late. By the time we got to Expedition Headquarters and past the junior officers to the door of the office where Ian was, Pel was already with Ian. I brushed aside the Force-Leader barring our way and walked in, followed by Moro. Pel was standing facing Ian, who sat at a desk surrounded by stacks of filmprints. He got to his feet as Moro and I appeared. "That'll be all right, Force-Leader," he said to the officer behind us. "Tom, I'm glad you're here. Mr. Mayor, though, if you don't mind waiting outside, I'll see you in a few minutes."

Moro had little choice but to go out again. The door shut behind him, Ian waved me to a chair beside Pel and sat down again himself. "Go ahead, General," he said to Pel. "Repeat what you'd started to tell me, for the benefit of Tom here."

Pel glanced savagely at me for a second out of the edge of his eyes before answering. "This doesn't have anything to do with the Police Commissioner of Blauvain," he said, "or anyone else of St. Marie."

"Repeat," said Ian again. He did not raise his voice. The word was simply an iron door dropped in Pel's way, forcing him to turn back.

Pel glanced once more grimly at me. "I was just saying," he said, "if Commander Graeme would go to the encampment and speak to the enlisted men there, he could probably get them to vote unanimously."

"Vote unanimously for what?" I asked.

"For a house-to-house search of the Blauvain area," Ian answered.

"The city's been cordoned," Pel said quickly. "A search like that would turn up the assassins in a matter of hours, with the whole Expeditionary force searching."

"Sure," I said, "and with the actual assassins, there'd be a few hundred suspected assassins, or people who fought or ran for the wrong reason, killed or wounded by the searchers. Even if the Blue Front didn't take advantage of the opportunity—which they certainly would—to start gunfights with the soldiers in the city streets."

"What of it?" said Pel, talking to Ian rather than to me. "Your troops can handle any Blue Front people. And you'd be doing St. Marie a favor to wipe them out."

"If the whole thing didn't develop into a wiping-out of the whole civilian population of the city," I said.

"You're implying, Tom," said Pel, "that the Exotic troops can't be controlled by—"

Ian cut him short. "Your suggestion, General," he said, "is the same one I've been getting from other quarters. Someone else is here with it right now. I'll let you listen to the answer I give him." He turned toward his desk annunciator. "Send in Groupman Whallo," he said.

He straightened up and turned back to us as the door to his office opened and in came the mercenary noncom I had brushed past out there. In the light, I saw it was the immigrant Dorsai of the Hunter Team I had encountered—the man who had been a Dorsai fourteen years. "Sir!" he said, stopping a few steps before Ian and saluting.

Uncovered himself, Ian did not return the salute. "You've got a message for me?" Ian said. "Go ahead. I want these gentlemen to hear it, and my answer."

"Yes, sir," said Whallo. I could see him glance at and recognize me out of the corner of his eyes. "As representative of the enlisted men of the Expedition, I have been sent to convey to you the results of our latest vote on orders. By unanimous vote, the enlisted men of this command have concurred in the need for a single operation."

"Which is?"

"That a house-to-house search of the Blauvain city area be made for the assassins of Field Commander Graeme," said Whallo. He nodded at Ian's desk, and for the first time I saw solidigraphs there —artist's impressions, undoubtedly, but looking remarkably life-like—of three men in civilian clothes. "There's no danger we won't recognize them when we find them."

Whallo's formal and artificial delivery was at odds with the way I had heard him speak when I had run into him at the Hunter Team site. There was, it occurred to me suddenly, probably military protocol even to matters like this—even to the matter of a man's death and the possible death of a city. It came as a little shock to realize it, and for the first time I began to feel something of what Padma had meant in saying that the momentum of forces involved here was massive. For a second it was almost as if I could feel those forces like great winds blowing on the present moment.

But Ian was already answering him. "Any house-to-house search involves possible military errors and danger to the civilian popu-lation," he was saying. "The military record of my brother is not to be marred after his death by any intemperate order from me."

"Yes, sir," said Whallo. "I'm sorry, sir, but the enlisted men of the Expedition had hoped that the action would be ordered by you. Their decision calls for six hours in which you may consider the matter before our Enlisted Men's Council takes the responsi-bility for the action upon itself. Meanwhile, the Hunter Teams will be withdrawn—this is part of the voted decision."

"That, too?" said Ian.

"I'm sorry, sir. But you know," said Whallo, "they've been at a dead end for some hours now. The trail was lost in traffic, and the men might be anywhere in the central part of the city."

"Yes," said Ian. "Well, thank you for your message, Groupman."

"Sir!" said Whallo. He saluted again and went out.

As the door closed behind him, Ian's head turned back to face Pel and me. "You heard, gentlemen," he said. "Now I've got work to do."

Pel and I left. In the corridor outside, Whallo was already gone and the young Force-Leader was absent. Only Moro stood waiting for us. Pel turned on me furiously. "Who asked you to show up here?" he demanded.

"Moro," I answered. "And a good thing, too. Pel, what's got into you? You act as if you had some personal axe to grind in seeing the Exotic mercenaries level Blauvain—"

He spun away from me. "Excuse me!" he snapped. "I've got things to do. I've got to call my Headquarters."

Puzzled, I watched him take a couple of long strides away from me and out of the outer office. Suddenly, it was as if the winds of those massive forces I had felt for a moment just past in Ian's office had blown my head strangely clean, clear and empty, so that the slightest sound echoed with importance. All at once, I was hearing the echo of Pel saying those identical words as Kensie was preparing to leave the mercenary encampment for the nonexistent victory dinner, and a half-recognized but long-held suspicion in me flared into a raging certainty.

I took three long strides after him and caught him. I whirled him around and rammed him up against a wall. "It was you!" I said. "You called from the encampment to the city just before we drove in. It was you who told the assassins we were on the way and to move into position to snipe at our car. You're Blue Front, Pel, and you set Kensie up to be murdered!"

My hands were on his throat, and he could not have answered if he had wanted to. But he did not need to. Then I heard the click of boot heels on the floor of the polished stone corridor outside the office, and let go of him, slipping my hand under my uniform jacket to my beltgun. "Say a word," I whispered to him, "or try anything . . . and I'll kill you before you can get the first syllable out. You're coming along with us!"

The Force-Leader entered. He glanced at the three of us curiously. "Something I can do for you gentlemen?" he asked.

"No," I said. "No, we're just leaving."

With one arm through Pel's and the hand of my other arm under my jacket on the butt of my beltgun, we went out as close as the old friends we had always been, Moro bringing up the rear. Out in the corridor, with the office door behind us, Moro caught up with me on the opposite side from Pel. "What are we going to do?" Moro whispered.

Pel had still said nothing, but his eyes were like the black shadows of meteor craters on the gray face of an airless moon.

"Take him downstairs and out to a locked room in the nearest police post," I said. "He's a walking stick of high explosive if any of the mercenaries find out what he did. Someone of his rank involved in Kensie's killing is all the excuse they need to run our streets red in the gutters."

We got Pel to a private back room in Post Ninety-six, a local police center less than three minutes' drive from the building where Ian had his office.

"But how can you be sure he—" Moro hesitated at putting it into words once we were safe in the room. He stood staring at Pel, who sat huddled in a chair, still without speaking.

"I'm sure," I said. "The Exotic, Padma—" I cut myself off as much as Moro had done. "Never mind. The main thing is he's Blue Front, he's involved—and what do we do about it?"

Pel stirred and spoke for the first time since I had almost strangled him. He looked up at Moro and me out of his gray-dead face. "I did it for St. Marie!" he said hoarsely. "But I didn't know they were going to kill him! I didn't know that. They said it was just to be shooting around the car—for an incident—"

"You hear?" I jerked my head at Moro. "Do you want more proof than that?"

"What'll we do?" Moro was staring in fascinated horror at Pel.

"That was my question," I reminded him. He stood there looking hardly in better shape than Pel. "But it doesn't look like you're going to be much help in answering it." I laughed, but not happily. "Padma said the choice was up to me."

"Who? What're you talking about? What choice?" asked Moro.

"Pel here"—I nodded at him—"knows where the assassins are hiding."

"No," said Pel.

"Well, you know enough so that we can find them," I said. "It makes no difference. And outside of this room, there's only two people on St. Marie we can trust with that information."

"You think I'd tell you anything?" Pel said. His face was still gray, but it had firmed up now. "Do you think even if I knew anything I'd tell you? St. Marie needs a strong government to survive, and only the Blue Front can give it to her. I was ready to give my life for that yesterday. I'm still willing. I won't tell you anything—and you can't make me. Not in six hours."

"What two people?" Moro asked me.

"Padma," I said, "and Ian."

"Ian!" said Pel. "You think he'll help you? He doesn't give a damn for St. Marie either way. Did you believe that talk of his about his brother's military record? He's got no feelings. It's his own military record he's concerned with, and he doesn't care if the mercenaries tear Blauvain up by the roots as long as it's done over his own objection. He's just as happy as any of the other mercenaries with that vote. He's just going to sit out his six hours and let things happen."

"And I suppose Padma doesn't care either?" Moro was beginning to sound a little ugly himself. "It was the Exotics sent us help against the Friendlies in the first place!"

"Who knows what Exotics want?" Pel retorted. "They pretend to go about doing nothing but helping other people, and never dirtying their hands with violence and so on; and somehow with all that they keep on getting richer and more powerful all the time. Sure, trust Padma, why don't you? Trust Padma and see what happens!"

Moro looked at me uncomfortably. "What if he's right?" Moro said.

"What if he's right?" I snarled at him. "Moro, can't you see this is what St. Marie's trouble has always been? Here's the troublemaker we always have around—someone like Pel—whispering that the devil's in the chimney; and you—like the rest of our people always do—starting to shake at the knees and wanting to sell him the house at any price! Stay here, both of you, and don't try to leave the room."

I went out, locking the door behind me. They were in one of a number of rooms set up behind the duty officer's desk, and I went up to the night sergeant on duty. He was a man I'd known back when I had been in detective training on the Blauvain force, an old-line policeman named Jaker Reales. "Jaker," I said, "I've got a couple of valuable items locked up in that back room. I hope to be back in an hour or so to collect them, but if I don't, make sure they don't get out and nobody gets in to them, or knows they're there. I don't care what kind of noises may seem to come out of there, it's all in the imagination for anyone who thinks he hears them, for twenty-four hours at least, if I don't come back."

"Got you, Tom," said Jaker. "Leave it up to me, sir."

"Thanks, Jaker," I said.

I went out and back to Expedition Headquarters. It had not occurred to me to wonder what Ian would do now that his Hunter Teams had been taken from him. I found Expedition Headquarters now quietly aswarm with officers—officers who clearly were most of them Dorsai. No enlisted men were to be seen.

I was braced to argue my way into seeing Ian, but the men on duty surprised me. I had to wait only four or five minutes outside the door of Ian's private office before six senior commandants, Charley ap Morgan among them, filed out. "Good," said Charley, nodding as he saw me, and then went on without any further explanation of what he meant. I had no time even to look after him. Ian was waiting.

I went in. Ian sat massively behind his desk waiting for me, and waved me to a chair facing him as I came in. I sat down. He was only a few feet from me, but again I had the feeling of a vast distance separating us. Even here and now, under the soft lights of this nighttime office, he conveyed more strongly than any Dorsai I had ever seen a sense of difference. Generations of men bred to war had made him, and I could not warm to him as Pel and others had warmed to Kensie. Far from kindling any affection in me, as he sat there, a cold wind like that off some icy and barren mountaintop seemed to blow from him to me, chilling me. I could believe Pel, that Ian was all ice and no blood; and there was no reason for me to do anything for him—except that as a man whose brother had been killed, he deserved whatever help any other decent, law-abiding man could give him.

But I owed something to myself too, and to the fact that we were not all villains like Pel on St. Marie. "I've got something to tell you," I said. "It's about General Sinjin."

He nodded slowly. "I've been waiting for you to come to me with that," he said.

I stared at him. "You knew about Pel?" I said.

"We knew someone from the St. Marie authorities had to be involved in what happened," he said. "Normally, a Dorsai officer is alert to any potentially dangerous situation. But there was the false dinner invitation, and then the matter of the assassins happening to be in just the right place at the right time, with just the right weapons. Also, our Hunter Teams found clear evidence the encounter was no accident. As I say, an officer like Field Commander Graeme is not ordinarily killed that easily."

It was odd to sit there and hear him speak Kensie's name that way. Title and name rang on my ears with the oddness one feels when somebody speaks of himself in the third person. "But Pel?" I said.

"We didn't know it was General Sinjin who was involved," Ian said. "You identified him yourself by coming to me about him just now."

"He's Blue Front," I said.

"Yes," said Ian, nodding.

"I've known him all my life," I said carefully. "I believe he's suffered some sort of nervous breakdown over the death of your brother. You know, he admired your brother very much. But he's still the man I grew up with, and that man can't be easily made to do something he doesn't want to do. Pel says he won't tell us anything that'll help us find the assassins, and he doesn't think we can make him tell us inside of the six hours left before your soldiers move in to search Blauvain. Knowing him, I'm afraid he's right."

I stopped talking. Ian sat where he was, behind the desk, looking at me, merely waiting.

"Don't you understand?" I said. "Pel can help us, but I don't know of any way to make him do it."

Still Ian said nothing.

"What do you want from me?" I almost shouted it at him at last.

"Whatever," Ian said, "you have to give."

For a moment it seemed to me that there was something like a crack in the granite mountain that he seemed to be. For a moment I could have sworn that I saw into him. But if this was true, the crack closed up immediately the minute I glimpsed it. He sat remote, icy, waiting there behind his desk.

"I've got nothing," I said, "unless you know of some way to make Pel talk."

"I have no way consistent with my brother's reputation as a Dorsai officer," said Ian remotely.

"You're concerned with reputations?" I said. "I'm concerned with the people who'll die and be hurt in Blauvain if your mercenaries come in to hunt door-to-door for those assassins. Which is more important, the reputation of a dead man, or the lives of living ones?"

"The people are rightly your concern, Commissioner," said Ian still remotely. "The professional reputation of Kensie Graeme is rightly mine."

"What will happen to that reputation if those troops move into Blauvain in less than six hours from now?" I demanded.

"Something not good," Ian said. "That doesn't change my personal responsibilities. I can't do what I shouldn't do, and I must do what I ought to do."

I stood up. "There's no answer to the situation, then," I said. Suddenly, the utter tiredness I had felt before was on me again. I was tired of the fanatic Friendlies who had come out of another solar system to exercise a purely theoretical claim to our revenues and world surface as an excuse to assault St. Marie. I was tired of the Blue Front and people like Pel. I was tired of off-world people of all kinds, including Exotics and Dorsais. I was tired, tired . . . It came to me then that I could walk out. I could refuse to make the decision that Padma had said I would make, and the whole matter would be out of my hands. I told myself to do that, to walk out, but my feet did not budge. In picking on me, events had chosen the right idiot as a pivot point. Like Ian, I could not do what I should not do, and I must do what I ought to do. "All right," I said, "Padma might be able to do something with him."

"The Exotics," said Ian, "force nobody." But he stood up.

"Maybe I can talk him into it," I said exhaustedly. "At least I can try."

Once more, I would have had no idea where to find Padma in a hurry. But Ian located him in a research enclosure, a carrel in the stacks of the Blauvain library, which like many libraries on all the eleven inhabited worlds had been Exotic-endowed. In the small space of the carrel Ian and I faced him, the two of us standing, Padma seated in the serenity of his blue robe and unchanging facial expression. I told him what we needed with Pel, and he shook his head. "Tom," he said, "you must already know that we who study the Exotic sciences never force anyone or anything. Not for moral reasons alone, but because using force would damage our ability to do the sensitive work we've dedicated our lives to doing. That's why we hire mercenaries to fight for us, and Cetan lawyers to handle our off-world business contracts. I am the last person on this world to make Pel talk."

"Don't you feel any responsibility to the innocent people of this city?" I said. "To the lives that will be lost if he doesn't?"

"Emotionally, yes," Padma said softly. "But there are practical limits to the responsibility of personal inaction. If I were to concern myself with all possible pain consequent upon the least single action of mine, I would have to spend my life like a statue. I was not responsible for Kensie's death, and I am not responsible for finding his killers. Without such a responsibility I can't violate the most basic prohibition of my life's rules."

"You knew Kensie," I said. "Don't you owe anything to him? And don't you owe anything to the same St. Marie people you sent an armed expedition to help?"

"We make it a point to give rather than take," Padma said, "just to avoid debts like that which could force us into doing what we shouldn't do. No, Tom. The Exotics and I have no obligation to your people, or even to Kensie."

"—And to the Dorsai?" asked Ian behind me.

I had almost forgotten he was there, I had been concentrating so hard on Padma. Certainly I had not expected Ian to speak. The sound of his deep voice was like a heavy bell tolling in the small room, and for the first time Padma's face changed. "The Dorsai . . ." he echoed. "Yes, the time is coming when there will be neither Exotics nor Dorsai, in the end when the final development is achieved. But we Exotics have always counted on our work as a step on the way to that end, and the Dorsai helped us up our step. Possibly, if things had gone otherwise, the Dorsai might never

have been, and we would still be where we are now. But things
went as they have, and our thread has been tangled with the
Dorsai thread from the time your many-times removed grandfather Cletus Graeme first freed all the younger worlds from the
politics of Earth . . ."

He stood up. "I'll force no one," he said. "But I will offer Pel
my help to find peace with himself, if he can, and if he finds such
peace, then maybe he will want to tell you willingly what you want
to know."

Padma, Ian and I went back to the police station where I had
left Pel and Moro locked up. We let Moro out and closed the door
upon the three of us with Pel. He sat in a chair, looking at us, pale,
pinch-faced and composed. "So you brought the Exotic, did you,
Tom?" he said to me. "What's it going to be? Some kind of
hypnosis?"

"No, Pel," said Padma softly, pacing across the room to him as
Ian and I sat down to wait. "I would not deal in hypnosis, particularly without the consent of the one to be hypnotized."

"Well, you sure as hell haven't got my consent!" said Pel.

Padma had reached him now and was standing over him.

Pel looked up into the calm face above the blue robe. "But try
it if you like," Pel said. "I don't hypnotize easily."

"No," said Padma. "I've said I would not hypnotize anyone, but
in any case, neither you nor anyone else can be hypnotized without his or her innate consent. All things between individuals are
done by consent. The prisoner consents to his captivity as the
patient consents to his surgery—the difference is only in degree
and pattern. The great, blind mass that is humanity in general is
like an amoebic animal. It exists by internal laws that cohere its
body and its actions. Those internal laws are based upon conscious
and unconscious, mutual consents of its atoms—ourselves—to work
with each other and cooperate. Peace and satisfaction come to each
of us in proportion to our success in such cooperation, in the
forward-searching movement of the humanity-creature as a whole.
Nonconsent and noncooperation work against the grain. Pain and
self-hate result from friction when we fight against our natural desire to cooperate . . ."

His voice went on. Gently but compellingly he said a great deal more, and I understood it all at the time; but beyond what I have quoted so far—and those first few sentences stay printed-clear in my memory—I do not recall another specific word. I do not know to this day what happened. Perhaps I half dozed without realizing I was dozing. At any rate, time passed, and when I reached a point where the memory record took up again, he was leaving and Pel had altered.

"I can talk to you some more, can't I?" Pel said as the Outbond rose to leave. Pel's voice had become clear-toned and strangely young-sounding. "I don't mean now. I mean, there'll be other times?"

"I'm afraid not," Padma said. "I'll have to leave St. Marie shortly. My work takes me back to my own world and then on to one of the Friendly planets to meet someone and wind up what began here. But you don't need me to talk to. You created your own insights as we talked, and you can go on doing that by yourself. Goodby, Pel."

"Goodby," said Pel. He watched Padma leave. When he looked at me again, his face, like his voice, was clear and younger than I had seen it in years. "Did you hear all that, Tom?"

"I think so . . ." I said, because already the memory was beginning to slip away from me. I could feel the import of what Padma had said to Pel, but without being able to give it exact shape. It was as if I had intercepted a message that had turned out not to be for me, and my mental machinery had already begun to cancel it out. I got up and went over to Pel. "You'll help us find those assassins now?"

"Yes," he said. "Of course I will."

He was able to give us a list of five locations that were possible hiding places for the three we hunted. He provided exact directions for finding each one.

"Now," I said to Ian when Pel was through, "we need those Hunter Teams of yours that were pulled off."

"We have Hunters," said Ian. "Those officers who are Dorsai are still with us and there are Hunters among them."

He stepped to the phone unit on the desk in the room and put a call in to Charley ap Morgan at Expeditionary Headquarters. When Charley answered, Ian gave him the five locations Pel had supplied us. "Now," he said to me as he turned away from the phone, "we'll go back to my office."

"I want to come," said Pel.

Ian looked at him for a long moment, then nodded without changing expression. "You can come," he said.

When we got back to the Expeditionary Headquarters building, the rooms and corridors there seemed even more aswarm with officers. As Ian had said, they were mostly Dorsai. But I saw some among them who might not have been. Apparently Ian commanded his own loyalty, or perhaps it was the Dorsai concept that commanded its own loyalty to whoever was commanding officer. We went to his office, and, sitting there, waited while the reports began to come in.

The first three locations to be checked out by the officer Hunter Teams drew blanks. The fourth showed evidence of having been used within the last twenty-four hours, although it was empty now. The last location to be checked also drew a blank.

The Hunter Teams concentrated on the fourth location and began to work outward from it, hoping to cross sign of a trail away from it. I checked the clock figures on my wrist unit. It was now nearing one A.M. in the morning, local time, and the six-hour deadline of the enlisted mercenaries was due to expire in forty-seven minutes. In the office where I waited with Ian, Pel, Charley ap Morgan and another senior Dorsai officer, the air was thick with the tension of waiting. Ian and the two other Dorsais sat still; even Pel sat still. I was the one who fidgeted and paced as the time continued to run out.

The phone on Ian's desk flashed its visual signal light. Ian reached out to punch it on. "Yes?" he said.

"Hunter Team Three," said a voice from the desk. "We have clear sign and are following now. Suggest you join us, sir."

"Thank you. Coming," said Ian.

We went, Ian, Charley, Pel and I, in an Expedition Command Car. It was an eerie ride through the patrolled and deserted streets of my city. Ian's Hunter Team Three was ahead of us and led us to an apartment hotel on the upper north side of the city in the oldest section.

The building had been built of poured cement faced with

Castlemane granite. Inside, the corridors were old-fashionedly narrow and close-feeling, with dark, thick carpeting and metal walls in imitation-oak woodgrain. The sound-proofing was good, however. We mounted to the seventh story and moved down the hall to suite number 415 without hearing any sound other than those we made ourselves.

"Here," finally said the leader of the Hunter Team, a lean, gnarled Dorsai senior commandant in his late fifties. He gestured to the door of 415. "All three of them."

"Ian," said Charley ap Morgan, glancing at his wrist unit, "the enlisted men start moving into the city in six minutes. You could go meet them to say we've found the assassins. The others and I—"

"No," said Ian. "We can't say we've found them until we see them and identify them positively." He stepped up to one side of the door, and, reaching out an arm, touched the door annunciator stud.

There was no response. Above the door, the half-meter-square annunciator screen stayed brown and blank.

Ian pressed the button again.

Again we waited, and there was no response.

Ian pressed the stud. Holding it down so that his voice would go with the sound of its announcing chimes to the ears of those within, he spoke. "This is Commander Ian Graeme," he said. "Blauvain is now under martial law, and you are under arrest in connection with the assassination of Field Commander Kensie Graeme. If necessary, we can cut our way in to you. However, I'm concerned that Field Commander Graeme's reputation be kept free of criticism in the matter of determining responsibility for his death. So I'm offering you the chance to come out and surrender." He released the stud and stopped talking.

There was a long pause. Then a voice spoke from the annunciator grille below the screen, although the screen itself remained blank. "Go to hell, Graeme," said the voice. "We got your brother, and if you try to blast your way in here, we'll get you too."

"My advice to you," said Ian—his voice was cold, distant and impersonal, as if this was something he did every day—"is to surrender."

"You guarantee our safety if we do?"

"No," said Ian. "I only guarantee that I will see that Field Commander Graeme's reputation is not adversely affected by the way you're handled."

There was no immediate answer from the screen. Behind Ian, Charley looked again at his wrist unit. "They're playing for time," he said. "But why? What good will that do them?"

"They're fanatics," said Pel shortly. "Just as much fanatics as the Friendly soldiers were, only for the Blue Front instead of for some puritan form of religion. Those three in there don't expect to get out of this alive. They're only trying to set a higher price on their own deaths—get something more for their dying."

Charley ap Morgan's wrist unit chimed. "Time's up," he said to Ian. "The enlisted men are moving into the suburbs of Blauvain now to begin their search."

Ian reached out and pushed the annunciator stud again, holding it down as he spoke to the men inside. "Are you coming out?"

"Why should we?" answered the voice that had spoken the first time. "Give us a reason."

"I'll come in and talk to you if you like," said Ian.

"No—" began Pel out loud. I gripped his arm, and he turned on me, whispering, "Tom, tell him not to go in! That's what they want."

"Stay here," I said.

I pushed forward until Charley ap Morgan put out an arm to stop me. I spoke across that arm to Ian. "Ian," I said in a voice safely low enough so that the door annunciator would not pick it up. "Pel says—"

"Maybe that's a good idea," said the voice from the annunciator. "That's right, why don't you come on in, Graeme? Leave your weapons outside."

"Tom," said Ian without looking either at me or Charley ap Morgan, "stay back. Keep him back, Charley."

"Yes, sir," said Charley. He looked into my face, eye to eye with me. "Stay out of this, Tom. Back up."

Ian stepped forward to stand square in front of the door, where a beam coming through it could go through him as well. He was taking off his sidearm as he went. He dropped it to the floor in full sight of the screen, through the blankness of which those inside would be looking out. "I'm unarmed," he said.

"Of that sidepiece, you are," said the annunciator. "Do you think we're going to take your word for the rest of you? Strip."

Without hesitation, Ian unsealed his uniform jacket and began to take off his clothes. In a moment or two, he stood naked in the hallway, but if the men in the suite had thought to gain some sort of morale advantage over him because of that, they were disappointed.

Stripped, he looked—like an athlete—larger and more impressive than he had, clothed. He towered over us all in the hall, even over the other Dorsais there, and with his darkly tanned skin under the lights he seemed like a massive figure carved in oak. "I'm waiting," he said after a moment, calmly.

"All right," said the voice from the annunciator. "Come on in."

He moved forward. The door unlatched and slid aside before him. He passed through and it closed behind him. For a moment we were left with no sound or word from him or the suite; then, unexpectedly, the screen lit up. We found ourselves looking over and past Ian's bare shoulders at a room in which three men, each armed with a rifle and a pair of sidearms, sat facing him. They gave no sign of knowing that he had turned on the annunciator screen, the controls of which would be hidden behind him now that he stood inside the door, facing the room.

The center one of the three seated men laughed. He was the big black-bearded man I had found vaguely familiar when I saw the solidigraphs of the three of them in Ian's office; and I recognized him now. He was a professional wrestler. He had been arraigned on assault charges four years ago, but lack of testimony against him had caused the charges to be dismissed. He was not as tall as Ian, but much heavier of body; and it was his voice we had been hearing, because now we heard it again as his lips moved on the screen. "Well, well, Commander," he said. "Just what we needed—a visit from you. Now we can rack up a score of two Dorsai commanders before your soldiers carry what's left of us off to the morgue, and St. Marie can see that even you people can be handled by the Blue Front."

We could not see Ian's face; but he said nothing and apparently his lack of reaction was irritating to the big assassin, because he dropped his cheerful tone and leaned forward in his chair. "Don't you understand, Graeme?" he said. "We've lived and died for the Blue Front, all three of us—for the one political party with the strength and guts to save our world. We're dead men no matter what we do. Did you think we don't know that? You think we don't know what would happen to us if we were idiots enough to surrender the way you said? Your men would tear us apart, and if there was anything left of us after that, the government's law would try us and then shoot us. We only let you in here so that we could lay you out like your twin brother before we were laid out ourselves. Don't you follow me, man? You walked into our hands here like a fly into a trap, never realizing."

"I realized," said Ian.

The big man scowled at him, and the muzzle of the heat gun he held in one thick hand came up. "What do you mean?" he demanded. "Whatever you think you've got up your sleeve isn't going to save you. Why would you come in here, knowing what we'd do?"

"The Dorsai are professional soldiers," said Ian's voice calmly. "We live and survive by our reputation. Without that reputation we could not earn our living. And the reputation of the Dorsai in general is the sum of the reputations of its individual men and women. So Field Commander Kensie Graeme's professional reputation is a thing of value, to be guarded even after his death. I came in for that reason."

The big man's eyes narrowed. He was doing all the talking and his two companions seemed content to leave it that way.

"A reputation's worth dying for?" he said.

"I've been ready to die for mine for eighteen years," said Ian's voice quietly. "Today's no different than yesterday."

"And you came in here—" the big man's voice broke off on a snort. "I don't believe it. Watch him, men!"

"Believe or not," said Ian. "I came in here, just as I told you, to see that the professional reputation of Field Commander Graeme was protected from events which might tarnish it. You'll notice—" his head moved slightly as if indicating something behind him and out of our sight, "I've turned on your annunciator screen, so that outside the door they can see what's going on in here."

The eyes of the three men jerked upwards to stare at the screen inside the suite, somewhere over Ian's head. There was a blur of motion that was Ian's tanned body flying through the air, a sound of something smashing and the screen went blank again.

We outside were left blind once again, standing in the hallway, staring at the unresponsive screen and door. Pel, who had stepped up next to me, moved toward the door itself.

"Stay!" snapped Charley.

The single sharp tone was like a command given to some domestic beast. Pel flinched at the tone, but stopped—and in that moment the door before us disintegrated to the roar of an explosion in the room.

"Come on!" I yelled, and flung myself through the now-open doorway.

It was like diving into a centrifuge filled with whirling bodies. I ducked to avoid the flying form of one of the men I had seen in the screen, but his leg slammed my head, and I went reeling, half-dazed and disoriented, into the very heart of the tumult. It was all a blur of action. I had a scrambled impression of explosions, of fire-beams lancing around me—and somehow in the midst of it all, the towering, brown body of Ian moving with the certainty and deadliness of a panther. All those he touched went down; and all who went down, stayed down.

Then it was over. I steadied myself with one hand against a half-burned wall and realized that only Ian and myself were on our feet in that room. Not one of the other Dorsai had followed me in. On the floor, the three assassins lay still. One had his neck broken. Across the room a second man lay obviously dead, but with no obvious sign of the damage that had ended his life. The big man, the ex-wrestler, had the right side of his forehead crushed in, as if by a club.

Looking up from the three bodies, I saw I was now alone in the room. I turned back into the corridor, and found there only Pel and Charley. Ian and the other Dorsai were already gone.

"Where's Ian?" I asked Charley. My voice came out thickly, like the voice of a slightly drunken man.

"Leave him alone," said Charley. "You don't need him now. Those are the assassins there; and the enlisted men have already been notified and pulled back from their search of Blauvain. What more is needed?"

I pulled myself together, and remembered I was a policeman.

"I've got to know exactly what happened," I said. "I've got to know if it was self-defense, or . . ."

The words died on my tongue. To accuse a naked man of anything else in the death of three heavily armed individuals who had threatened his life, as I had just heard them do over the annunciator, was ridiculous.

"No," said Charley. "This was done during a period of martial law in Blauvain. Your office will receive a report from our command about it; but actually it's not even something within your authority."

Some of the tension that had been in him earlier seemed to leak out of him, then. He half-smiled and became more like the friendly officer I had known before Kensie's death.

"But that martial law is about to be withdrawn," he said. "Maybe you'll want to get on the phone and start getting your own people out here to tidy up the details."

And he stood aside to let me go.

One day later, the professional soldiers of the Exotic Expeditionary Force showed their affection for Kensie in a different fashion.

His body had been laid in state for a public review in the open main-floor lobby of the Blauvain City Government building. Beginning in the gray dawn and throughout the cloudless day—the sort of hard, bright day that seems impatient with those who will not bury their dead and get on to further things—the mercenaries filed past the casket holding Kensie, who was visible at full length in dress uniform under the transparent cover. Each one as he passed touched the casket lightly with his fingertips, or said a word to the dead man, or both. There were over ten thousand soldiers passing one at a time. They were unarmed, in field uniforms, and their line seemed endless.

But that was not the end of it. The civilians of Blauvain had formed along either side of the street down which the line of troops wound on its way to the place where Kensie lay waiting for them. The civilians had formed in the face of strict police orders against doing any such thing, and my men could not drive them away. The situation could not have offered a better opportunity for the Blue Front to cause trouble. One heat grenade tossed into that line of slowly moving, unarmed soldiers, for example . . . But nothing happened.

By the time noon came and went without incident, I was ready to make a guess why not. It was because there was something in the mood of the civilian crowd itself that forbade terrorism here and now. Any Blue Front members trying such a thing would have been smothered by the very civilians around them in whose name they were doing it.

Something of awe and pity, and almost of envy, seemed to be stirring the souls of the Blauvain people, those same people of mine who had huddled in their houses twenty hours before in undiluted fear of the very men now lined up before them and moving slowly to the City Government building. Once more, as I stood on a balcony above the lobby holding the casket, I felt those winds of vast movement I had sensed first for a moment in Ian's office, the winds of those forces of which Padma had spoken to me. The Blauvain people were different today and showed the difference. Kensie's death had changed them.

Then, something more happened. As the last of the soldiers passed, Blauvain civilians began to fall in behind them, extending the line. By midafternoon, the last soldier had gone by and the first figure in civilian clothes passed the casket, neither touching it nor speaking to it, but pausing to look with an unusual, almost shy curiosity upon the face of the body inside, in the name of which so much might have happened.

Already behind that one man, the line of civilians was half again as long as the line of soldiers had been.

It was nearly midnight, long past the time when it had been planned to shut the gates of the lobby, when the last of the civilians had gone and the casket could be transferred to a room at Expeditionary Headquarters from which it would be shipped back to the Dorsai. This business of shipping a body home happened seldom, even in the case of mercenaries of the highest rank, but there had never been any doubt that it would happen in the case of Kensie. The enlisted men and officers of his command had contributed the extra funds necessary for the shipment. Ian, when his time came, would undoubtedly be buried in the earth of whatever world on which he fell. Only if he happened to be at home when the time came, would that earth be soil of the Dorsai.

"Do you know what's been suggested to me?" asked Moro, as he, Pel and I, along with several of the Expedition's senior officers —Charley ap Morgan among them—stood watching Kensie's casket being brought into the room at Expedition HQ. "There's a proposal to get the city government to put up a statue of him, here in Blauvain. A statue of Kensie."

Neither Pel nor I answered. We stood watching the placing of the casket. For all its massive appearance, four men handled it and the body within easily. The apparently thick metal sides were actually hollow to reduce shipping weight. The soldiers settled it, took off the transparent weather cover and carried it out. The body of Kensie lay alone, uncovered, the profile of his face, seen from where we stood, quiet and still against the light-pink cloth of the casket's lining. The senior officers who were with us and who had not been in the line of soldiers filing through the lobby, now began to go into the room, one at a time, to stand for a second at the casket before coming out again.

"It's what we never had on St. Marie," said Pel, after a long moment. He was a different man since Padma had talked to him. "A leader. Someone to love and follow. Now that our people have seen there is such a thing, they want something like it for themselves." He looked up at Charley ap Morgan, who was just coming back out of the room. "You Dorsai changed us," Pel said.

"Did we?" said Charley, stopping. "How do you feel about Ian now, Pel?"

"Ian?" Pel frowned. "We're talking about Kensie. Ian's just— what he always was."

"What you all never understood," said Charley, looking from one to the other of us.

"Ian's a good man," said Pel. "I don't argue with that. But there'll never be another Kensie."

"There'll never be another Ian," said Charley. "He and Kensie made up one person. That's what none of you ever understood. Now half of Ian is gone into the grave."

Pel shook his head slowly. "I'm sorry," he said. "I can't believe that. I can't believe Ian ever needed anyone—even Kensie. He's never risked anything, so how could he lose anything? After Kensie's death he did nothing but sit on his spine here insisting that he couldn't risk Kensie's reputation by doing anything—until events forced his hand. That's not the action of a man who's lost the better half of himself."

"I didn't say better half," said Charley, "I only said half—and just half is enough. Stop and try to feel for a moment what it would be like. Stop for a second and feel how it would be if you were amputated down the middle—if the life that was closest to you was wrenched away, shot down in the street by a handful of self-deluded, crackpot revolutionaries from a world you'd come to rescue. Suppose it was like that for you; how would you feel?"

Pel had gone a little pale as Charley talked. When he answered, his voice had a light echo of the difference and youngness it had had after Padma had talked to him. "I guess . . ." he said very slowly and ran off into silence.

"Yes?" said Charley. "Now you're beginning to understand, to feel as Ian feels. Suppose you feel like this, and just outside the city where the assassins of your brother are hiding, there are six battalions of seasoned soldiers who can turn that same city—who can hardly be held back from turning that city—into another Rochmont, at one word from you. Tell me, is it easy, or is it hard, not to say that one word that will turn them loose?"

"It would be . . ."—the words seemed dragged from Pel—"hard . . ."

"Yes," said Charley grimly, "as it was hard for Ian."

"Then why did he do it?" demanded Pel.

"He told you why," said Charley. "He did it to protect his brother's military reputation so that not even after his death should Kensie Graeme's name be an excuse for anything but the highest and best of military conduct."

"But Kensie was dead. He couldn't hurt his own reputation!"

"His troops could," said Charley. "His troops wanted someone to pay for Kensie's death. They wanted to leave a monument to

Kensie and their grief for him, as long-lasting a monument as Rochmont has been to Jacques Chrétien. There was only one way to satisfy them, and that was if Ian himself acted for them— as their agent—in dealing with the assassins. Because nobody could deny that Kensie's brother had the greatest right of all to represent all those who had lost with Kensie's death."

"You're talking about the fact that Ian killed the men person- ally," said Moro. "But there was no way he could know he'd come face to face—" He stopped, halted by the thin, faint smile on Charley's face.

"Ian was our Battle Op, our strategist," said Charley. "Just as Kensie was Field Commander, our tactician. Do you think that a strategist of Ian's ability couldn't lay a plan that would bring him face to face, alone, with the assassins once they were located?"

"What if they hadn't been located?" I asked. "What if I hadn't found out about Pel, and Pel hadn't told us what he knew?"

Charley shook his head. "I don't know," he said. "Somehow Ian must have known this way would work—or he would have done it differently. For some reason he counted on help from you, Tom."

"Me!" I said. "What makes you say that?"

"He told me so." Charley looked at me strangely. "You know, many people thought that because they didn't understand Ian, that Ian didn't understand them. Actually, he understands other people unusually well. I think he saw something in you, Tom, he could rely on. And he was right, wasn't he?"

Once more, the winds I had felt of the forces of which Padma had spoken, blew through me, chilling and enlightening me. Ian had felt those winds as well as I had—and understood them better. I could see the inevitability of it now. There had been only one pull on the many threads entangled in the fabric of events here, and that pull had been through me to Ian.

"When he went to that suite where the assassins were holed up," said Charley, "he intended to go in to them alone and un- armed. And when he killed them with his bare hands, he did what every man in the Expeditionary Force wanted to do. So, when that was done, the anger of the troops was lightning-rodded. Through Ian, they all had their revenge, and then they were free. Free just to mourn for Kensie as they're doing today. So Blauvain escaped, and the Dorsai reputation has escaped stain, and the state of affairs between the inhabited worlds hasn't been upset by an incident here on St. Marie that could make enemies out of the worlds, like the Exotic and the Dorsai, and St. Marie, who should all be friends."

He stopped talking. It had been a long speech for Charley, and none of us could think of anything to say. The last of the senior officers, all except Ian, had gone past us now, in and out of the room, and the casket was alone.

Then Pel spoke. "I'm sorry," he said, and he sounded sorry. "But even if what you say is all true, it only proves what I always said about Ian. Kensie had two men's feelings, but Ian hasn't any. He's ice and water with no blood in him. He couldn't bleed if he wanted to. Don't tell me any man torn apart emotionally by his twin brother's death could sit down and plan to handle a situation so cold-bloodedly and efficiently."

"People don't always bleed on the outside where you can see—" Charley broke off, turning his head.

We looked where he was looking, down the corridor behind us, and saw Ian coming, tall and alone. He strode up to us, nodded briefly at us and went past into the room. We saw him walk to the side of the casket.

He did not speak to Kensie, or touch the casket gently as the soldiers passing through the lobby had done. Instead he closed his big hands, those hands that had killed three armed men, almost casually on the edge of it, and looked down into the face of his dead brother.

Twin face gazed to twin face, the living and the dead. Under the lights of the room, with the motionless towering figure of Ian, it was as if both were living, or both were dead—so little difference there was to be seen between them. Only, Kensie's eyes were closed and Ian's open; Kensie slept while Ian waked. And the oneness of the two of them was so solid and evident a thing, there in that room, that it stopped the breath in my chest.

For perhaps a minute or two Ian stood without moving. His face did not change. Then he lifted his gaze, let go of the casket and turned about. He came walking toward us, out of the room, his hands at his sides, the fingers curled into his palms.

"Gentlemen," he said, nodding to us as he passed, and went down the corridor until a turn in it took him out of sight.

Charley left us and went softly back into the room. He stood a moment there, then turned and called to us. "Pel," he said, "come here."

Pel came, and the rest of us after him.

"I told you," Charley said to Pel, "some people don't bleed on the outside where you can see it."

He moved away from the casket and we looked at it. On its edge were the two areas where Ian had laid hold of it with his hands while he stood looking down at his dead brother. There was no mistaking the places, for at both of them, the hollow metal side had been bent in on itself and crushed with the strength of a grip that was hard to imagine. Below the crushed areas, the cloth lining of the casket was also crumpled and rent; and where each fingertip had pressed, the fabric was torn and marked with a dark stain of blood.

THE MOTHBALLED SPACESHIP

by Harry Harrison

I began writing Deathworld in 1956 in Mexico, continued it in England and Italy, and finally finished it in New
York in 1957. All along the way it was a collaboration with John
Campbell. Since I had already sold him a short story or two, I
felt bold enough to ask him to comment on an outline of a novel
—my first—that I was struggling with. His answering letter was
longer than my outline. He suggested ideas I had never considered,
permutations never thought of—and all within the structure of
my outline. Emboldened, I wrote 10,000 words and sent them to
him and received comment afresh. Still fearful of the novel
length, I sent him 30,000 words when I had done them, only to
receive an irate grumble that he thought this was the whole thing
and was put out he couldn't finish reading it. With this firm kick I
finally finished the thing and took it to the post office and re-

*ceived, practically by return mail, a check for $2,100. I had sold
my first serial to* Astounding.

The Deathworld *trilogy appeared in* ASF, *after the first serial,
as* The Ethical Engineer *and* The Horse Barbarians. *It is the
continuing story of real supermen, people who live on a high-
gravity planet where the deadly life forms continually war on
them. Eventually they leave this world to settle on an equally
deadly planet named Felicity. "The Mothballed Spaceship" takes
place after this last conquest, and is the only* Deathworld *story
written without the aid, advice, comment, criticism and good-
humored assistance of John Campbell.*

I wish it could have been otherwise.

"I'LL JUST swing in a bit closer," Meta said, touching the
controls of the Pyrran spacer.

"I wouldn't if I were you," Jason said resignedly, knowing that
a note of caution was close to a challenge to a Pyrran.

"Let us not be afraid *this* far away," Kerk said, as Jason had predicted. Kerk leaned close to look at the viewscreen. "It is big, I'll
admit, three kilometers long at least, and probably the last space
battleship existing. But it is over five thousand years old, and we
are two hundred kilometers away from it . . ."

A tiny orange glow winked into brief existence on the distant
battleship, and at the same instant the Pyrran ship lurched heavily.
Red panic lights flared on the control panel.

"How old did you say it was?" Jason asked innocently, and received in return a sizzling look from the now-silent Kerk.

Meta sent the ship turning away in a wide curve and checked
the warning circuitry. "Port fin severely damaged, hull units out in
three areas. Repairs will have to be made in null-G before we can
make a planetfall again."

"Very good. I'm glad we were hit," Jason dinAlt said. "Perhaps
now we will exercise enough caution to come out of this alive with
the promised five hundred million credits. So set us on a course
to the fleet commander so we can find out all the grisly details

they forgot to tell us when we arranged this job by jump-space communication."

Admiral Djukich, the commander of the Earth forces, was a small man who appeared even smaller before the glowering strength of the Pyrran personality. Shrinking back when Kerk leaned over his desk toward him and spoke coldly. "We can leave and the Rim Hordes will sweep through this system and that will be the end of you."

"No, it will not happen. We have the resources. We can build a fleet, buy ships, but it will be a long and tedious task. Far easier to use this Empire battleship."

"Easy?" Jason asked, raising one eyebrow. "How many have been killed attemping to enter it?"

"Well, easy is not perhaps the correct word. There are difficulties, certain problems . . . forty-seven people in all."

"Is that why you sent the message to Felicity?" Jason asked.

"Yes, assuredly. Our heavy-metals industry has been purchasing from your planet; they heard of the Pyrrans: how less than a hundred of you conquered an entire world. We thought we would ask you to undertake this task of entering the ship."

"You were a little unclear as to who was aboard the ship and preventing any one else from coming near."

"Yes, well, that is what you might call the heart of our little problem. There's no one aboard . . ." His smile had a definite artificial quality as the Pyrrans leaned close. "Please, let me explain. This planet was once one of the most important under the old Empire. Although at least eleven other worlds claim themselves as the first home of mankind, we of Earth are much more certain that we are the original. This battleship seems proof enough. When the Fourth War of Galactic Expansion was over, it was mothballed here and has remained so ever since, unneeded until this moment."

Kerk snorted with disbelief. "I will not believe that an unmanned, mothballed ship five millennia old has killed forty-seven people."

"Well, I will," Jason said. "And so will you as soon as you give it a little thought. Three kilometers of almost indestructible fighting ship propelled by the largest engines ever manufactured—which means the largest spaceship atomic generators as well. And of course the largest guns, the most advanced defensive and offensive weaponry ever conceived with secondary batteries, parallel fail-safe circuitry, battle computers—ahh, you're smiling at last. A Pyrran dream of heaven—the most destructive single weapon ever conceived. What a pleasure to board a thing like this, to enter the control room, to *be* in control."

Kerk and Meta were grinning happily, eyes misty, nodding their heads in total agreement. Then the smiles faded as he went on. "But this ship has now been mothballed. Everything shut down and preserved for an emergency—everything, that is, except the power plant and the ship's armament. Part of the mothballing was obviously provision for the ship's computer to be alert and to guard the ship against meterorites and any other chance encounters in space. In particular against anyone who felt he needed a spare battleship. We were warned off with a single shot. I don't doubt that it could have blasted us out of space just as easily. If this ship were manned and on the defensive, then nothing could be done about getting near it, much less entering. But this is not the case. We must outthink a computer, a machine, and while it won't be easy, it should be possible." He turned and smiled at Admiral Djukich. "We'll take the job. The price has doubled. It will be one billion credits."

"Impossible! The sum is too great; the budget won't allow . . ."

"Rim Hordes, coming closer, bent on rapine and destruction. To stop them you order some spacers from the shipyard; schedules are late; they don't arrive on time; the Horde fleet descends. They break down this door and here, right in this office, blood . . ."

"Stop!" the Admiral gasped weakly, his face blanched white. A desk commander who had never seen action—as Jason had guessed. "The contract is yours, but you have a deadline, thirty days. One minute after that and you don't get a deci of a credit. Do you agree?"

Jason looked up at Kerk and Meta who, with instant warrior's decision, made their minds up, nodding at the same time.

"Done," he said. "But the billion is free and clear. We'll need supplies, aid from your space navy, material and perhaps men as well to back us up. You will supply what we need."

"It could be expensive," Admiral Djukich groaned, chewing at his lower lip. "Blood . . ." Jason whispered, and the Admiral broke into a fine sweat as he reluctantly agreed. "I'll have the papers drawn up. When can you begin?"

"We've begun. Shake hands on it and we'll sign later." He pumped the Admiral's weak hand enthusiastically. "Now, I don't suppose you have anything like a manual that tells us how to get into the ship?"

"If we had that we wouldn't have called you here. We have gone to the archives and found nothing. All the facts we did discover are on record and available to you for what they are worth."

"Not much if you killed forty-seven volunteers. Five thousand years is a long time, and even the most efficient bureaucracy loses things over that kind of distance. And, of course, the one thing you cannot mothball are instructions how to *un*-mothball a ship. But we will find a way; Pyrrans never quit, never. If you will have the records sent to our quarters, my colleagues and I will now withdraw and make our plans for the job. We shall beat your deadline."

"How?" Kerk asked as soon as the door of their apartment had closed behind them.

"I haven't the slightest idea," Jason admitted, smiling happily at their cold scowls. "Now, let us pour some drinks and put our thinking caps on. This is a job that may end up needing brute force, but it will have to begin with man's intellectual superiority over the machines he has invented. I'll take a large one with ice if you are pouring, darling."

"Serve yourself," Meta snapped. "If you had no idea how we were to proceed, why did you accept?"

Glass rattled against glass and strong beverage gurgled. Jason sighed. "I accepted because it is a chance for us to get some ready cash, which the budget is badly in need of. If we can't crack into the damn thing, then all we have lost is thirty days of our time." He drank and remembered the hard-learned lesson that reasoned argument was usually a waste of time with Pyrrans and that there were better ways to quickly resolve a situation. "You people aren't scared of this ship, are you?"

He smiled angelically at their scowls of hatred, the sudden tensing of hard muscles, the whine of the power holsters as their guns slipped toward their hands, then slid back out of sight.

"Let us get started," Kerk said. "We are wasting time and every second counts. What do we do first?"

"Go through the records, find out everything we can about a ship like this, then find a way in."

"I fail to see what throwing rocks at that ship can do," Meta said. "We know already that it destroys them before they get close. It is a waste of time. And now you want to waste food as well, all those animal carcasses . . ."

"Meta, sweet, shut up, I'm hinting. There is method to the apparent madness. The navy command ship is out there with radars beeping happily, keeping a record of every shot fired, how close the target was before it was hit, what weapon fired the shot and so forth. There are thirty spacers throwing spacial debris at the battleship in a steady stream. This is *not* the usual thing that happens to a mothballed vessel and it can only have interesting results. Now, in addition to the stone-throwing, we are going to launch these sides of beef at our target, each space-going load of steak to be wrapped with twenty kilos of armlite plastic. They are being launched on different trajectories with different speeds, and if any one of them gets through to the ship, we will know that a man in a plastic spacesuit made of the same material will get through as well. Now, if all that isn't enough burden on the ship's computer, a good-sized planetoid is on its way now in an orbit aimed right at our mothballed friend out there. The computer will either have to blow it out of space, which will take a good deal of energy—if it is possible at all—or fire up the engines or something. *Anything* it does will give us information, and any information will give us a handle to grab the problem with."

"First side of beef on the way," Kerk announced from the controls where he was stationed. "I cut some steaks off while we were loading them; have them for lunch. We have a freezerful now.

Prime cuts only from every carcass, maybe a kilo each; won't affect the experiment."

"You're turning into a crook in your old age," Jason said.

"I learned everything I know from you. There goes the first one." He pointed to a tiny blip of fire on the screen. "Flare powder on each, blows up when they hit. Another one. They're getting closer than the rocks—but they're not getting through."

Jason shrugged. "Back to the drawing board. Let's have the steaks and a bottle of wine. We have about two hours before the planetoid is due, and that is an event we want to watch."

The expected results were anticlimactic, to say the least. Millions of tons of solid rock put into collision orbit at great expense, as Admiral Djukich was fond of reminding them, soared majestically in from the black depths of space. The battleship's radar pinged busily and, as soon as the computer had calculated the course, the main engines fired briefly so that the planetoid flashed by the ship's stern and continued on into interstellar space.

"Very dramatic," Meta said in her coldest voice.

"We gained information!" Jason was on the defensive. "We know the engines are still in good shape and can be activated at a moment's notice."

"And of what possible use is that information?" Kerk asked.

"Well, you never know; might come in handy . . ."

"*Communication control to Pyrrus One. Can you read me?*" Jason was at the radio instantly, flicking it on. "This is *Pyrrus One*. What is your message?"

"*We have received a signal from the battleship on the 183.4 wavelength. Message is as follows. Nederuebla al navigacio centro. Kroniku ĉi tio ŝanĝon . . .*"

"I cannot understand it," Meta said.

"It's Esperanto, the old Empire language. The ship simply sent a change-of-course instruction to navigation control. And we know its name now, the *Indestructible*."

"Is this important?"

"Is it!" Jason yipped with joy as he set the new wavelength into the communication controls. "Once you get someone to talk to you, you have them half sold. Ask any salesman. Now, absolute silence, if you please, while I practice my best and most military

Esperanto." He drained his wine glass, cleared his throat and turned the radio on. "Hello, *Indestructible*, this is Fleet Headquarters. Explain unauthorized course change."

"Course change authorized by instructions 590-L to avoid destruction."

"Your new course is a navigational hazard. Return to old course."

Silent seconds went by as they watched the screen—then the purple glow of a thrust drive illuminated the battleship's bow.

"You did it!" Meta said happily, giving Jason a loving squeeze that half crushed his rib cage. "It's taking orders from you. Now tell it to let us in."

"I don't think it is going to be that easy—so let me sneak up on the topic in a roundabout way." He spoke Esperanto to the computer again. "Course change satisfactory. State reasons for recent heavy expenditure of energy."

"Meteor shower. All meteors on collision orbit were destroyed."

"It is reported that your secondary missile batteries were used. Is this report correct?"

"It is correct."

"Your reserves of ammunition will be low. Resupply will be sent."

"Resupply not needed. Reserves above resupply level."

"Argumentative for a computer, isn't it?" Jason said, his hand over the microphone. "But I shall pull rank and see if that works. "Headquarters overrides your resupply decision. Resupply vessel will arrive your cargo port in seventeen hours. Confirm."

"Confirmed. Resupply vessel must supply override mothball signal before entering two-hundred kilometer zone."

"Affirmative, signal will be sent. What is current signal?"

There was no instant answer—and Jason raised crossed fingers as the silence went on for almost two seconds.

"Negative. Information cannot be supplied."

"Prepare for memory check of override mothball signal. This is a radio signal only?"

"Affirmative."

"This is a spoken sentence."

"Negative."

"This is a coded signal."

"Affirmative."

"Pour me a drink," Jason said with the microphone off. "This playing twenty questions may take some time."

It did. But patient working around the subject supplied, bit by bit, the needed information. Jason turned off the radio and passed over the scribbled sheet. "This is something at least. The code signal is a ten-digit number. If we send the correct number, all the mothballing activity stops instantly and the ship is under our control."

"And the money is ours," Meta said. "Can our computer be programmed to send a series of numbers until it hits on the right one?"

"It can—and just the same thought crossed my mind. The *Indestructible* thinks that we are running a communications check and tells me that it can accept up to seven hundred signals a second for repeat and verification. Our computer will read the returned signal and send an affirmative answer to each one. But of course all the signals will be going through the discrimination circuits, and if the correct signal is sent, the mothball defenses will be turned off."

"That seems like an obvious trick that would not fool a five-year-old," Kerk said.

"Never underestimate the stupidity of a computer. You forget that it is a machine with zero imagination. Now, let me see if this will do us any good." He punched keys rapidly, then muttered a curse and kicked the console. "No good. We will have to run nine to the tenth power numbers and, at seven hundred a second, it will take us about five months to do them all."

"And we have just three weeks left."

"I can still read a calendar, thank you, Meta. But we'll have to try in any case. Send alternate numbers from one up and counting from 9,999,999,999 back down. Then we'll get the navy code department to give us all their signals to send as well; one of them might fit. The odds are still about five to one against hitting the right combination, but that is better than no odds at all. And we'll keep working to see what else we can think of."

The navy sent over a small man named Shrenkly who brought a large case of records. He was head of the code department, and a cipher and puzzle enthusiast as well. This was the greatest challenge of his long and undistinguished career, and he hurled himself into it. "Wonderful opportunity, wonderful. The ascending and descending series are going out steadily. In the meantime I am taping permutations and substitutions of signals which will—"

"That's fine, keep at it," Jason said, smiling enthusiastically and patting the man on the back. "I'll get a report from you later, but right now we have a meeting to attend. Kerk, Meta, time to go."

"What meeting?" Meta asked as he tried to get her through the door.

"The meeting I just made up to get away from that bore," he said when he finally got her into the corridor. "Let him do his job while we see if we can find another way in."

"I think what he has to say is very interesting."

"Fine. You talk to him—but not while I am around. Let us now spur our brains into action and see what we can come up with."

What they came up with was a number of ideas of varying quality and uniform record of failure. There was the miniature flying robot fiasco where smaller and smaller robots were sent and blasted out of existence, right down to the smallest, about the size of a small coin. Obsessed by miniaturization, they constructed a flying-eye apparatus no larger than the head of a pin that dragged a threadlike control wire after it that also supplied current for the infinitesimal ion drive. This sparked and sizzled its way to within fifteen kilometers of the *Indestructible* before the all-seeing sensors detected it and neatly blasted it out of existence with a single shot. There were other suggestions and brilliant plans, but none of them worked out in practice. The great ship floated serenely in space reading seven hundred numbers a second and, in its spare time, blowing into fine dust any object that came near it. Each attempt took time, and the days drifted by steadily. Jason was beginning to have a chronic headache and had difficulty sleeping. The problem seemed insoluble. He was feeding figures about destruction distances into the computer when Meta looked in on him. "I'll be with Shrenkly if you need me," she said.

"Wonderful news."

"He taught me about frequency tables yesterday, and today he is going to start me on simple substitution ciphers."

"How thrilling."

"Well, it *is*—to me. I've never done anything like this before. And it has some value: we are sending signals and one of them could be the correct one. It certainly is accomplishing more than you are with all your flying rocks. With two days to go, too."

She stalked out and slammed the door, and Jason slumped with fatigue, aware that failure was hovering close. He was pouring himself a large glass of Old Fatigue Killer when Kerk came in. "Two days to go," Kerk said.

"Thanks. I didn't know until you told me. I know that a Pyrran never gives up, but I am getting the sneaking suspicion that we are licked."

"We are not beaten yet. We can fight."

"A very Pyrran answer—but it won't work this time. We just can't barge in there in battle armor and shoot the place up."

"Why not? Small-arms fire would just bounce off us as well as the low-power rays. All we have to do is dodge the big stuff and bull through."

"That's all! Do you have any idea how we are going to arrange that?"

"No. But you will figure something out. But you better hurry."

"I know, two days. I suppose it's easier to die than admit failure. We suit up, fly at the battleship behind a fleet of rocks that are blasted by the heavy stuff. Then we tell the enemy discrimination circuits that we are not armored spacesuits at all, but just a couple of jettisoned plastic beer barrels that they can shoot up with the small-caliber stuff. Which then bounces off us like hail and we land and get inside and get a billion credits and live happily ever after."

"That's the sort of thing. I'll go get the suits ready."

"Before you do that, just consider one thing in this preposterous plan. How do we tell the discrimination circuitry . . ." Jason's voice ran down in midsentence, and his eyes opened wide—then he clapped Kerk on the back. Heavily too, he was so excited, but the Pyrran seemed completely unaware of the blow. "That's it, that's how we do it!" Jason chortled, rushing to the computer console. Kerk waited patiently while Jason fed in figures and muttered over the tapes of information. The answer was not long in coming.

"Here it is!" Jason held up a reel of tape. "The plan of attack—and it is going to work. It is just a matter of remembering that the computer on that battleship is just a big dumb adding machine that counts on its fingers, but very fast. It *always* performs in the same manner because it is programmed to do so. So here is what happens. Because of the main drive tubes the area with the least concentration of fire power is dead astern. Only one hundred and fourteen gun turrets can be trained that way. Their slew time varies—that is, the time it takes a turret to rotate one hundred and eighty degrees in azimuth. The small ones do it in less than a second; the main batteries need six seconds. This is one factor. Other factors are which targets get that kind of attention. Fastest-moving rocks get blasted first, even if they are farther away than a larger, slower-moving target. There are other factors like rate of fire, angle of depression of guns and so forth. Our computer has chomped everything up and come up with *this!*"

"What does it reveal?"

"That we can make it. We will be in the center of a disk of flying rocks that will be aimed at the rear of the *Indestructible*. There will be a lot of rock, enough to keep all the guns busy that can bear on the spot. Our suits will be half the size of the smallest boulder. We will all be going at the same speed, in the same direction, so we should get the small-caliber stuff. Now, another cloud of rock, real heavy stuff, will converge on the stern of the ship from a ninety-degree angle, but it will not hit the two-hundred-kilometer limit until after the guns start blasting at us. The computer will track it and as soon as our wave is blasted will slew the big guns to get rid of the heavy stuff. As soon as these fire, we *accelerate* toward the stern tubes. We will then become prime targets, but, before the big guns can slew back, we should be inside the tubes."

"It sounds possible. What is the time gap between the instant we reach the tubes and the earliest the guns can fire?"

"We leave their cone of fire exactly six-tenths of a second before they can blast us."

"Plenty of time. Let us go."

Jason held up his hand. "Just one thing. I'm game if you are. We carry cutting equipment and weapons. Once inside the ship there should not be too many problems. But it is not a piece of cake by any means. The two of us go. But we don't tell Meta—and she stays here."

"Three have a better chance than two to get through."

"And two have a better chance than one. I'm not going unless you agree."

"Agreed. Set the plan up."

Meta was busy with her new-found interest in codes and ciphers; it was a perfect time. The Earth navy ships were well trained in precision rock-throwing—as well as being completely bored by it. They let the computers do most of the work. While the preparations were being made, Kerk and Jason suited up in the combat suits: more tanks than suits, heavy with armor and slung about with weapons. Kerk attached the special equipment they would need while Jason short-circuited the airlock indicator so Meta, in the control room, would not know they had left the ship. Silently they slipped out.

No matter how many times you do it, no matter how you prepare yourself mentally, the sensation of floating free in space is not an enjoyable one. It is easy to lose orientation, to have the sensation that all directions are up—or down—and Jason was more than slightly glad of the accompanying bulk of the Pyrran.

"Operation has begun."

The voice crackled in their earphones, then they were too busy to be concerned about anything else. The computer informed them that the wall of giant boulders was sweeping toward them—they could see nothing themselves—and gave them instructions to pull aside. Then the things were suddenly there, floating ponderously by, already shrinking into the distance as the jets fired on the spacesuits. Again following instructions, they accelerated to the correct moving spot in space and fitted themselves into the gap in the center of the floating rock field. They had to juggle their jets until they had the same velocity as the boulders; then, power cut off, they floated free.

"Do you remember the instructions?" Jason asked.

"Perfectly."

"Well, let me run through them again for the sake of my morale, if you don't mind." The battleship was visible now far ahead, like a tiny splinter in space. "We do nothing at all to draw attention as we come in. There will be plenty of activity around us, but we don't use power except in an extreme emergency. And we get hit by small-caliber fire—the best thing that can happen to us because it means the big stuff is firing at something else. Meanwhile the other attack of flying rocks will be coming in from our flank. We won't see them—but our computer will. It is monitoring the battleship as well, and the instant the big guns fire on the second wave, it will send the signal go. Then we go. Full power on the rockets toward the main drive tube. When our suit radar says we are eleven hundred meters from the ship, we put on full reverse thrust because we will be inside the guns. See you at the bottom of the tube."

"What if the computer fires the tube to clear us out?"

"I have been trying not to think about that. We can only hope that it is not programmed for such a complex action and that its logic circuits will not come up with the answer . . ."

Space around them exploded with searing light. Their helmet visors darkened automatically, but the explosions could still be clearly seen, they were so intense. And silent. A rock the size of a small house burned and vaporized soundlessly not a hundred meters from Jason, and he cringed inside the suit. The silent destruction continued—but the silence was suddenly shattered by deafening explosions, and his suit vibrated with the impact.

He was being hit! Even though he expected it, wanted it, the jarring was intense and unbelievably loud. Then it stopped as suddenly as it had begun, and dimly, he heard a weak voice say go.

"Blast, Kerk, blast!" he shouted as he jammed on full power.

The suit kicked him hard, numbing him, slowing his fingers as they grappled for the intensity control on the helmet and turned it off. He winced against the glare of burning matter but could just make out the disk of the spaceship's stern before him, the main tube staring like a great black eye. It grew quickly until it filled space and the sudden red glow of the preset radar said he had passed the eleven-hundred-meter mark. The guns couldn't touch him here—but he could crash into the battleship and demolish himself. Then the full blast of the retrojets hit him, slamming him against the suit, stunning him again, making control almost impossible. The dark opening blossomed before him, filling his vision, blacking out everything else.

He was inside it, the pressure lessening as the landing circuits took over and paced his rate of descent. Had Kerk made it? He had stopped, floating free, when something plummeted from above, glanced off him and crashed heavily into the end of the tube.

"Kerk!" Jason grabbed the limp figure as it rebounded after the tremendous impact, grappled it and turned his lights on it. "Kerk!" No answer. Dead?

"Landed . . . faster than I intended."

"You did indeed. But we're here. Now let's get to work before the computer decides to burn us out."

Spurred by this danger, they unshipped the molecular unbinder torch, the only thing that would affect the tough tube liners, and worked a circular line on the wall just above the injectors. It took almost two minutes of painstaking work to slowly cut the opening, and every second of the time they waited for the tube to fire.

It did not. The circle was completed, and Kerk put his shoulder to it and fired his jets. The plug of metal and the Pyrran instantly vanished from sight—and Jason dived in right behind him into the immense, brightly lit engine room, made suddenly brighter by a flare of light behind him. Jason spun about just in time to see the flames cut off, the flames leaping from the hole they had just cut. The end of a microsecond blast. "A smart computer," he said weakly. "Smart indeed."

Kerk had ignored the blast and dived into a control room to one side. Jason followed him—and met him as he emerged with a large chart in a twisted metal frame. "Diagram of the ship. Tore it from the wall. Central control this way. Go."

"All right, all right," Jason muttered, working to keep pace with the Pyrran's hurtling form. This was what Pyrrans did best, and it was an effort to keep up the pace. "Repair robots," he said when they entered a long corridor. "They won't bother us . . ."

Before he had finished speaking, the two robots had raised their welding torches and rushed to the attack. But even as they moved, Kerk's gun blasted twice, and they exploded into junk. "Good computer," Kerk said. "Turn anything against us. Stay alert and cover my back."

There was no more time for talking. They changed their course often, since it was obvious that they were heading toward central control. Every machine along the way wanted to kill them. Housekeeping robots rushed at them with brooms, TV screens exploded as they passed, airtight doors tried to close on them, floors were electrified if they were touched. It was a battle, but really a one-sided one as long as they stayed alert. Their suits were invulnerable to small-scale attack, insulated from electricity. And Pyrrans are the best fighters in the galaxy. In the end they came to the door marked CENTRA KONTROLO, and Kerk offhandedly blasted it down and floated through. The lights were lit, the room and the controls were spotlessly clean.

"We've done it," Jason said, cracking his helmet and smelling the cool air. "One billion credits. We've licked this bucket of bolts . . ."

"THIS IS A FINAL WARNING!" the voice boomed and their guns nosed about for the source before they realized it was just a recording. "THIS BATTLESHIP HAS BEEN ENTERED BY ILLEGAL MEANS. YOU ARE ORDERED TO LEAVE WITHIN THE NEXT FIFTEEN SECONDS OR THE ENTIRE SHIP WILL BE DESTROYED. CHARGES HAVE BEEN SET TO ASSURE THAT THIS BATTLESHIP DOES NOT FALL INTO ENEMY HANDS. FOURTEEN . . ."

"We can't get out in time!" Jason shouted.

"Shoot up the controls!"

"No! The destruction controls won't be here."

"TWELVE"

"What can we do?"

"Nothing! Absolutely nothing at all . . ."

"EIGHT"

They looked at each other wordlessly. Jason put out his armored hand and Kerk touched it with his own.

"SEVEN"

"Well, goodby," Jason said, and tried to smile.

"FOUR . . . errrk. THREE . . ."

There was silence, then the mechanical voice spoke again, a different voice. "*De-mothballing activated. Defenses disarmed. Am awaiting instructions.*"

"What . . . happened?" Jason asked.

"*De-mothballing signal received. Am awaiting instructions.*"

"Just in time," Jason said, swallowing with some difficulty. "Just in time."

"You should not have gone without me," Meta said. "I shall never forgive you."

"I couldn't take you," Jason said. "I wouldn't have gone myself if you had insisted. You are worth more than a billion credits to me."

"That's the nicest thing you ever said to me." She smiled now and kissed him while Kerk looked on with great disinterest.

"When you are through, would you tell us what happened?" Kerk said. "The computer hit the right number?"

"Not at all. I did it." She smiled into the shocked silence, then kissed Jason again. "I told you how interested I am now in codes and ciphers. Simply thrilling, with wartime applications too, of course. Well, Shrenkly told me about substitution ciphers and I tried one, the most simple. Where the letter A is one, B is two and so forth. And I tried to put a word into this cipher and I did, but it came out 81122021, but that was two numbers short. Then Shrenkly told me that there must be two digits for each letter or there would be transcription problems, like you have to use 01 for A instead of just the number 1. So I added a zero to the two one-digit numbers, and that made ten digits, so for fun I fed the number into the computer and it was sent and that was that."

"The jackpot with your first number—with your first try?" Jason asked hollowly. "Wasn't that pretty lucky?"

"Not really. You know military people don't have much imagination; you've told me that a thousand times at least. So I took the simplest possible, looked it up in the Esperanto dictionary . . ."

"*Haltu?*"

"That's right; encoded it and sent it and that was that."

"And just what does the word mean?" Kerk asked.

"Stop," Jason said, "just plain *stop*."

"I would have done the same thing myself," Kerk said, nodding in agreement. "Let us collect the money and go home."

BLACK SHEEP ASTRAY

by Mack Reynolds

> This story is the third and last of a series laid in North Africa, where I lived for three or four years. The first, "Black Man's Burden," tells of educated American Blacks who return to Africa to help bring that dark continent into the present world (circa 2000 A.D.). Buffeted by the conflicting interests of the United States of the Americas, the Soviet Complex and the Arab Union, they come to the conclusion that what the area needs is a temporary strong man, always realizing that such strong men usually wind up being clobbered. Doctor Homer Crawford, sociologist, becomes the mysterious El Hassan with the dream of uniting all North Africa. The serial was so successful that John Campbell ordered a sequel, "Border, Breed Nor Birth," which describes the coming of El Hassan to power.
>
> Like a good many of the longer stories that appeared in Analog,

these were written at a suggestion of John Campbell's and whole chunks of them were based on his ideas. I don't mean that he necessarily agreed with a great deal in them, but, as always, John liked to throw a handful of mud in the fan just to stir up controversy and get the folk to thinking. As a matter of fact, he very often disagreed with what I had to say—but would defend to the death the right to say it . . . or anything else!

> *We're little black sheep*
> *Who've gone astray,*
> *Baa-aa-aa!*
> > *—Kipling*

HOMER CRAWFORD, better known as El Hassan, tyrant of all of North and much of Central Africa for twenty years, was at bay. He sat in his heavy wooden chair at the end of the conference table, a recoilless, high-velocity .10-caliber Tommy-Noiseless before him. He was alone. Even the palace bodyguard had deserted in the face of the oncoming rebel hover-tanks. Happily, Isobel and the children were up in Switzerland on a skiing vacation. Had she known and had time, she would have returned, he realized. But the coup had come very quickly.

The military revolt had been well planned. It should have been, he thought bitterly. He himself had trained the leaders.

Back over the years came the words of Abe Baker, onetime friend, who had first suggested that Doctor Homer Crawford, sociologist from the University of Michigan, become El Hassan and unite North Africa. "These North Africans aren't going to make it, not in the short time that we want them to, unless a leader appears on the scene. They are just beginning to emerge from the tribal society. In the tribes, people live by rituals and taboos, by traditions. But at the next step in the evolution of the society they follow a Hero—and the traditions are thrown overboard. It's one step up the ladder of cultural evolution. Just for the record, the Heroes almost invariably get clobbered in the end, since a Hero must be perfect. Once he's found wanting in any respect, he's a false prophet, a cheat, and a new, perfect and fault-less Hero must be found.

"Okay. At this stage we need a Hero to unite North Africa, but this time we need a real super-hero. In this modern age, the old-style one won't do. We need one with education and altruism, one with the dream. We need a man who has no affiliations, no preferences for Tuareg, Teda, Chaambra, Dogon, Moor or what-ever. He's got to be truly neutral. O.K., you're it. You're an Ameri-can Black, educated, competent, widely experienced. You're a natural for the job. You even speak Arabic, French, Tamaheq, Songhai and Swahili."

El Hassan sighed. Abe Baker had been correct. The heroes wind up being clobbered when the people find them with feet of clay. He was being clobbered. Outside the palace, coming ever nearer, were the sounds of explosives. Probably the jets were bombing, in close cooperation with the advancing tanks. He wondered sourly who was left to bomb. His forces had melted away, or defected.

The years had taken their toll of Homer Crawford at the age of half a century; however, in spite of hair all but gray and a weari-ness of facial expression brought on by decades spent largely in stress and tension, he was still an outstanding specimen of man-hood, straight and in as good physical shape as can be maintained at fifty.

The guns were coming closer. He stirred restlessly in his chair. Perhaps he should be out leading the defense. But he grunted self-deprecation. There was no defense. And even if there was, his presence would at best prolong the agony and lead to even greater death. "*Sic semper tyrannis*," he muttered.

But then he shook his head. He did not regret what he had done. He had done what he had to do. Back to him came Byron's verse.

> The tyrant of the Chersonese
>   Was freedom's best and bravest friend.
> That tyrant was Miltiades,
>   Oh that the present hour would lend
> Another despot of the kind
> Such bonds as his were sure to bind.

He wished, somewhat sourly still, that he had encouraged more the trend toward democratic institutions. But it is ever difficult for him who holds power to give it up, to hand it over to others. He who holds power is ever of the belief that no one else is quite capable of taking his place. It had not been a matter of his ambitions; he was long since weary of the work and responsibility. Indeed, he had never wanted the position in the first place. His team of agents of the Sahara Division, African Development Project of the Reunited Nations, had talked him into making the play.

Outside, the firing and bombing fell off, finally melting away to single individual shots from time to time.

Suddenly the door flung open, and two in uniform strode in. Both carried guns, but they were holstered.

Homer Crawford nodded. "I've been expecting you, Field Marshal. But I thought you were up farther north, Colonel Allen. You must have wanted to be in on the kill."

"The north has been pacified," Bey-ag-Akhamouk, he who wore the field marshal's uniform, said. "Your Fort Laperrine here and your palace were the last holdouts."

"And now they've fallen, Homer," Elmer Allen said. His face was both weary and wan. Elmer Allen, old member of Crawford's Reunited Nations team, had been one of the first to urge him to assume the El Hassan role.

Bey-ag-Akhamouk, another of the original team, wasn't happy either, but his Tuareg face was trained not to betray emotion. He alone of their original group was of Saharan birth, but he had been taken at an early age to the States and had become an American citizen. Like all the team, he held a doctorate in the social sciences, but combat had brought out the fact that he was a genius of intuitive generalship.

"You look tired, Bey," Homer Crawford said as the other two men took chairs across from him. They ignored his gun. "You're to be congratulated on your efficiency. I didn't know about your coup until three days ago."

Bey said emptily, "It's all over, Homer. El Hassan is through."

Crawford nodded. "You two are making a big mistake."

Elmer Allen shook his head. "No, we're not, Homer. When El

Hassan first took over, he accomplished miracles in uniting and advancing Africa, but now he stands in the way of progress. We've got to industrialize, encourage foreign capital, request aid from the great powers."

Homer Crawford looked at him. "You should be a better socioeconomist than that. Those steps will be the end of real progress in this part of Africa, not the beginning."

Both of the other two shook their heads at him. "We're still backward peoples," Elmer Allen said. "We've got to industrialize. We've got the raw materials, we've got the manpower, and the schools are beginning to turn out the needed technicians."

Crawford said, "It's a mistake they began to make back about 1950. The cry went up to industrialize the underdeveloped nations. So-called aid went out, particularly from the United States and Soviet Russia. The voices of such as Vance Packard, in his *The Waste Makers*, went unheeded. He pointed out that bringing the underdeveloped countries up to the level of the United States and Western Europe was impossible. There wasn't enough of such essential metals as copper, lead and zinc in the world to accomplish it. Already in 1950 the United States, with a small fraction of the earth's population, was consuming some one half of the raw materials produced. In 1940 the United States had been the largest exporter of copper in the world; by 1950 she was the largest importer. It applied to a good many other essentials needed for her throwaway, waste-making economy. That cry for ever more gross national product was a cry for disaster."

"What are you building up to?" Elmer Allen said.

"The most highly advanced nations today, the United States of the Americas, the Soviet Complex, Common Europe and Japan have had it so far as their own resources are concerned. To keep their top-heavy economies going, they are forced to milk us of ours. We mustn't stand for it. Give them the wedge to move in and we're sunk."

"What do you mean, so-called aid?" Bey demanded. "We've already had offers from those first three powers you named. Massive aid. Until now, only El Hassan stood in the way."

"Aid always was 'so called,' " Crawford said grimly. "An optical illusion. They lend a backward nation a billion dollars—at interest, by the way. In return they specify that the money must be spent in their country. Very well, with the billion you build a railroad network and airports. But then when your equipment begins to wear out and you need some new locomotives and aircraft, you have to buy them from that country who gave you the aid originally, because the equipment needed is not manufactured elsewhere. You also have to pay back the loan. Meanwhile, your supposedly generous aid-giving country has wrung various concessions from you. The right to mine your copper, the right to pump your oil. You're poor, they're rich, and before you know it, their capital dominates every industry you have that is worth dominating. And that's what we're faced with now."

"What's the alternative?" Bey demanded. "We're backward. We need the products of industry."

Homer Crawford shook his head all over again. "But we don't have to build manufacturing centers to achieve them. There's enough industry in the world already. Why should we build airplanes, for instance, when America and Common Europe can do it better? They're desperate for our raw materials and for our agricultural products. Very well. We'll put those products on the world market, letting them compete for what they so desperately must have. With the international exchange we realize, we'll buy what manufactured products we need, and we'll also buy the necessary equipment to exploit our resources and develop our agriculture. We won't have them dominated by foreign powers who, if they could, would pay us off with peanuts as they once did the Arab countries for their oil. What started off with so-called aid to the Near East oil countries wound up with a situation where the big oil cosmocorps, the multinational corporations, made hundreds of billions of dollars, pounds and francs."

Bey said wearily, "However, Homer, it's not the way the people feel. They want the good things, but quick, and lifting ourselves by our own bootstraps won't get them quick."

Homer Crawford said flatly, "And you think the army speaks for the people?"

"It certainly does as much as El Hassan did," Elmer Allen said sharply. "I say, what do you know about the people and what they want?"

"Touché." Crawford sighed. He looked from one of them to the other. "What now, Bey, Elmer? The firing squad?"

"Oh, come off it, old chap," Elmer Allen said in indignation, his West Indies–British accent coming through.

Bey said, "We've got a plane waiting for you. Four of my officers will fly you to Casablanca under guard, though Casablanca is in our hands and there is no danger. There you are free to take an international carrier to any place you wish. I assume that will be Common Europe. Isobel is in Switzerland with the boys, isn't she? You will be granted a pension which you will receive so long as you refrain from ever returning to Africa."

Homer Crawford stood. "I doubt that I'll want to," he said. "I suspect this country will be in a shambles within a few years."

II

They left the palace, and Homer Crawford was hurried into one of his own hover-limousines, driven by an army lieutenant he didn't recognize.

Elmer Allen was apologetic. "We're not going to be able to give you time to pack, Homer. We're afraid that some of the blokes are on the bitter side. Some have been against you for donkey's years. We want to get you out of town while there is still confusion."

"All right," Crawford said. He watched out the window from where he sat between his two former comrades. His capital town, which he had deliberately located in the deepness of the Sahara to keep himself mysteriously remote, was crawling with soldiers. However, there didn't seem to be any looting going on. That would be Bey-ag-Akhamouk's influence. Now that he had won, Bey wanted stability. He wanted to play the liberator's role, not antagonize anyone. Homer Crawford suspected there would be an almost immediate amnesty for all who had sided with El Hassan. If any, he added to himself wryly.

From time to time as they progressed, he was recognized by civilians and sometimes soldiers. One major, formerly of his palace guard, turned his back, evidently in embarrassment. His men had

been some of the first to defect as Bey's column approached from
the west.

There was no demonstration against him, possibly, he thought,
because the car traveled too fast for one to develop. He could have
expected some thrown rocks, or whatever. One doesn't remain
ruler of a country for twenty years without developing some types
who would like to throw rocks at you.

Bey possibly read some of his thoughts. He said, "I'd suggest
you get on out of Casablanca as quickly as possible. You never
know."

"No," Homer said. "You never know. Even your best friends
might get around to stabbing you in the back."

Neither of them answered him, but Elmer Allen winced.

Very well, let him wince. They had been in the clutch together
so many times that Crawford could not have counted them. He
had saved the other's life on at least a half-dozen occasions. They
had all been part of the close-knit team in the old days.

At the airport, the aircraft which was to transport El Hassan
from his country was cordoned off by infantry with two hover-
tanks nearby.

Bey-ag-Akhamouk and Elmer Allen strode with him quickly to
the plane. There were four officers standing before it, two captains,
two majors. They all wore sidearms. They snapped to the salute
when the Field Marshal and Colonel approached, but ignored
Homer Crawford. He had never, in his memory, seen any of them
before, but by their appearance two were Egyptians, two Algerians.
All four must have been under thirty, which meant they had been
educated in the schools he had inaugurated, trained in his military
academy. And all, of course, had once sworn allegience to him.
He wondered, vaguely, what had brought them to revolt. They
were probably Moslems, and he knew that the elders, in particular,
of that religion were far from enthusiastic about El Hassan, who
had drastically changed such institutions as the University of Fez,
where nothing but the Koran had been taught previously.

Bey didn't bother to introduce him to his guard. He turned to
Homer and said, his usually impassive face working slightly, "We
won't shake hands, Homer. It wouldn't look good to the men

watching. Goodbye, good luck, my regards to Isobel and the boys."

"Goodbye," Homer said.

Elmer Allen took a deep breath. "I wish it could have been different, Homer."

"So do I."

III

The aircraft was an upper-echelon airforce staff plane, which seated eight in the swank passenger compartment in the comfortable easy chairs. There was even a small bar to the rear. The two majors Homer Crawford had pegged as Algerians went into the pilot's compartment. The two Egyptian captains sat with Homer in back. One was directly facing him, the other to one side.

When they were airborne, the one across brought forth his gun and held it nonchalantly in his lap. The other unbuttoned his holster but left the gun in it.

Homer Crawford said sourly, "Aren't you being a bit melodramatic, Captain?" to the one with the gun in hand.

"Orders from the Field Marshal," the other returned curtly. "It would seem that he considers you a very dangerous man." There was a quality of the sneer in his voice.

"Even so, it would hardly seem very sensible for me to hinder you in any manner. I obviously have no desire to do anything but expedite our arrival in Casablanca."

"A very dangerous man," the other Egyptian said. "Our orders are not to shoot you unless you attempt to escape."

There was something in the other's voice that Homer Crawford didn't like. He had not become ruler of half a continent without the ability to read men. He said softly, "Where in the world would I escape to, Captain?"

The Egyptian officer grinned without humor. "Who can say? Perhaps you believe, inaccurately, that you have adherents between Tamanrasset and Casablanca. You might plan to parachute down to them and attempt a counter-coup."

The captain with the gun was possibly twenty-five. When one is twenty-five and in his physical prime, one is inclined to be scornful of the physical abilities of a graying man of twice his years.

There was another element of which Homer Crawford was aware. The Moslem does not, as a rule, go for hand-to-hand combat. He is raised not to like to be touched by another man, nor to touch one. Hence boxing is not a Moslem sport, nor is wrestling. Knives, swords, yes, but not the bare hand. Karate and judo have never taken hold in the lands of Islam.

On top of all else, the captain could not have dreamed of the reflexes of which Homer Crawford, even at this point in life, boasted. They were as abnormal as those of a *numero uno* matador.

Homer Crawford flung across the small compartment in a blur. Before the captain's gun was half up, he had chopped the wrist in a vicious karate blow. Before the captain's eyes had even had the time to bug, he had swung again, slammed him with the flat of his hand across the jawbone and was already swinging to take on the other, who was clawing for his holster. Homer turned American and slugged the man with his fist—but not on the jaw, in the throat. He could feel the cartilage crush. He hadn't wanted to do it, but he could take no chances on a shout which would alert the two pilots.

He could hear the man gasping his breathless life away, even as he scooped up the gun and the other captain's gun as well. That worthy was beginning to come out of it, so Homer Crawford kicked him in the side of the head.

He headed for the pilot's compartment, opened the door and confronted the two startled Algerians, one pistol directed at each of them.

He snarled at the co-pilot, "Okay. Get into the back here, and get parachutes on yourself and those two in there. One of them is probably dead, and so will you be unless you move chop-chop. I'm going to stand here in this passageway where I can cover all of you at once."

The major's lips whitened. "We can't jump here. There's nothing but the erg below, nothing but sand."

"And there's nothing but me and two guns up here," Homer Crawford said grimly, relieving him of his gun, making his collection three, and shortly four. "Your boys in the back just let me know that they had no intention of taking me as far as Casablanca.

I assume that you two were in on the plot. I doubt that the Field Marshal and Colonel Allen knew about it. If they wanted me dead, they could have done it there in the palace. Get into those damn parachutes and take your chances below. You've got split seconds of life if you don't. If necessary, I can pilot this plane." The last was a lie, but he doubted that they knew that. African boys of their age had been raised in the belief that El Hassan could do anything, and better than anybody else could do it.

He watched the process of parachuting up with narrowed eyes.

When the co-pilot got to the captain Homer Crawford had hit in the throat, he looked up and said, "He's dead."

"I know," Crawford said grimly. "I killed him."

The other was surly. "Then what is the point of putting a parachute on him?"

"You aren't very sharp, Major, even as majors go. When we land, I wouldn't want to be embarrassed by corpses all over the place. Some airport officials take a dim view of such. What we'll do is this. You'll jump with him in your arms. Pull his rip cord, drop him, and then pull your own." Crawford turned and looked at the other captain, the one he had first hit. "Our boy is reviving. He'll be able to pull his own rip cord."

When the three were gone, Crawford went over to the little bar at the rear of the compartment and poured himself a husky cognac. He had noted, cynically, that the major hadn't bothered to pull the dead man's rip cord, had simply dropped him once they were out of the plane. Allah was going to be awfully upset when he received this warrior into the Moslem paradise. He was going to be smashed all to hell and gone and not much good for those eight houris the Koran promises to the faithful.

He returned to the pilot's compartment and slid into the co-pilot's seat. He had already relieved the pilot of his sidearm and now kept his own gun trained on the other. He said, "All right. We'll set a course for southern Spain. They have an airport at Malaga."

The other said, "I haven't enough fuel to get to Spain."

Homer Crawford, some of the pressure off him now, chuckled. "You know, when I was a boy, we had an institution known as airplane highjacking. It became a regular fad. Invariably, the pilot would have some argument to give the highjacker, chief among them that he didn't have enough fuel to get to Cuba or wherever the highjacker wanted to go. Often, he was lying. So today we'll assume you're lying. We'll head for Spain. If we don't make it, we'll probably crash somewhere in the Atlas Mountains. You're an Arab, I take it. The Rif people in that country don't like Arabs; they've had trouble with them since the Prophet's boys swept across there centuries ago. On the other hand, they like El Hassan. I doubt if the Rifs are in on the revolt against me. So, if at all possible, I advise you, Major, to get across the Atlases and to Spain."

IV

By the time they reached Malaga, on the Mediterranean Costa del Sol, Homer Crawford had put away the better part of the bottle of Napoleon brandy, but, on the surface at least, it didn't seem to have fazed him. He caught the pilot looking at him from the side of his eyes a few times and once chuckled, "Don't try it, Major. You'd be surprised just how fast and how good I am with this shooter."

He had little trouble with the authorities in Spain. The revolt was too new for the outside world to have a very clear idea of what was going on in Africa. That there was fighting had leaked through, but not the information that El Hassan was defeated and on the run.

He claimed diplomatic immunity and chartered a plane for Switzerland before the major could get around to putting over the idea that El Hassan was a fugitive and that the new government might want to extradite him.

He had picked up another bottle, this time of Spanish Fundador brandy, at the airport and now relaxed with it, and with his thoughts, as they flew over the Pyrenees en route to Switzerland. They didn't land in France. In his time, El Hassan had had his difficulties with the French who had once dominated so much of North Africa. They had hated to give up the privileges they had retained even after their pull-out from Algeria and the other former colonies.

Isobel was at a chalet near Interlaken. Homer Crawford had the plane land at Lucerne and took a cab to the mountain resort.

He was feeling his exhaustion by the time he confronted her in her apartment. She hurried to him, her face in emotional agony. Obviously, she had been getting the confused news from broadcasts.

In her forties, Isobel Crawford was an even more beautiful woman than she had been twenty years before, when she had been an agent of the Africa For Africans Association, an organization with many of the same goals as Homer's own, but independent of the Reunited Nations.

Even as they embraced, she said, "Darling, I've been frantic. I was about to make arrangements to fly to Tamanrasset."

"It's just as well that you didn't," he told her. "It's all over. My forces collapsed. The army has taken over."

"Bey-ag-Akhamouk?"

"Yes, and Elmer Allen. They've formed a military junta. It swept the country. I was a fool."

"But what about that computer program to keep track of everyone who might try to overthrow your regime? To warn you of subversives?"

He said bitterly, "I put it in the charge of Elmer. It must have informed him that Bey was the most dangerous man to El Hassan in the country and that he, Elmer Allen, was the second most. Where are the boys? Are they all right?"

"Of course. Nothing ever happens to anyone in Switzerland. Tom and Cliff are out on the slopes. Abe is in his room, I believe."

A voice from behind them said, "Hello, Father. We've been worried about you."

Homer Crawford turned to the newcomer.

Abraham Crawford was an eighteen-year-old edition of his parent. Slighter in build, as became his age, and not quite so tall as yet, but much in the way of a carbon copy, short of hair, very black of complexion, sincere of face, well proportioned.

The two men shook hands.

Abe said, "We've been trying to follow developments, but the news broadcasts are confusing."

"No wonder," Homer said. "This morning I was still in the palace in Tamanrasset."

"You managed to escape?" Isobel said.

"In a way. Bey and Elmer sent me off with an escort to Casablanca from where I was to fly up here to Common Europe. But evidently some of his followers don't see eye to eye with Bey about the deserved fate of El Hassan. They were going to finish me. So I had to take steps to divert the plane from Casablanca to Spain." He went over to a sideboard where he had spotted bottles and glasses and poured himself a long drink.

Isobel looked at him worriedly. "You've been drinking, Homer. It's not like you, especially when under stress."

He said sourly, "I had nothing else to do." He knocked back part of the drink and grinned at his son. "Possibly those anti-El Hassan petitions you and your schoolmates circulated had some effect, Abe. When all the chips were down, I didn't seem to have many followers, students or otherwise."

Abe frowned. "The petitions and demonstrations were against the dictatorship, not against you personally, Father. Certainly not so far as I was concerned."

Homer Crawford laughed ruefully and took another pull at the drink. Now that he was relaxing from the strain of the past hours, he could feel the alcohol creeping up on him. "I know it, Son. You came to honorable decisions based on your own studies and experiences. I didn't agree with them, but I didn't hold any grudge when I had you expelled from the Dakar University and ordered you to attend the Sorbonne in Paris instead."

"You *were* a dictator, Father. That was what I was against."

Crawford nodded wearily. He slumped into an easy chair, drink in hand, and the other two sat facing him. Isobel's face was still concerned but held less worry now.

"It's an elastic term, Abe. You see, over a period of time a people deserve and get the kind of government they want. Sometimes they want a dictatorship, in spite of what I used to think to the contrary when I was your age. They wanted an El Hassan twenty years ago, before you were born, and I supplied the desire. They wanted a symbol to follow, someone they thought could lead them to the promised land. But I only led them part way, I'm afraid. But, even then, you know, a single man is never really a complete dictator. He heads a team. He has to have a competent team backing him up, doing most of the work, making most of the decisions. Caesar wasn't alone; neither was Napoleon, nor Hitler. Even Lenin had his Old Bolsheviks, a strong, capable body of men. When Stalin took over, he clobbered them and brought in his own team. My team was composed almost exclusively of idealistic American Blacks who had returned to Africa to help its development."

"But you stood in the way of developing democracy," the boy said.

Crawford finished his drink. "That's an elastic word, too," he said with a sigh. "There's more talk about it than reality. However, for some years now I've been planning to introduce it, perhaps slowly, in North Africa. Perhaps a different type of democracy from that which allegedly prevails in the United States of the Americas. Certainly different from the alleged democracy that prevails in the Soviet Complex."

"But you didn't, Father."

Homer Crawford was slightly irritated. He came to his feet to acquire another drink. "No, I didn't, but I don't think that you're going to find much more of it under rule by a military junta than you did under El Hassan."

v

Isobel Crawford came into her husband's supposed study and eyed in distress the body slumped on the couch. It was hardly noon. An empty bottle lay on its side on the floor beside the couch. An empty bottle, she thought tiredly. He doesn't even bother to use a glass any more.

Only six months of dissipation, of letting completely go, had worked surprisingly on Homer Crawford. His face had a bloated quality, and he had put on possibly twenty pounds. She knew what motivated him, though the knowledge did her concern little good. He deemed himself a failure in his life's work. On top of that, he was a man of action, used to as much as sixteen hours of work a day every day in the week. Now, all of a sudden, there was nothing.

She went over and gently shook his shoulder.

He opened his eyes and looked up at her. They were bloodshot.

He sat up and muttered, "Oh. Sorry, Isobel. Must have fallen asleep." That didn't seem to be enough, so he added, "Been working out some ideas on those memoirs of mine we discussed."

She took a straight chair across from him. "Have you heard the news, Homer?"

He looked at her. "You know I never watch Tri-Di. Can't stand it."

She said, "Bey-ag-Akhamouk's junta has been overthrown."

He stared at her. "By whom? My adherents?"

"No. By Abd-el-Kader and a group of colonels, evidently largely from the Ouled Toyameur clan of the Chaambra tribe, and the Egyptians."

He shook his head in an attempt to clear away the liquor fumes. "Damn! I knew I should have had that character shot back when we had him."

She said, "Too late now, Homer. When he led that Arab revolt, the only thing you could do was compromise. You weren't strong enough, as yet, to clash head-on with him."

He rubbed the back of his hand over his mouth. "What happened to Bey?"

"They lined him up against the nearest wall and shot him, of course."

"Yes, of course. And Elmer Allen?"

"Nobody seems to know. The revolt was evidently a complete success. After all, the Moslems predominated in the army. It's possible he is in hiding, or possible that he is dead. Elmer would have gone down fighting."

"Yes. Elmer would have gone down fighting, whatever the odds." He came to his feet, kicked, in a sudden rage, the empty bottle at his feet, sending it spinning across the room. He went to the window and stared out. "At least Elmer and Bey had the dream," he muttered. "I didn't agree with them, but they weren't opportunists."

Isobel said, her voice level, "Homer, what do you plan to do with yourself?"

He turned and looked at her questioningly. "I didn't plan to do anything with myself. I considered myself retired. I was going to spend out the rest of our days here in Switzerland, seeing the boys got good schooling, possibly writing my memoirs. I haven't been doing so good thus far, but those were my plans."

"Even they are impossible now, including the boys' schooling."

He scowled at her. "How do you mean?"

"That pension of yours. I rather doubt that your old enemy Abd-el-Kader is likely to honor it. And we have no other resources, Homer. When I suggested it some years ago, you refused to deposit a sizable amount in a numbered account here in Switzerland in case just such an emergency as this came up."

Crawford growled, "I'm not the type to milk the people to deposit a nest egg in a Swiss bank."

"No. I know. But what do we do now?"

"Let me think, Isobel. Think about it. We can't go back to the States. The corporations there with their lickspittle politicians hate my guts for thwarting them when they wanted mining and oil concessions in North Africa. They'd dredge up some charges against me, and I wouldn't have the funds to fight."

"All right, darling."

VI

It was two days later when Homer, Isobel and Abe Crawford were in the living room that the doorbell rang. Homer had been staring out the window unseeingly, as he had been doing so often of late. He growled, "More newspapermen, probably. Get it, will you, Abe?"

"Yes, sir." The boy got up from his chair and left.

Homer said to his wife apologetically, "Sorry I suggested we let the maids go. Now we have to do everything ourselves, including answering the door."

She shook her head. "It was an obvious economy measure. If it wasn't for the fact that the rent is paid in advance, I'd suggest we move to a cheaper place."

Abe returned, looking strange. "It's Uncle Elmer, uh, that is, Mr. Allen. Do you want to see him, Father?"

"Elmer!" Homer Crawford was startled. "Why . . . of course. See him in."

Elmer Allen entered from the *entrada*. His clothes looked as though they'd been slept in more than once, and his left arm was in a sling.

The two men looked at each other, Elmer Allen ruefully. He said, "You were right, Homer. Or at least partially so."

"Your arm. Has it had proper medical care?"

"Yes, thank you very much. Could I have a drink?"

Abe went over to the well-stocked sideboard. "Whiskey, Uncle Elmer?"

"Scotch, if you have it, Abe. Thanks." The newcomer slumped into a chair as though exhausted.

"What happened?" Homer Crawford said.

"Lucky for me, I was in Rabat trying to cool the student riots when Abd-el-Kader made his play. I was able to make it through to Tangier under a load of produce in a truck, and from Tangier got a fisherman to take me over to Gibraltar."

"Bey?"

"Our whole junta was shot." With a stiff-wristed motion Elmer Allen knocked back the drink Abe brought him, after saying, "Cheers."

The boy looked at his father. "Would you like one, sir?"

"No." Homer Crawford looked at his old comrade in arms. "What student riots?"

"I say, old boy, you haven't been keeping up on the news. We've tried to suppress most of the press accounts, but some of it has leaked through. They've been demonstrating, rioting, off and on, ever since Bey and I took over." Elmer Allen looked at Abe. "It's largely that outfit you belonged to before your father lowered the boom on you."

"Student Africans for Democracy?"

Elmer Allen grunted. "If you ask me, a better title would be Student Africans for Socialism."

Even at eighteen, Abe Crawford was not the type to kowtow. He said, "SAD believes that the means of production should be democratically owned and operated, by and for the people. What 'socialism' means today is so elastic that we don't use the word."

Homer sat down across from the former member of his Re-united Nations team. "What's going to happen now, Elmer?"

Elmer Allen took a deep breath. "You know the Abd-el-Kader type. They'll loot the country white. They'll graft wholesale. The students aren't the only ones demonstrating. A lot of the more advanced workers in the cities and the farmers are. One of the planks in the platform of this cabal of colonels is to break up the new cooperative farms into small plots and distribute them to individual farmers."

"That will be the end of modern farming in North Africa," Homer muttered. "We were just beginning to get to the point where we could compete with the super-farms in America and the Soviet Complex."

"But first there'll be the bloodbath. Bey and I tried to cool the students and any others who were opposed to us. Abd-el-Kader is sure as hell going to cut them down. He can't afford to show any weakness, or the demonstrations would double in size over-night. Another position he's taken is to return the universities to the control of the marabouts. That was to get the support of the orthodox Moslems. Within the year, I'll lay you money that they'll be back to teaching nothing but the Koran. It'll be as though Oxford, the Sorbonne and Harvard taught nothing but the Bible."

Homer said wearily, "What's happened to Kenny Ballalou?"

Elmer said, evidently surprised by the question, "Bey and I continued to support him in his African import-export business in San Francisco. But, of course, that will fold now. The colonels will have their own men sucking up the profits of foreign trade."

"And Cliff Jackson?"

"Well, Cliff was your representative to the Reunited Nations in New York, of course. He stuck to El Hassan and resigned when we wanted him to represent us. I don't know what happened to him."

"I know where I could locate him," Isobel said. She and Cliff Jackson had worked together in the old days.

"And Jake Armstrong?"

"He, as your ambassador to America, also supported El Hassan and resigned."

Isobel, mystified at her husband's questions, said, "Cliff would know where to find him."

"And Rex Donaldson?"

"He's probably on the run," Elmer Allen said. "He grudgingly came over to Bey and me, and we had him working down in the Dogon country. But I doubt that he could stick Abd-el-Kader."

Homer Crawford took a deep breath. "Okay. The first job is to get in touch with them."

All eyes were on him.

Homer Crawford said, "El Hassan is returning from Elba."

Isobel's eyes widened.

Homer Crawford said, "We've got to reassemble what's left of the team."

Isobel said quickly, "I'm coming too."

He shook his head. "No. You've got the boys to take care of. Besides, I need you in New York. You're Minister Extraordinary to the Reunited Nations, representing El Hassan. You just might be able to stir up some support. Not all nations recognized the overthrow of my government. Jake Armstrong will stay in Greater Washington as my representative. He's too old to go into the field."

Abe Crawford said tightly, "I'm going."

The father looked at his eldest son emptily. "We can use every man." His eyes went back to Elmer Allen. "You're in with us?"

"Of course, old chap."

"Are there any troops at all stationed at Bidon Cinq?"

"Where Ralph Sandell has his afforestation headquarters? No. It's not of any military interest."

"Then we'll rendezvous there. We gave Ralph all-out support under my regime. He'd want to see the return of El Hassan."

VII

Homer and Abe Crawford and Elmer Allen filtered in from the southwest. They flew down to Tenerife in the Canary Islands, Homer Crawford's head swathed in bandages as though he had been in an accident. His face alone would have been recognized. Elmer Allen had always remained in the background, even when he was one of El Hassan's closest associates. And Abe was unknown, since his father had made a policy of keeping his family out of the public eye. In actuality, many of his people had not even known El Hassan was a married man. It was part of his mystery pose.

In Tenerife, Abe was sent out with what little remained of their resources. It had been necessary to turn over to Isobel most of what remained of the Crawford funds. Abe rented a plane in his own name, since he was the only one of the three to carry a pilot's license.

They flew south and slightly east, and landed in the desert just north of Bamako in what had once been the nation of Mali before the advent of El Hassan.

In this region, Homer had long ago operated as Omar ben Crawf, and though it had been years since he'd had occasion to visit the area, he had a backlog of native friends, some of whom owed him their lives. Many, he now found, were dead; but not all.

He and his two companions were able to acquire Tuareg dress: loose baggy trousers of dark indigo-blue cotton cloth, a loose, nightgown-like white cotton shirt, and over this a *gandoura* outer garment. Most important of all, a *teguelmoust* turban-veil, since the Targui men, reversing usual Moslem custom, go veiled while their women do not. It was a vanity come down through the ages. The Tuareg considers himself a Caucasian in spite of the fact that he is as black as his Bantu neighbors, and theoretically is protecting his complexion. Homer Crawford, along with his two followers, was able to keep his face completely shrouded. They were now getting into areas where Elmer Allen, as well as El Hassan, might be recognized.

They took a desert bus from Bamako to Mopti and, at Mopti, the Niger River boat to Gao. From Gao they hitched a ride on a hover-lorry to Bourem and there, after a two-day wait, were able to make arrangements for an old-fashioned wheeled truck to take them up to Ralph Sandell's afforestation project at Bidon Cinq.

Bidon Cinq was suitably named. Long decades before, when the French engineers were pushing their way across the wastes of the ergs of the Sahara, they found it impossible to build a road in the ordinary sense of the word. The sand would blow over it before it was completed. So they adopted a policy of routing themselves over the areas most covered with gravel and rock and leaving, from time to time, a *bidon* or can: an empty oil drum full of rocks so that it could not blow away. A traveler across the desert simply went from one oil drum to the other all the way from Bourem on the Niger to Colomb-Bechar in Algeria, the farthest point south to which they had been able to push a narrow-gauge railroad. Bidon Cinq had been so named because it was the fifth of these oil drums and also a fuel point.

Today, Bidon Cinq was a far cry from the two gasoline tanks sunk in the sand and the single quonset hut, half submerged, that once had housed the two Arab attendants who remained there for the winter months while traffic was possible over the erg.

Some 750 kilometers north of Bourem on the Niger, it was 1,229 kilometers south of Colomb-Bechar, the nearest thing to a city in southern Algeria. Under the original Sahara Afforestation Project of the Reunited Nations, it had been discovered that the water table in the vicinity of Bidon Cinq was considerably higher than had once been thought. Even artesian wells were possible in some localities. More practical still were springs and wells exploited by the new solar-powered pumps that in their tens of thousands were driving back the sands of the world's largest desert.

Bidon Cinq itself was centered in an oasis of several square miles. It was a showplace, often visited by the skeptical, who doubted the possibility of ever bringing the Sahara back to the semitropical lushness which it enjoyed during the last Ice Age. It supported in profusion palm trees, fruit trees, lumber pines, shade trees. All about, in all directions for miles, were the transplants and seedlings which Ralph Sandell was carefully bringing to maturity, trees suited to the desert such as *Acacia tortila* and, in the more rocky areas, pinyon, which would take a fantastic beating but were on the slow-growing side. There were also acres upon acres of slash pine, eucalyptus and black locust, all quick-growing dry-climate trees.

Bidon Cinq was but one of the afforestation project areas. From Mauritania on the Atlantic, the trees were being pushed in, utilizing the new chemical methods of sweetening sea water. From the Nile, the Egyptians and Sudanese were driving their new forests both east and west. From the Niger, utilizing the eleventh-largest river in the world, the afforestation teams were pushing both north and south, using the most modern of irrigation methods.

It had been one of El Hassan's pet plans, the long-term afforestation of a desert as large as Europe. Now he was afraid it would go by the board. Such as Abd-el-Kader would never appropriate the enormous sums involved.

The truck dropped them off at the oasis administration building and pressed on, wending its way toward far Poste Weygand.

The three entered the main office, a long room with its half dozen or so staff workers typing, punching cards, sorting, collating, going through the endless routine involved in the planting, watering and nursing of the world's largest artificial forest.

Both Homer and Elmer Allen had been here before, but not for some years. They approached the desk of the aging Ralph Sandell, who had held his position through thick and thin and through all political changes for some thirty years.

He looked up at the seeming three Targui somewhat impatiently. "*La bas,*" he said in Tamaheq, the Tuareg tongue. "There is no evil. If you are looking for shelter for the night, the quarters are down that path in front."

Homer Crawford dropped his *teguelmoust* just enough that the other could recognize him, then raised it immediately. He said nothing.

Ralph Sandell put his hands against the edge of his desk as though pushing and leaned back in his swivel chair. His dark eyes in his dark face were wide. He said finally, "I see. Come with me into the other room."

They followed him wordlessly into a smaller office. The others in the large office had been only mildly interested and didn't bother to look up from their work. A good many Targui worked on the project, especially in more menial jobs. They were no rarity in Bidon Cinq.

Ralph Sandell carefully closed the door behind him before blurting, "Crawford!"

Homer Crawford said, "You know Elmer Allen, and this is my son, Abraham."

Sandell ignored the introduction. "What are you doing here, man? You're in danger! I thought El Hassan had fled to Switzerland!"

"He's come back," Homer Crawford said grimly. "It seems that there's work to be done."

"What are your plans?"

"We'll stay here, with your permission, until some of the rest of my former team show up. Then we'll head into the erg. No word must get out that we're here. If Abd-el-Kader hears about it, he'll land on us like the proverbial ton of bricks."

Ralph Sandell, who was no man of action, was nevertheless no coward. "You can stay in my private quarters," he said.

VIII

Cliff Jackson showed up three days later. He had landed at Dakar in the guise of an American businessman looking for native handicrafts for gift shops in New York. That had made it possible for him to depart into the interior, even though he was wearing a Western-style business suit. Since El Hassan had originally come to power, Jackson had spent practically all his time in either Common Europe or the United States of the Americas representing his leader. His face was an unknown in this area, and he had no need for disguise.

Although it had been twenty years since they had briefly met at a meeting of Amcrican Blacks working at their various projects to modernize the Sahara, Ralph Sandell immediately recognized Jackson and hurried him back to his bungalow-type house, which was set off in an isolated part of the oasis.

Homer Crawford, Elmer Allen and Cliff Jackson went through the usual routine of trying to crush each other's hands and pounding each other drastically on the back.

"So," the big man, who looked like nothing so much as a middle-aged Joe Louis, said sourly, "El Hassan rides again."

Homer Crawford grinned ruefully. "At this stage of the game, he's only walking. We don't even have a hover-lorry to start out with."

Ralph Sandell was scurrying around finding them chairs. He still wasn't quite used to the presence of these men, undoubtedly the most wanted in Africa. He said, "Beer? I have ice-cold Tuborg in the fridge."

"Oh, man," Jackson said.

"Not for me," Homer Crawford said. "In the past six months I did enough drinking to last the rest of my life. Cliff, what's the latest news?"

Cliff Jackson, his beer in hand, looked at their host. "The latest news concerns you, Sandell. You're out of a job."

"How . . . how do you mean?"

"Abd-el-Kader has just informed the Reunited Nations that unless they pony up the money to continue the afforestation of the Sahara, he's going to let the project lapse. The yearly sum he's requested is astronomical; they'll never come through."

"But . . . the trees. Without continued care, my seedlings and transplants will be so much kindling in a few months."

"Argue it out with Abd-el-Kader, not me," Jackson said. "On second thought, you'd better not approach him. He's beginning to make anti-American noises."

"What's that?" Homer Crawford said.

Cliff Jackson looked at him. "Abd-el-Kader knows damn well that the educated American Blacks who were El Hassan's main support, his equivalent of brain trusters, his scientists and educators, are superior to that Arab bastard's own followers. He's probably afraid that, if he lets them remain in Africa, sooner or later they'll get to him. So he's going to run out even those in key positions in industry, education and agriculture."

Elmer Allen said, "The country'll be in a fouled-up mess within weeks."

Jackson looked at Abe Crawford. "Those students you used to be active with are putting up a big beef, but they aren't going to get anywhere with it. I suspect that old Abd is getting ready to hit them hard. What few newspapermen are still allowed in the country are getting rumors that troops are concentrating in the university cities such as Dakar, Rabat and so forth."

Abe groaned in despair.

Kenneth Ballalou, also of Homer Crawford's original Reunited Nations team, showed up two days later. He had entered Africa by air and landed in the Union of South Africa, figuring he would be less conspicuous coming from the south than from the west. He'd had even fewer difficulties than he had expected. The colonels' cabal wasn't as well organized as all that as yet. They were seemingly still feeling their way, and their main strength was in the north, particularly in the areas along the Mediterranean.

By coincidence, he had run into Rex Donaldson in Mopti, and now they showed up together at Bidon Cinq. Donaldson, in disgust at developments, had decided to leave Africa and return to his Nassau home in the Bahamas. In the old days he had done much the same type of work Homer Crawford's team did, though he worked alone and under the sponsorship of the British rather than the Reunited Nations. He was the oldest of them all, probably in his early sixties, but, as ever, as wiry and dried out as a desert rat. It seemed unlikely that he would be the first to drop behind when the going got rough.

Kenny Ballalou, pushing fifty, had gone slightly to paunch, Homer Crawford noted. Well, perhaps so had they all to one degree or the other. A few weeks in the desert and they'd lose the softness of civilization. In the old times Kenny Ballalou had been as good a man as there was on the team.

IX

It was the following day, with everyone supposedly rested, that Homer Crawford sat them all down around Ralph Sandell's dining-room table, maps of the area before him.

"This is the last chance to drop out, men."

"Hell," Kenny Ballalou said, "I didn't come this far to chicken out. Besides, that business of mine fell flat on its kisser when El Hassan collapsed." He grinned. "The way I see it, I'll have to get him in again to escape bankruptcy."

"And I kind of got used to that job of mine as representative to the Reunited Nations. Lots of parties," Cliff Jackson said.

Nobody else bothered to say anything.

Homer Crawford sighed and looked at Ralph Sandell. "Do you mind if we liberate a couple of your hover-lorries? We'll need transportation."

"Why, no, I suppose not. From what Jackson reported, this installation is due for folding up anyway. And we've got on hand various other equipment you might need."

"Guns?"

"Why, yes, some. For hunting, and, in the past, for a threat against any marauding Bedouin."

Homer Crawford looked at Elmer Allen. "Do you know how much of a force is at Tessalit?"

Elmer looked at him. "Very small detachment of second-rate caliber. As we've said before, most of Abd-el-Kader's best forces are to the north."

"We're going to have to take them."

"Take them!" Kenny Ballalou blurted. "Half a dozen middle-aged men capture an army post?"

"Yes. Happily, they won't be expecting it. If I know these remote desert army posts, they'll have already deteriorated in discipline and morale. There's possibly even some *cafard* among them. We'll hit them quick and hard. According to what tribes they come from, we might even get some recruits. These southerners are probably none too in love with that group of ruling colonels."

"But why?" Cliff said. "Here we'd be sticking our necks out, taking chances, before we even get going."

"It's our way of getting going," Homer said. "We've got to let the world know that El Hassan is back on the war path. Above all, we've got to let our people in the desert know it. They can't rally around us until they know we're available to rally around. On top of that, we need the guns and other military equipment they'll have, both for ourselves and to supply our hoped-for followers."

"You think there'll be any?" Rex Donaldson said dryly.

Homer Crawford looked at him. "Yes. The same who followed us before. The young men, no. Most of them have left the nomadic life and gone to the cities or agricultural centers, to the schools and industries. But you don't change a way of life completely in twenty years. Especially tribes such as the Ahaggar

Tuareg still hang on to the old way. They were always supporters of El Hassan, and I think most of them will continue to be." His eyes swept them all, one by one, the old El Hassan personality there, dominating them.

Abe said softly, "I suspect you'll be leading them to their slaughter. Abd-el-Kader has your former army, and it was modernly equipped. How will desert tribesmen, rifle armed, prevail against hover-tanks and bombing planes?"

His father looked at him. "That's the field we veterans know best, Son. What do you think the most effective weapon is against the most ultramodern field equipment?"

"Why . . . I suppose artillery."

Homer Crawford shook his head. "No. It's a man on foot, well acquainted with the vicinity, who has a pocketful of sugar cubes, a pair of pliers, perhaps some baling wire, preferably some dynamite or other explosives, a trench knife in his belt and possibly a shotgun in his hands."

"Sugar?" Ralph Sandell said blankly.

Cliff Jackson said, "A handful of sugar in the tank of any gasoline-operated vehicle ruins the engine beyond the point of repair."

"Baling wire?" Abe said, also blank.

Kenny Ballalou grinned at him. "You stretch a line of wire across a road at night, at the height of a man's head on a motorcycle or mechanized transport vehicle. It's invisible at night and it cuts off their heads very neatly when they come beating down the road."

Crawford said, "Long since, Abe, Tito's guerrillas in Yugoslavia and the Viet Cong in Indochina, among others, proved that the most modern of armies are just short of helpless against the guerrilla."

"After Tessalit is taken, what do we do?" Cliff Jackson said.

"We separate. I go up into Tuareg country, the Great Erg, with Elmer. You go over to Teda country and try to find our old followers there, with Kenny. Donaldson goes south to his old stamping grounds to try and raise a column there among the Dogon. Our base of operations will be the camp of the Taitoq Tuareg, who were always El Hassan's most devoted followers."

Abe said, frowning, "And where do I go, sir? With you?"

His father looked at him. "No. You go to the university in Dakar."

"Dakar!"

"Yes." Homer looked around at his old companions in arms. "You see, Abe, the rest of us have always known something that hasn't occurred to you. It was one thing for a handful of men in their prime, along with your mother, Isobel, to raise the tribes and unite all North Africa. How does the old poem go?

> One man with a dream, at pleasure,
> Can go forth and conquer a crown.
> And three with a new song's measure
> Can trample an empire down.

"But there is no road to the past, Son. El Hassan's day is over."

The boy was staring at him. "Then you don't expect to succeed?"

"No. You see, we're going to be a diversion. You need time, Abe. We're going to try and give it to you. When Abd-el-Kader hears that El Hassan has reappeared on the scene, he's going to head for the Great Erg with every man at his command to try and root us out. It'll take him time, the Great Erg being the Great Erg. The longer we can stretch it out, the better."

"What do you *mean*, I need time? I don't know what you're talking about!"

"You go first to Dakar and locate those student friends of yours who are raising such a stink. You form an organization and contact the other universities and those other groups that are demonstrating and rioting against the cabal of colonels."

"But what do I tell them? What is your program?"

"It's not my program, it's yours. I can't dictate to your generation what it must do. Revolution is a young man's game. I am no longer a young man. It's up to you and your generation to find answers to today's problems. Good luck at it."

They were all silent now. The old team had accepted his words, as he knew they would. They had pretended that they expected to fight themselves back to power again, but in actuality they had no illusions. There is no return from Elba.

Homer Crawford looked unseeingly at a far corner. His final words with Isobel came back to him now. They had been in the bedroom, packing his things for his trip back to Africa.

Isobel was as much the veteran as he. She said softly to his back, "You won't return this time, will you, Homer?"

He turned and faced her and put his hands on her shoulders and looked into the eyes of the woman he loved. He waited a long time before saying, "No. I probably won't be back this time, Isobel."

EPILOG

by Clifford D. Simak

When Harry Harrison suggested I write a final City story for this memorial volume, I found myself instinctively shying away from it. Over the years a writer's perspectives and viewpoints shift and his techniques change. I was fairly certain that in the thirty years since the tales were written I had probably traded for other writing tools the tools that I had used to give them the texture that served to distinguish them from my other work. Yet I realized that if I were to write a story for this book it should be a City story, for those stories were more deeply rooted in the old Astounding era than anything I had ever done.

The eight previous stories, with one exception, were published in John Campbell's Astounding and told the story of the Webster family, the Webster robots and dogs. The tales recounted the breakdown of the city, the development of the Dog civilization by *the Websters, the launching of the Ant society by the mad mutant, Joe. Finally, in order not to interfere with the culture being developed by the Dogs, the Websters left their old ancestral home. Staying behind, however, was the ancient robot, Jenkins, who served as mentor for the Dogs until they too went to one of the alternate Earths when the Ants began taking over.*

The other stories recorded the saga of the Websters and the Dogs. This final tale is Jenkins' story. It also is the last story I shall ever write for John. It is my hope it can stand as a small tribute to a man who deserves a much larger one and who was a greater friend to all of us than we may have known.

THINGS HAPPENED all at once on that single day, although what day it might have been is not known, for Jenkins . . .

As Jenkins walked across the meadow, the Wall came tumbling down . . .

Jenkins sat on the patio of Webster House and remembered that long-gone day when the man from Geneva had come back to Webster House and had told a little Dog that Jenkins was a Webster, too. And that, Jenkins told himself, had been a day of pride for him . . .

Jenkins walked across the meadow to commune with the little meadow mice, to become one with them and run for a time with them in the tunnels they had constructed in the grass. Although there was not much satisfaction in it. The mice were stupid things, unknowing and uncaring, but there was a certain warmth to them, a quiet sort of security and well-being, since they lived quite alone in the meadow world and there was no danger and no threat. There was nothing left to threaten them. They were all there were, aside from certain insects and worms that were fodder for the mice.

In time past, Jenkins recalled, he had often wondered why the mice had stayed behind when all the other animals had gone to join the Dogs in one of the cobbly worlds. They could have gone, of course. The Dogs could have taken them, but there had been no wish in them to go. Perhaps they had been satisfied with where they were; perhaps they had a sense of home too strong to let them go.

The mice and I, thought Jenkins. For he could have gone as well. He could go even now if he wished to go. He could have gone at any time at all. But like the mice, he had not gone, but stayed. He could not leave Webster House. Without it, he was only half a being.

So he had stayed and Webster House still stood. Although it would not have stood, he told himself, if it had not been for him. He had kept it clean and neat; he had patched it up. When a stone began to crumble, he had quarried and shaped another and had carefully replaced it, and while it may for a while have seemed new and alien to the house, time took care of that—the wind and sun and weather and the creeping moss and lichens.

He had cut the lawn and tended the shrubs and flower beds. The hedges he'd kept trimmed. The woodwork and the furniture well-dusted, the floors and paneling well-scrubbed—the house still stood. Good enough, he told himself with some satisfaction, to house a Webster if one ever should show up. Although there was no hope of that. The Websters who had gone to Jupiter were no longer Websters, and those at Geneva still were sleeping if, in fact, Geneva and the Websters in it existed any longer.

For the Ants now held the world. They had made of the world one building, or so he had presumed, although he could not really know. But so far as he did know, so far as his robotic senses reached (and they reached far), there was nothing but the great senseless building that the Ants had built. Although to call it senseless, he reminded himself, was not entirely fair. There was no way of knowing what purpose it might serve. There was no way one might guess what purpose the Ants might have in mind.

The Ants had enclosed the world, but had stopped short of Webster House, and why they had done that there was no hint at all. They had built around it, making Webster House and its adjoining acres a sort of open courtyard within the confines of the building—a five-mile circle centered on the hill where Webster House still stood.

Jenkins walked across the meadow in the autumn sunshine, being very careful where he placed his feet for fear of harming mice.

Except for the mice, he thought, he was alone, and he might almost as well have been alone, for the mice were little help. The Websters were gone and the Dogs and other animals. The robots gone as well, some of them long since having disappeared into the Ants' building to help the Ants carry out their project, the others blasting for the stars. By this time, Jenkins thought, they should have gotten where they were headed for. They all had been long gone, and now he wondered, for the first time in many ages, how long it might have been. He found he did not know and now would never know, for there had been that far-past moment when he had wiped utterly from his mind any sense of time. Deliberately he had decided that he no longer would take account of time, for as the world then stood, time was meaningless. Only later had he understood that what he'd really sought had been forgetfulness. But he had been wrong. It had not brought forgetfulness; he still remembered, but in scrambled and haphazard sequences.

He and the mice, he thought. And the Ants, of course. But the Ants did not really count, for he had no contact with them. Despite the sharpened senses and the new sensory abilities built into his birthday body (now no longer new) that had been given by the Dogs so long ago, he had never been able to penetrate the walls of the Ants' great building to find out what might be going on in there. Not that he hadn't tried.

Walking across the meadow, he remembered the day when the last of the Dogs had left. They had stayed much longer than loyalty and common decency had demanded, and although he had scolded them mildly for it, it still kindled a warm glow within him when he remembered it.

He had been sitting in the sun, on the patio, when they had come trailing up the hill and ranged themselves before him like a gang of naughty boys. "We are leaving, Jenkins," the foremost one of them had said. "Our world is growing smaller. There is no longer room to run."

He had nodded at them, for he'd long expected it. He had wondered why it had not happened sooner.

"And you, Jenkins?" asked the foremost Dog.

Jenkins shook his head. "I must stay," he'd said. "This is my place. I must stay here with the Websters."

"But there are no Websters here."

"Yes, there are," said Jenkins. "Not to you, perhaps. But to me. For me they still live in the very stone of Webster House. They live in the trees and the sweep of hill. This is the roof that sheltered them; this is the land they walked upon. They can never go away."

He knew how foolish it must sound, but the Dogs did not seem to think that it was foolish. They seemed to understand. It had been many centuries, but they still seemed to understand.

He had said the Websters still were there, and at the time they had been. But he wondered as he walked the meadow if now they still were there. How long had it been since he had heard footsteps going down a stairs? How long since there had been voices in the great, fireplaced living room and, when he'd looked, there'd been no one there?

And now, as Jenkins walked in the autumn sunshine, a great crack suddenly appeared in the outer wall of the Ants' building, a mile or two away. The crack grew, snaking downward from the top in a jagged line, spreading as it grew, and with smaller cracks moving out from it. Pieces of the material of which the wall was fashioned broke out along the crack and came crashing to the ground, rolling and bouncing in the meadow. Then, all at once, the wall on both sides of the crack seemed to come unstuck and came tumbling down. A cloud of dust rose into the air, and Jenkins stood there looking at the great hole in the wall.

Beyond the hole in the wall, the massive building rose like a circular mountain range, with peaks piercing upward here and there above the plateau of the structure.

The hole stood gaping in the wall and nothing further happened. No ants came pouring out, no robots running frantically. It was as though, Jenkins thought, the Ants did not know, or knowing, care, as if the fact that at last their building had been breached held no significance.

Something had happened, Jenkins told himself with some astonishment. Finally, in this Webster world, an event had come to pass.

He moved forward, heading for the hole in the wall, not moving fast, for there seemed no need to hurry. The dust settled slowly, and now and then additional chunks of the wall broke loose and fell. He came up to the broken place, and, climbing the rubble, walked into the building.

The interior was not as bright as it was outdoors, but considerable light still filtered through what might be thought of as the ceiling of the building. For the building, at least in this portion of it, was not partitioned into floors, but was open to the upper reaches of the structure, a great gulf of space soaring to the topmost towers.

Once inside, Jenkins stopped in amazement, for it seemed at first glance that the building was empty. Then he saw that was not the case, for while the greater part of the building might be empty, the floor of it was most uneven, and the unevenness, he saw, was made up of monstrous ant hills, and on top of each of them stood a strange ornament made of metal that shone in the dim light coming through the ceiling. The hills were crisscrossed here and there by what appeared to be tiny roads, but all of them were out of repair and broken, parts of them wiped out by the miniature landslides that scarred the hills. Here and there, as well, were chimneys, but no smoke poured out of them; some had fallen and others were plainly out of plumb and sagging.

There was no sign of ants.

Small aisles lay between the anthills, and, walking carefully, Jenkins made his way between them, working deeper into the building. All the hills were like the first one—all of them lay dead, with their chimneys sagging and their roads wiped out and no sign of any life.

Now, finally, he made out the ornaments that stood atop each hill, and for perhaps the first time in his life, Jenkins felt laughter shaking him. If he had ever laughed before, he could not remember it, for he had been a serious and a dedicated robot. But now he stood between the dead hills and held his sides, as a laughing man might hold his sides, and let the laughter rumble through him.

For the ornament was a human foot and leg, extending midway from the thigh down through the foot, with the knee bent and the foot extended, as if it were in the process of kicking something violently.

Joe's foot! The kicking foot of the crazy mutant, Joe!

It had been so long ago that he had forgotten it, and he was a little pleased to find there had been something that he had forgotten, that he was capable of forgetting, for he had thought that he was not.

But he remembered now the almost legendary story from the far beginning, although he knew it was not legendary but had really happened, for there had been a mutant human by the name of Joe. He wondered what had happened to such mutants. Apparently not too much. At one time there had been a few of them, perhaps too few of them, and then there had been none of them, and the world had gone on as if they'd never been.

Well, not exactly as if they'd never been, for there was the Ant world and there was Joe. Joe, so the story ran, had experimented with an ant hill. He had covered it with a dome and had heated it and perhaps done other things to it as well—certain things that no one knew but Joe. He had changed the ants' environment and in some strange way had implanted in them some obscure spark of greatness, and in time they had developed an intellectual culture, if ants could be said to be capable of intelligence. Then Joe had come along and kicked the hill, shattering the dome, devastating the hill, and had walked away with that strange, high, almost insane laughter that was characteristic of him. He had destroyed the hill and turned his back upon it, not caring any longer. But he had kicked the ants to greatness. Facing adversity, they had not gone back to their old, stupid, antlike ways, but had fought to save what they had gained. As the Ice Age of the Pleistocene had booted the human race to greatness, so had the swinging foot of the human mutant, Joe, set the ants upon their way.

Thinking this, a suddenly sobering thought came to Jenkins. How could the Ants have known? What ant or ants had sensed or seen, so long ago, the kick that had come out of nothingness? Could some ant astronomer, peering through his glass, have seen it all? And that was ridiculous, for there could have been no ant astronomers. But otherwise how could they have tied up the connection between the blurred shape that had loomed, momentarily, so far above them, and the true beginning of the culture they had built?

Jenkins shook his head. Perhaps this was a thing that never

would be known. But the ants, somehow, had known, and had built atop each hill the symbol of that mystic shape. A memorial, he wondered, or a religious symbol? Or perhaps something else entirely, carrying some obscure purpose or meaning that could be conceived by nothing but an ant.

He wondered rather idly if the recognition by the ants of the true beginning of their greatness might have anything to do with their not overrunning Webster House, but he did not follow up the thought because he realized it was too nebulous to be worth the time.

He went deeper into the building, making his way along the narrow paths that lay between the hills, and with his mind he searched for any sign of life, but there was none—there was no life at all, not even the feeblest, smallest flicker denoting the existence of those tiny organisms that should be swarming in the soil.

There was a silence and a nothingness that compounded into horror, but he forced himself to continue on his way, thinking that surely he would find, just a little farther on, some evidence of life. He wondered if he should shout in an attempt to attract attention, but reason told him that the ants, even were they there, would not hear a shout, and aside from that, he felt a strange reluctance to make any kind of noise. As if this were a place where one should stay small and furtive.

Everything was dead.

Even the robot that he found.

It was lying in one of the paths, propped up against a hill, and he came upon it as he came around the hill. It dangled and was limp, if it could be said that a robot could be limp, and Jenkins, at the sight of it, stood stricken in the path. There was no doubt that it was dead; he could sense no stir of life within the skull, and in that moment of realization it seemed to him the world stumbled to a halt.

For robots do not die. Wear out, perhaps, or be damaged beyond possible repair, but even then the life would keep ticking in the brain. In all his life he had never heard of a robot dead, and if there had been one, he surely would have heard of it.

Robots did not die, but here one lay dead, and it was not only this one, something seemed to tell him, but all the robots who had served the ants. All the robots and all the ants and still the building stood, an empty symbol of some misplaced ambition, of some cultural miscalculation. Somewhere the ants had gone wrong, and had they gone wrong, he wondered, because Joe had built a dome? Had the dome become a be-all and an end-all? Had it seemed to the ants that their greatness lay in the construction of a dome, that a dome was necessary for them to continue in their greatness?

Jenkins fled. And as he fled, a crack appeared in the ceiling far overhead, and there was a crunching, grating sound as the crack snaked its way along.

He plunged out of the hole in the wall and raced out into the meadow. Behind him he heard the thunder of a part of the roof collapsing. He turned around and watched as that small portion of the building tore itself apart, great shards falling down into all those dead ant hills, toppling the emblems of the kicking human foot that had been planted on their tops.

Jenkins turned away and went slowly across the meadow and up the hill to Webster House. On the patio, he saw that for the moment the collapse of the building had been halted. More of the wall had fallen, and a great hole gaped in the structure held up by the wall.

In this matchless autumn day, he thought, was the beginning of the end. He had been here at the start of it, and he still was here to see the end of it. Once again he wondered how long it might have been and regretted, but only a small regret, that he had not kept track of time.

Men were gone and Dogs were gone, and except for himself, all the robots, too. Now the ants were gone, and the Earth stood lonely except for one hulking robot and some little meadow mice. There might still be fish, he thought, and other creatures of the sea, and he wondered about those creatures of the sea. Intelligence, he thought. But intelligence came hard and it did not last. In another day, he thought, another intelligence might come from the sea, although deep inside himself he knew it was most unlikely.

The ants had shut themselves in, he thought. Their world had been a closed world. Was it because there was no place for them to go that they had failed? Or was it because their world had been a closed one from the start? There had been ants in the world as early as the Jurassic, 180 million years, and probably before that. Millions of years before the forerunners of man had existed, the ants had established a social order. They had advanced only so far; they had established their social order and been content with it—content because it was what they wanted, or because they could go no further? They had achieved security, and in the Jurassic and for many millions of years later, security had been enough. Joe's dome had served to reenforce that security, and it had then been safe for them to develop further if they held the capacity to develop. It was quite evident, of course, that they had the capability, but, Jenkins told himself, the old idea of security had continued to prevail. They had been unable to rid themselves of it. Perhaps they never even tried to rid themselves of it, had never recognized it as something that should be gotten off their backs. Was it, Jenkins wondered, that old, snug security that had killed them?

With a booming crash that went echoing around the horizon, another section of the roof fell.

What would an ant strive for, Jenkins wondered. A maintenance of security, and what else? Hoarding, perhaps. Grubbing from the earth everything of value and storing it away against another day. That in itself, he realized, would be no more than another facet to the fetish of security. A religion of some sort, perhaps—the symbols of the kicking foot that stood atop the hills could have been religious. And again security. Security for the souls of ants. The conquest of space? And perhaps the ants had conquered space, Jenkins told himself. For a creature the size of an ant the world itself must have appeared to be a quite sufficient galaxy. Conquering one galaxy with no idea that an even greater galaxy lay beyond. And even the conquering of a galaxy might be another sort of security.

It was all wrong, Jenkins realized. He was attributing to ants the human mental process, and there might be more to it than that. There might lie in the minds of ants a certain ferment, a strange direction, an unknown ethical equation which had never been a part, or could never be a part, of the minds of men.

Thinking this, he realized with horror that in building a picture of an ant he'd built the picture of a human.

He found a chair and sat down quietly to gaze across the meadow to the place where the building of the ants still was falling in upon itself.

But Man, Jenkins remembered, had left something behind him. He had left the Dogs and robots. What, if anything, had the ants left? Nothing, certainly, that was apparent, but how was he to know?

A man could not know, Jenkins told himself, and neither could a robot, for a robot was a man, not blood and flesh as was a man, but in every other way. The ants had built their society in the Jurassic or before and had existed within its structure for millions of years, and perhaps that was the reason they had failed—the society of the hill was so firmly embedded in them they could not break away from it.

And I? he asked himself. How about me? I am embedded as deeply in man's social structure as any ant in hers. For less than a million years, but for a long, long time, he had lived in, not the structure of man's society, but in the memory of that structure. He had lived in it, he realized, because it had offered him the security of an ancient memory.

He sat quietly, but stricken at the thought—or at least at the fact that he could allow the thought.

"We never know," he said aloud. "We never know ourselves."

He leaned far back in the chair and thought how unrobot-like it was to be sitting in a chair. He never used to sit. It was the man in him, he thought. He allowed his head to settle back against the rest and let his optic filters down, shutting out the light. To sleep, he wondered—what would sleep be like? Perhaps the robot he had found beside the hill—but no, that robot had been dead, not sleeping. Everything was wrong, he told himself. Robots neither sleep nor die.

Sounds came to him. The building still was breaking up, and out in the meadow the autumn breeze was rustling the grasses. He strained a little to hear the mice running in their tunnels, but for once the mice were quiet. They were crouching, waiting. He could sense their waiting. They knew somehow, he thought, that there was something wrong.

And another sound, a whisper, a sound he'd never heard before, an entirely alien sound.

He snapped his filters open and sat erect abruptly, and out in front of him he saw the ship landing in the meadow.

The mice were running now, frightened, running for their lives, and the ship came to rest like floating thistledown, settling in the grass.

Jenkins leaped to his feet and stabbed his senses out, but his probing stopped at the surface of the ship. He could no more probe beyond it than he could the building of the ants before it came tumbling down.

He stood on the patio, utterly confused by this unexpected thing. And well he might be, he thought, for until this day there had been no unexpected happenings. The days had all run together, the days, the years, the centuries, so like one another there was no telling them apart. Time had flowed like a mighty river, with no sudden spurts. And now, today, the building had come tumbling down and a ship had landed.

A hatch came open in the ship and a ladder was run out. A robot climbed down the ladder and came striding up the meadow toward Webster House. He stopped at the edge of the patio. "Hello, Jenkins," he said. "I thought we'd find you here."

"You're Andrew, aren't you?"

Andrew chuckled at him. "So you remember me."

"I remember everything," said Jenkins. "You were the last to go. You and two others finished up the final ship, and then you left the Earth. I stood and watched you go. What have you found out there?"

"You used to call us wild robots," Andrew said. "I guess you thought we were. You thought that we were crazy."

"Unconventional," said Jenkins.

"What is conventional?" asked Andrew. "Living in a dream? Living for a memory? You must be weary of it."

"Not weary . . ." said Jenkins, his voice trailing off. He began again. "Andrew, the ants have failed. They're dead. Their building's falling down."

"So much for Joe," said Andrew. "So much for Earth. There is nothing left."

"There are mice," said Jenkins. "And there is Webster House."

He thought again of the day the Dogs had given him a brand-new body as a birthday gift. The body had been a lulu. A sledge hammer wouldn't dent it, and it would never rust, and it was loaded with sensory equipment he had never dreamed of. He wore it even now, and it was good as new, and when he polished the chest a little, the engraving still stood out plain and clear: To Jenkins From the Dogs.

He had seen men go out to Jupiter to become something more than men, and the Websters to Geneva for an eternity of dreams, the Dogs and other animals to one of the cobbly worlds, and now, finally, the ants gone to extinction.

He was shaken to realize how much the extinction of the ants had marked him. As if someone had come along and put a final period to the written story of the Earth.

Mice, he thought. Mice and Webster House. With the ship standing in the meadow, could that be enough? He tried to think: Had the memory worn thin? Had the debt he owed been paid? Had he discharged the last ounce of devotion?

"There are worlds out there," Andrew was saying, "and life on some of them. Even some intelligence. There is work to do."

He couldn't go to the cobbly world that the Dogs had settled. Long ago, at the far beginning, the Websters had gone away so the Dogs would be free to develop their culture without human interference. And he could do no less than Websters, for he was, after all, a Webster. He could not intrude upon them; he could not interfere.

He had tried forgetfulness, ignoring time, and it had not worked, for no robot could forget.

He had thought the ants had never counted. He had resented them, at times even hated them, for if it had not been for them, the Dogs would still be here. But now he knew that all life counted.

There were still the mice, but the mice were better left alone. They were the last mammals left on Earth, and there should be no interference with them. They wanted none and needed none, and they'd get along all right. They would work out their own destiny, and if their destiny be no more than remaining mice, there was nothing wrong with that.

"We were passing by," said Andrew. "Perhaps we'll not be passing by again."

Two other robots had climbed out of the ship and were walking about the meadow. Another section of the wall fell, and some of the roof fell with it. From where Jenkins stood, the sound of falling was muted and seemed much farther than it was.

So Webster House was all, and Webster House was only a symbol of the life that it once had sheltered. It was only stone and wood and metal. Its sole significance, Jenkins told himself, existed in his mind, a psychological concept that he had fashioned.

Driven into a corner, he admitted the last hard fact: He was not needed here. He was only staying for himself.

"We have room for you," said Andrew, "and a need of you."

So long as there had been ants, there had been no question. But now the ants were gone. And what difference did that make? He had not liked the ants.

Jenkins turned blindly and stumbled off the patio and through the door that led into the house. The walls cried out to him. And voices cried out as well from the shadow of the past. He stood and listened to them, and now a strange thing struck him. The voices were there, but he did not hear the words. Once there had been words, but now the words were gone and, in time, the voices as well? What would happen, he wondered, when the house grew quiet and lonely, when all the voices were gone and the memories faded? They were faded now, he knew. They were no longer sharp and clear; they had faded through the years.

Once there had been joy, but now there was only sadness, and it was not, he knew, alone the sadness of an empty house; it was the sadness of all else, the sadness of the Earth, the sadness of the failures and the empty triumphs.

In time the wood would rot and the metal flake away; in time the stone be dust. There would, in time, be no house at all, but only a loamy mound to mark where a house had stood.

It all came from living too long, Jenkins thought—from living too long and not being able to forget. That would be the hardest part of it; he never would forget.

He turned about and went back through the door and across the patio. Andrew was waiting for him, at the bottom of the ladder that led into the ship.

Jenkins tried to say goodbye, but he could not say goodbye. If he could only weep, he thought, but a robot could not weep.

INTERLUDE

by George O. Smith

Venus Equilateral Relay Station, to give it the full name, was a manned satellite that occupied the libration point sixty degrees ahead of Venus along the planet's orbit. It relayed radio messages among the three inner planets when the Sun intervened.

Its usefulness was often misunderstood, since many persons think that the intervention of the Sun means the physical presence of the obscuring mass dead in line. This is not so. The Sun is a tremendous generator of radiothermal noise, and since communication fails when the signal-to-noise ratio becomes untenable, the relay station becomes useful, or at least expedient, long before and long after solar syzygy.

Venus Equilateral and the persons who worked there were first reported as fiction in 1942 in Astounding Science Fiction under the title "QRM Interplanetary," the QRM signal being wireless *telegrapher's code meaning, "I am being interfered with." The report was popular; this was the beginning of a series that ran for three years and through thirteen novelettes.*

IT IS TWENTY-SEVEN years since Don Channing and his merry men invented Venus Equilateral out of a job and closed the relay station after one last "Mad Holiday." The matter transmitter, which turned out to be a duplicator, ruined the economy because it provided everyone with anything he wanted or needed, and work became a nasty four-letter monosyllable.

But if one expected the chaos to last indefinitely, one does not understand human nature very well. For the matter duplicator and its library of recordings became more than a household appliance: It became a way of life. For with its belly filled, its person housed, and its back clothed, the human race cast about for new mountains to climb, new follies to indulge, new mischief to get into, and new happiness to pursue.

New problems arose. When the maw of the home duplicator needed only to be filled with rubbish when its owner wanted something, backyard and landscape began to look like a strip mine. Ecology, this time in favor of beauty, arose once more. There was, said ecology with bony forefinger pointed, plenty of usable rubbish in the Solar System if one would only make use of it. And so, with the duplicator to provide and maintain a habitable environment, the satellites of the Outer Planets, and Pluto itself, were colonized.

Some miles south of Bifrost Bridge, which spans the River Styx between the twin cities of Mephisto and Hell, on the newly transformed and settled Pluto, there is an island some acres in area. Upon it is a gracious, rambling house that is flanked by the squat form of a workshop—matched on the other side by the silver sphere of an aging spacecraft, the *Relay Girl*. On the day in question a bright green copter was sitting on the pad next to it, indicating that the Channings had guests.

"Have some more of the champagne," Don Channing said, pouring the two glasses full again. "After all—it isn't every day that we discover we are going to be mutual grandfathers of twins."

"A good excuse," Walter Franks said, sipping at the bubbly. "Better pour another glass for Jeffery and call him over. He doesn't seem too enthused by the obstetrical conversation the women get such pleasure in."

Jeffery Franks smiled at the invitation, gave his wife Diane a warm kiss to make up for his absence, and hurried over as the last drop was poured. "The bitter dregs?" he asked, draining them without too much show of unhappiness. "You wouldn't happen to have any more of this vintage around, would you, Mr. Channing?"

"A universe full. Since you are the youngest and most able, I leave you the responsibility of tossing the special recording, reserved for special occasions, into the duplicator so you can run us off a magnum of special champagne."

Jeffery exited willingly on the errand, and Walt looked down at the diagrams that were spread on the grass around Don's chair. "What's all this, Don?"

"Puzzle I've been working on for some time."

"Puzzle? What's it about?"

"Something that has been bugging me for quite a while. Way back when we invented us out of the economic mess that we had duplicated ourselves into, why, that old big-mouthed Keg Johnson told me that the matter transmitter we had invented wasn't that at all. We scan a solid, send a signal analog of the thing particle by particle, then reconstitute it at the receiving end. That's why we can record the signal and make a million duplicates. Keg wants something that will transmit a certified unique and keep it certifiable as a unique, since it will be the same object—not a faithful replica."

"Some problem," Walt said, his eyes going out of focus as he mused over it.

Jeffery Franks returned with the champagne bucket and, after expertly twirling the bottle, he as efficiently extracted the cork and topped up glasses all around, the ladies included.

Handing out the glasses, Jeffery paused to look at the diagram as

Don proposed a toast to the imminent, and inescapable, event. After the first polite sip, Jeffery said, "I hate to sound rash, but—er, you er—were all born too early."

"Meaning what?" demanded his father.

"Well, Dad, you and Mr. Channing were running Venus Equilateral on *vacuum tubes*. Thermionic devices. Power klystrons and wideband traveling wave tubes, and things like that. Why, you didn't even know about parametric amplifiers."

"So—?"

"Look," said Jeffery, "back in those olden days, when you started to design some doodad, you went out and got tubes and resistors and capacitors and all sorts of junk. You actually *built* flipflops and-or gates and monostable multivibrators. You're still thinking that way."

Don shook his head. "I'm afraid so. We dogs are both too old to be taught a lot of new tricks. So, you tell us what you are thinking about."

"Well, the advent of the solid state device opened up a whole new concept. The old electron tube was as crude as opening an oyster with a hammer. But once the semiconductor came in, quantum mechanics stuck its nose in the tent like the proverbial camel, and like the camel, it took over the tent. Now, let's review what we know about the tunnel diode."

"You tell us."

"Well, sir, Werner Heisenberg once pointed out that under some circumstances, the exact position of the electron can be determined, but not its energy, and under other conditions, the exact energy can be measured, but then its position becomes uncertain. Between these extremes, the laws of probability take over, and if the conditions are right, one can assume with some degree of confidence that the electron has as probable a chance of existing on the mythical planet of Aldebaran as it has of being in this living room.

"In the tunnel diode," he went on, "there is the interface between the two terminals, and for some small distance across this interface there is a so-called forbidden gap in which the electron cannot exist. But bias the tunnel diode properly, and the electrons will slyly disappear from one side and reappear on the other—as if they'd passed through a tunnel, hence the name. In other words, there is a flow of current across the gap."

"And you're suggesting that if this can take place with electrons, we ought to make out with heavier stuff?"

"Yes."

Don eyed his son-in-law with amusement. "There is a lot of your old man in you, Jeff. No man but a Franks could cross the credibility gap by leaping from a harebrained idea to a foregone conclusion."

Christine Franks looked at Arden and pointed at the men. "I think we've lost our husbands for another session."

"Not for a while," replied Arden. "They're still babbling about it. We can enjoy their company through the first phase, which always begins with that old hackneyed phrase—'Let us repair to the bar,' where there are always new tablecloths and nice black pencils."

The first operation, once the tablecloth session closed, was a bit of hardware-building in the workshop. This produced a large model of the tunnel diode—which is usually quite small—made with the terminals movable and constructed of coupled crystals.

Now, the undoing of Venus Equilateral as a communications relay had been the coupled crystal effect. With the matter duplicator, exactly identical replicas of anything could be produced. By the philosophy of Einsteinian Reasoning that argues that if no measurement can be made to show a difference between two things, they are then manifestations of the same thing, two identically duplicated crystals are one and the same. Twitch one and the other says "Ouch!"

Progress was slow. The tunnel diode as conceived, and built by the tens of millions, is a solid state device, meaning that it comes in one chunk. The problem was to separate the terminal semiconducting elements at their interface—the forbidden gap—and do what was necessary to keep the flow of tunneling electrons across it.

There was a minor celebration when their meters registered the trickle of a current across a gap of a thousandth of a millimeter.

The celebration was minor because the thing worked as predicted. Since the theory of the tunnel diode is sound, they all *knew* that the Heisenberg Uncertainty Principle ruled over electrons crossing a physical gap, as it did over electrons crossing a mere forbidden gap at the interface between two semiconductors in physical contact.

Then the gap was increased to a millimeter, to a centimeter, and finally the micrometer screw was removed, the two terminals remounted on separated stands, and separated by meters. It was unnerving at first to walk between the two, knowing that there was a statistical flow of electrons passing hidden from one to the other. But they were not only hidden from sight or detection, they disappeared physically from one terminal and reappeared physically at the other. The men felt nothing: nothing but uneasiness.

Then the "other" terminal, that is, the receptor, was moved from the Channing workshop to the Franks attic, some eight kilometers distant.

Next came nuclei; protons and deuterons are easy to come by; the ion source has been known since long before the cyclotron. They are also easy to detect and to identify; the Aston Mass Spectrograph was a commercially available instrument in the middle of the twentieth century. And after protons and deuterons came helium nuclei, and then the heavier ions: singly ionized oxygen and nitrogen.

Carbon dioxide was the first molecule to tunnel the gap. And at this point, Don Channing said, "We may be overlooking something."

"You mean that everything that goes over has to be ionized?"

"No," said Don. "That doesn't bother me. Once we get to trying gross matter, we can simply slap an electrostatic charge on it. What bothers me is that we're not really zapping something solid over there. So far as I know, it still may be 'flowing' as a stream of electrons flow. In fact, I'm sure of it."

"What have you in mind?" asked Franks.

"Well, we are about to rebuild these things anyway. Let's put a couple of small cabinets at either end and try an all-at-once zap of a gas volume."

"How small?" asked Walt quietly.

"Couple of cubic centimeters."

"Shucks. Why not a full cubic meter?"

"I'm a little concerned—"

"Let's compromise," suggested Walt Franks.

Don eyed his lifelong friend. "From long years of close experience," he said, "I think I'm about to be outmaneuvered. Walter, what, for example, is the size of the cabinet you've been building in your attic?"

"Twenty by thirty by forty centimeters. And—"

"It just so happens that you have it in your copter?"

"I did want to show it to you, Don. It's an heirloom. Dad used to use it to keep the beer cold. Great fisherman, my father."

"And you've been cherishing Father's ice chest all these decades so we could use it for our matter transporter? Wonderful! How sentimental! How truly thoughtful! And, I suppose, the scion of the Franks family, that despoiler of my daughter's innocence, is now connecting its duplicate to the receiving terminal at your place."

"Why, yes. It just so happens—"

"Walt, less circumlocution and more action. Go bring in Pappy's ice chest."

Walt went out; he reappeared a moment later with a metal cabinet complete with door and latch. "Connecting it up is no problem, Don. Father, you see, had plans to convert it to an electrical refrigerator, so he equipped it with connectors."

"And so thoughtful of him to use those high-voltage insulators for the feet. That's what I call foresight."

"One more point," said Walt. "Let's toss this in for good old empirical information."

He held up a large, sixty-degree prism of some transparent material which he identified as one of the synthetic glasses with a high index of refraction. "Jeff has measured everything about this to fifteen or twenty decimal places," he said. "If we zap it over there in one piece, he can measure it, and if it goes all right, we're several steps ahead."

"Okay," said Don, with a shrug. "Here goes."

"You push the button."

"Nope," said Don. "It's *your* father's ice chest. *You* push."

"Okay. One! Two! Three!—and *Fire!*"

At the word, all hell broke out. The cabinet imploded with an ear-shattering, high-pitched *Crack!* and for a moment there came the whistling screech of air rushing in through jagged cracks in metal.

Over at the Franks place, the receiving cabinet exploded with an equally shattering blast that ripped the cabinet apart along the corners and seams and bulged the flat surfaces outward. A roughly rectangular hole marked the exit of the cabinet door through the wall, and every window in the room was shattered outward.

They were surveying the ruin when Arden came rushing in. "Migawd," she blurted. "What happened?"

"My dear," said Don. "At this end, Walter has just demonstrated that old Torricellian remark that Nature abhors a vacuum. At the other end, our son-in-law has most likely been observing the truth of that statement that two things cannot occupy the same place at the same time."

"I have the unpleasant notion that someone is going to be pessimistic," Walt said. "I'm about to be lectured about safety and about looking ahead, and about planning, when the important point, being grossly overlooked if not blatantly ignored, is that we did indeed transmit matter."

"Arden, get on the pipe and ask Jeff if we did indeed zap that prism over there."

"One problem I foresee," said Walt. "Are we going to have to pull a hard vacuum on these cabinets, or conduct all transport operations from the surface of airless satellites?"

"Neither sounds eminently acceptable," said Don. "But I think we can make it run quietly by arranging a double switch, swapping what's in that cabinet for what's in this."

"Jeff's on the intercom," said Arden.

She flipped a switch, and the loudspeaker said, "I'm half deaf. Someone blew the roof off the joint."

"Forget the roof," said his father. "We needed a new one anyway. The important thing is that prism. Did it come over?"

There were rummaging sounds on the intercom, and then Jeff returned. "If someone likes solid-problem jigsaws made of cut glass, and doesn't mind a few hundred missing pieces, and has a lot of time and infinite patience, one might be able to restore it—partially. It sort of got fractured."

"Okay, Jeff," said Don. "Call in the clean-up crew and the roofing contractor, and then let's all have lunch. Walt, you get out the crystal ball and make contact with Madame Ouija and ask her to get the specifications for that ice chest from your father's blithe spirit."

"Oh," said Walt Franks airily, "those were duplicates. I have a lot of them. Thought they might come in handy. Now, about that lunch?"

The economy had been ruined by the matter duplicator; when the turn of a switch, using the proper recording, can produce anything from Sunday dinner, steaming hot, to a new tire for the family wagon, not only does man get lazy, but nothing remains worth anything. No, Hilda the maid doesn't wear faithful replicas of the crown jewels; Hilda just isn't the maid any more.

And nothing is worth anything as a medium of exchange.

Then Wes Farrell discovered the synthetic element called identium which exploded with ruinous violence when it was touched by the scanning beam of the matter transmitter-duplicator. Identium became the medium of exchange, and the stuff upon which contracts and binding agreements were inscribed.

Of course, once something is uncovered to the amazement of all, the next thing is to find it on every hand. On the satellites of the Outer Planets and upon Pluto itself, crystals and minerals born of extreme cold and lack of pressure—the opposite of the diamond—were discovered, and many of these refused dissection under the scanning beam.

Keg Johnson's spaceline carried humans, and as he put it, "the mail," and then these precious minerals that could not be scanned and transmitted, nor recorded and reproduced, and Life Went On in an Oddball Economy. But then, all economy is oddball.

So with the success at zapping solid matter across the forbidden gap of about eight kilometers, Channing contacted Keg Johnson over the coupled crystal communicator. "Keg—?" asked Channing. "Brace yourself. We're about to bankrupt you again."

"I'm scared," said Keg cheerfully. "Don, you and your crew could always solve problems, but you always waited until they hit you between the eyes before you bent a brain cell. Singly or collectively, you fellows couldn't program a fight in an Irish bar on Boylston Street in Boston on the Eve of Saint Patrick. Now, what have you blithering geniuses cooked up, and why do you think I'm ruined?"

"You chided me, twenty-five years ago, for not building a *real* matter transmitter," Don said with some pleasure. "Keg, we're going to transmit not only identium, but any other certified

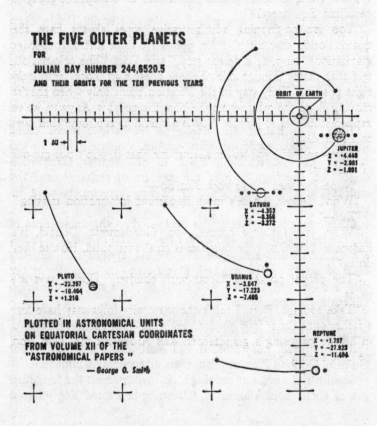

THE FIVE OUTER PLANETS
FOR
JULIAN DAY NUMBER 244,6520.5
AND THEIR ORBITS FOR THE TEN PREVIOUS YEARS

1 AU

ORBIT OF EARTH

JUPITER
X = +4.449
Y = -2.981
Z = -1.001

SATURN
X = -4.353
Y = -6.360
Z = -3.272

PLUTO
X = -23.257
Y = -18.464
Z = +1.216

URANUS
X = -3.647
Y = -17.223
Z = -7.495

NEPTUNE
X = +1.797
Y = -27.923
Z = -11.484

PLOTTED IN ASTRONOMICAL UNITS
ON EQUATORIAL CARTESIAN COORDINATES
FROM VOLUME XII OF THE
"ASTRONOMICAL PAPERS "
—George O. Smith

unique. Not a facsimile, nor the analog-scan signal, but the item itself. Once you get your receiver plugged in, we can pour anything into the hopper and zap it across the Solar System. The *thing*, the *stuff*, the *artifact*, itself."

"Well, I knew you'd do it sometime," Keg said. "But have you taken the Walt Franks habit of extreme extrapolation? How do you know your devil machine will cross space?"

"Oh, we set up a station on Neptune's moon, Triton. Neptune, you'll recall, has been the outermost planet since Pluto crossed its orbit in the Seventies, but Neptune is a goodly heliocentric angle ahead of Pluto—like fifty-five degrees."

"Damned near libration point." Keg chuckled. "Tell me, Don, is Pluto going to be 'Neptune Equilateral' or is Neptune going to be 'Pluto Equilateral'?"

"You ground-gripping administrative types always have the quaint notion that the libration points are some sort of four-space gravitational cusp, or a detent stop," said Don. "The celestial object that passes through one of them doesn't go 'Zock!' into lock-tight position. They stay in the libration point only when they're moving along the orbit where the libration point is. Anyway, we've zapped stuff over to Triton. Now we intend to zap some stuff over to Earth. Okay?"

"Sure—and will you wager against me that it won't put me out of business?"

"Nope. I've seen you at work, Keg. So—"

"Whoa, fellow. There's more important information missing."

"But—"

"Why, you supreme egotist, you. Goddammit, Donald, it's known all over that your daughter is great with child. How're they doing?"

"The proper phrase is 'Great with children.' Doctor says it's twins."

"Take courage, Don. I think the maternity folks may have lost a father once about four hundred years ago—but there is no record in history of losing a grandfather. Kiss Arden for me, Don, and we'll be a-seein' you."

*   *   *

Walt Franks entered with a wire cage containing three small field mice. "These animiles are hard to find on Pluto," he said. "I think when we zap these micers to Wes Farrell, on Triton, we'll be cutting the mice population of Pluto by half."

Don chuckled. "Keg is going to get a shock when he finds out that his spaceline isn't going to have anything to carry."

"Still don't bet against Keg," said Walt. "Communication takes two terminals, and Keg's spaceline may be the last means by which we can plant a receiver on Ugggthubbbb."

"On what?"

"The only colonizable planet in the Alpha Centauri system. Now, which of these little fellows do you like for the first?"

"Walt, when you've seen one mouse, you've seen 'em all. Sashay that cage to the cabinet door and let the most curious mouser venture forth. I—"

Channing was interrupted by a screech that might have been heard on Uranus if interplanetary space hadn't existed. The screecher was Arden, who ran out of breath, inhaled deeply, and then said, "Get those things out of here!"

"This we propose to do—via tunnel transport."

"Well, so long as you get rid of them—and who's going to be on the receiving end?" she asked suspiciously. "Diane?"

"No, we're not about to relieve me of this gran'pa kick by scaring her out of—of—of—forget it. We're zapping these small rodents over to Triton, where our old pal Wes Farrell is running the receiving end."

Channing poked the intercom button and said, "Wes? Stand by for the live one. Ready?"

"Ready," replied Farrell.

The mouse, running aimlessly about the floor of the transmitting cabinet in the way of mice, quietly disappeared, and reappeared roaming about the receiving cabinet.

"Live one received," reported Wes Farrell. "I doubt that he can appreciate being the first live one to be zapped across about twenty-eight astronomical units of wide open interplanetary space."

"Okay. Give me a minute by minute report."

At the end of the first minute, Farrell reported that the mouse was still acting typically mouselike. At minute two, the mouse had been proffered a bit of fairly high cheese, and had taken it in with mouselike enthusiasm. At minute three, the mouse had relieved himself—in one end and out the other. At four, no change. But at the end of five minutes—

"Don, our mouse friend has suddenly slowed down. He's not squealing as if in pain, it's more like he just simply got tired. Run out of energy. Now he's stopped cold; lain down. Flat. I've nudged him with a stick, but he didn't respond. I'm little judge of mice-life, Don, and wouldn't know what to do with a mouse-sized stethoscope if I had one, but I'm very much inclined to think that we have one dead mouse on our hands."

"We'll zap him back," said Don, "and have Mephisto Medical take a look. Stand by for Number Two."

An ordinary citizen, entering a large medical clinic with three very deceased mice and asking that they examine the trio of specimens for the cause of death, would either be curtly invited to leave or quietly invited to become a member of the smile-in ward. But when the citizen bearing the specimens happens to be a well-known scientific type, the director of any such clinic knows that something is going on over and above the development of a new way to dispose of the rodent menace.

His report, made the following morning, was negative. "Mr. Channing," said the director, "there is absolutely no reason for these mice to die. There are signs of anoxia, but no apparent cause."

"Now, since I can carve my medical knowledge on the head of a pin with a dull hatchet, you'll have to explain."

"Suffocation," said the doctor, "to the layman implies fighting for breath in a smoke-filled room or having his windpipe plugged by a blanket. Drowning means gurgling water and not being able to breathe. Fact is, suffocation is a failure of the blood to carry oxygen in and carbon dioxide out of the body. So far okay?"

"Yes. Go on."

"First, there is no trace of poison. Your associate on Triton reported that he fed these mice some of the cheese left over from a sandwich, and that the water was from the drinking-water supply. Scratch out poison, Mr. Channing.

"But let's consider suffocation. Veinous blood is notably blue; arterial blood is bright red. Laymen seldom observe veinous blood because hemoglobin acts so fast that if a vein is cut, it reacts with the oxygen of the air and instantly turns red. In monoxide poisoning, for example, the carbon monoxide molecule latches on with—so to speak—both hands, and the veinous blood from the victim is bright red. In cases of oxygen shut-off, there is no supply and arterial blood runs blue. That's oversimplified, of course, but your mice show no such anomalies."

"Just like hell," mumbled Channing.

"What was that?" asked the doctor sharply.

"Oh, in the technical world, hell is where all the parts function properly but nothing works. Well, back to the old drawing board."

It was, indeed, back to the old drawing board, but this problem was not to be solved. Animals flipped over to the station on Triton all died, in about the same mysterious pattern. Upon their return, when they could be compared in autopsy to the carefully made pre-trip examinations, no reason could be found.

But in the three weeks that followed the first failure, the old drawing board brought forth a new success. A large packing case was deposited on Keg Johnson's lawn, with an ornate label carrying his name as the addressee. On the six flat sides was a large two-colored stencil that couldn't have been missed at ninety meters in a high fog:

CERTIFIED UNIQUES

In the case was a batch of smaller boxes, each containing some real or synthetic mineral—including a sheaf of identium documents—that either refused or reacted violently to the matter scanning beam. The sheaf of identium documents was, upon examination, the certification papers and a copy of an application for a patent for a true artifact transmitter.

As Keg Johnson was reading the details, Walt Franks entered. "How do you like these apples?" he asked Keg.

"Looks like you fellows did it." Keg nodded. "Only two things bother me. First, how much is it going to cost me to buy a piece of this action; and second, do humans merely walk into a booth and dial their destination, or do we go through that old 'Fasten Seat Belts, No Smoking' routine?"

Walt shook his head. "First, we haven't formed any company yet; and second, while getting there may be half the fun, staying alive once you've arrived is more so." Walt explained in some detail. "So until we lick this problem, we're not going to offer passenger service."

"Well, let me know when you begin to get these two things off and running. I want in. Now to other items. How come an old duffer like you came a-spacing across the System?"

"I was elected by default." Walt chuckled. "Don's busy with the experimental work. Since Neptune is at about fifty-five degrees heliocentric angle from Pluto, it would take Wes Farrell the same time to cross the arc as it takes to run from Pluto to Earth. So I took the good old *Relay Girl* and loaded up with parts for a one-cubic-meter transporter, built the thing here on Earth, and received that humble package for you. I'm expendable in this imminent maternity case, you know. Grandfathers are less important than fathers."

Keg chuckled. "Actually, the father isn't important at the time, but none of them believe it. How's things going?"

"Routine, if you believe the medico. Says it's a shame to take his valuable time."

"Sounds fine. We'll keep in touch, Walt. I think I am about to draw up a proposal to incorporate. Both you and Channing are too interested in playing with the nuts and bolts to give serious thought to business. There's always that one way to become useful: Be very adept at something distasteful to the other guy."

"I'd be in favor of it," said Walt. "All you can get is a refusal, and what you say about our interest is true. Try it for size."

On the link between Pluto and Triton, Don Channing said, "Wes, we're slowly running the mice population to zero over here. How're they on Triton?"

"Oh, we can catch a few."

"Okay, go catch, and we'll zap a few this direction. Send their examination records along. I think we'd best keep the same autopsy crew operating."

"Will do," replied Farrell on Triton.

Channing had never observed the death of a transported animal. He was a fairly gentle man who had no cruel streak; he felt it deplorable that things should cease to live after being transported, and felt it necessary to continue until they found out why. But there was not enough morbid interest in him to suggest—until now—that the transport process be reversed.

So he watched with as near to a clinical interest as his training for electronics and hardware permitted, ran off the by now customary reel of videotape, and then packaged the dead mouse, videotape and the reel of examination records and headed for the copter parked in his heliport. Half way to the machine, he was stopped by a hail from the house: Arden, dressed for the city, on a stiff walk.

"What gives?" he asked.

"Where are you heading?"

"Mephisto Medical. Got another dead one."

"I hate to use the old cliché. 'Killing two birds' makes me nervous. But we're all heading for the same hospital."

"Great! When did the word come and how far along?"

"Jeffery called about ten minutes ago. He's been wearing a course in the carpet for about three hours. Delivery room attendants say it might be within the hour."

Don landed on the hospital roof, although the heliport there was supposed to be for special equipment and emergencies. His small helicopter was immediately hauled over to a far corner, and he and Arden parted: she toward Maternity and he toward Analysis with his package.

When he was finished with his business, he went to Maternity, where he found Arden, Jeffery and the family doctor, Farnum, in a three-way.

Farnum turned to Don. "Channing," he asked, "has any of your family any record of Rh negative blood?"

"Not that I know of."

"Well, we've a problem. It's turned up. The kids—fraternal twins, one of each—are Rh negative."

"How serious is this?"

"For the immediate instant, no more than mildly serious. But as time wears on, and nothing is done, it becomes terminal."

"So what must be done?"

"The standard practice is to give the infant a complete, whole blood replacement with a compatible type."

"So let's go," said Don impatiently. "We don't need a high-level conference to come to a sensible decision."

"The decision has been made," said Doctor Farnum. "The problem is implementing it. First, compatible whole blood of their type is fairly rare, but there is a reasonable probability that, by a general broadcast plea, we can get enough to do the trick. Second, we are set up to do it, but it's a process that we seldom face because the incidence of Rh negative offspring from a positive mother is low; and further, there is usually a history of mixed Rh in the family to make plans beforehand—such cases usually are sent early enough in their terms to make preparation."

"Well, if we have time enough, I can get a spacecraft from Keg Johnson."

"How long will it take?"

"Pluto is thirty astronomical units out," said Don, pulling his minicomputer out. "Under one g drive, it would take about eight and a half days to midflight and another eight and a half to the Inner System."

"That's seventeen days. Out of the question."

"Well, if we double the drive to two g, we—"

"Halve the time," finished Doctor Farnum for him, "and also halve the survival time, since higher g force means greater strain on the breathing and blood systems."

"When we're really in a hurry," said Don, "we load up on gravanol and take it at five or six g."

"And suffer the pangs of hell for a week afterward," added the doctor. "But we're not dealing with hardy adults, especially those kept in fair training." He eyed the perceptible bulge around Channing's midsection. "We're dealing with two newly born infants and one mother who's still dopey and pardonably weak."

Distantly, a telephone rang, and an attendant came up. "Mr.

Channing? Doctor Wilburs in Analysis would like to speak to you."

"Apologize to Doctor Wilburs for me," said Don. "We've a more personal problem than a dead mouse."

"Dead mouse," said Doctor Farnum. "I've been hearing waiting-room tales about this. What is with this matter transmitter of yours?"

"It does fine on minerals and the like, but kills life."

"I wonder—would that include whole blood?"

"I don't know at what level one can say, 'Here life begins.' But I do know that all of our experiments end the same way. Appearance of anoxia but no evidence of any change in the blood."

"I'll make the arrangements," said Doctor Farnum. "You get your crew alert."

Arrangements. First was a full hour of wideband transmission of every characteristic of the compatible blood type that was, to date, known to medical science. Next, the word was broadcast, and whole-blood banks were shipping that blood type to Central Medical Center. Helicopters especially contrived to transport whole blood carried the precious fluid to the transporting station built by Walter Franks.

A Doctor Knowles was in charge. "First, we test for compatibility, he explained. "We'll do this two ways; they're sending a sample this way, and we're sending a sample from the banks that way. We'll test on either end for compatibility before we risk this many canisters."

"Okay," said Franks nervously. He put the sample in the chamber and pressed the button. The transfer was instantaneous, and a second later, he handed the sample from Pluto to Doctor Knowles.

"Got it, Don," said Franks.

"Ditto," replied Channing on Pluto.

"My God!" exploded Doctor Knowles. "Compatible? This reacts as if they weren't even within the same gross blood types. Quick coagulation. Odd—"

He deposited a small drop on either end of a slide, one from the sample from Pluto, the other from the banks on Earth.

"Observe," he said tensely. "The whole blood from our banks here on Earth is red; veinous blood turned red upon contact with atmospheric oxygen. The sample from Pluto remains blue. It is not reacting with atmospheric oxygen."

He reached for the telephone; it rang as his hand touched it. The caller was Doctor Farnum on Pluto. "Doctor," Farnum said, "we've an odd incompatibility here—and the sample from your blood banks does not react—"

"No," said Doctor Knowles, "it's the sample from Pluto that remains blue."

"Let's both check this."

The samples were reswapped, and as they were all waiting for the result, Don Channing's hand strayed into his side pocket. An envelope. He'd been handed it as he left Maternity with his mind awhirl with plans to set up this blood transmission, and he'd abruptly shoved it in his pocket. With nothing else to do, and with nervous tension making his hands itch, he opened the envelope and read,

> Channing:
> The last mouse also died of anoxia—but with this difference: The hemoglobin did not react with oxygen. How do you explain this? None of the others acted that way.
>
> Finholdt—Analysis

The speaker blurted into life, "Farnum? Hate to question you, but there is not only complete compatibility, but that sample you alleged to be inert is nicely red when exposed."

Doctor Farnum looked up from his test table. "I was about to report the same thing."

Channing whistled. "Walt—you heard that?"

"Yes. And if you're thinking what I'm thinking, then we've got the problem licked. Both problems."

Channing poked another button. "Stand by, Walt. Conference

call." Wes Farrell's voice came in to confirm. "Wes, we think we're on to something. Stand by five."

He went to a wall-plate and began to unscrew it. Doctor Farnum asked, "What are you up to, Channing?"

"I've got us an idea," said Don. He returned to the machine with two small machine screws in his hand. "Now," he said, "I have two standard wall-plate machine screws, here and ready to go. The first goes direct to Earth. While I'm zapping it off, Wes, I'm sending the other to you. Take a look at it, and then fire it off to Walt."

"I hear you, but I don't understand."

"Wes, in all our experiments—except the last—we returned the dead ones to the point of origin for examination. Making a two-trip each?"

"Yes, now that you mention it. But—"

"Here she goes."

On Earth, Walt Franks said, "It's here—but left-hand threaded."

On Triton, Wes Farrell said, "She's here, but left-hand threaded."

On Earth, Walt Franks said, "The second one arrived. It's as natural as anyone rolling a three-and-four."

"All right," said Don, with a smile. "Walt, get another blood sample, and *transport it to Triton*. Wes, when it arrives, waste no time, but re-zap it over here."

"I still don't follow."

Don said, "Somewhere I've heard that there are more than forty times ten to the six-hundredth power ways of arranging the components that compose the hemoglobin molecule—and of that monstrous figure, only one way has ever been found in life. Mightn't a mirror image of the real thing be equal to one of the wrong ways?"

"We'll look into that when we have better time," said Doctor Farnum. "But since we now have complete compatibility"—he held up the blood sample under test—"let's get along with this."

"One moment," interrupted Jeffery Franks. "You claim the facilities are superior on Earth?"

"That's undeniably true."

"Then think of this," said Jeffery slowly and calmly. "I'm the only one present that has total authority. No matter what you decide to do for the twins, my permission must be received. It is to my best interest to see them alive and healthy, and it is your medical opinion that they'll receive superior care on Earth. We'll take the chance. Double-zap the twins to Earth."

And so the first to survive the zap from Pluto to Triton to Earth were the twin grandchildren of the men and women who once manned the Venus Equilateral Relay Station, beaming radio communications among the Inner Planets. To do so, they traversed two nearly equal legs of what Keg Johnson promptly called "The External Triangle."

HELIX THE CAT

by Theodore Sturgeon

There are times when one wonders, about one's own life and affairs, "Who writes this plot?"

Over here is your editor, assiduously trying to round up original stories for what amounts to being a final issue of the olden, golden Astounding Stories. Back in the dim past is a story I wrote called "Helix the Cat," which John Campbell had seen and rejected, not because he didn't like it, but because it fell too exactly between ASF and his fantasy magazine Unknown. I do not remember writing the story, but to reason from the return address on the manuscript (Seaman's Church Institute, New York) it must have been written while I was at sea as a teen-aged ordinary seaman, in 1938 or 1939, picking up my mail there whenever I was in port. In 1940 I got married and moved to Staten Island, renting the second floor of a little house in West New

Brighton. The landlady was a nice quiet mind-her-own-business kind of person; I remember her particularly for the time when my wife was in the hospital for our first baby, and I proudly showed her the bassinet I had built. She went right to work with her sewing machine and covered it for me in pink sateen and dotted swiss, complete with a canopy; it was so beautiful my wife cried when she saw it.

We went off then to run a hotel in the West Indies, and the war broke out while we were there, and all our stuff was put in storage. But a few things remained in the attic, and life went on, and we all lost track of one another. Then, just about the time your editor was beginning to gig the "Golden Age" writers for originals, this same Mrs. Myers, from Staten Island and more than thirty years back, wrote to my agent that she had a box of old papers of mine and did I want them. Want them I did, and in the box was "Helix the Cat."

The temptation to edit and rewrite and undate and polish has been enormous, but after torturous consideration I have decided to give you what John Campbell read—and liked, and didn't buy— so you can share for a moment his eyes and his reaction. For me, it has brought him back for a moment. It may for you too.

DID YOU see this in the papers?

BURGLAR IS CAT

Patrolman and Watchman
Shoot "Safe-cracker"

It was a strange tale that George Murphy, night watchman for a brokerage firm, and Patrolman Pat Riley had to tell this morning.

Their report states that the policeman was called from his beat by Murphy, who excitedly told him that someone was opening the safe in the inner office. Riley followed him into the building, and they tiptoed upstairs to the offices.

"Hear him?" Murphy asked the policeman. The officer swears that he heard the click of the tumblers on the old safe. As they gained the doorway there was a scrambling sound, and a voice called out of the darkness, "Stand where you are or I plug you!"

The policeman drew his gun and fired six shots in the direction of the voice. There was a loud feline yowl and more scrambling, and then the watchman found the light switch. All they saw was a big black cat thrashing around —two of Riley's bullets had caught him. Of the safe-cracker there was no sign. How he escaped will probably always remain a mystery. There was no way out of the office save the door from which Riley fired.

The report is under investigation at police head-quarters.

I can clear up that mystery.

It started well over a year ago, when I was developing my new flexible glass. It would have made me rich, but—well, I'd rather be poor and happy.

That glass was really something. I'd hit on it when I was fooling with a certain mineral salt—never mind the name of it. I wouldn't want anyone to start fooling with it and get himself into the same kind of jam that I did. But the idea was that if a certain complex sulphide of silicon is combined with this salt at a certain tempera-ture, and the product carefully annealed, you get that glass. In-expensive, acid-proof, and highly flexible. Nice. But one of its properties—wait till I tell you about that.

The day it all started, I had just finished my first bottle. It was standing on the annealer—a rig of my own design; a turntable, shielded, over a ring of Bunsen burners—cooling slowly while I was turning a stopper from the same material on my lathe. I had to step the lathe up to twenty-two thousand before I could cut the stuff, and Helix was fascinated by the whine of it. He always liked to watch me work, anyway. He was my cat, and more. He was my friend. I had no secrets from Helix.

Ah, he was a cat. A big black tom, with a white throat and white mittens, and a tail twice as long as that of an ordinary cat.

He carried it in a graceful spiral—three complete turns—and hence his name. He could sit on one end of that tail and take two turns around his head with the other. Ah, he was a cat.

I took the stopper off the lathe and lifted the top of the annealer to drop it into the mouth of the bottle. And as I did so—*whht!*

Ever hear a bullet ricochet past your ear? It was like that. I heard it, and then the stopper, which I held poised over the rotating bottle, was whipped out of my hand and jammed fast on the bottle mouth. And all the flames went out—*blown* out! I stood there staring at Helix, and noticed one thing more:

He hadn't moved!

Now you know and I know that a cat—any cat—can't resist that short, whistling noise. Try it, if you have a cat. When Helix should have been on all fours, big yellow eyes wide, trying to find out where the sound came from, he was sitting sphinxlike, with his eyes closed, his whiskers twitching slightly, and his front paws turned under his forelegs. It didn't make sense. Helix's senses were unbelievably acute—I knew. I'd tested them. Then—

Either I had heard that noise with some sense that Helix didn't possess, or I hadn't heard it at all. If I hadn't, then I was crazy. No one likes to think he is crazy. So you can't blame me for trying to convince myself that it was a sixth sense.

Helix roused me by sneezing. I took his cue and turned off the gas.

"Helix, old fellow," I said when I could think straight, "what do you make of this? Hey?"

Helix made an inquiring sound and came over to rub his head on my sleeve. "Got you stopped too, has it?" I scratched him behind the ear, and the end of his tail curled ecstatically around my wrist. "Let's see. I hear a funny noise. You don't. Something snatches the stopper out of my hand, and a wind comes from where it's impossible for any wind to be, and blows out the burners. Does that make sense?" Helix yawned. "I don't think so either. Tell me, Helix, what shall we do about this? Hey?"

Helix made no suggestion. I imagine he was quite ready to forget about it. Now, I wish I had.

I shrugged my shoulders and went back to work. First I slipped a canvas glove on and lifted the bottle off the turntable. Helix slid under my arm and made as if to smell the curved, flexible surface. I made a wild grab to keep him from burning his nose, ran my bare hand up against the bottle, and then had to make another grab to keep it off the floor. I missed with the second grab—the bottle struck dully, bounced, and—landed right back on the bench? Not only on it, but in the exact spot from which I had knocked it!

And—get this, now—when I looked at my hand to see how big my hypothetical seared spot might be, it wasn't there! That bottle was *cold*—and it should have been hot for hours yet! My new glass was a very poor conductor. I almost laughed. I should have realized that Helix had more sense than to put his pink nose against the bottle if it were hot.

Helix and I got out of there. We went into my room, closed the door on that screwy bottle, and flopped down on the bed. It was too much for us. We would have wept aloud purely for self-expression, if we hadn't forgotten how, years ago, Helix and I.

After my nerves had quieted a bit, I peeped into the laboratory. The bottle was still there—but it was *jumping!* It was hopping gently, in one place.

"Come on in here, you dope. I want to talk to you."

Who said that? I looked suspiciously at Helix, who, in all innocence, returned my puzzled gaze. Well, I hadn't said it. Helix hadn't. I began to be suspicious as hell of that bottle.

"Well?"

The tone was drawling and not a little pugnacious. I looked at Helix. Helix was washing daintily. But—Helix was the best watchdog of a cat that ever existed. If there had been anyone else—if he had *heard* anyone else—in the lab, he'd have let me know. Then he hadn't heard. And I had. "Helix," I breathed—and he looked right up at me, so there was nothing wrong with his hearing—"we're both crazy."

"No, you're not," said the voice. "Sit down before you fall down. I'm in your bottle, and I'm in to stay. You'll kill me if you take me out—but just between you and me I don't think you can get me out. Anyway please don't try . . . what's the matter with you? Stop popping your eyes, man!"

"Oh," I said hysterically, "there's nothing the matter with me. No, no, no. I'm nuts, that's all. Stark, totally, and completely nuts, balmy, mentally unbalanced, and otherwise the victim of psychic loss of equilibrium. Me, I'm a raving lunatic. I hear voices. What does that make me, Joan of Arc? Hey, Helix. Look at me. I'm Joan of Arc. You must be Beucephalus, or Pegasus, or the great god Pasht. First I have an empty bottle, and next thing I know it's full of djinn. Hey, Helix, have a lil drink of djinn . . ." I sat down on the floor and Helix sat beside me. I think he was sorry for me. I know I was—very.

"Very funny," said the bottle—or rather, the voice that claimed it was from the bottle. "If you'll only give me a chance to explain, now—"

"Look," I said, "maybe there is a voice. I don't trust anything any more—except you, Helix. I know. If you can hear him, then I'm sane. If not, I'm crazy. Hey, Voice!"

"Well?"

"Look, do me a favor. Holler 'Helix' a couple of times. If the cat hears you, I'm sane."

"All right," the voice said wearily. "Helix! Here, Helix!"

Helix sat there and looked at me. Not by the flicker of a whisker did he show that he had heard. I drew a deep breath and said softly, "Helix! Here, Helix!"

Helix jumped up on my chest, put one paw on each shoulder, and tickled my nose with his curving tail. I got up carefully, holding Helix. "Pal," I said, "I guess this is the end of you and me. I'm nuts, pal. Better go phone the police."

Helix purred. He could see I was sad about something, but what it was didn't seem to bother him any. He was looking at me as if my being a madman didn't make him like me any the less. But I think he found it interesting. He had a sort of quizzical look in his glowing eyes. As if he'd rather I stuck around. Well, if he wouldn't phone the law, I wouldn't. I wasn't responsible for myself any more.

"Now, *will* you shut up?" said the bottle. "I don't want to give you any trouble. You may not realize it, but you saved my life. Don't be scared. Look. I'm a soul, see? I was a man called Gregory

—Wallace Gregory. I was killed in an automobile accident two hours ago—"

"You were killed two hours ago. And I just saved your life. You know, Gregory, that's just dandy. On my head you will find a jeweled turban. I am now the Maharajah of Mysore. Goo. Da. And flub. I—"

"You are perfectly sane. That is, you are right now. Get hold of yourself and you'll be all right," said the bottle. "Yes, I was killed. My body was killed. I'm a soul. The automobile couldn't kill that. But They could."

"They?"

"Yeah. The Ones Who were chasing me when I got into your bottle."

"Who are They?"

"We have no name for Them. They eat souls. There are swarms of Them. Any time They find a soul running around loose, They track it down."

"You mean—any time anyone dies, his soul wanders around, running away from Them? And that sooner or later, They catch it?"

"Oh, no. Only some souls. You see, when a man realizes he is going to die, something happens to his soul. There are some people alive today who knew, at one time, that they were about to die. Then, by some accident, they didn't. Those people are never quite the same afterward, because that something has happened. With the realization of impending death, a soul gets what might be called a protective covering, though it's more like a change of form. From then on, the soul is inedible and undesirable to Them."

"What happens to a protected soul, then?"

"That I don't know. It's funny . . . people have been saying for millennia that if only someone could come back from death, what strange things he could relate . . . well, I did it, thanks to you. And yet I know very little more about it than you. True, I died, and my soul left my body. But then, I only went a very little way. A protected soul probably goes through stage after stage . . . I don't know. Now, I'm just guessing."

"Why wasn't your soul 'protected'?"

"Because I had no warning—no realization that I was to die. It happened so quickly. And I haven't been particularly religious. Religious people, and freethinkers if they think deeply, and philosophers in general, and people whose work brings them in touch with deep and great things—these may all be immune from Them, years before they die."

"Why?"

"That should be obvious. You can't think deeply without running up against a realization of the power of death. 'Realization' is a loose term, I know. If your mind is brilliant, and you don't pursue your subject—*any* subject—deeply enough, you will never reach that realization. It's a sort of dead end to a questing mind— a *ne plus ultra*. Batter yourself against it, and it hurts. And that pain is the realization. Stupid people reach it far easier than others—it hurts more, and they are made immune easier. But at any rate, a man can live his life without it, and still have a few seconds just before he dies for his soul to undergo the immunizing change. I didn't have those few seconds."

I fumbled for my handkerchief and mopped my face. This was a little steep. "Look," I said, "this is—well, I'm more or less of a beginner. Just what *is* a soul?"

"Elementally," said the bottle, "it is matter, just like everything else in the universe. It has weight and mass, though it can't be measured by earthly standards. In the present stage of the sciences, we haven't run up against anything like it. It usually centers around the pineal gland, although it can move at will throughout the body, if there is sufficient stimulus. For example—"

He gave me the example, and it was very good. I saw his point.

"And anger, too," the bottle went on. "In a fit of fury, one's soul settles momentarily around the adrenals, and does what is necessary. See?"

I turned to Helix. "Helix," I said, "we're really learning things today." Helix extended his claws and studied them carefully. I suddenly came to my senses, realizing that I was sitting on the floor of my laboratory, holding a conversation with an empty glass bottle; that Helix was sitting in my lap, preening himself, listening without interest to my words, and *not hearing* those from the bottle. My mind reeled again. I *had* to have an answer to that.

"Bottle," I said hoarsely, "why can't Helix hear you?"

"Oh. That," said the bottle. "Because there is no sound."

"How can I hear you?"

"Direct telepathic contact. I am not speaking to you, specifically, but to your soul. Your soul transmits my message to you. It is functioning now on the nerve-centers controlling your hearing— hence you interpret it as sound. That is the most understandable way of communication."

"Then—why doesn't Helix get the same messages?"

"Because he is on a different—er—wavelength. That's one way of putting it, though thoughtwaves are not electrical. I can—that is, I believe I can—direct thoughts to him. Haven't tried. It's a matter of degree of development."

I breathed much easier. Astonishing, what difference a rational explanation will make. But there were one or two more things—

"Bottle," I said, "what's this about my saving your life? And what has my flexible glass to do with it?"

"I don't quite know," said the bottle. "But, purely by accident, I'm sure, you have stumbled on the only conceivable external substance which seems to exclude—Them. Sort of an insulator. I sensed what it was—so did They. I can tell you, it was nip and tuck for a while. They can really move, when They want to. I won, as you know. Close. Oh, yes, I was responsible for snatching the stopper out of your hand. I did it by creating a vacuum in the bottle. The stopper was the nearest thing to the mouth, and you weren't holding it very tightly."

"Vacuum?" I asked. "What became of the air?"

"That was easy. I separated the molecular structure of the glass, and passed the air out that way."

"What about Them?"

"Oh, They would have followed. But if you'll look closely, you'll see that the stopper is now fused to the bottle. That's what saved me. Whew! —Oh, by the way, if you're wondering what cooled the bottle so quickly, it was the vacuum formation. Expanding air, you know, loses heat. Vacuum creation, of course, would create intense cold. That glass is good stuff. Practically no thermal expansion."

"I'm beginning to be glad, now, that it happened. Would have been bad for you . . . I suppose you'll live out the rest of your life in my bottle."

"The rest of my life, friend, is—eternity."

I blinked at that. "That's not going to be much fun," I said. "I mean—don't you ever get hungry, or—or anything?"

"No. I'm fed—I know that. From outside, somehow. There seems to be a source somewhere that radiates energy on which I feed. I wouldn't know about that. But it's going to be a bit boring. I don't know—maybe some day I'll find a way to get another body."

"What's to prevent your just going in and appropriating someone else's?"

"Can't," said the bottle. "As long as a soul is in possession of a body, it is invulnerable. The only way would be to convince some soul that it would be to its advantage to leave its body and make room for me."

"Hmm . . . say, Bottle. Seems to me that by this time you must have experienced that death-realization you spoke about a while back. Why aren't you immune from Them now?"

"That's the point. A soul must draw its immunity from a body which it possesses at the time. If I could get into a body and possess it for just one split second, I could immunize myself and be on my way. Or I could stay in the body and enjoy myself until it died. By the way, stop calling me Bottle. My name's Gregory— Wallace Gregory."

"Oh. Okay. I'm Pete Tronti. Er—glad to have met you."

"Same here." The bottle hopped a couple of times. "That can be considered a handshake."

"How did you do that?" I asked, grinning.

"Easy. The tiniest of molecular expansion, well distributed, makes the bottle bounce."

"Neat. Well—I've got to go out and get some grub. Anything I can get for you?"

"Thanks, no, Tronti. Shove along. Be seeing you."

*   *   *

Thus began my association with Wally Gregory, disembodied soul. I found him a very intelligent person; and though he had cramped my style in regard to the new glass—I didn't fancy collecting souls in bottles as a hobby—we became real friends. Not many people get a break like that—having a boarder who is so delightful and so little trouble. Though the initial cost had been high—after all, I'd almost gone nuts!—the upkeep was negligible. Wally never came in drunk, robbed the cash drawer, or brought his friends in. He was never late for meals, nor did he leave dirty socks around. As a roommate, he was ideal, and as a friend, he just about had Helix topped.

One evening about eight months later I was batting the wind with Wally while I worked. He'd been a great help to me—I was fooling around with artificial rubber synthesis at the time, and Wally had an uncanny ability for knowing exactly what was what in a chemical reaction—and because of that, I began to think of his present state.

"Say, Wally—don't you think it's about time that we began thinking about getting a body for you?"

Wally snorted. "That's about all we can do—think about it. How in blazes do you think we could ever get a soul's consent for that kind of a transfer?"

"I don't know—we might try kidding one of them along. You know—put one over on him."

"What—kid one along when he has the power of reading every single thought that goes through a mind? Couldn't be done."

"Now, don't tell me that every soul in the universe is incapable of being fooled. After all, a soul is a part of a human being."

"It's not that a soul is phenomenally intelligent, Pete. But a soul reasons without emotional drawbacks—he deals in elementals. Any moron is something of a genius if he can see clearly to the roots of a problem. And any soul can do just that. That is, if it's a soul as highly developed as that of a human being."

"Well, suppose that the soul isn't that highly developed? That's an idea. Couldn't you possess the body of a dog, say, or—"

"Or a cat . . . ?"

I stopped stirring the beakerful of milkweed latex and came around the table, stopping in front of the bottle. "Wally—not

Helix. Not that cat! Why, he's—he's a friend of mine. He trusts me. We *couldn't* do anything like that. My gosh, man—"

"You're being emotional," said Wally scornfully. "If you've got any sense of values at all, there'll be no choice. You can save my immortal soul by sacrificing the life of a cat. Not many men have that sort of an opportunity, especially at that price. It'll be a gamble. I haven't told you, but in the last couple of months I've been looking into Helix's mentality. He's got a brilliant mind for a cat. And it wouldn't do anything to him. He'd cease to exist— you can see that. But his soul is primitive, and has been protected since he was a kitten, as must be the case with any primitive mentality. Man needs some powerful impetus to protect his soul, because he has evolved away from the fear of death to a large degree—but a cat has not. His basic philosophy is little different from that of his wild forebears. He'll be okay. I'd just step in and he'd step out, and go wherever it is that good cats go when they die. You'd have him, in body, the same as you have now; but he'd be motivated by my soul instead of his own. Pete, you've *got* to do it."

"Gosh, Wally . . . look, I'll get you another cat. Or . . . say! How's about a monkey?"

"I've thought about all that. In the first place, a monkey would be too noticeable, walking around by himself. You see, my idea is to get into some sort of a body in which I can go where I please, when I please. In the second place, I have a headstart with Helix. It's going to be a long job, reconditioning that cat to my needs, but it can be done. I've been exploring his mind, and by now I know it pretty well. In the third place, you know him, and you know me—and he knows me a little now. He is the logical subject for something which, you must allow, is going to be a most engrossing experiment."

I had to admire the way Wally was putting it over. Being dissociated from emotionalism like that must be a great boon. He had caused me to start the conversation, and probably to put forward the very objections to which he had prepared answers. I began to resent him a little—but only a little. That last point of his told. It *would* be a most engrossing experiment—preparing a feline body and mind to bear a human soul, in such a way that the soul could live an almost normal life . . . "I won't say yes or no, Wally," I said. "I want to talk it over a little . . . Just how would we go about it, in case I said yes?"

"Well—" Wally was quiet a minute. "First we'd have to make some minor changes in his physique, so that I could do things that are impossible for a cat—read, write, speak and memorize. His brain would have to be altered so that it could comprehend an abstraction, and his paws would have to be made a little more manageable so that I could hold a pencil."

"Might as well forget the whole thing, then," I told him. "I'm a chemist, not a veterinary surgeon. There isn't a man alive who could do a job like that. Why—"

"Don't worry about that. I've learned a lot recently about myself, too. If I can once get into Helix's brain, I can mess around with his metabolism. I can stimulate growth in any part of his body, in any way, to any degree. I can, for instance, atrophy the skin between his toes, form flesh and joints in his claws. Presto—hands. I can—"

"Sounds swell. But how are you going to get in there? I thought you couldn't displace his soul without his consent. And—what about Them?"

"Oh, that will be all right. I can get in there and work, and his soul will protect me. You see, I've been in contact with it. As long as I am working to increase the cat's mental and physical powers, his soul won't object. As for getting in there, I can do it if I move fast. There are times when none of Them are around. If I pick one of those times, slide out of the bottle and into the cat, I'll be perfectly safe. My one big danger is from his soul. If it wants me out of there, it can bring a tremendous psychic force into play—throw me from here to the moon, or farther. If that happened—that will finish me. They wouldn't miss a chance like that."

"Golly . . . listen, friend, you'd better not take the chance. It's a swell idea, but I don't think it's worth it. As you are now, you're safe for the rest of time. If something goes wrong—"

"Not worth it? Do you realize what you're saying, man? I have my choice between staying here in this bottle forever—and that's an awful long time, if you can't die—or fixing up Helix so that he can let me live a reasonable human existence until he dies. Then I can go, protected, into wherever it is I should go. Give me a break, Pete. I can't do it without you."

"Why not?"

"Don't you see? The cat has to be educated. Yes, and civilized. You can do it, partly because he knows you, partly because that is the best way. When we can get him speaking, you can teach him orally. That way we can keep up our mental communication, but he'll never know about it. More important, neither will his soul. Pete, can't you see what this means to me?"

"Yeah. Wally, it's a shabby trick on Helix. It's downright dirty. I don't like it—anything about it. But you've got something there . . . all right. You're a rat, Wally. So am I. But I'll do it. I'd never sleep again if I didn't. How do we start?"

"Thanks, Pete. I'll never be able to thank you enough . . . First, I've got to get into his brain. Here's what you do. Think you can get him to lick the side of the bottle?"

I thought a minute. "Yes. I can put a little catnip extract—I have some around somewhere—on the bottle. He'll lick it off . . . Why?"

"That'll be fine. See, it will minimize the distance. I can slip through the glass and be into his brain before one of Them has a chance at me."

I got the little bottle of extract and poured some of it on a cloth. Helix came running when he smelled it. I felt like a heel—almost tried to talk Wally out of it. But then I shrugged it off. Fond as I was of the big black cat, Wally's immortal soul was more important.

"Hold it a minute," said Wally. "One of Them is smelling around."

I waited tensely. Helix was straining toward the cloth I held in my right hand. I held him with the other, feeling smaller and smaller. He *trusted* me!

"Let 'er go!" snapped Wally. I slapped the cloth onto the side of the bottle, smeared it. Helix shot out of my grip, began licking the bottle frantically. I almost cried. I said, "May God have mercy on his soul . . ." Don't know why . . .

"Good lad!" said Wally. "I made it!" After a long moment,

"Pete! Give him some more catnip! I've got to find out what part of his brain registers pleasure. That's where I'll start. He's going to enjoy every minute of this."

I dished up the catnip. Helix, forgive me!

Another long pause, then, "Pete! Pinch him, will you? Or stick a pin in him."

I chose the pinch, and it was a gentle one. It didn't fool Wally. "Make him holler, Pete! I want a real reaction."

I gritted my teeth and twisted the spiral tail. Helix yowled. I think his feelings were hurt more than his caudal appendage.

And so it went. I applied every possible physical and mental stimulus to Helix—hunger, sorrow, fright, anger (that was a hard one. Old Helix just wouldn't get sore!), heat, cold, joy, disappointment, thirst and insult. Hate was impossible. And Wally, somewhere deep in the cat's mind, checked and rechecked; located, reasoned, tried and erred. Because he was tireless, and because he had no sidetracking temptations to swerve him from his purpose, he made a perfect investigator. When he finally was ready to emerge, Helix and I were half dead from fatigue. Wally was, to hear him talk, just ready to begin. I got him back into his bottle without mishap, using the same method; and so ended the first day's work, for I absolutely refused to go on until the cat and I had had some sleep. Wally grumbled a bit and then quieted down.

Thus began the most amazing experiment in the history of physiology and psychology. We made my cat over. And we made him into a—well, guess for yourself.

Inside of a week he was talking. I waited with all the impatience of an anxious father for his first word, which was, incidentally, not "Da-da" but "Catnip." I was so tickled that I fed him catnip until he was roaring drunk.

After that it was easy; nouns first, then verbs. Three hours after saying "Catnip" he was saying "How's about some more catnip?"

Wally somehow stumbled onto a "tone control" in Helix's vocal cords. We found that we could give him a loud and raucous voice, but that by sacrificing quantity to quality, something approximating Wally's voice (as I "heard" it) could be achieved. It was quiet, mellow and very expressive.

After a great deal of work in the anterior part of Helix's brain, we developed a practically perfect memory. That's one thing that the lower orders are a little short on. The average cat lives almost entirely in the present; perhaps ten minutes of the past are clear to him; and he has no conception of the future. What he learns is retained more by muscular or neural memory than by aural, oral or visual memory, as is the case with a schoolchild. We fixed that. Helix needed no drills or exercises; to be told once was enough.

We hit one snag. I'd been talking to Wally the way I'd talk to anyone. But as Helix came to understand what was said aloud, my long talks with no one began to puzzle and confuse him. I tried hard to keep my mouth shut while I talked with Wally, but it wasn't until I thought of taping my mouth that I succeeded. Helix was a little surprised at that, but he got used to it.

And we got him reading. To prove what a prodigy he was, I can say that not one month after he started on his ABC's he had read and absorbed the Bible, Frazer's *Golden Bough* in the abridged edition, *Alice in Wonderland* and four geography texts. In two months he had learned solid geometry, differential calculus, the fourteen basic theories of metempsychosis, and every song on this week's Hit Parade. Oh, yes; he had a profound sense of tone and rhythm. He used to sprawl for hours in front of the radio on Sunday afternoons, listening to the symphony broadcasts; and after a while he could identify not only the selection being played and its composer, but the conductor as well.

I began to realize that we had overdone it a bit. Being a cat, which is the most independent creature on earth, Helix was an aristocrat. He had little, if any, consideration for my comparative ignorance—yes, ignorance; for though I had given him, more or less, my own education, he had the double advantage of recent education and that perfect memory. He would openly sneer at me when I made a sweeping statement—a bad habit I have always had—and then proceed to straighten me out in snide words of one syllable. He meant me no harm; but when he would look over his whiskers and say to me, "You don't really know very much, do you?" in that condescending manner, I burned. Once I had to go so far as to threaten to put him on short rations; that was one thing that would always bring him around.

Wally would spring things on me at times. He went and gave

the cat a craving for tobacco, the so-and-so. The result was that Helix smoked up every cigarette in the house. I had a brainstorm, though, and taught him to roll his own. It wasn't so bad after that. But he hadn't much conception of the difference between "mine" and "thine." My cigarettes were safe with Helix—as long as he didn't feel like smoking.

That started me thinking. Why, with his mental faculties, couldn't he learn not to smoke my last cigarette? Or, as happened once, eat everything that was on the table—my dinner as well as his—while I was phoning? I'd told him not to; he couldn't explain it himself. He simply said, "It was there, wasn't it?"

I asked Wally about it, and I think that he hit the right answer.

"I believe," he told me, "that it's because Helix has no conception of generosity. Or mercy. Or any of those qualities. He is completely without conscience."

"You mean that he's got no feeling toward me? That bringing him up, feeding him, educating him, has done nothing to—"

Wally sounded amused. "Sure, sure. He likes you—you're easy to get along with. Besides, as you just said, you're the meal ticket. You mustn't forget, Tronti, that Helix is a cat, and until I take possession, always will be. You don't get implicit obedience from any cat, no matter how erudite he may be, unless he damn well pleases to give it to you. Otherwise, he'll follow his own sweet way. This whole process has interested him—and I told you he'd enjoy it. But that's all."

"Can't we give him some of those qualities?"

"No. That's been bothering me a little. You know, Helix has a clever and devious way of his own for going about things. I'm not quite sure how he—his soul—stands on this replacement business. He might be holding out on us. I can't do much more than I've done. Every attribute we have developed in him was, at the beginning, either embryonic or vestigial. If he were a female, now, we might get an element of mercy, for instance. But there's none in this little tiger here; I have nothing to work on." He paused for a moment.

"Pete, I might as well confess to you that I'm a little worried. We've done plenty, but I don't know that it's enough. In a little while now he'll be ready for the final stage—my entrance into his psyche. As I told you, if his soul objects, he can sling mine out of the solar system. And I haven't a chance of getting back. And here's another thing. I can't be sure that he doesn't know just why we are doing this. If he does—Pete, I hate to say this, but are you on the level? Have you told Helix anything?"

"Me?" I shouted. "Why, you—you ingrate! How could I? You've heard every single word that I've said to that cat. You never sleep. You never go out. Why, you dirty—"

"All right—all right," he said soothingly. "I just asked, that's all. Take it easy. I'm sorry. But—if only I could be sure! There's something in his mind that I can't get to . . . Oh, well. We'll hope for the best. I've got a lot to lose, but plenty to gain—everything to gain. And for heaven's sake don't shout like that. You're not taped up, you know."

"Oh—sorry. I didn't give anything away, I guess," I said silently. "But watch yourself, Gregory. Don't get me roiled. Another crack like that and I throw you and your bottle into the ocean, and you can spend the rest of eternity educating the three little fishies. *Deve essere cosi.*"

"In other words, no monkey business. I took Italian in high school," sneered the voice from the bottle. "Okay, Pete. Sorry I brought it up. But put yourself in my place, and you'll see what's what."

The whole affair was making me increasingly nervous. Occasionally I'd wake up to the fact that it was a little out of the ordinary to be spending my life with a talking bottle and a feline cum laude. And now this friction between me and Wally, and the growing superciliousness of Helix—I didn't know whose side to take. Wally's, Helix's, or, by golly, my own. After all, I was in this up to my ears and over. Those days were by no means happy ones.

One evening I was sitting morosely in my easy chair, trying to inject a little rationality into my existence by means of the evening paper. Wally was sulking in his bottle, and Helix was spread out on the rug in front of the radio, in that hyperperfect relaxation that only a cat can achieve. He was smoking sullenly and making passes at an occasional fly. There was a definite tension in the air, and I didn't like it.

"Helix," I said suddenly, hurling my paper across the room, "what ails you, old feller?"

"Nothing," he lied. "And stop calling me 'old feller.' It's undignified."

"Ohh! So we have a snob in our midst! Helix, I'm getting damn sick of your attitude. Sometimes I'm sorry I ever taught you anything. You used to show me a little respect, before you had any brains."

"That remark," drawled the cat, "is typical of a human being. What does it matter where I got anything I have? As long as any talents of mine belong to me, I have every right to be proud of them, and to look down on anyone who does not possess them in such a degree. Who are you to talk? You think you're pretty good yourself, don't you? And just because you're a member of the cocky tribe of"—and here his words dripped the bitterest scorn—"Homo sapiens."

I knew it would be best to ignore him. He was indulging in the age-old pastime of the cat family—making a human being feel like a fool. Every inferiority complex is allergic to felinity. Show me a man who does not like cats and I'll show you one who is not sure of himself. The cat is a symbol of aloneness superb. And with man, he is not impressed.

"That won't do you any good, Helix," I said coldly. "Do you realize how easy it would be for me to get rid of you? I used to think I had a reason for feeding you and sheltering you. You were good company. You certainly are not now."

"You know," he said, stretching out and crushing his cigarette in the rug because he knew it annoyed me, "I have only one deep regret in my life. And that is that you knew me before my little renaissance. I remember little about it, but I have read considerably on the subject. It appears that the cat family has long misled your foolish race. And yet the whole thing is summed up in a little human doggerel:

I love my dear pussy, his coat is so warm,
And if I don't hurt him, he'll do me no harm.

"There, my friend and"—he sniffed—"benefactor, you have our basic philosophy. I find that my actions previous to your fortuitous intervention in my mental development, led you to exhibit a sad lack of the respect which I deserve. If it were not for that stupidity on my part, during those blind years—and I take no responsibility on myself for that stupidity; it was unavoidable— you would now treat me more as I should be treated, as the most talented member of a superlative race.

"Don't be any more of a fool than you have to be, Pete. You think I've changed. I haven't. The sooner you realize that, the better for you. And for heaven's sake stop being emotional about me. It bores me."

"Emotional?" I yelled. "Damn it, what's the matter with a little emotion now and then? What's happening around here, anyway? Who's the boss around here? Who pays the bills?"

"You do," said Helix gently, "which makes you all the more a fool. You wouldn't catch me doing anything unless I thoroughly enjoyed it. Go away, Pete. You're being childish."

I picked up a heavy ashtray and hurled it at the cat. He ducked it gracefully. "Tsk tsk! *What* an exhibition!"

I grabbed my hat and stormed out, followed by the cat's satiric chuckle.

Never in my life have I been so completely filled with helpless anger. I start to do someone a favor, and what happens? I begin taking dictation from him. In return for that I do him an even greater favor, and what happens? He corrupts my cat. So I start taking dictation from the cat too.

It wouldn't matter so much, but I had loved that cat. Snicker if you want to, but for a man like me, who spends nine-tenths of his life tied up in test tubes and electrochemical reactions, the cat had filled a great gap. I realized that I had kidded myself—Helix was a conscienceless parasite, and always had been. But I had loved him. My error. Nothing in this world is quite as devastating as the realization of one's mistaken judgment of character. I could have loved Helix until the day he died, and then cherished his memory. The fact that I would have credited him with qualities that he did not possess wouldn't have mattered.

Well, and whose fault was it? Mine? In a way; I'd given in to Wally in his plan to remake the cat for his use. But it was more Wally's fault. Damn it, had I asked him to come into my house and bottle? Who did he think he was, messing up my easy, uncomplicated life like that? . . . I had someone to hate for it all, then. Wallace Gregory, the rat.

Lord, what I would have given for some way to change everything back to where it was before Gregory came into my life! I had nothing to look forward to now. If Wally succeeded in making the change, I'd still have that insufferable cat around. In his colossal ego there was no means of expressing any of the gentler human attributes which Wally might possess. As soon as he fused himself with the cat, Helix would disappear into the cosmos, taking nothing but his life force, and leaving every detestable characteristic that he had—and he had plenty. If Wally couldn't make it, They would get him, and I'd be left with that insufferable beast. What a spot!

Suppose I killed Helix? That would be one way . . . but then what about Wally? I knew he had immense potentialities; and though that threat of mine about throwing him into the ocean had stopped him once, I wasn't so sure of myself. He had a brilliant mind, and if I incurred his hatred, there's no telling what he might do. For the first time I realized that Wally Gregory's soul was something of a menace. Imagine having to live with the idea that as soon as you died, another man's soul would be laying for you, somewhere Beyond.

I walked miles and hours that night, simmering, before I hit on the perfect solution. It meant killing my beloved Helix; but, now, that would be a small loss. And it would free Wallace Gregory. Let the man's soul take possession of the cat, and then kill the cat. They would both be protected then; and I would be left alone. And, by golly, at peace.

I stumbled home after four, and slept like a dead man. I was utterly exhausted and would have slept the clock around. But that would not have suited Helix. At seven-thirty that morning he threw a glass of ice water over me. I swore violently.

"Get up, you lazy pig," he said politely. "I want my breakfast."

Blind with fury, I rolled out and stood over him. He stood quite still, grinning up at me. He was perfectly unafraid, though I saw him brace his legs, ready to move forward or back or to either side if I made a pass at him. I couldn't have touched him, and he knew it, damn him.

And then I remembered that I was going to kill him, and my throat closed up. I turned away with my eyes stinging. "Okay, Helix," I said when I could speak. "Comin' up."

He followed me into the kitchen and sat watching me while I boiled us some eggs. I watched them carefully—Helix wouldn't eat them unless they were boiled exactly two minutes and forty-five seconds—and then took his out and cut them carefully in cubes, the way he liked them. And then I put a little shot of catnip extract over them and dished them up. Helix raised his eyebrows at that. I hadn't given him any catnip for weeks. I'd only used it as a reward when he had done especially well. Recently I hadn't felt like rewarding him.

"Well!" he said as he wiped his mouth delicately, "I see that little session of ambulating introspection in which you indulged after your outbreak last night did you good. There never need be any friction between us, Pete, if you continue to behave this way. I can overlook almost anything but familiarity."

I choked on a piece of toast. Of all the colossal gall! He thought he had taught me a lesson! For a moment I was tempted to rub him out right then and there, but managed to keep my hands off him. I didn't want him to be suspicious.

Suddenly he swept his cup off the table. "Call this coffee?" he said sharply. "Make some more immediately, and this time be a little careful."

"You better be careful yourself," I said. "I taught you to say 'please' when you asked for anything."

" 'Please' be damned," said my darling pet. "You ought to know by this time how I like my coffee. I shouldn't have to tell you about things like that." He reached across the table and sent my cup to the floor too. "Now you'll have to make more. I tell you, I won't stand for any more of your nonsense. From now on this detestable democracy is at an end. You're going to do things *my* way. I've taken too much from you. You offend me. You eat sloppily, and I never did care particularly for your odor. Hereafter keep away from me unless I call. And don't speak unless you are spoken to."

I drew a deep breath and counted to ten very, very slowly. Then I got two more cups out of the closet, made more coffee, and poured it. And while Helix was finishing his breakfast, I went out and bought a revolver.

When I got back I found Helix sleeping. I tiptoed into the kitchen to wash the dishes, but found them all broken. His idea of a final whimsical touch. I ground my teeth and cleaned up the mess. Then I went into the laboratory and locked the door. "Wally!" I called.

"Well?"

"Listen, fella, we've got to finish this up now—today. Helix has gotten it into his head that he owns the place, me included. I won't stand for it, I tell you! I almost killed him this morning, and I will yet if this nonsense keeps up. Wally, is everything ready?"

Wally sounded a little strained. "Yes . . . Pete, it's going to be good! Oh, God, to be able to walk around again! Just to be able to read a comic strip, or go to a movie, or see a ball game! Well— let's get it over with. What was that about Helix? Did you say he's a little—er—intractable?"

I snorted. "That's not the word for it. He has decided that he is a big shot. Me, I only work here."

"Pete, did he say anything about—about me? Don't get sore now, but—do you think it's safe? If what you say is true, he's asserting his individuality; I wouldn't like that to go too far. You know, They have a hunch that something's up. The last time you got me into Helix's mind, there were swarms of Them around. When they sensed that I was making a change, They all drew back as if to let me get away with it. Pete, They have something up Their sleeve, too."

"What do you mean, 'too'?" I asked quickly.

"Why, nothing. Helix is one, They are another. Too. What's the matter with that?"

It didn't relieve me much. Wally probably knew I was planning to kill the cat as soon as he made the change, thus doing him out of several years of fleshly enjoyment before he went on his way. He wasn't saying anything, though. He had too much to lose.

I took the bottle out of the laboratory into the kitchen and washed it, just by way of stalling for a minute. Then I set it down on the sink and went and got my gun, loaded it and dropped it into a drawer in the bench. Next I set the bottle back on the bench—I was pretty sure Wally hadn't known about the gun, and I didn't want him to—and went for Helix.

I couldn't find him.

The cushion where he had been sleeping was still warm; what was he up to now?

I hunted feverishly all through the apartment, without success. This was a fine time for him to do a blackout! With an exasperated sigh I went back into the laboratory to tell Wally.

Helix was sitting on the bench beside the bottle, twirling his whiskers with his made-over right paw and looking very amused. "Well, my good man," he greeted me, "what seems to be the trouble?"

"Damn it, cat," I said irritably, "where have you been?"

"Around," he said laconically. "You are as blind as you are stupid. And mind your tone."

I swallowed that. I had something more important to think about. How was I going to persuade him to lick the bottle? Mere catnip wouldn't do it, not in his present frame of mind. So—

"I suppose," Helix said, "that you want me to go through the old ritual of bottle-cataglottism again. Pardon the pun."

"Why, yes," I said, surprised but trying not to show it. "It's to your benefit, you know."

"Of course," said the cat. "I've always known that. If I didn't get something out of it, I'd have stopped doing it long ago."

That was logical, but I didn't like it. "All right," I said. "Let's go!"

"Pete!" Wally called. "This time, I want you to hold him very firmly, with both hands. Spread your fingers out as far as possible, and if you can get your forearms on him too, do it. I think you'll learn something—interesting."

A little puzzled, I complied. Helix didn't object, as I thought he might. Wally said, "Okay. They're drawing away now. Get him to lick the bottle."

"All right, Helix," I whispered tightly.

The pink tongue flashed out and back. The bottle tipped the tiniest bit. Then there was a tense silence.

"I . . . think . . . I'll . . . make it . . ."

We waited, Helix and I.

Suddenly something deep within me wrenched sickeningly. I almost dropped with the shock of it. And there was a piercing shriek deep within my brain—Wally's shriek, dwindling off into the distance. And faintly, then, there was a rending, tearing sound. It was horrible.

I staggered back and leaned against the lathe, gasping. Helix lay unmoving where I had left him. His sides were pumping in and out violently.

Helix shook himself and came over to me. "Well," he said, looking me straight in the eye, "they got your friend."

"Helix! How did you know about that?"

"Why must you be so consistently stupid, Pete? I've known about that all along. I'll give you a little explanation, if you like. It might prove to you that a human being is really a very, very dull creature."

"Go ahead," I gulped.

"You and I have just been a part of a most elaborately amusing compound double cross." He chuckled complacently. "Gregory was right in his assumption that I could not overhear his conversations with you—and a very annoying thing it was, too. I knew there was something off-color somewhere, because I didn't think that you were improving me so vastly just out of the goodness of your heart. But—someone else was listening in, and knew everything."

"Someone else?"

"Certainly. Have you forgotten Them? They were very much interested as to the possibilities of getting hold of our mutual friend Mr. Gregory. Being a lower order of spirit, They found it a simple matter to communicate with me. They asked me to toss Mr. Gregory's soul out to Them." He laughed nastily.

"But I was getting too much out of it. See what a superior creature I am! I told Them to stand by; that They would have a chance at Gregory when I was through using him, and not before. They did as I said, because it was up to me to give what They wanted. That's why They did not interfere during the transfers."

"Why, you heel!" I burst out. "After all Wally did for you, you were going to do that?"

"I wouldn't defend him, if I were you," the cat said precisely.

"He was double-crossing you too. I know all about this soul-replacement business; needn't try to hide that from me. He was sincere, at first, about using my body, but he couldn't help thinking that yours would suit his purpose far better. Though why he'd prefer it to mine—oh, well. No matter. However, his idea was to transfer himself from the bottle to me, and then to you. That's why he told you to hold me firmly—he wanted a good contact."

"How—how the devil do you know that?"

"He told me himself. After I had reached a satisfactory stage of development, I told him that I was wise. Oh, yes, I fooled him into developing a communication basis in me! He thought it was a taste for alcohol he was building up! However, he caught wise in time to arrest it, but not before it was good enough to communicate with him. If he'd gone a little farther, I'd have been able to talk with you that way too. At any rate, he was a little dampened by my attitude; knew he'd never get a chance to occupy me. I suggested to him, though, that we join forces in having him possess *you*."

"*Me!*" I edged toward the drawer in the bench. "Go on, Helix."

"You can see why I did this, can't you?" he asked distantly. "It would have been embarrassing to have him, a free soul, around where he might conceivably undo some of the work he had done on me. If he possessed you, you would be out of the way—They would take care of that—and he would have what he wanted. An ideal arrangement. You had no suspicion of the plan, and he had a good chance of catching your soul off-guard and ousting it. He knew how to go about it. Unfortunately for him, your soul was a little too quick. It was *you* who finally killed Wallace Gregory, not I. Neat, eh?"

"Yes," I said slowly, pulling the gun out of the drawer and sighting down the barrel, right between his eyes. "Very neat. For a while I thought I'd be sorry to do this. Now, I'm not." I drew a deep breath; Helix did not move. I pulled the trigger four times, and then sagged back against the bench. The strain was too much.

Helix stretched himself and yawned. "I knew you'd try something like that," he said. "I took the trouble of removing the bullets from your gun before the experiment. Nice to have known you!"

I hurled the gun at him but I was too slow. In a flash he was out of the laboratory, streaking for the door. He reached for the knob, opened the door, and was gone before I could take two steps.

There was a worrisome time after that, once I had done all the hysterical things anyone might do—pound out, run left, run right, look up and back and around. But this was a *cat* I was chasing, and you don't catch even an ordinary cat that does not in some way want to be caught.

I wonder why he decided to crack a safe.

No, I don't. I know how his head works. Worked. He had plans for himself—you can be sure of that, and unless I'm completely wrong, he had plans for all of us, ultimately. There have been, in human history, a few people who had the cold, live-in-the-present, me-first attitude of a cat, and humanity has learned a lot of hard lessons from them. But none of them was a cat.

Helix may have made a try or two to get someone to front for him—I wouldn't know. But he was smart enough to know that there was one tool he could use that would work—money. Once he had that, who knows how he would have operated? He could write, he could use a telephone. He would have run a lethal and efficient organization more frightening than anything you or I could imagine.

Well—he won't do it now. As for me, I'll disappear into research again. Flexible glass would be a nice patent to own and enjoy, but thank you, I'm glad to pass on that one.

But Helix . . . damn him, I miss him.

PROBABILITY ZERO!
THE POPULATION IMPLOSION

by Theodore R. Cogswell

In the early 1940s, in Astounding, there was a small department called "Probability Zero!" that ran short-short stories. Or items. Or lies. Things. These short pieces were usually funny and always impossible—echoing the description of the title. They read just like this . . .

H. H.

JUST AS more radioactivity is released into the atmosphere by the burning of fossil fuels than by a properly designed nuclear power plant (all coal containing substances other than hydrocarbons, some of which are radioactive), so also is the present world population a mere drop in the bucket compared with what it was only one thousand years ago. In fact, the population of our planet has been shrinking geometrically since the time of Christ. It is true that local urban clusters such as New York, Los Angeles and Chinchilla, Pennsylvania, have been expanding rapidly during the last few decades, but if one considers the entire land mass, a quick examination of available genealogical statistics will show that the average population per square mile is steadily and rapidly decreasing.

The key to the proof of this is the geometrical expansion in the number of ancestors one has as one moves back generation by generation. Assuming no inbreeding, your four grandparents had eight parents, who in turn had sixteen, etc. For purposes of demonstration, assume that each generation produces a new one in twenty-five years. Using 1950 as a convenient starting point, 1850 would see a generation of 16 ancestors; 1750: 256; 1650: 4,096; 1550: 65,536; 1450: 1,048,576; 1350: 16,777,136; 1250: 268,434,176; 1150: 4,294,946,816; 1050: 68,719,149,056; and A.D. 1000: 274,876,596,224.

Now two hundred and seventy-four billion-plus great-grandparents is a sizable number to have, especially if, as in my case, they were all Anglo-Saxon, miscegenation with Normans and other breeds without the law who slipped over from the Continent during the temporary alien quota relaxation of 1066 always having been frowned on by my progenitors.

I assume that the 50,874-square-mile land area of England proper hasn't changed substantially since the year 1000, so simple division will establish that there were 4,872,913 of my people jammed into every square mile of that little country. This works out to an average of a little less than six square feet per person, or a six-by-six-foot lot for each family of six, with no provision for throughways, supermarkets, jails, churches and other amenities of gracious living. Certainly the population problem then, especially the disposal of sewage, makes that of today shrink to nothingness in comparison. There were certain compensations, however.

Nobody ever got lonely. With an average of 7,642 persons per acre, computer dating and singles bars were unnecessary.

Where the other gentry lived, let alone the lower classes and the Scottish, Welsh and Irish servants, I haven't the slightest idea. But with my kin alone, the population density per square mile of all of England was some sixty-six times that of Manhattan today. The only obvious conclusion that can be drawn from this is that there has been a fantastic population implosion during the last thousand years.

Take England alone. If you divide her present population of some forty-four million by the almost 275 billion living there in the year 1000, you'll note that today she has only about 1.6 ten-thousandths of the population she had ten centuries ago, a shrinkage of 6,250 percent. If we assume that some of the original population and I are not related, the latter figure is greatly inflated and the shrinkage becomes even more astronomical.

Since English and American birth rates are roughly the same, we can take the English historical experience as an approximate analog of what is happening in America. So the next time you hear a prophet of doom moaning about the horrible future that awaits us if something isn't done to defuse the population bomb, laugh in his face. Statistics show that you have nothing to worry about.

AFTERWORD

by Harry Harrison

In the early summer of 1971 I was asked to write a brief obituary to be published in *Analog*. I began it this way:

> *It is with the most profound sadness that I must report that John W. Campbell is dead.*
>
> *For thirty-four years he was the editor of this magazine, guiding it with a firm hand from its origins in the pulps of a past era to its present stature. In shaping this journal he shaped all of modern science fiction, so that, in many ways, this entire body of literature is his memorial.*

This book is a memorial of a different kind. It is a group project, a spontaneous decision by a number of writers who decided that a special tribute was needed for this editor and friend who had been such a large part of our lives. John Campbell loved his work, and it is obvious that his magazine was as much a part of him as he was of it. What better tribute could there be than to bring out what might be called the last issue of the magazine he edited, an anthology of stories that might, perhaps, echo more of *Astounding* and *Unknown* than of *Analog*. History chose the writers who are represented here, and they in turn wrote the kind of stories they knew best how to do. If there is more than a hint of nostalgia in these pages, it is no accident. We wanted it that way. It has been my pleasure to assemble these stories in book form and to handle the mechanics of preparation for book publication. My responsibility stops there; we would have it no other way.

You see, we all know who the real editor was.

About the Editor

HARRY HARRISON is one of the best-known editors in the field of science fiction, as well as being a distinguished writer. Born in Stamford, Connecticut, he now lives in San Diego, California.